image comics presents

THE WALKING DEAD™

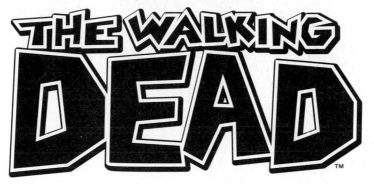

ROBERT KIRKMAN
CREATOR, WRITER

CHARLIE ADLARD
PENCILER

STEFANO GAUDIANO
INKER

CLIFF RATHBURN
GRAY TONES

RUS WOOTON
LETTERER

CHARLIE ADLARD
&
DAVE STEWART
COVER

SEAN MACKIEWICZ
EDITOR

SKYBOUND™

For SKYBOUND ENTERTAINMENT
Robert Kirkman - CEO
David Alpert - President
Sean Mackiewicz - Editorial Director
Shawn Kirkham - Director of Business Development
Brian Huntington - Online Editorial Director
June Alian - Publicity Director
Rachel Skidmore - Director of Media Development
Jon Moisan - Editor
Arielle Basich - Assistant Editor
Dan Petersen - Operations Manager
Sarah Effinger - Office Manager
Nick Palmer - Operations Coordinator
Genevieve Jones - Production Coordinator
Andres Juarez - Graphic Designer
Stephan Murillo - Business Development Coordinator
International inquiries: foreign@skybound.com
Licensing inquiries: contact@skybound.com
WWW.SKYBOUND.COM

IMAGE COMICS, INC.
Robert Kirkman – Chief Operating Officer
Erik Larsen – Chief Financial Officer
Todd McFarlane – President
Marc Silvestri – Chief Executive Officer
Jim Valentino – Vice-President
Eric Stephenson – Publisher
Corey Murphy – Director of Sales
Jeff Boison – Director of Publishing Planning & Book Trade Sales
Jeremy Sullivan – Director of Digital Sales
Kat Salazar – Director of PR & Marketing
Emily Miller – Director of Operations
Branwyn Bigglestone – Senior Accounts Manager
Sarah Mello – Accounts Manager
Drew Gill – Art Director
Jonathan Chan – Production Manager
Meredith Wallace – Print Manager
Briah Skelly – Publicity Assistant
Sasha Head – Sales & Marketing Production Designer
Randy Okamura – Digital Production Designer
David Brothers – Branding Manager
Ally Power – Content Manager
Addison Duke – Production Artist
Vincent Kukua – Production Artist
Tricia Ramos – Production Artist
Jeff Stang – Direct Market Sales Representative
Emilio Bautista – Digital Sales Associate
Leanna Caunter – Accounting Assistant
Chloe Ramos-Peterson – Administrative Assistant
IMAGECOMICS.COM

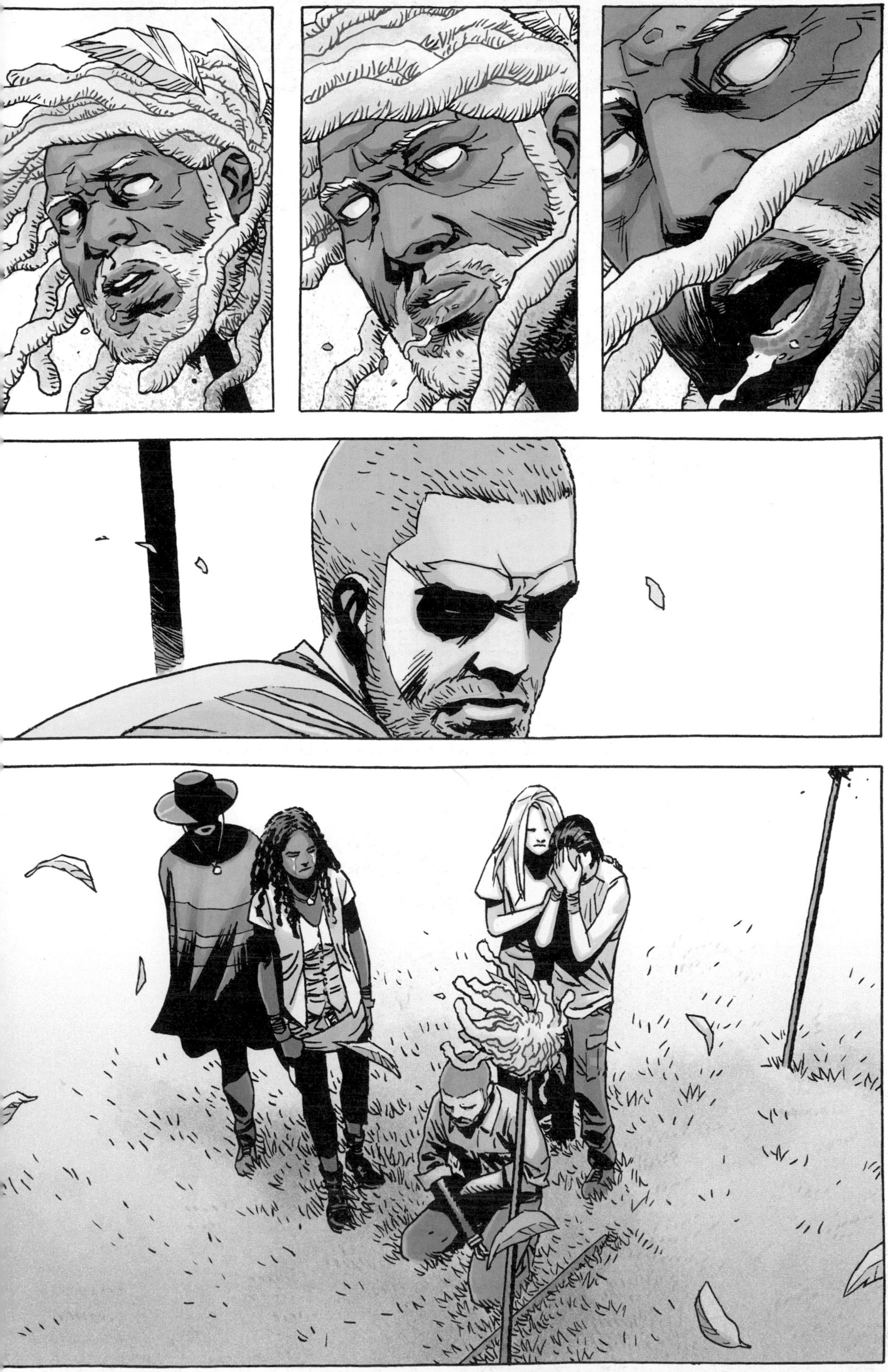

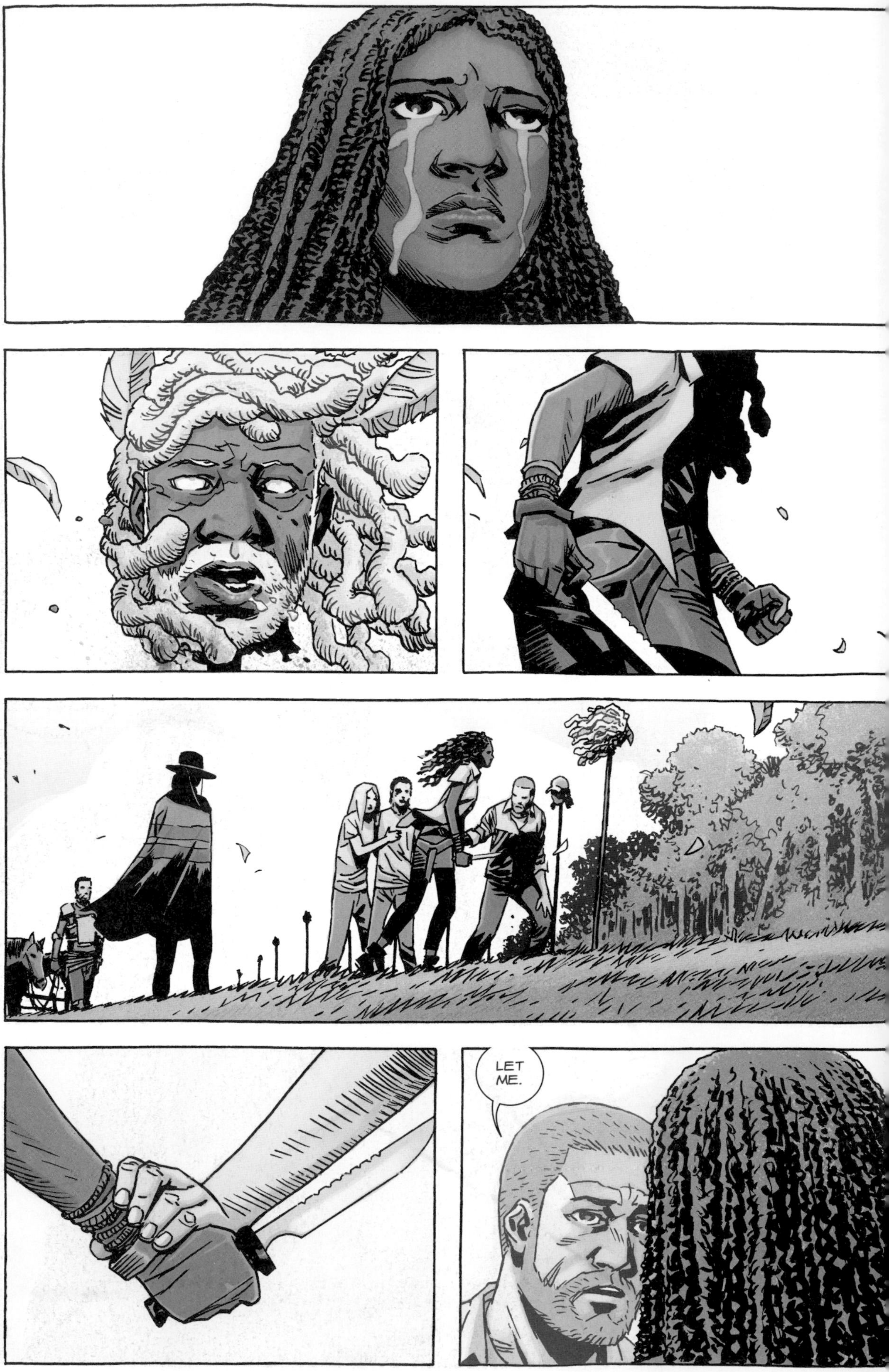
LET ME.

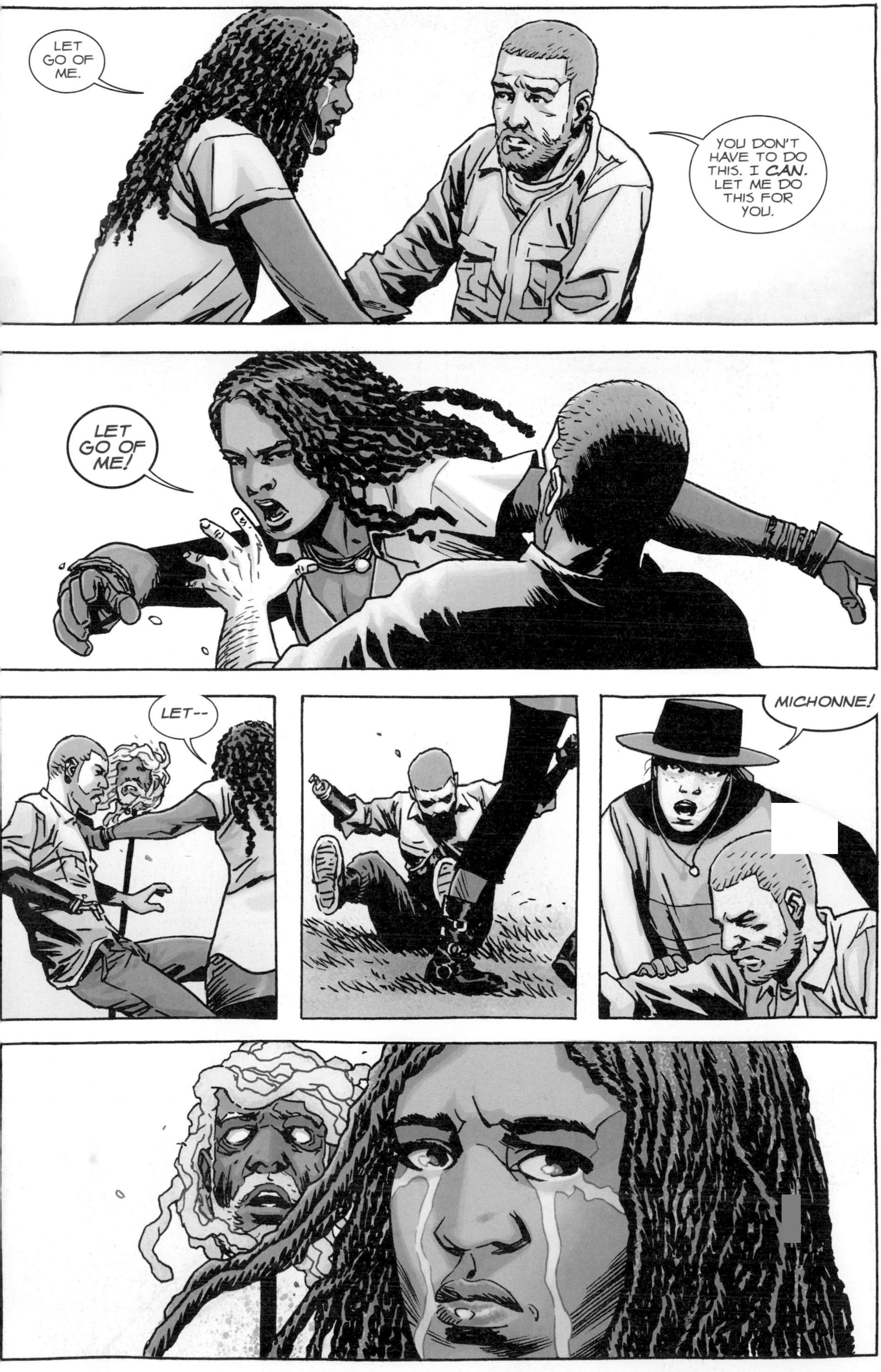
LET GO OF ME.
YOU DON'T HAVE TO DO THIS. I *CAN.* LET ME DO THIS FOR YOU.
LET GO OF ME!
LET--
MICHONNE!

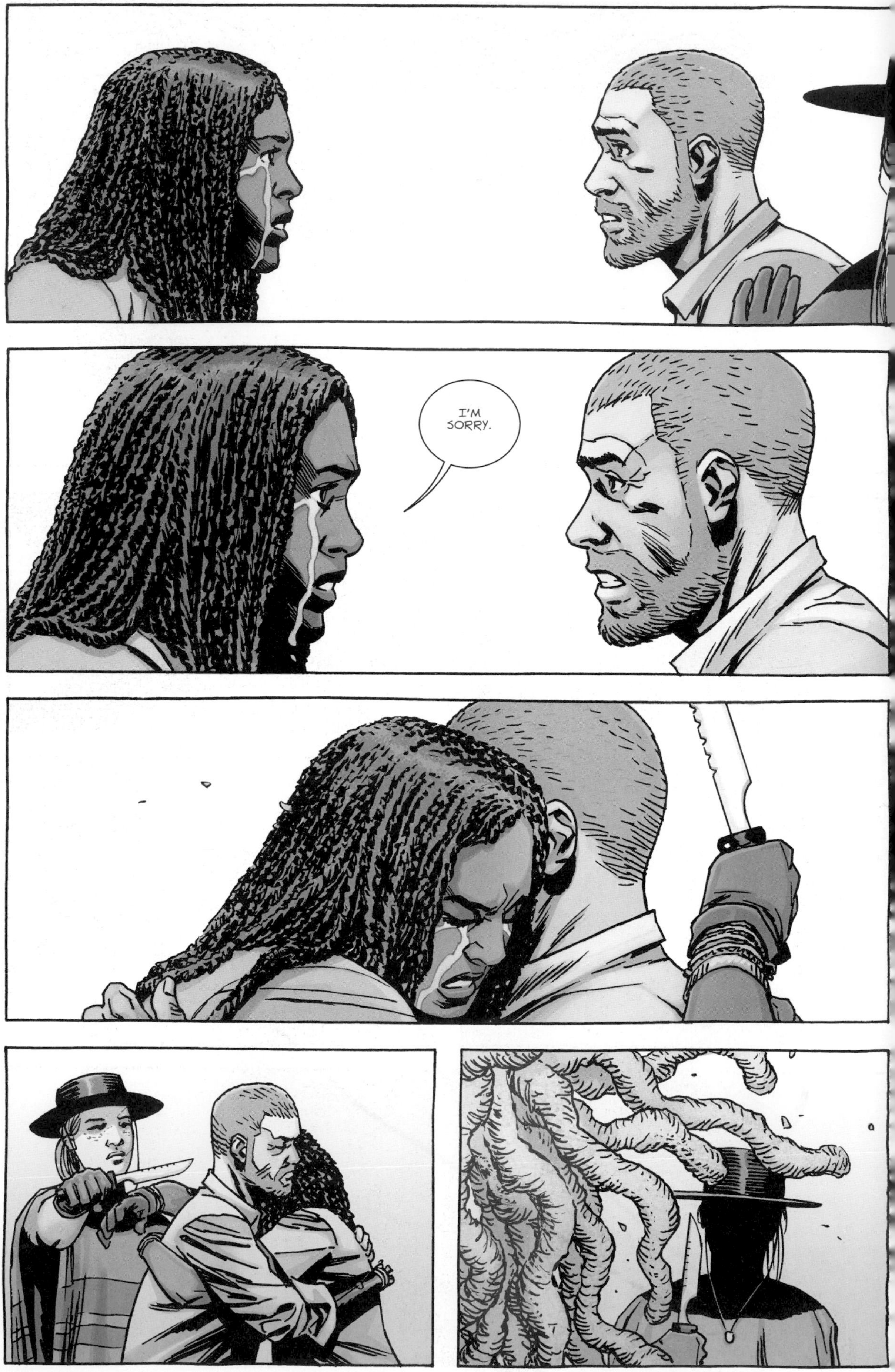
I'M SORRY.

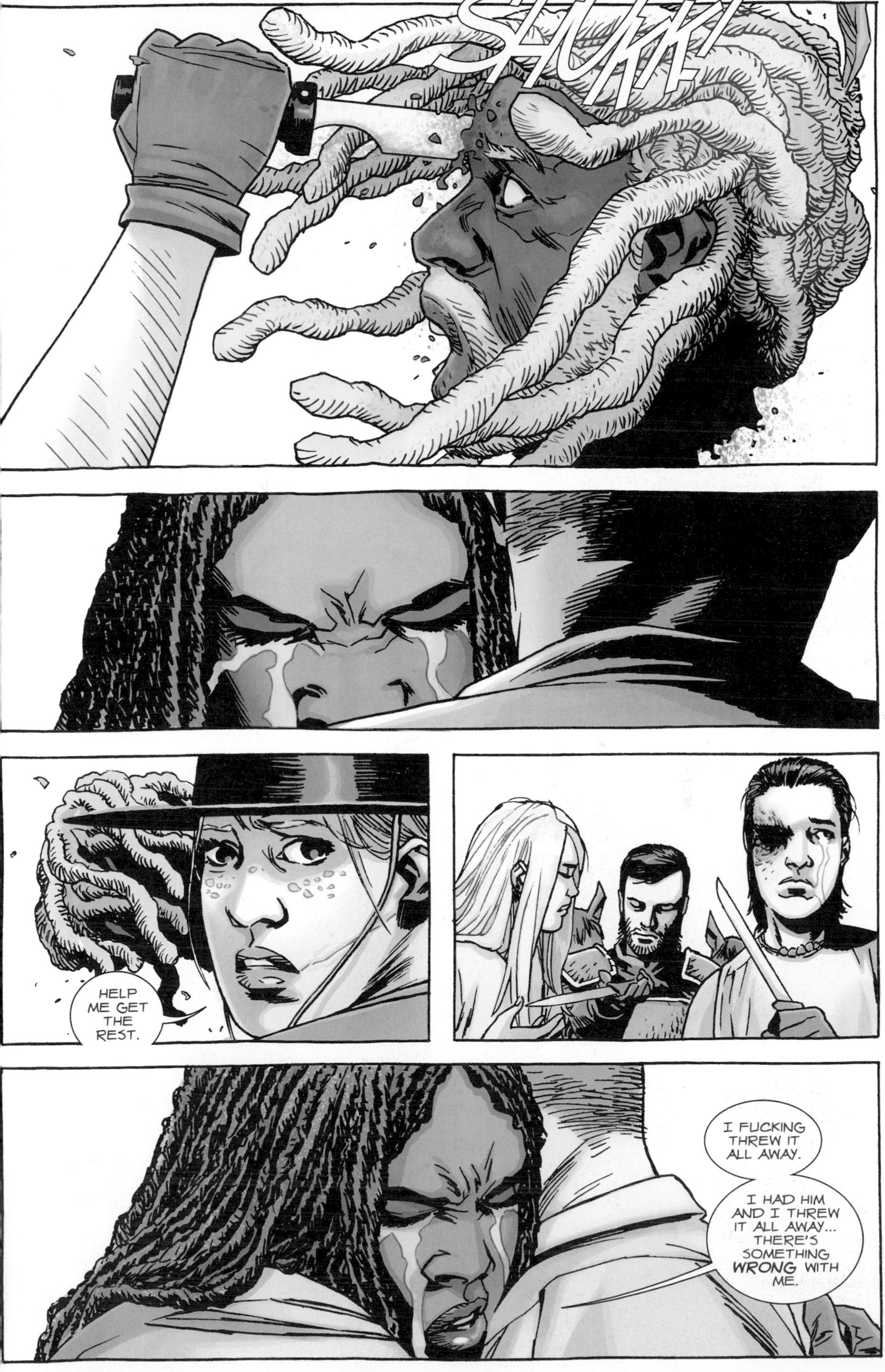
SHUKK!
HELP ME GET THE REST.
I FUCKING THREW IT ALL AWAY.
I HAD HIM AND I THREW IT ALL AWAY... THERE'S SOMETHING WRONG WITH ME.

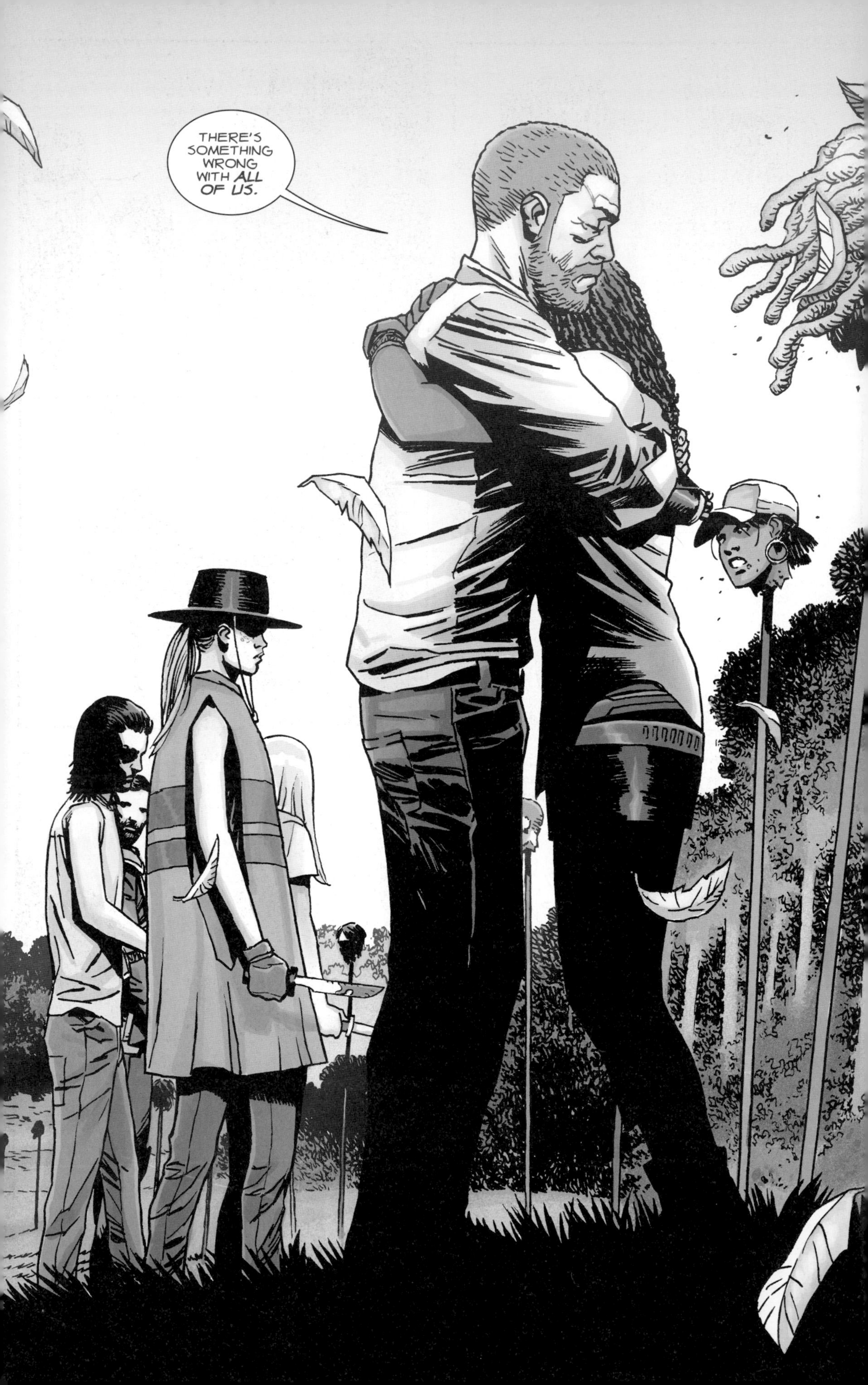
THERE'S SOMETHING WRONG WITH ALL OF US.

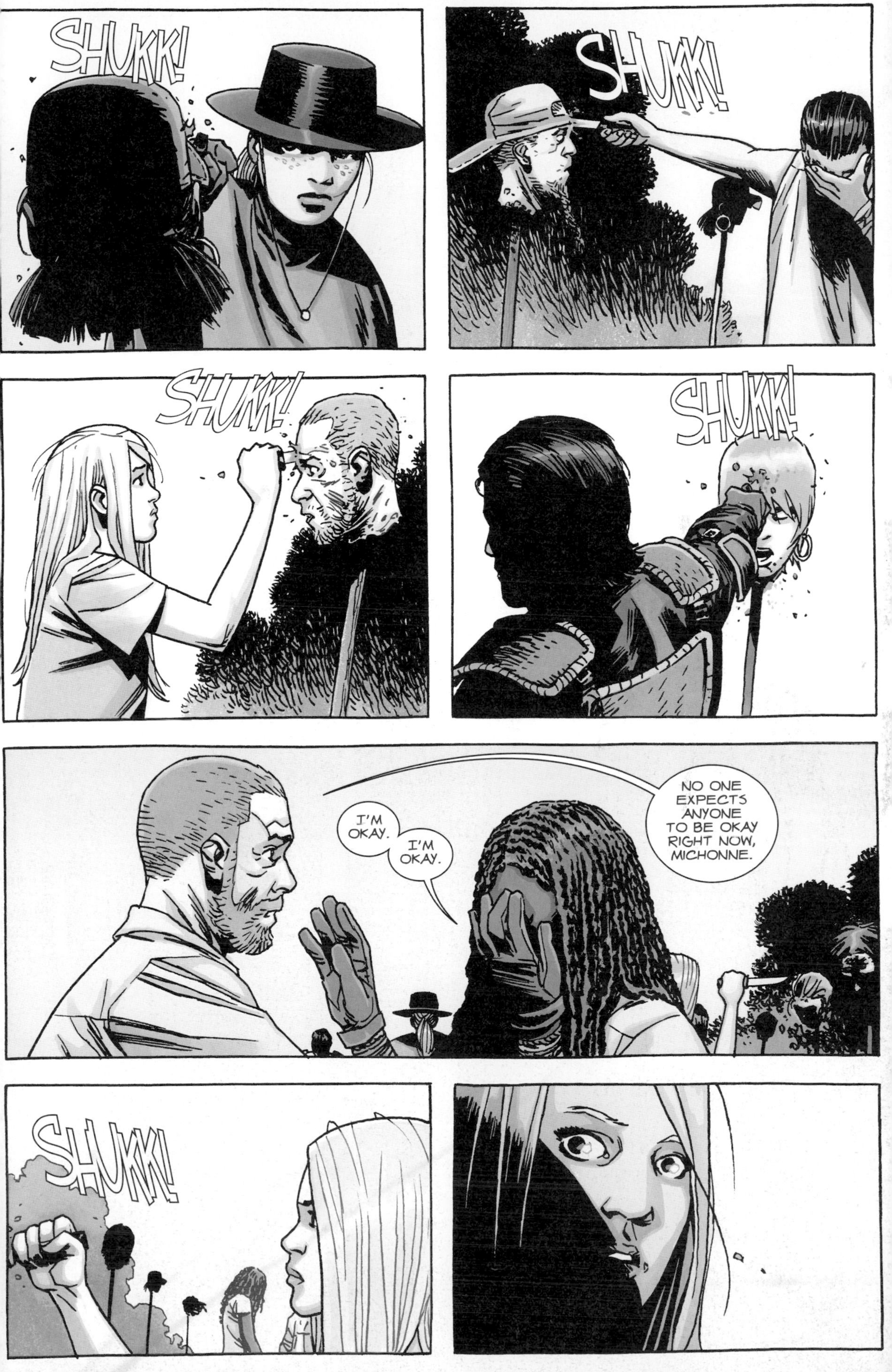
SHUKK!
SHUKK!
SHUKK!
SHUKK!
I'M OKAY.
I'M OKAY.
NO ONE EXPECTS ANYONE TO BE OKAY RIGHT NOW, MICHONNE.
SHUKK!

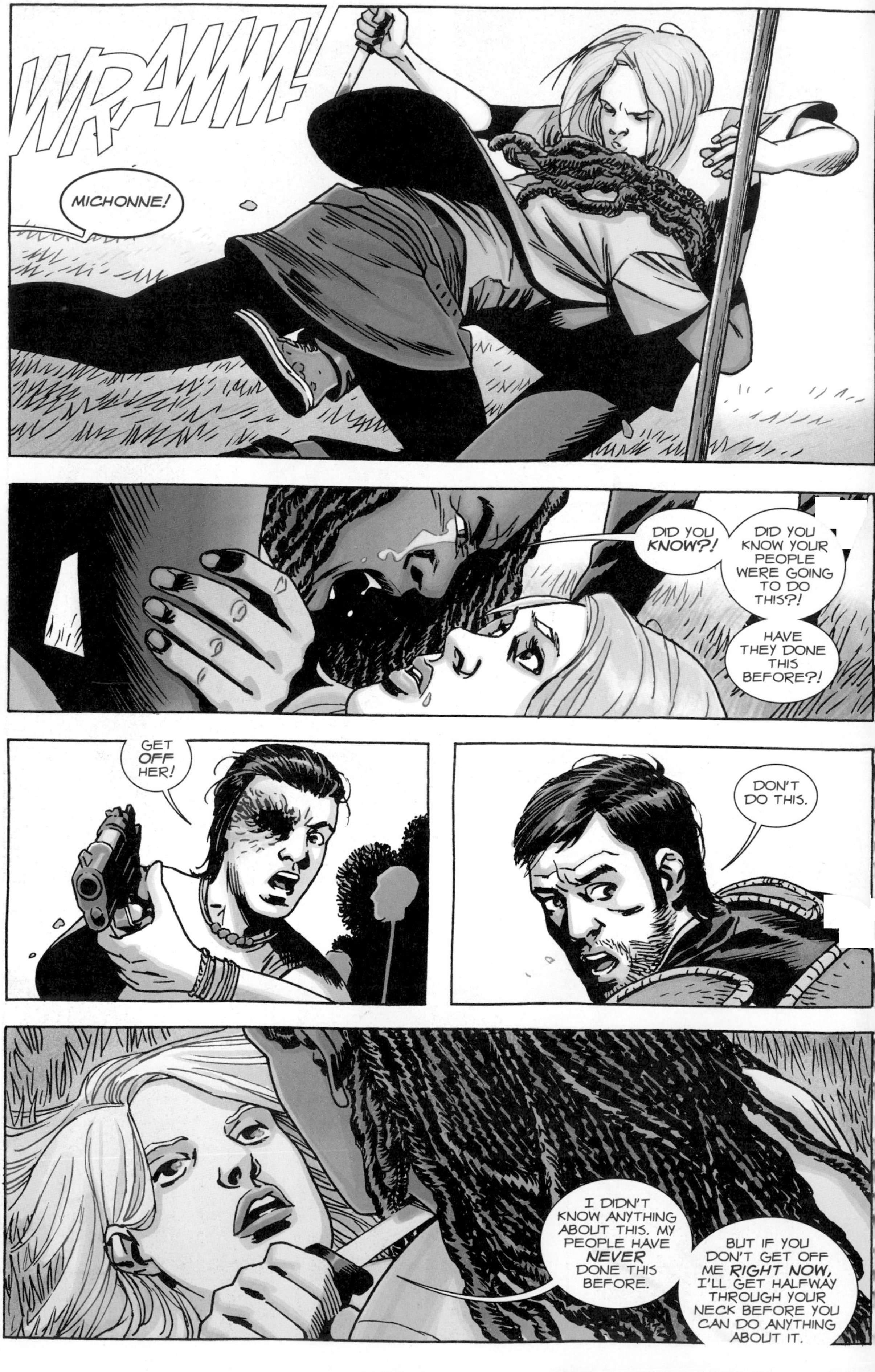
WRAMM!
MICHONNE!
DID YOU KNOW?!
DID YOU KNOW YOUR PEOPLE WERE GOING TO DO THIS?!
HAVE THEY DONE THIS BEFORE?!
GET OFF HER!
DON'T DO THIS.
I DIDN'T KNOW ANYTHING ABOUT THIS. MY PEOPLE HAVE NEVER DONE THIS BEFORE.
BUT IF YOU DON'T GET OFF ME RIGHT NOW, I'LL GET HALFWAY THROUGH YOUR NECK BEFORE YOU CAN DO ANYTHING ABOUT IT.

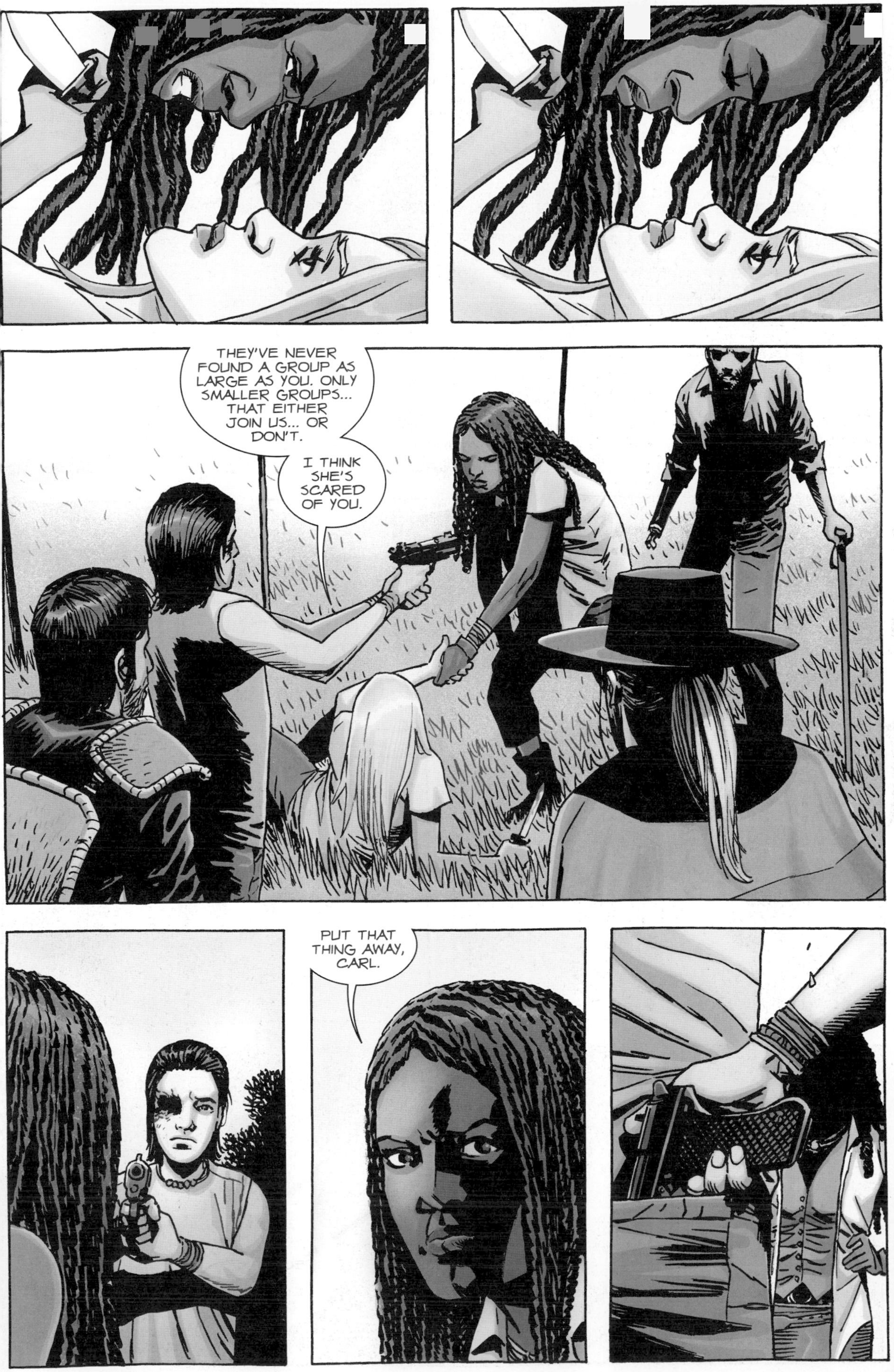
THEY'VE NEVER FOUND A GROUP AS LARGE AS YOU. ONLY SMALLER GROUPS... THAT EITHER JOIN US... OR DON'T.
I THINK SHE'S SCARED OF YOU.
PUT THAT THING AWAY, CARL.

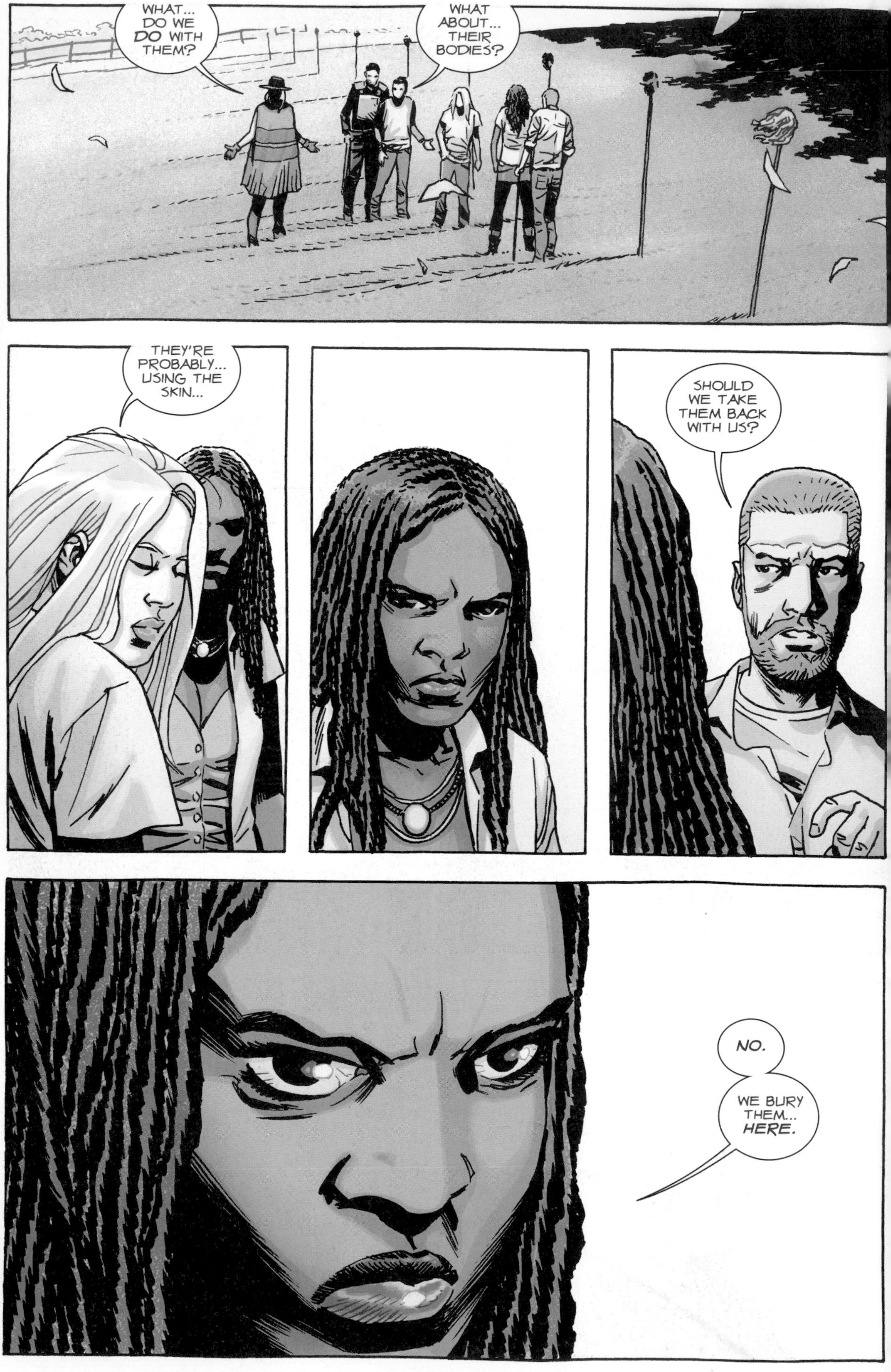
WHAT... DO WE DO WITH THEM?
WHAT ABOUT... THEIR BODIES?
THEY'RE PROBABLY... USING THE SKIN...
SHOULD WE TAKE THEM BACK WITH US?
NO.
WE BURY THEM... HERE.

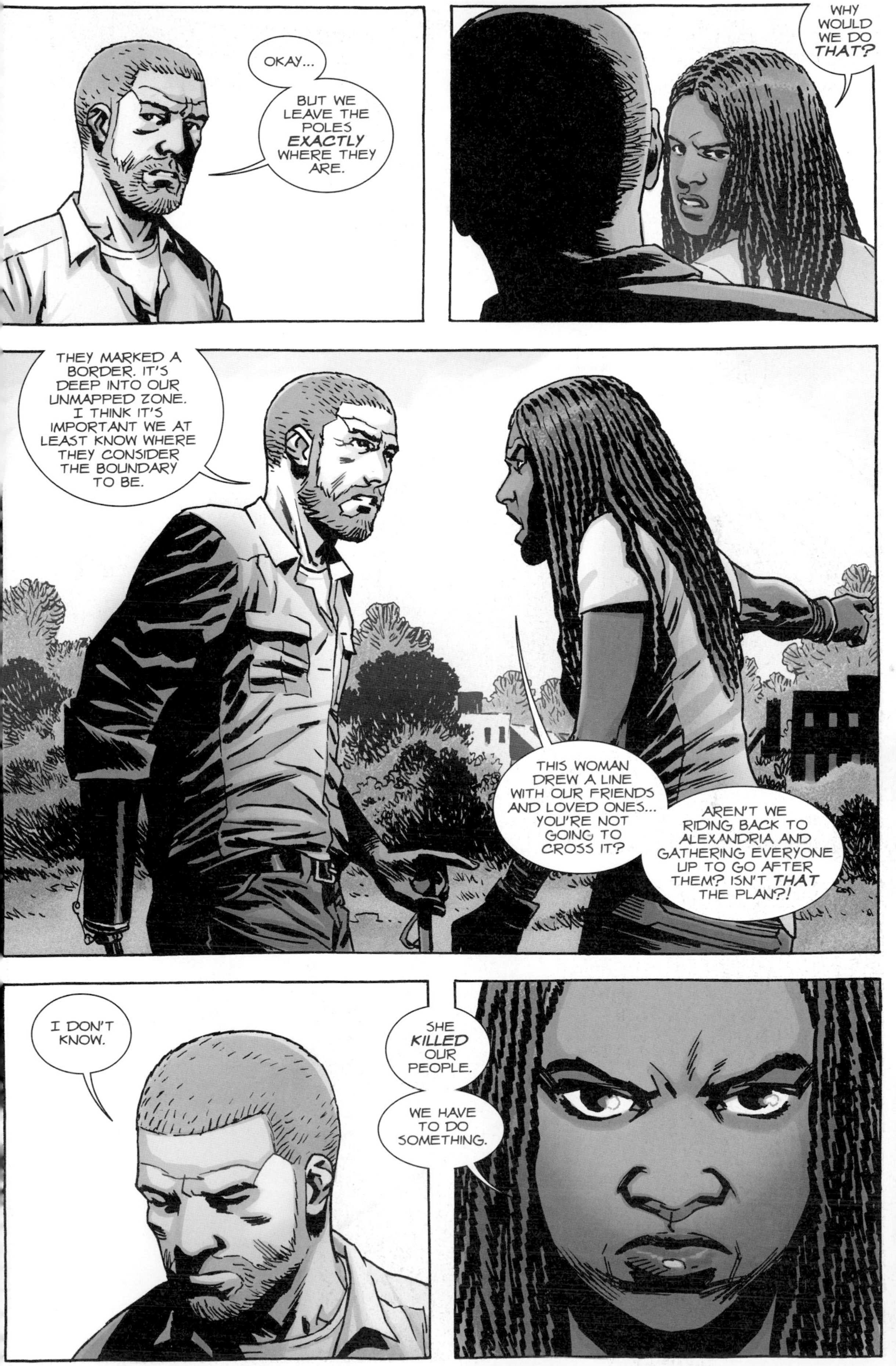
OKAY...
BUT WE LEAVE THE POLES *EXACTLY* WHERE THEY ARE.
WHY WOULD WE DO *THAT?*
THEY MARKED A BORDER. IT'S DEEP INTO OUR UNMAPPED ZONE. I THINK IT'S IMPORTANT WE AT LEAST KNOW WHERE THEY CONSIDER THE BOUNDARY TO BE.
THIS WOMAN DREW A LINE WITH OUR FRIENDS AND LOVED ONES... YOU'RE NOT GOING TO CROSS IT?
AREN'T WE RIDING BACK TO ALEXANDRIA AND GATHERING EVERYONE UP TO GO AFTER THEM? ISN'T *THAT* THE PLAN?!
I DON'T KNOW.
SHE *KILLED* OUR PEOPLE.
WE HAVE TO DO SOMETHING.

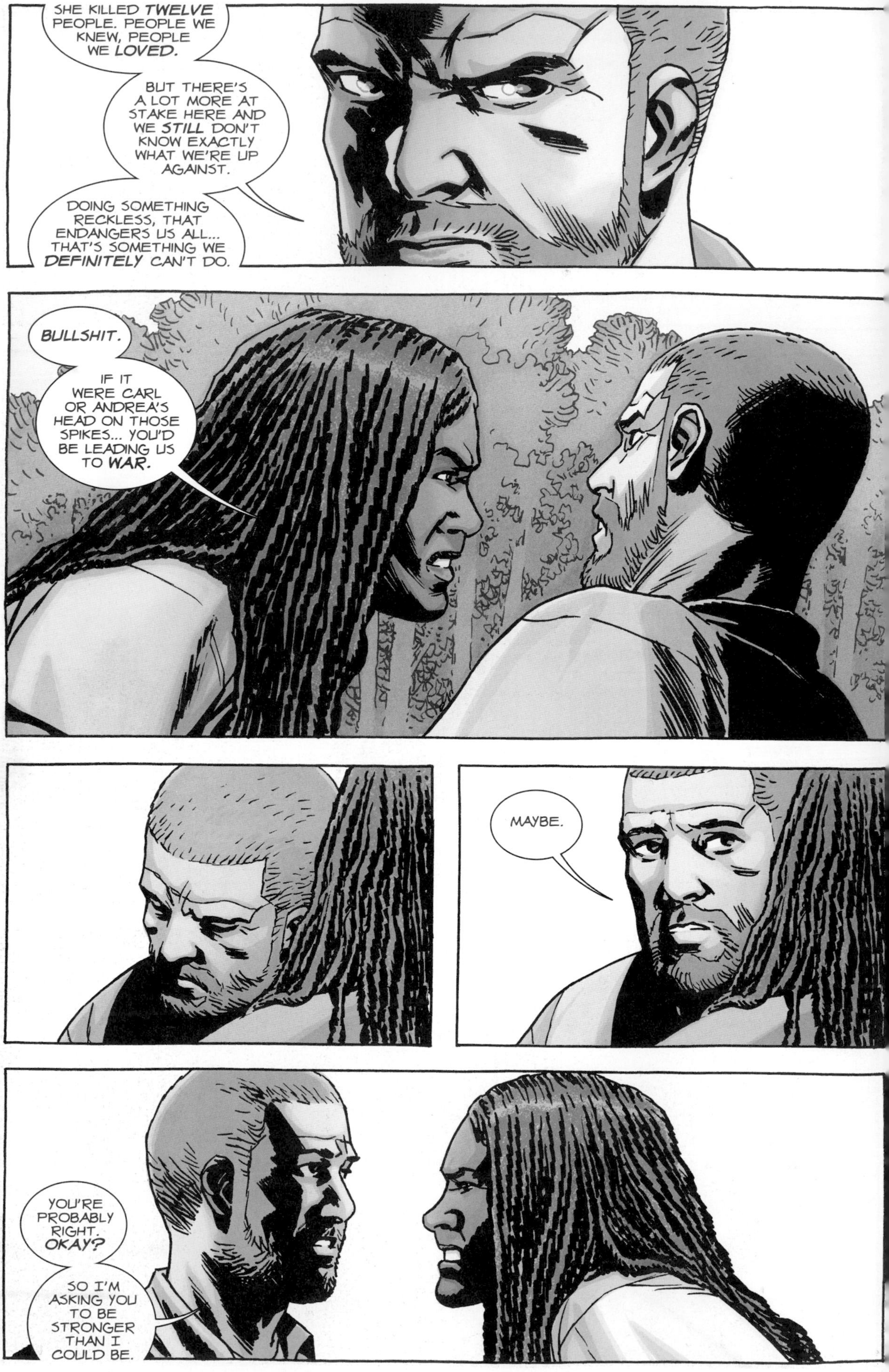

SHE KILLED TWELVE PEOPLE. PEOPLE WE KNEW, PEOPLE WE LOVED.
BUT THERE'S A LOT MORE AT STAKE HERE AND WE STILL DON'T KNOW EXACTLY WHAT WE'RE UP AGAINST.
DOING SOMETHING RECKLESS, THAT ENDANGERS US ALL... THAT'S SOMETHING WE DEFINITELY CAN'T DO.
BULLSHIT.
IF IT WERE CARL OR ANDREA'S HEAD ON THOSE SPIKES... YOU'D BE LEADING US TO WAR.
MAYBE.
YOU'RE PROBABLY RIGHT. OKAY?
SO I'M ASKING YOU TO BE STRONGER THAN I COULD BE.

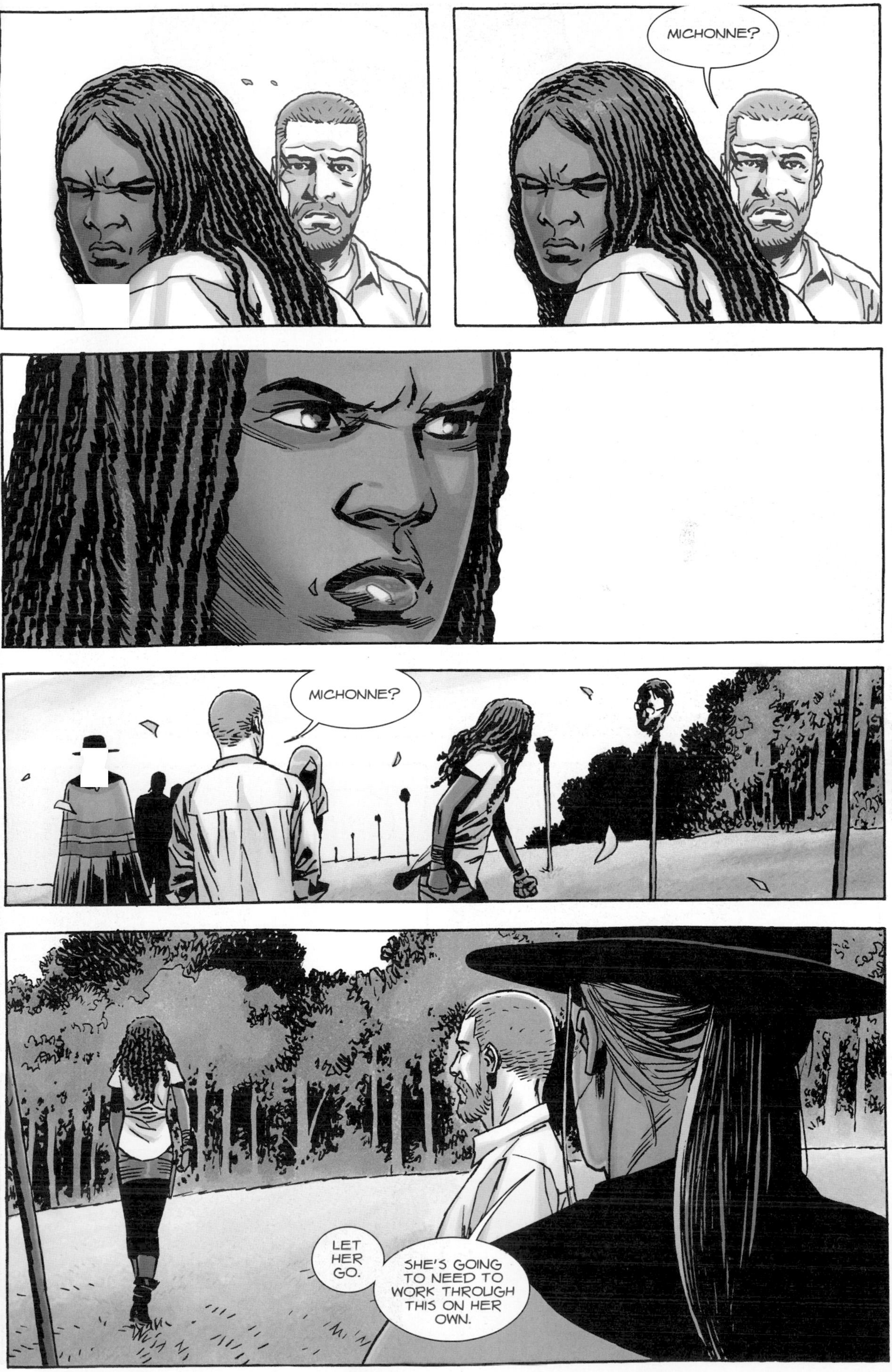
MICHONNE?
MICHONNE?
LET HER GO.
SHE'S GOING TO NEED TO WORK THROUGH THIS ON HER OWN.

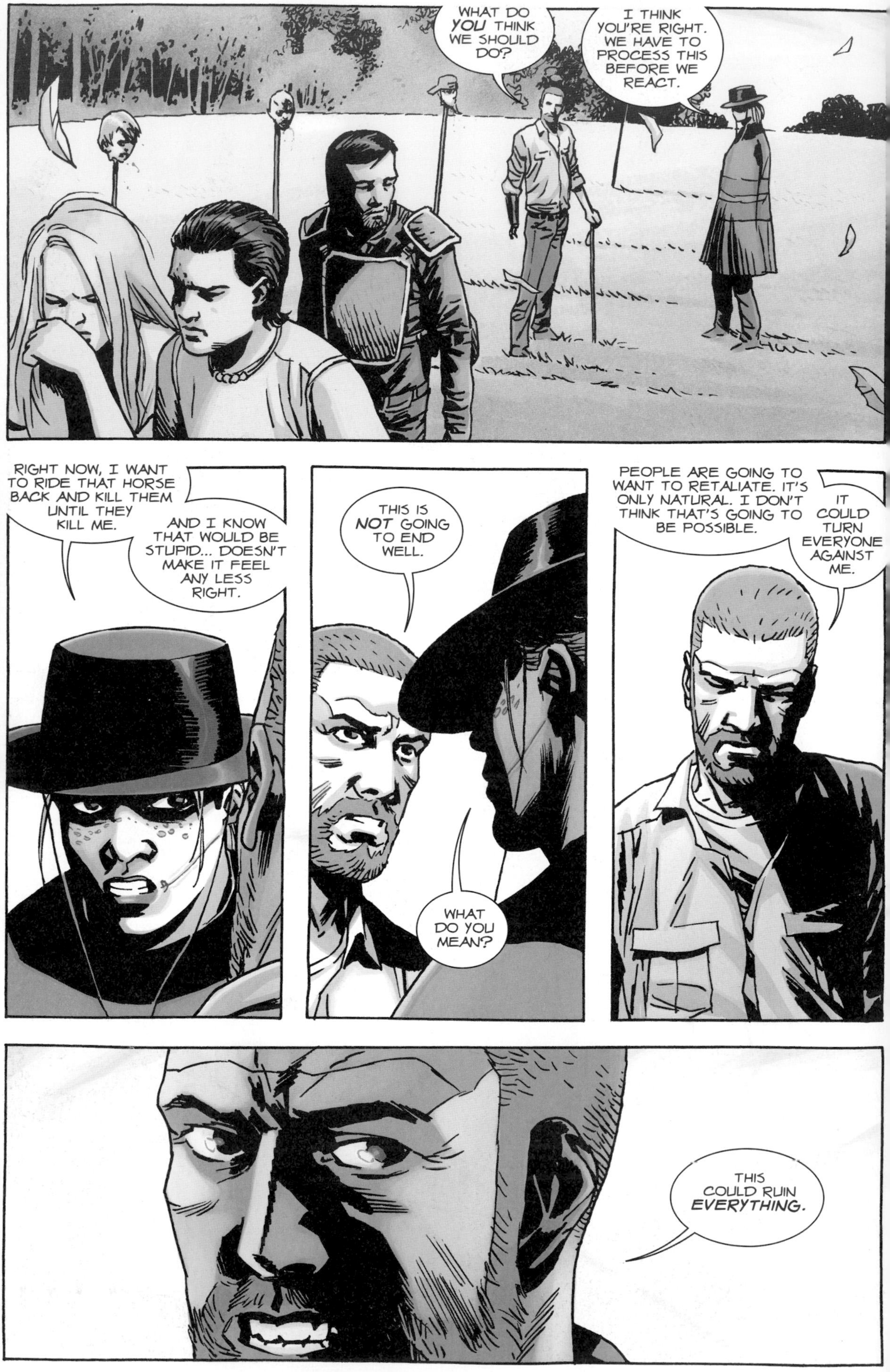
WHAT DO YOU THINK WE SHOULD DO?
I THINK YOU'RE RIGHT. WE HAVE TO PROCESS THIS BEFORE WE REACT.
RIGHT NOW, I WANT TO RIDE THAT HORSE BACK AND KILL THEM UNTIL THEY KILL ME.
AND I KNOW THAT WOULD BE STUPID... DOESN'T MAKE IT FEEL ANY LESS RIGHT.
THIS IS NOT GOING TO END WELL.
WHAT DO YOU MEAN?
PEOPLE ARE GOING TO WANT TO RETALIATE. IT'S ONLY NATURAL. I DON'T THINK THAT'S GOING TO BE POSSIBLE.
IT COULD TURN EVERYONE AGAINST ME.
THIS COULD RUIN EVERYTHING.

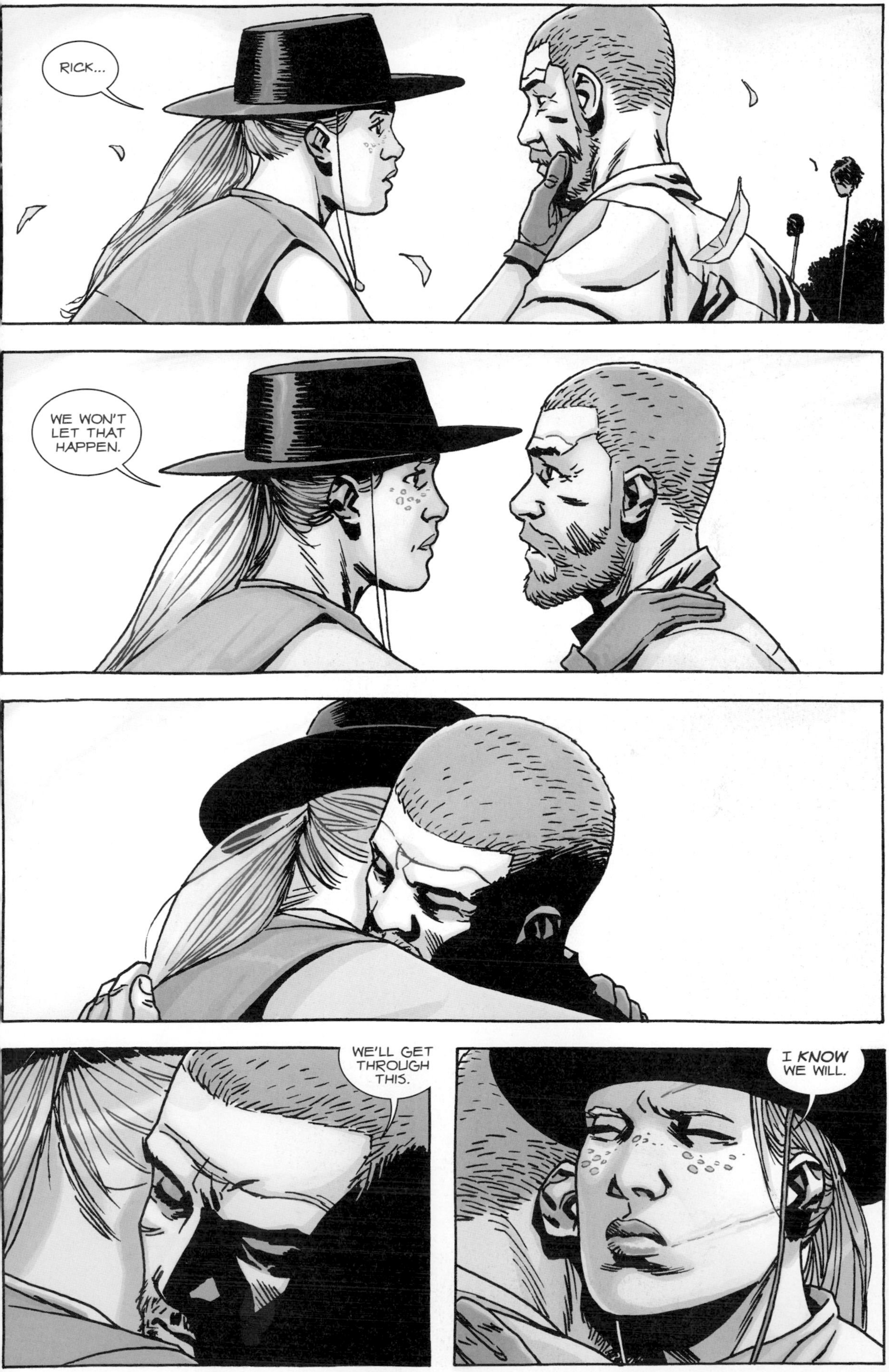
RICK...
WE WON'T LET THAT HAPPEN.
WE'LL GET THROUGH THIS.
I KNOW WE WILL.

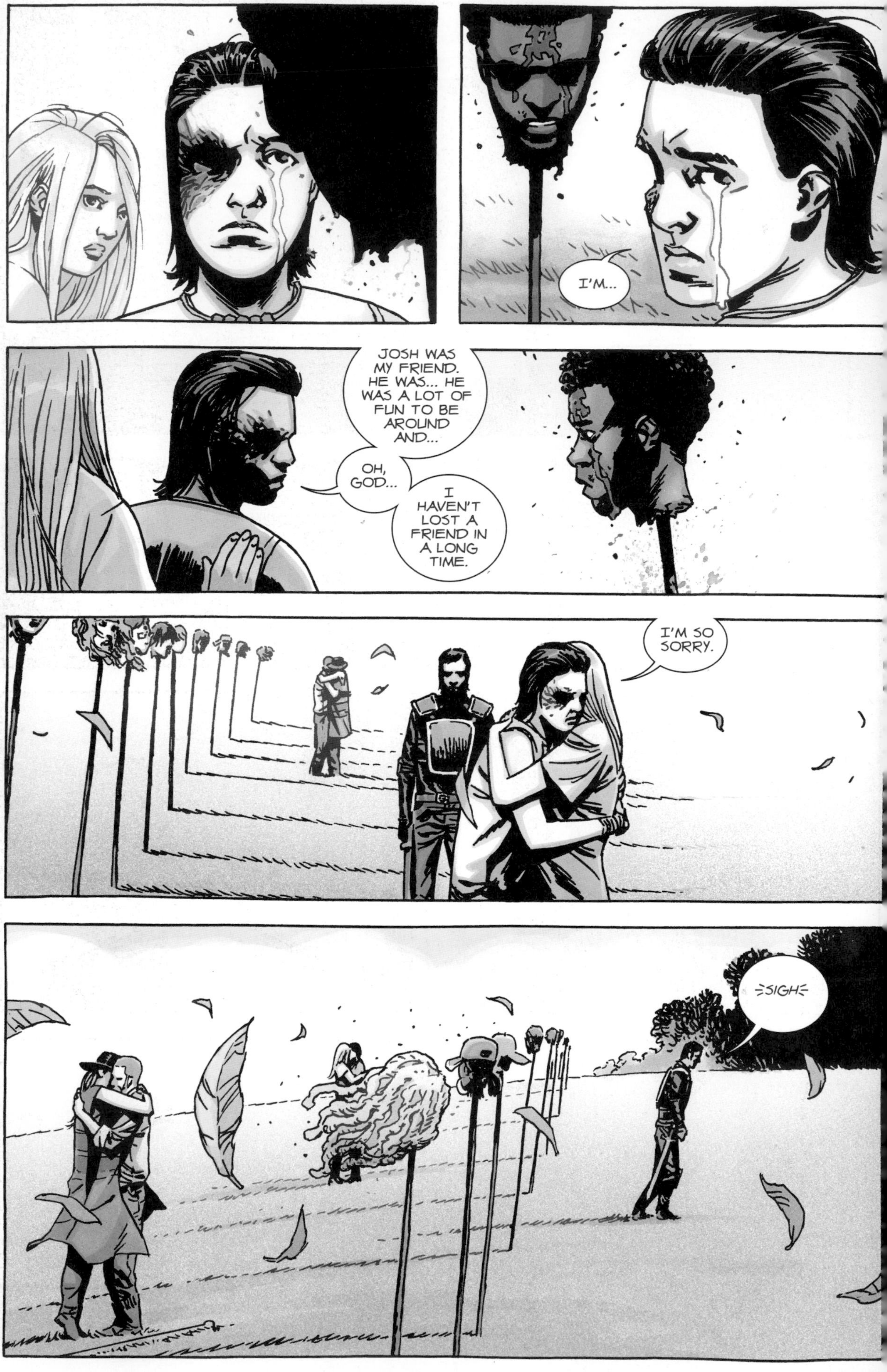
I'M...
JOSH WAS MY FRIEND. HE WAS... HE WAS A LOT OF FUN TO BE AROUND AND...
OH, GOD...
I HAVEN'T LOST A FRIEND IN A LONG TIME.
I'M SO SORRY.
SIGH

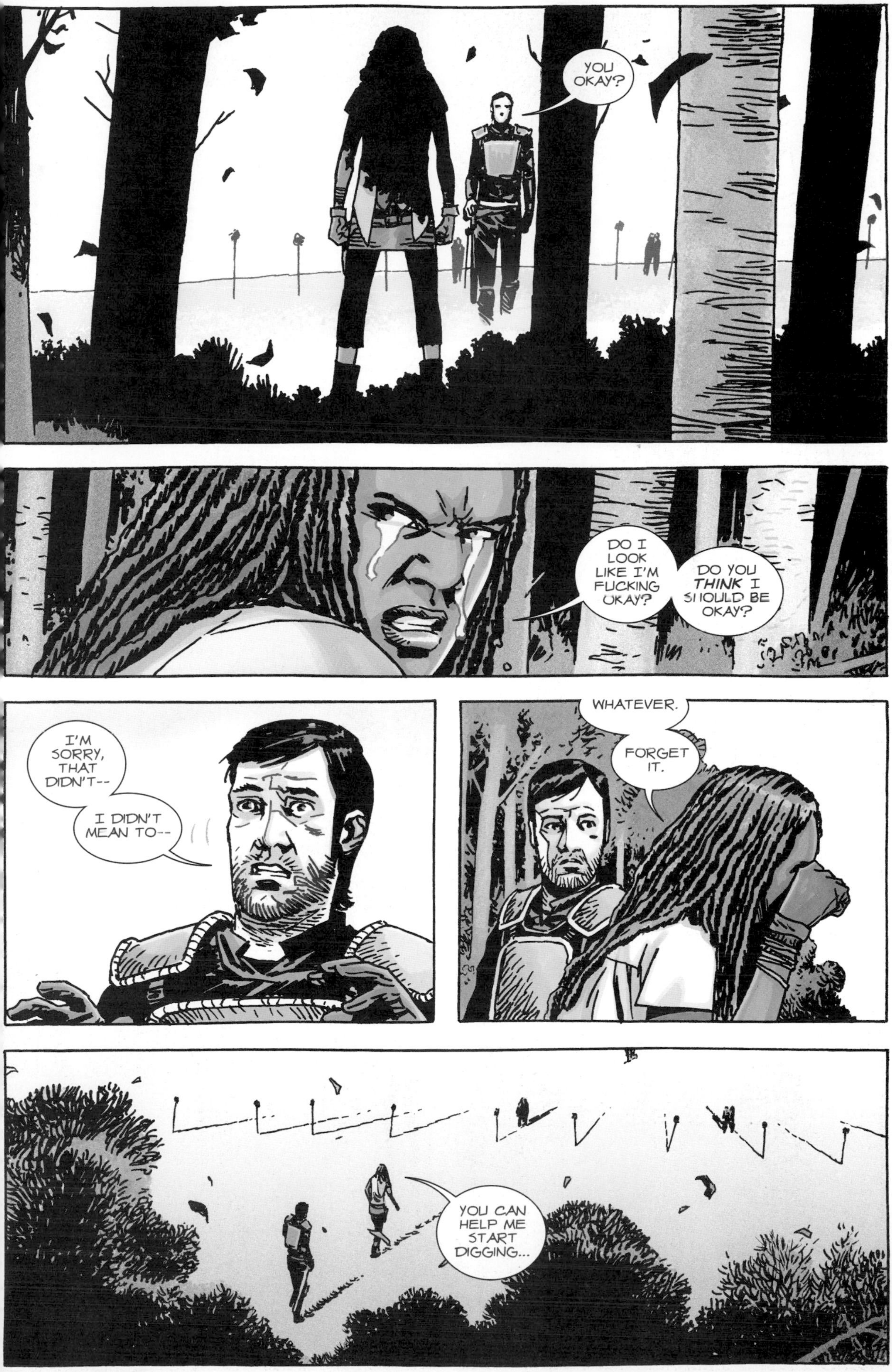
YOU OKAY?
DO I LOOK LIKE I'M FUCKING OKAY?
DO YOU *THINK* I SHOULD BE OKAY?
I'M SORRY, THAT DIDN'T--
I DIDN'T MEAN TO--
WHATEVER.
FORGET IT.
YOU CAN HELP ME START DIGGING...

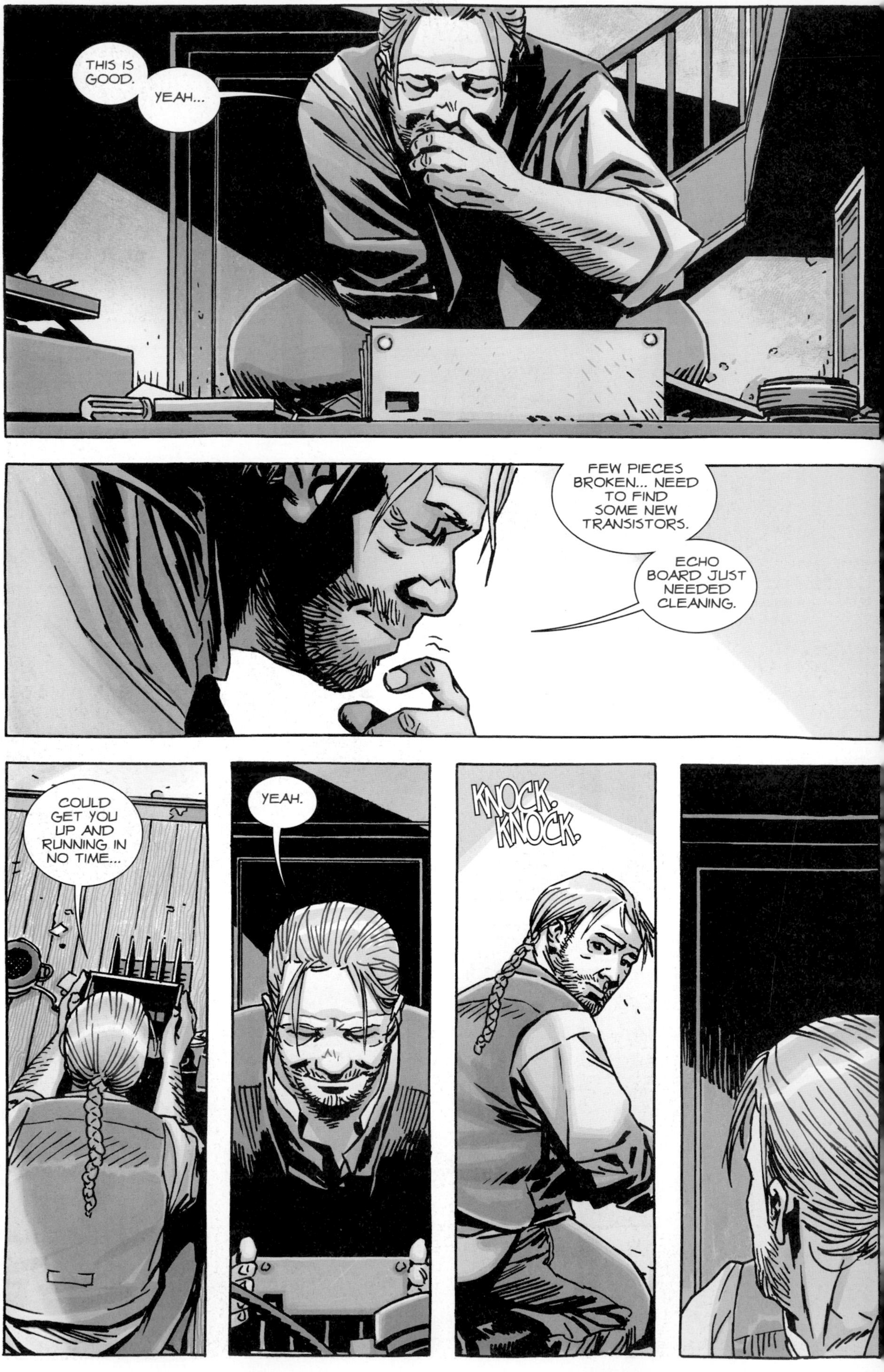
THIS IS GOOD.
YEAH...
FEW PIECES BROKEN... NEED TO FIND SOME NEW TRANSISTORS.
ECHO BOARD JUST NEEDED CLEANING.
COULD GET YOU UP AND RUNNING IN NO TIME...
YEAH.
KNOCK. KNOCK.

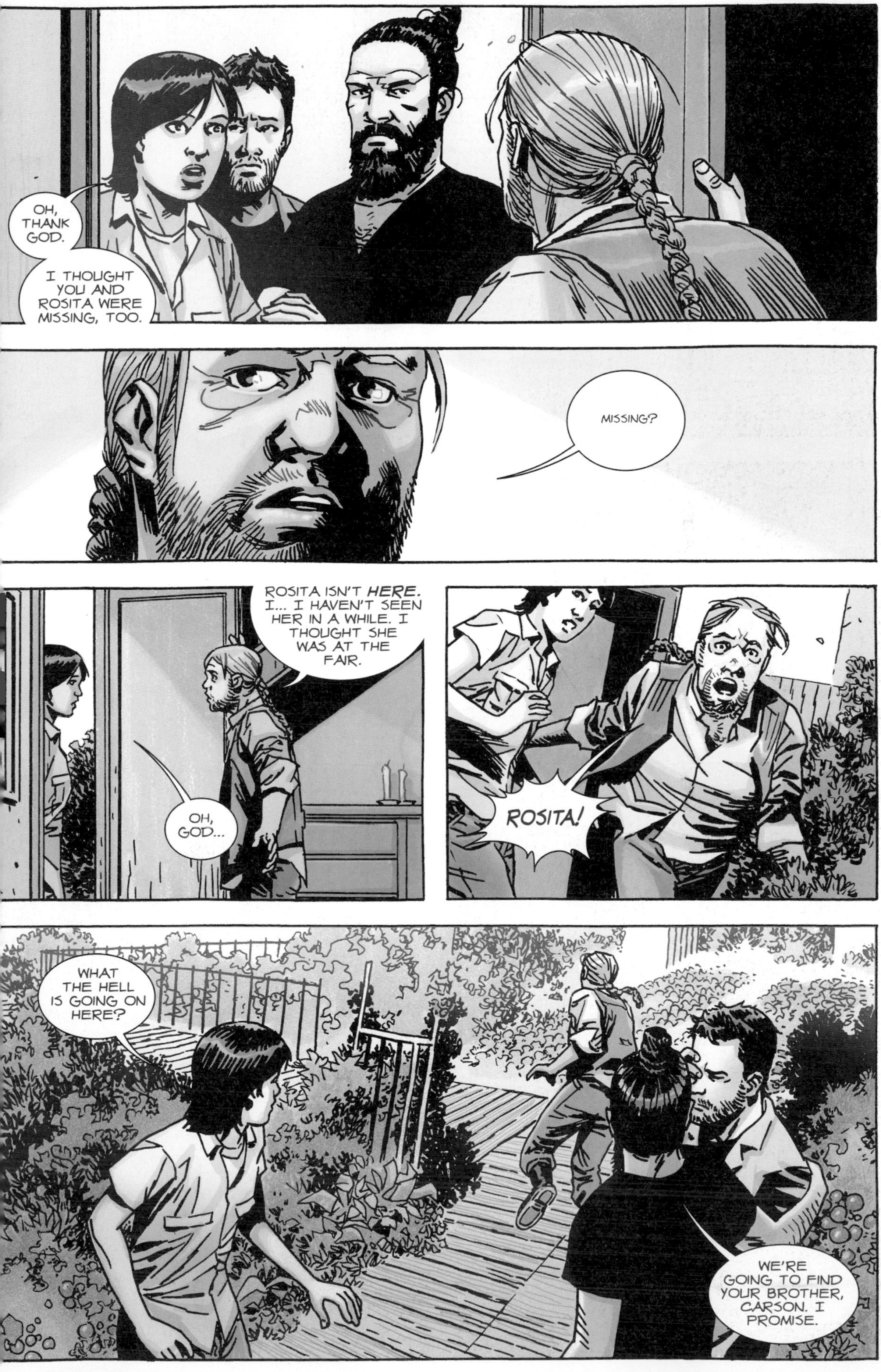
OH, THANK GOD.
I THOUGHT YOU AND ROSITA WERE MISSING, TOO.
MISSING?
ROSITA ISN'T *HERE.* I... I HAVEN'T SEEN HER IN A WHILE. I THOUGHT SHE WAS AT THE FAIR.
OH, GOD...
ROSITA!
WHAT THE HELL IS GOING ON HERE?
WE'RE GOING TO FIND YOUR BROTHER, CARSON. I PROMISE.

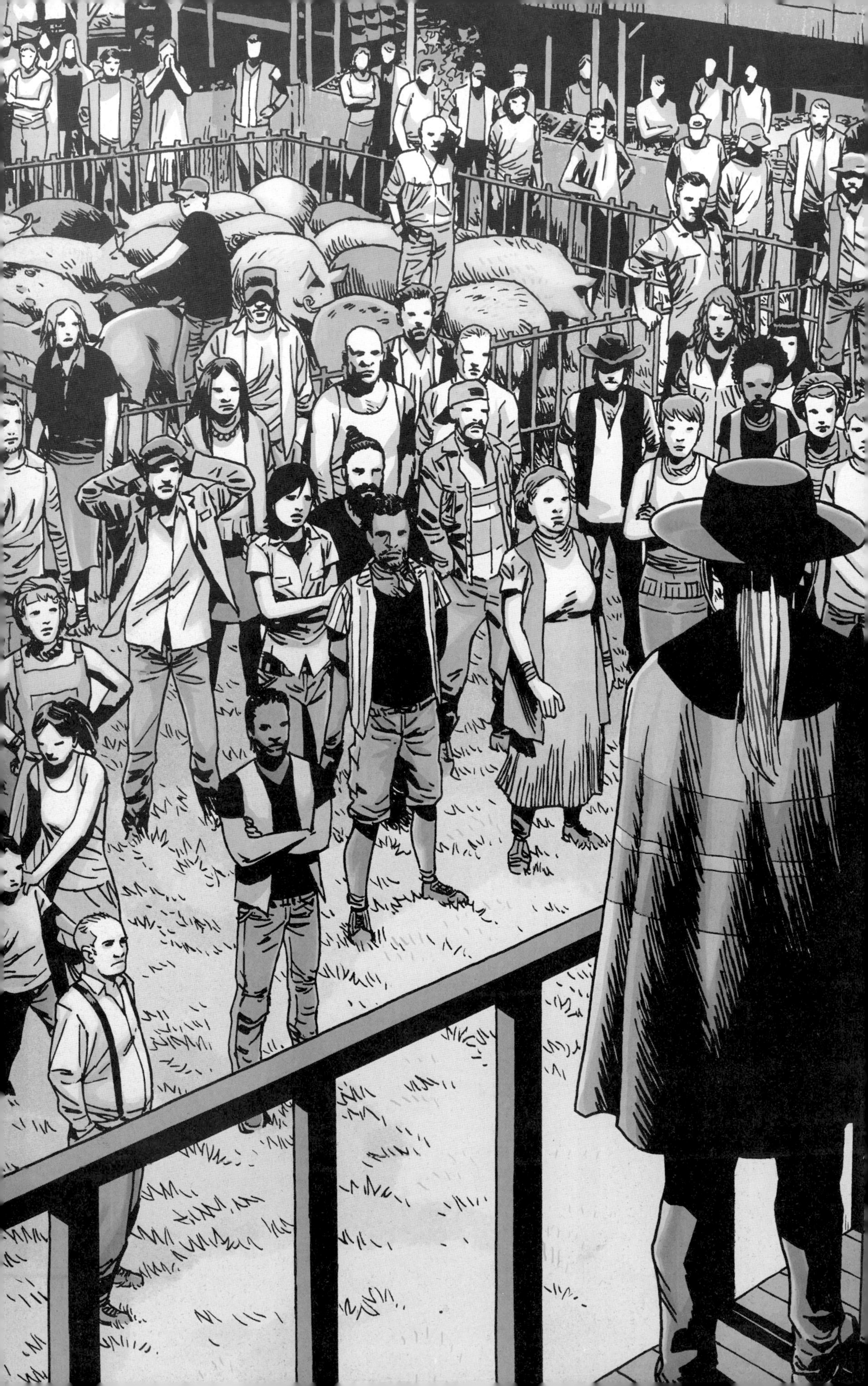

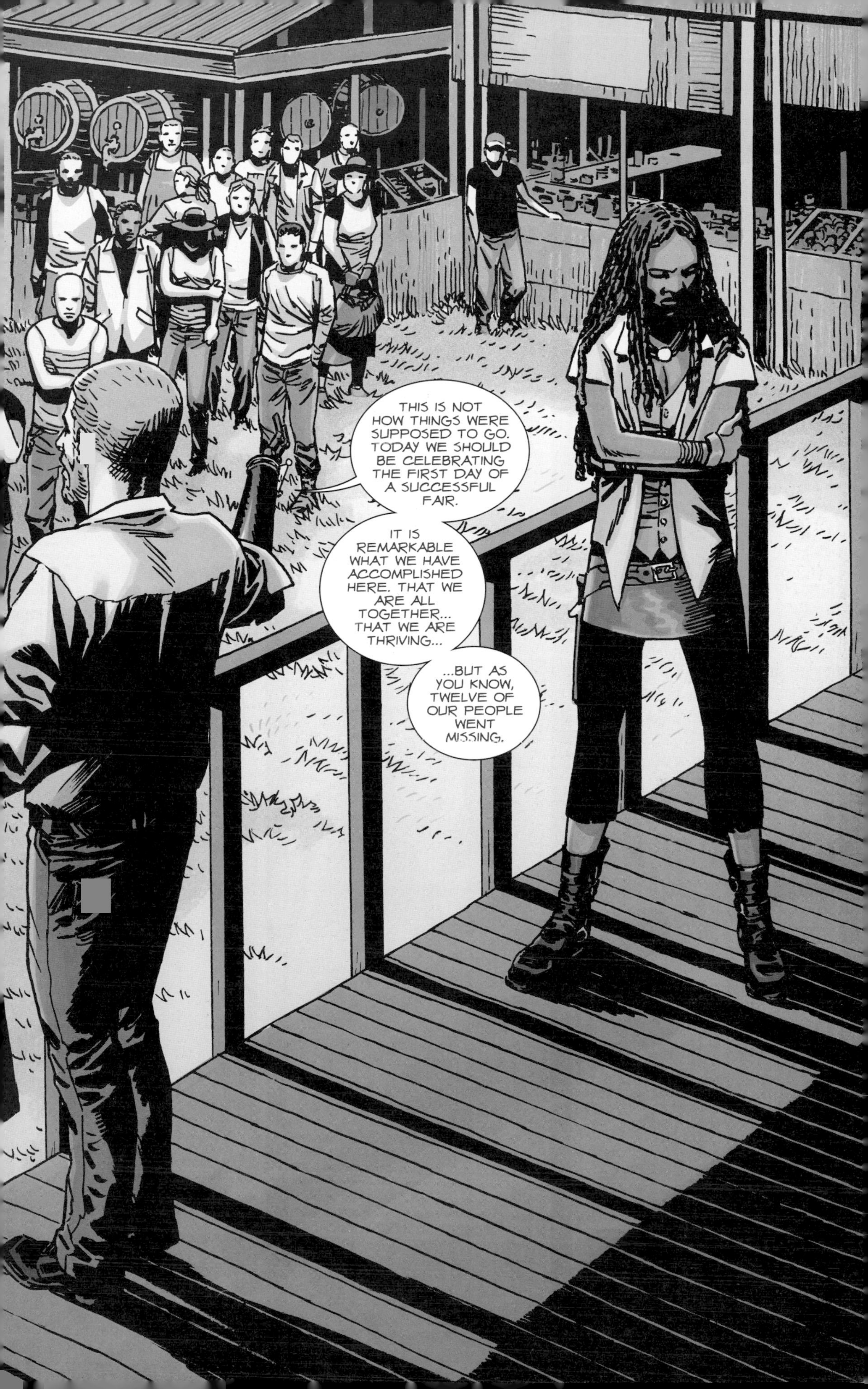
THIS IS NOT HOW THINGS WERE SUPPOSED TO GO. TODAY WE SHOULD BE CELEBRATING THE FIRST DAY OF A SUCCESSFUL FAIR.
IT IS REMARKABLE WHAT WE HAVE ACCOMPLISHED HERE. THAT WE ARE ALL TOGETHER... THAT WE ARE THRIVING...
...BUT AS YOU KNOW, TWELVE OF OUR PEOPLE WENT MISSING.

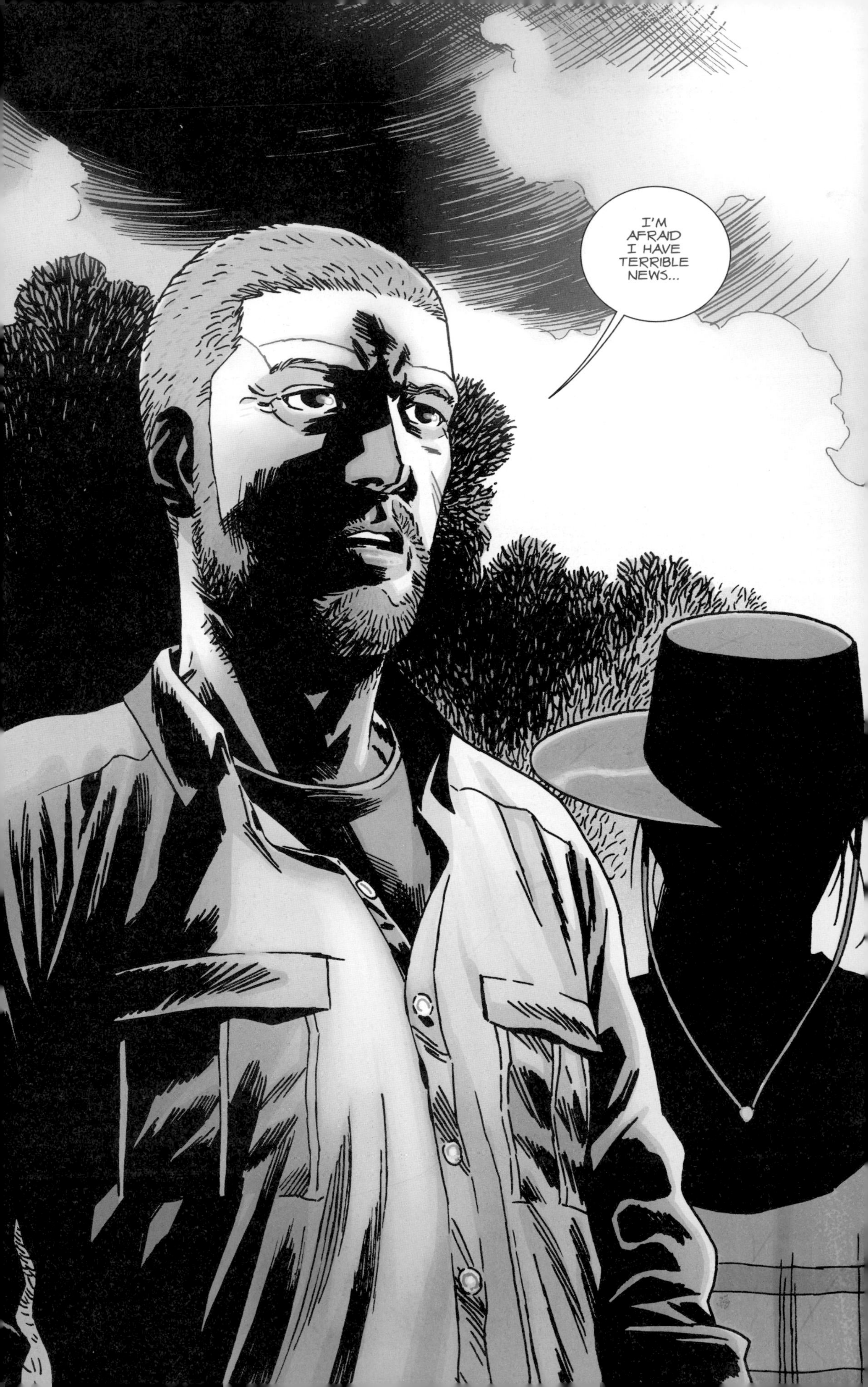
I'M AFRAID I HAVE TERRIBLE NEWS...

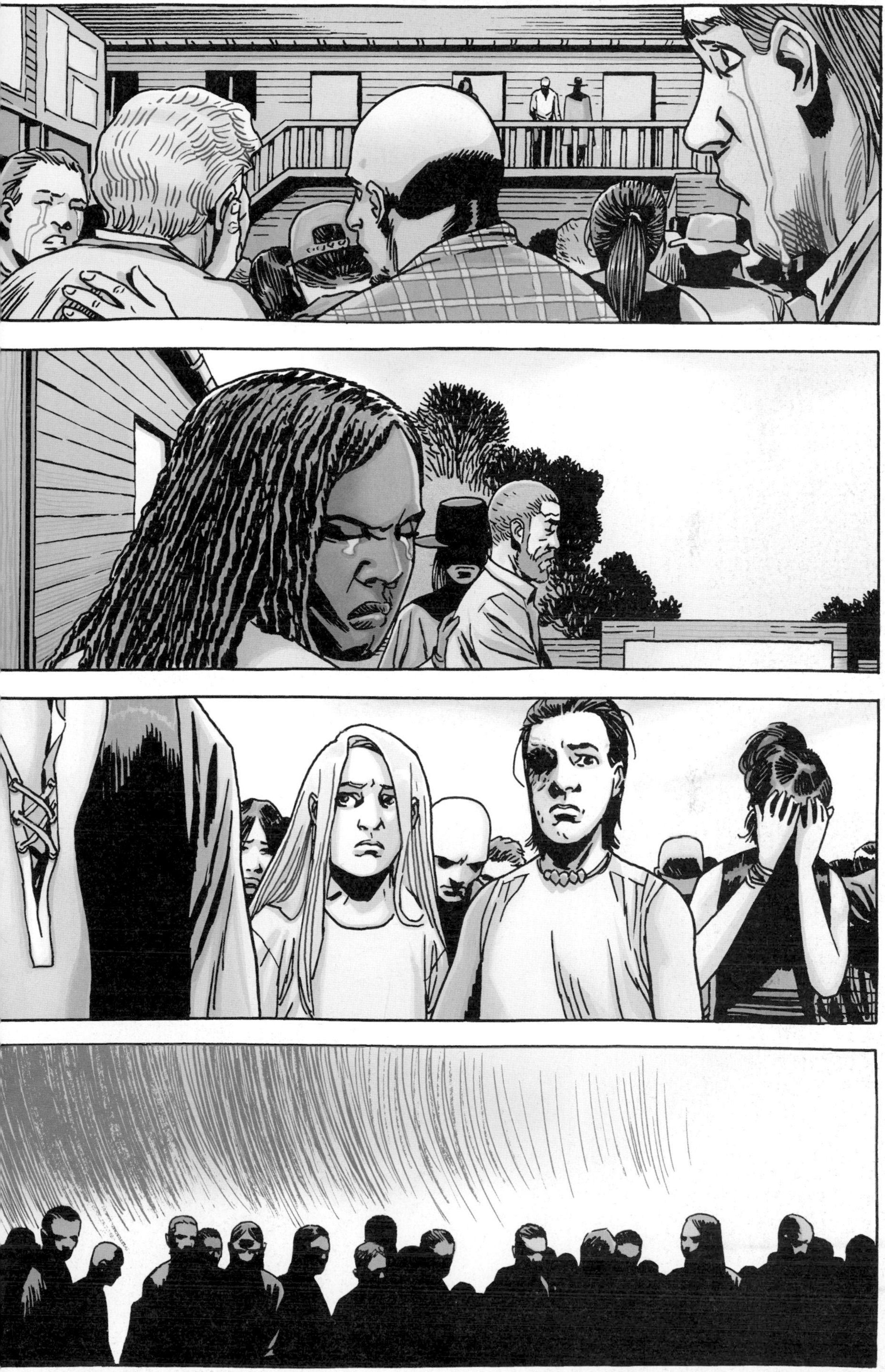

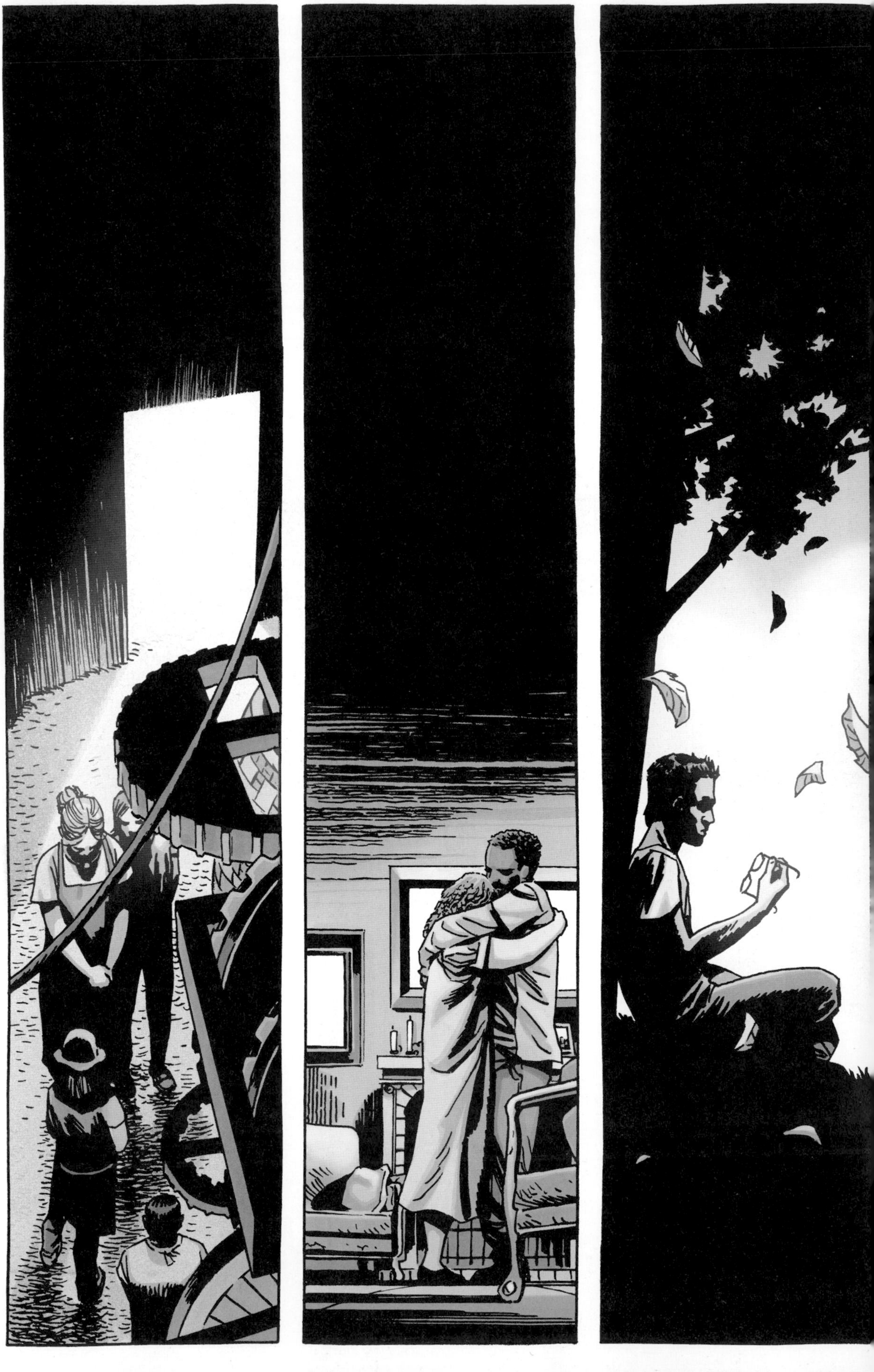

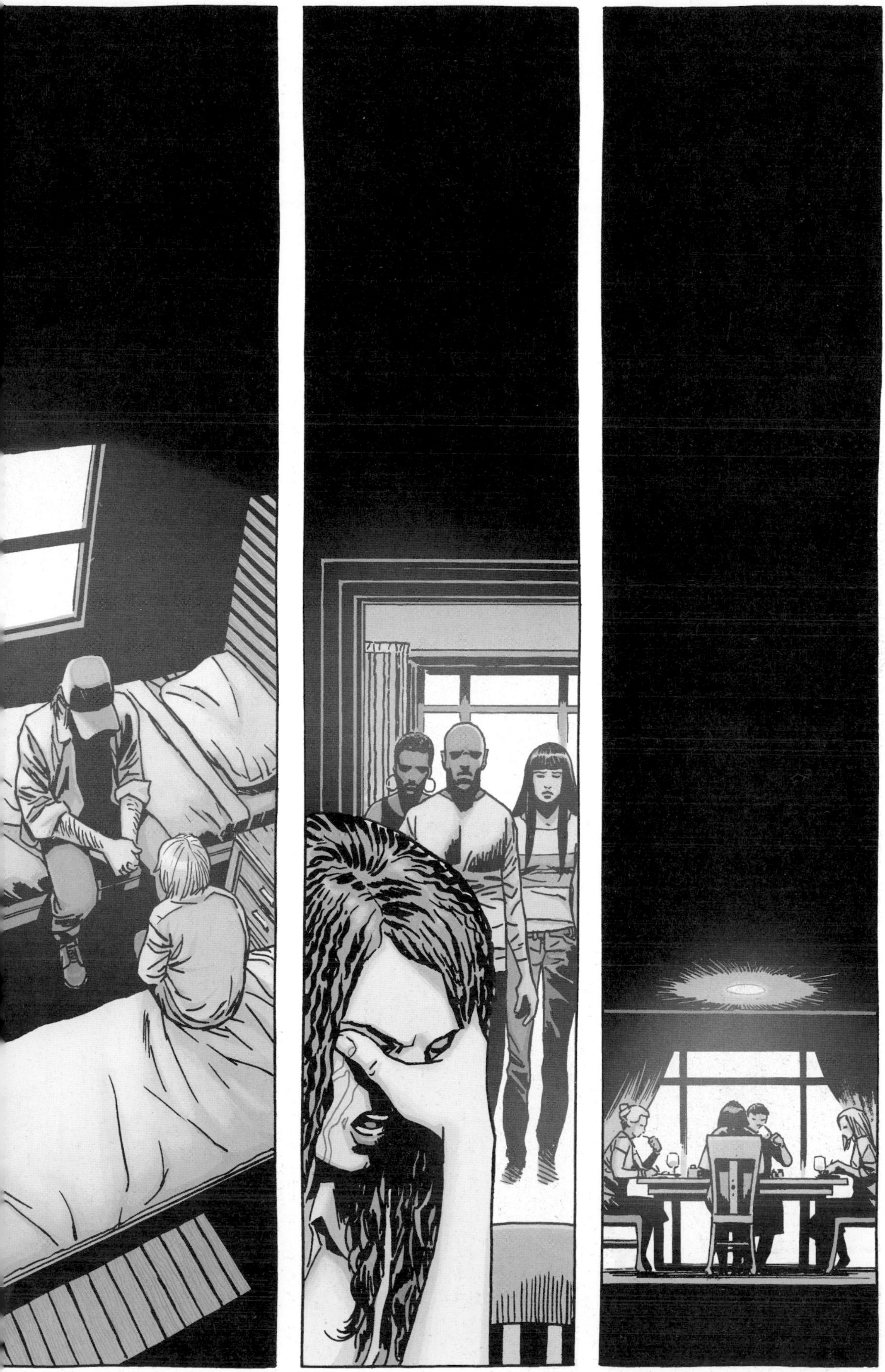

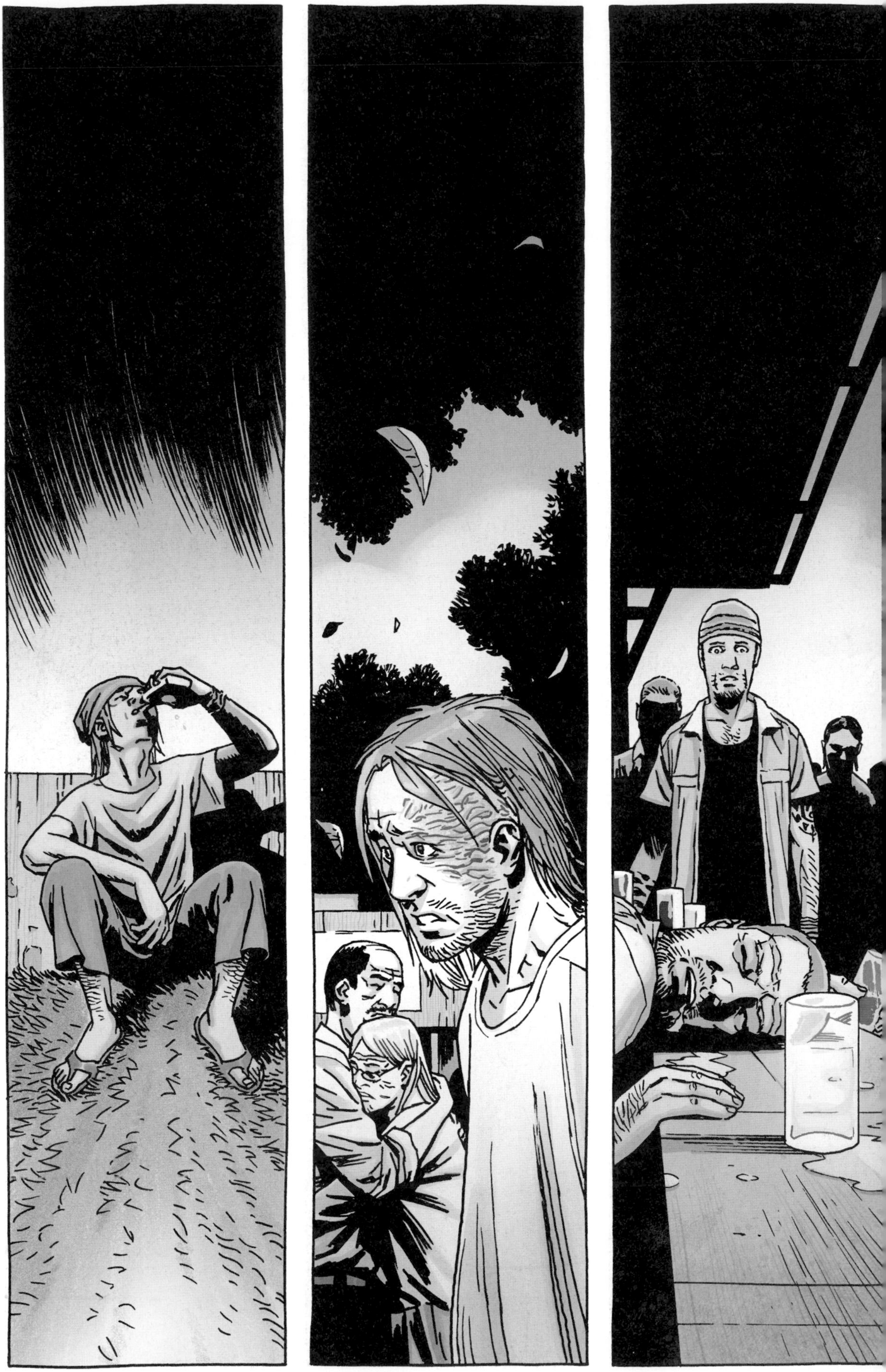

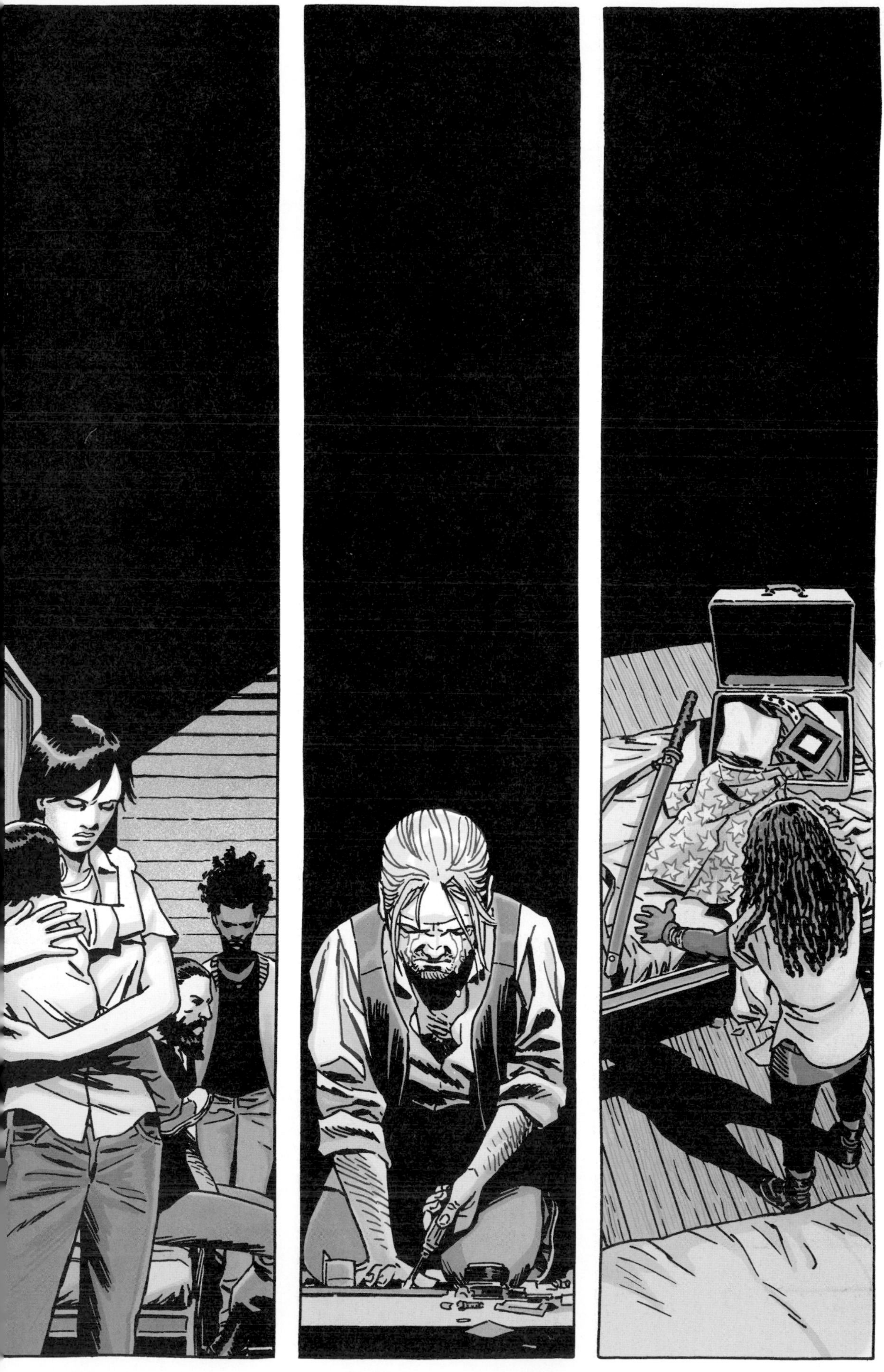

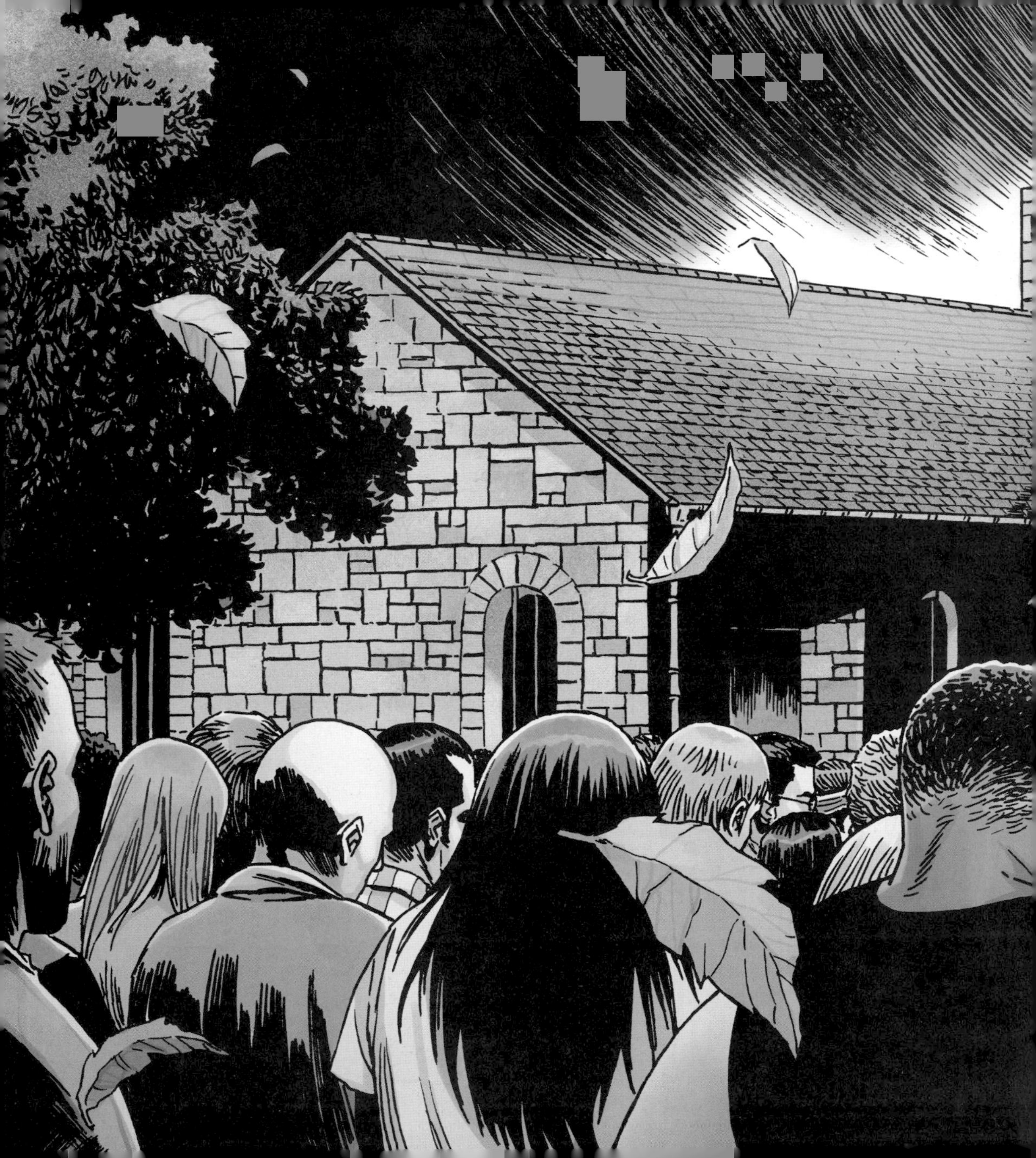

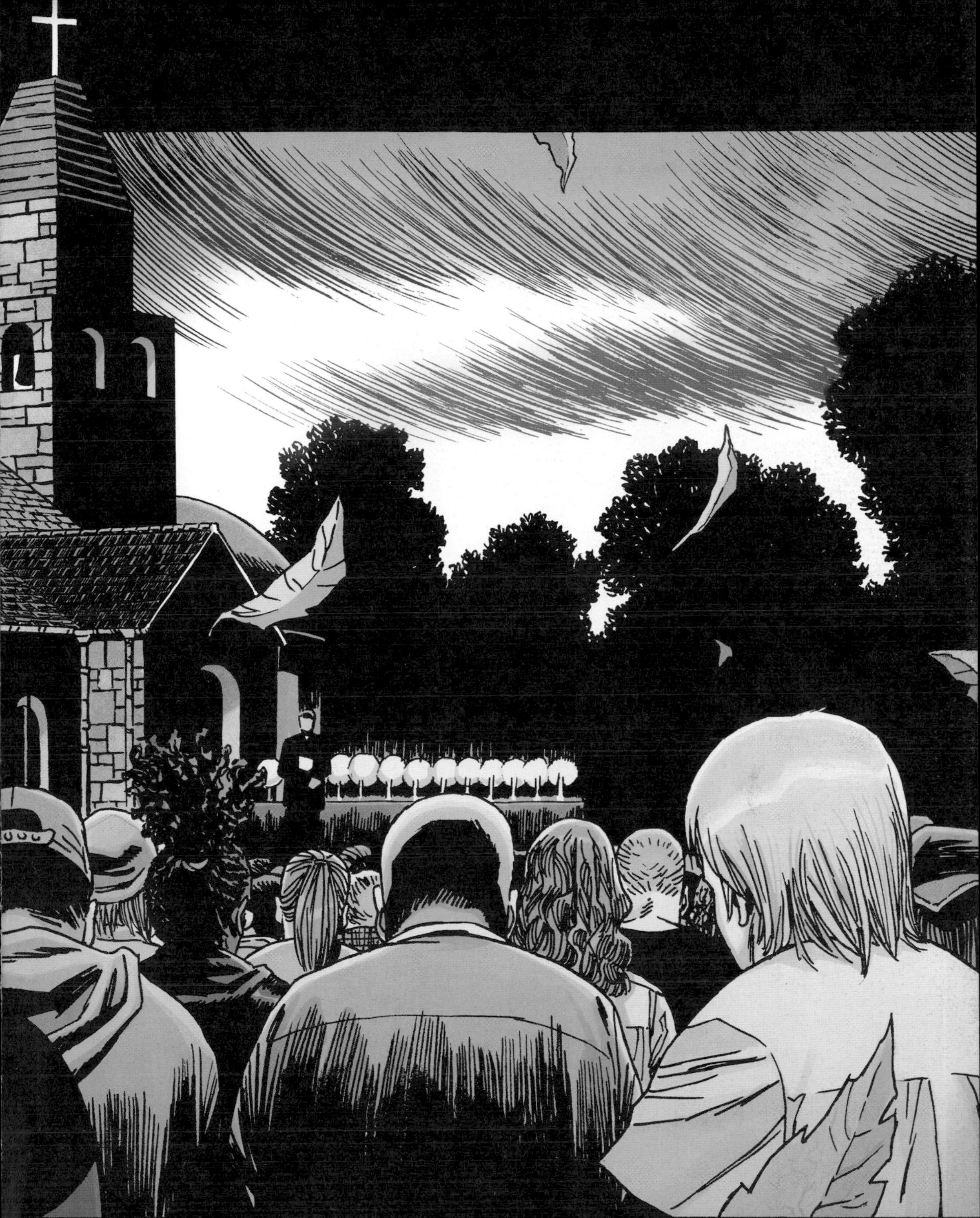

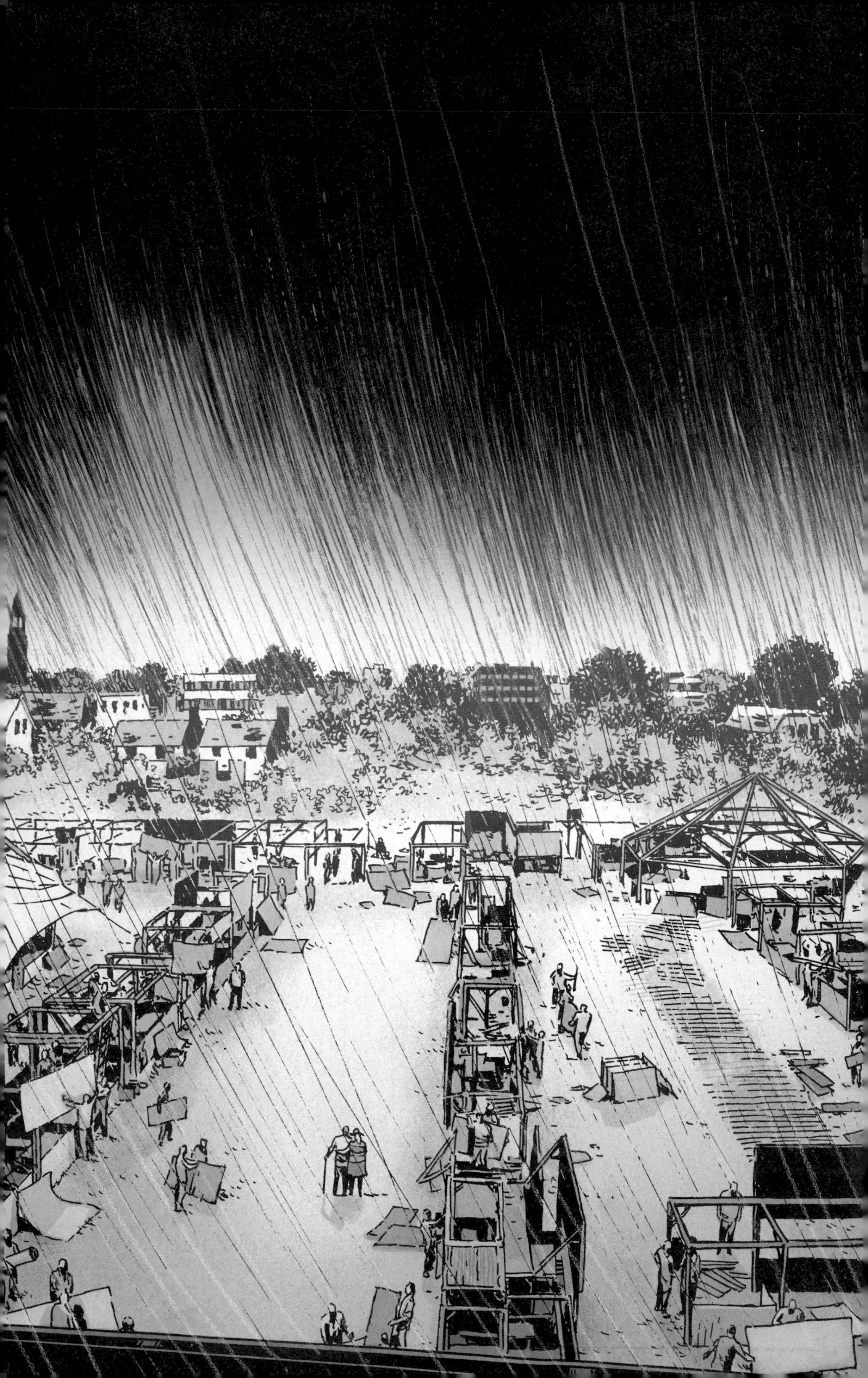

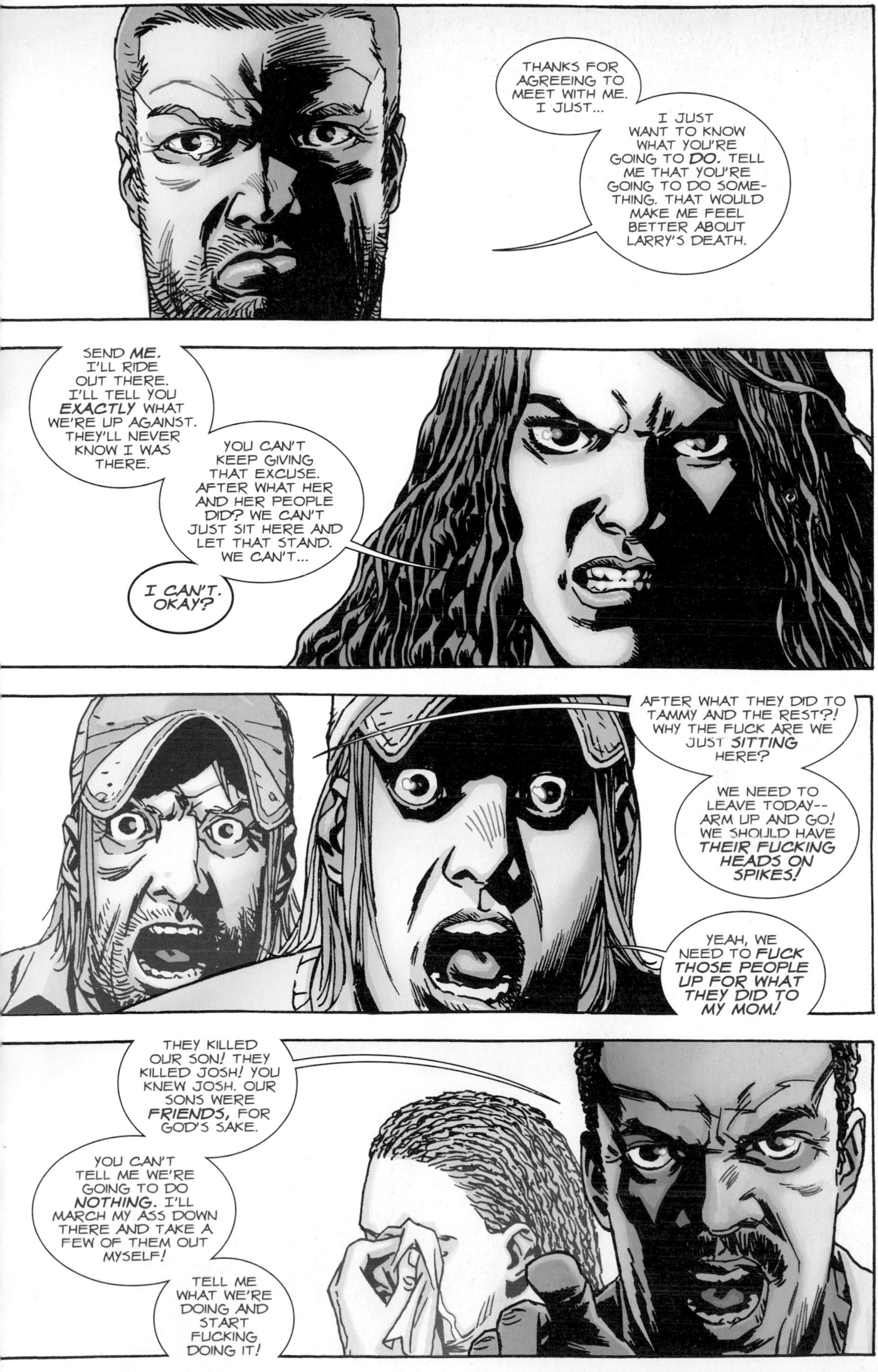
THANKS FOR AGREEING TO MEET WITH ME. I JUST...
I JUST WANT TO KNOW WHAT YOU'RE GOING TO DO. TELL ME THAT YOU'RE GOING TO DO SOME-THING. THAT WOULD MAKE ME FEEL BETTER ABOUT LARRY'S DEATH.
SEND ME. I'LL RIDE OUT THERE. I'LL TELL YOU EXACTLY WHAT WE'RE UP AGAINST. THEY'LL NEVER KNOW I WAS THERE.
YOU CAN'T KEEP GIVING THAT EXCUSE. AFTER WHAT HER AND HER PEOPLE DID? WE CAN'T JUST SIT HERE AND LET THAT STAND. WE CAN'T...
I CAN'T. OKAY?
AFTER WHAT THEY DID TO TAMMY AND THE REST?! WHY THE FUCK ARE WE JUST SITTING HERE?
WE NEED TO LEAVE TODAY-- ARM UP AND GO! WE SHOULD HAVE THEIR FUCKING HEADS ON SPIKES!
YEAH, WE NEED TO FUCK THOSE PEOPLE UP FOR WHAT THEY DID TO MY MOM!
THEY KILLED OUR SON! THEY KILLED JOSH! YOU KNEW JOSH. OUR SONS WERE FRIENDS, FOR GOD'S SAKE.
YOU CAN'T TELL ME WE'RE GOING TO DO NOTHING. I'LL MARCH MY ASS DOWN THERE AND TAKE A FEW OF THEM OUT MYSELF!
TELL ME WHAT WE'RE DOING AND START FUCKING DOING IT!

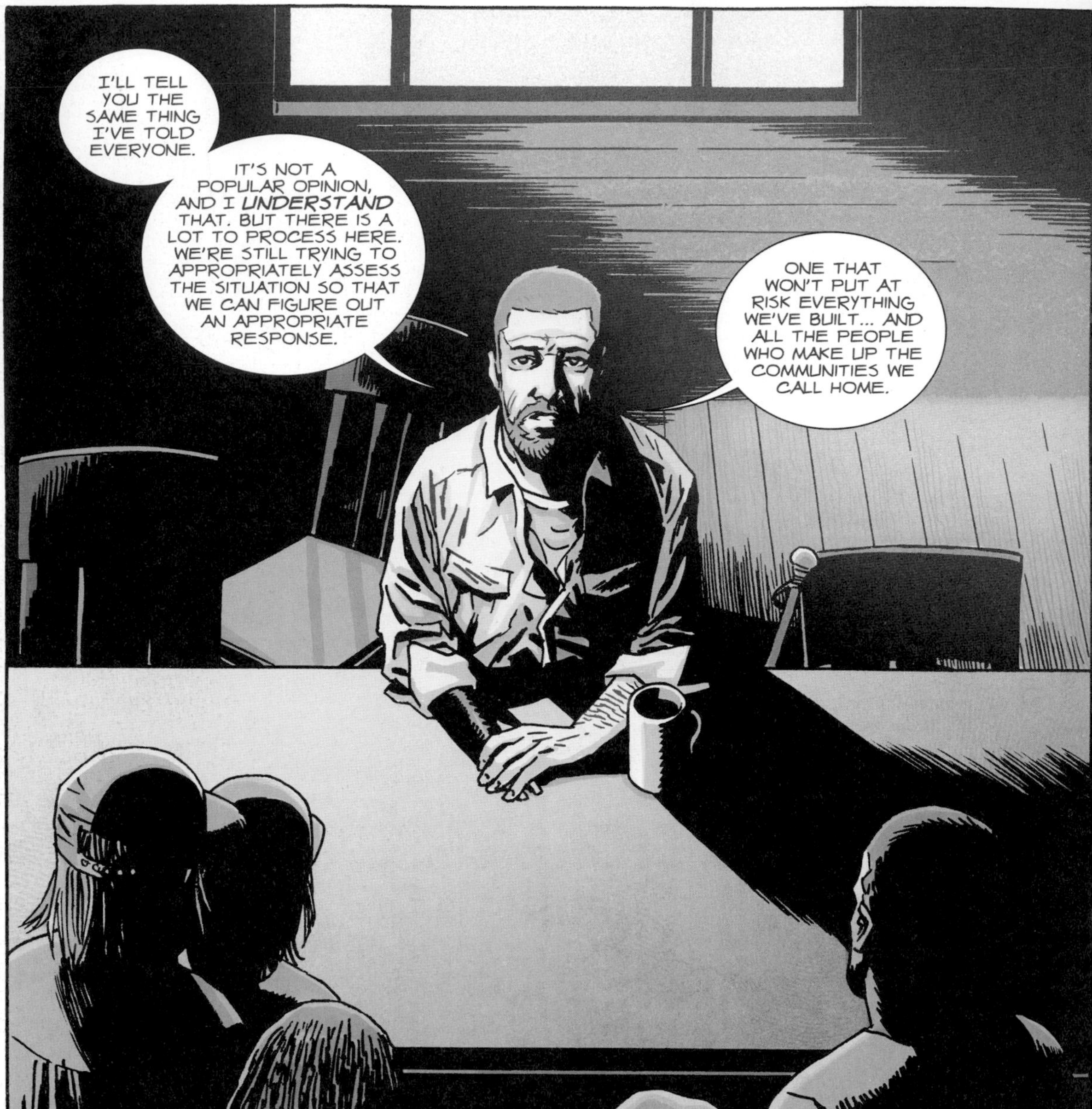
I'LL TELL YOU THE SAME THING I'VE TOLD EVERYONE.
IT'S NOT A POPULAR OPINION, AND I *UNDERSTAND* THAT. BUT THERE IS A LOT TO PROCESS HERE. WE'RE STILL TRYING TO APPROPRIATELY ASSESS THE SITUATION SO THAT WE CAN FIGURE OUT AN APPROPRIATE RESPONSE.
ONE THAT WON'T PUT AT RISK EVERYTHING WE'VE BUILT... AND ALL THE PEOPLE WHO MAKE UP THE COMMUNITIES WE CALL HOME.

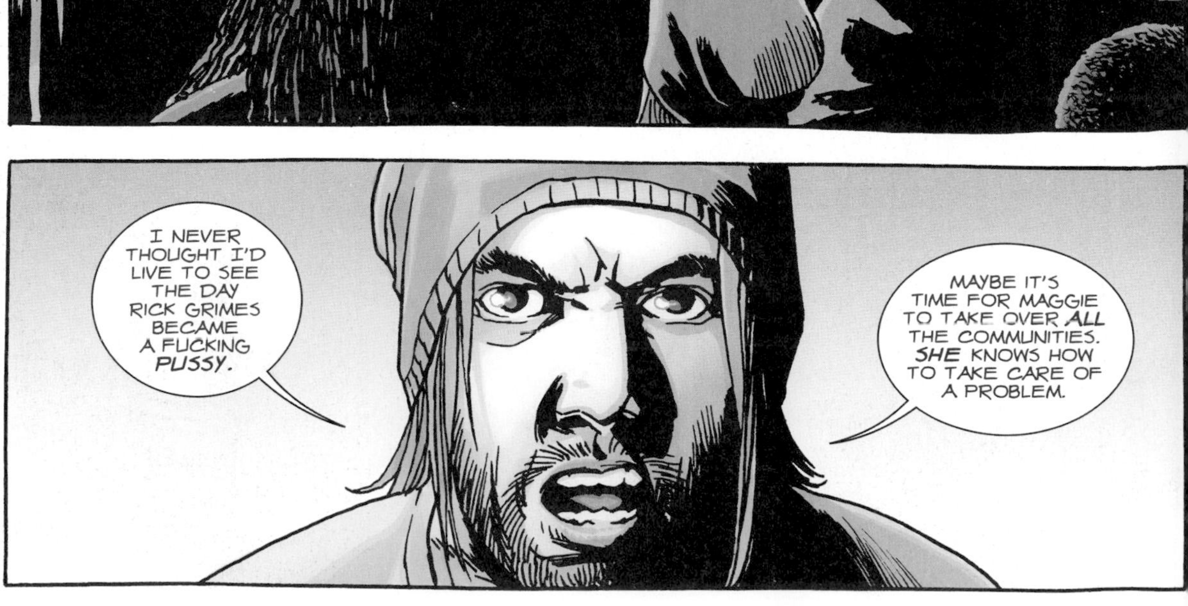
I NEVER THOUGHT I'D LIVE TO SEE THE DAY RICK GRIMES BECAME A FUCKING *PUSSY*.
MAYBE IT'S TIME FOR MAGGIE TO TAKE OVER *ALL* THE COMMUNITIES. *SHE* KNOWS HOW TO TAKE CARE OF A PROBLEM.

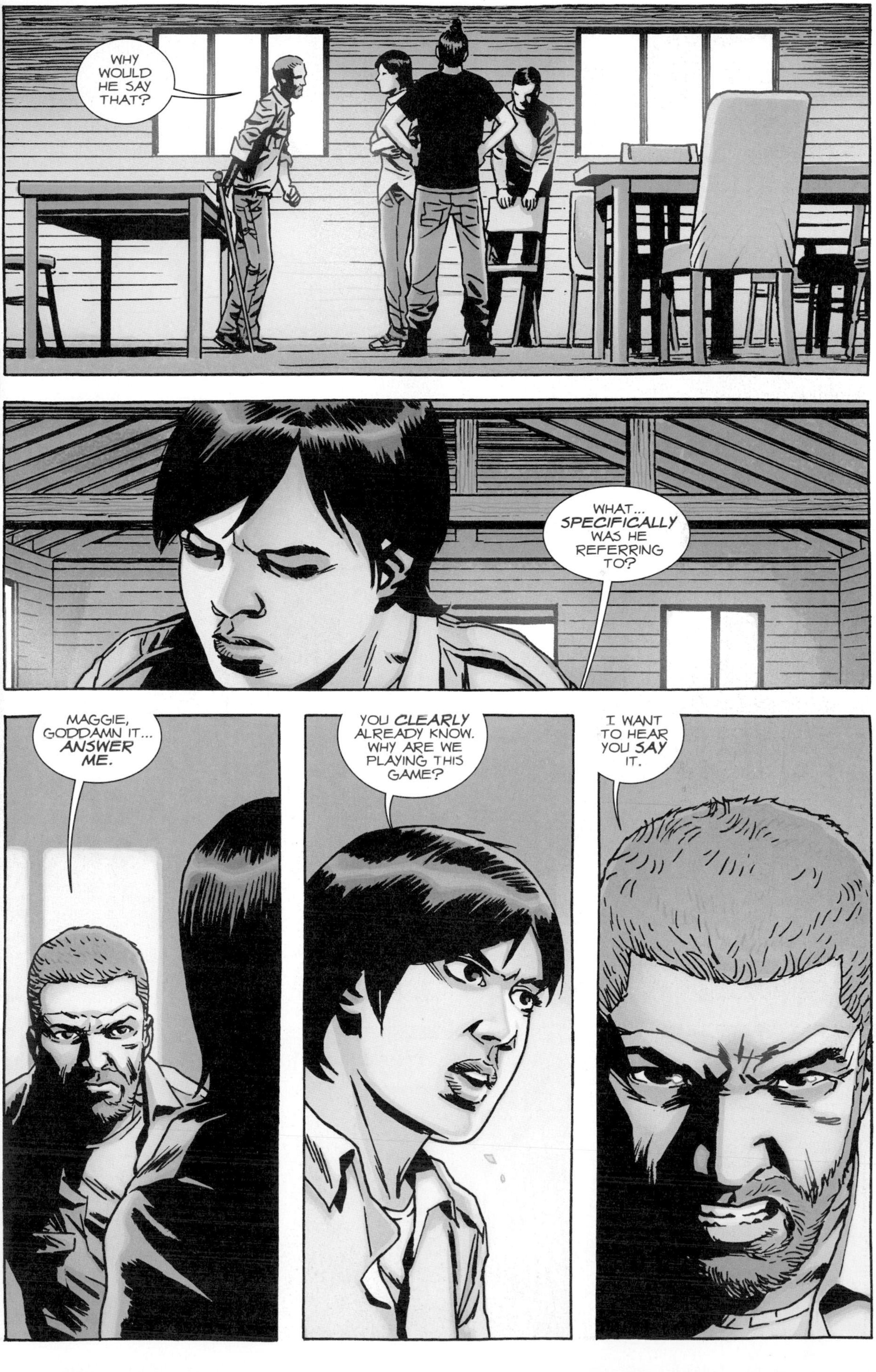
WHY WOULD HE SAY THAT?
WHAT... SPECIFICALLY WAS HE REFERRING TO?
MAGGIE, GODDAMN IT... ANSWER ME.
YOU CLEARLY ALREADY KNOW. WHY ARE WE PLAYING THIS GAME?
I WANT TO HEAR YOU SAY IT.

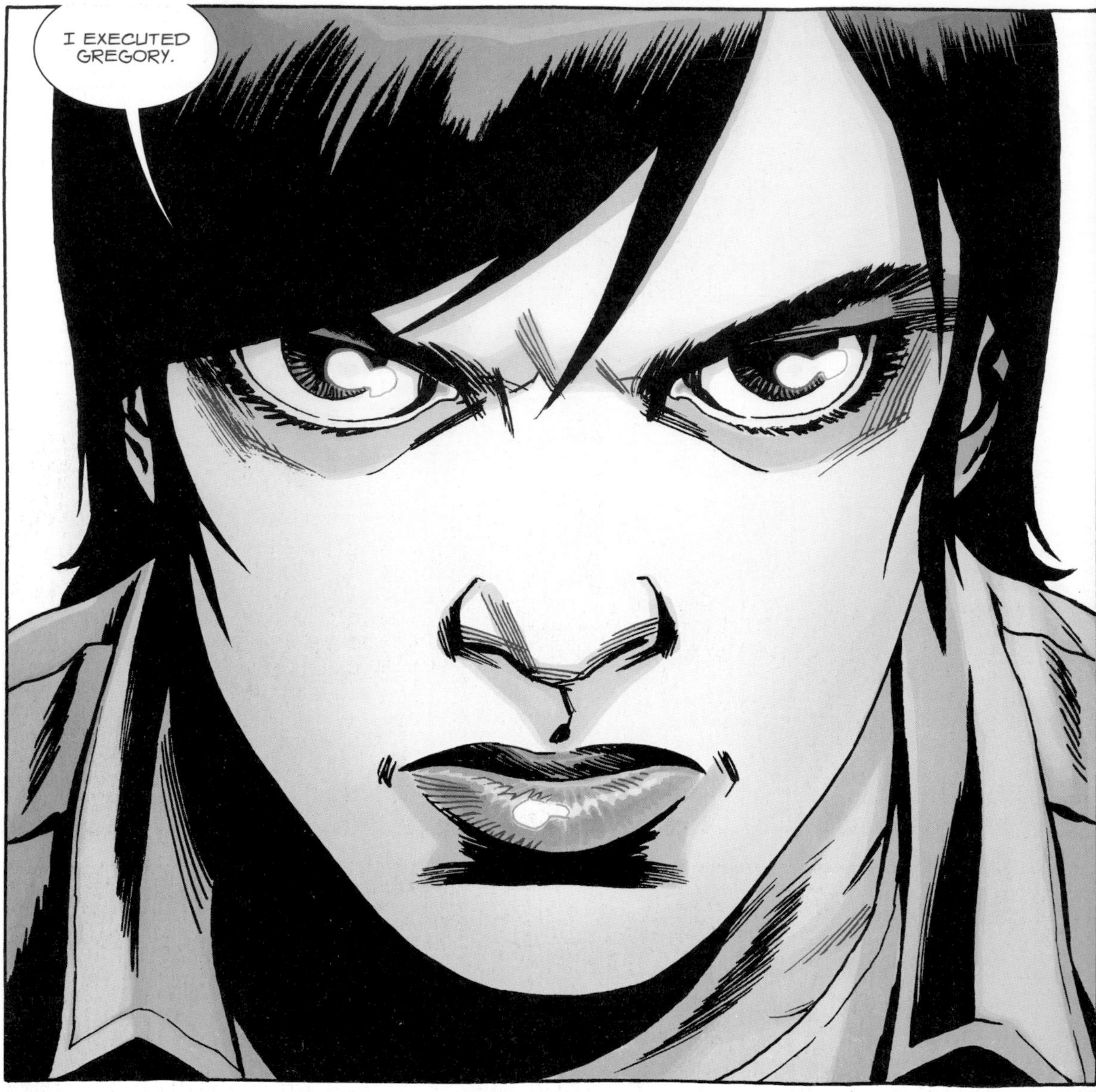
I EXECUTED GREGORY.

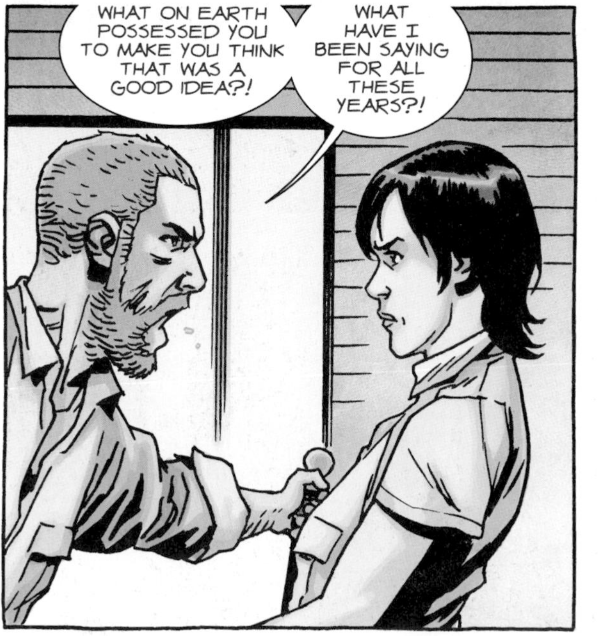
WHAT ON EARTH POSSESSED YOU TO MAKE YOU THINK THAT WAS A GOOD IDEA?!
WHAT HAVE I BEEN SAYING FOR ALL THESE YEARS?!

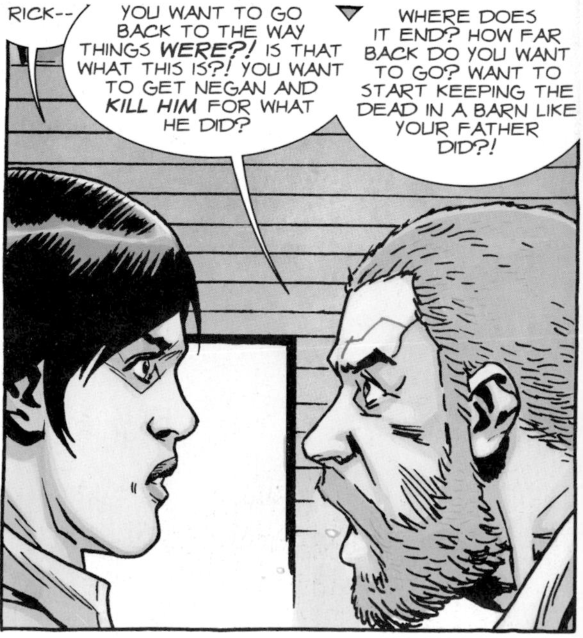
RICK--
YOU WANT TO GO BACK TO THE WAY THINGS *WERE?!* IS THAT WHAT THIS IS?! YOU WANT TO GET NEGAN AND *KILL HIM* FOR WHAT HE DID?
WHERE DOES IT END? HOW FAR BACK DO YOU WANT TO GO? WANT TO START KEEPING THE DEAD IN A BARN LIKE YOUR FATHER DID?!

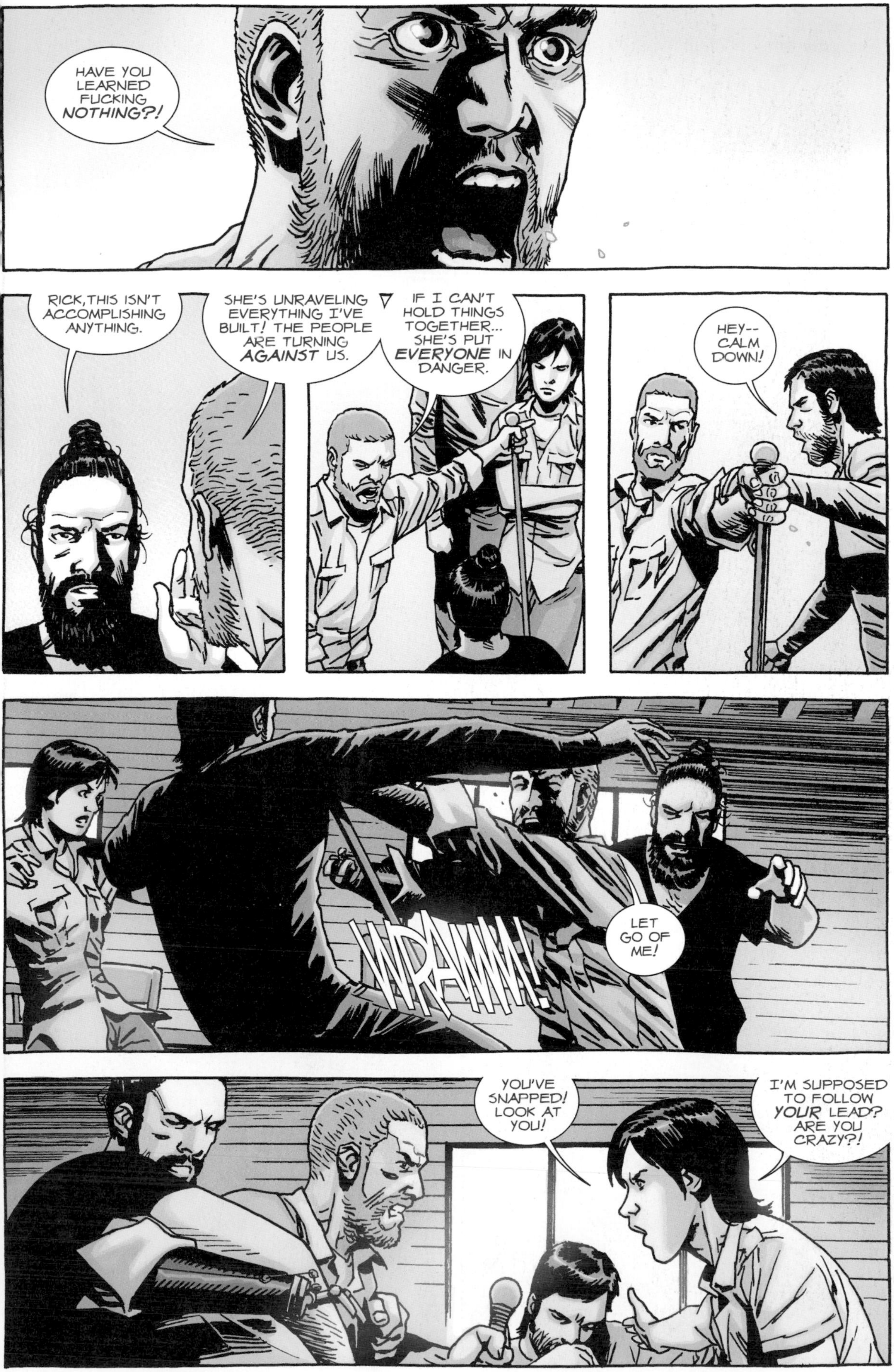
HAVE YOU LEARNED FUCKING NOTHING?!
RICK, THIS ISN'T ACCOMPLISHING ANYTHING.
SHE'S UNRAVELING EVERYTHING I'VE BUILT! THE PEOPLE ARE TURNING AGAINST US.
IF I CAN'T HOLD THINGS TOGETHER... SHE'S PUT EVERYONE IN DANGER.
HEY-- CALM DOWN!
WRANNN!
LET GO OF ME!
YOU'VE SNAPPED! LOOK AT YOU!
I'M SUPPOSED TO FOLLOW YOUR LEAD? ARE YOU CRAZY?!

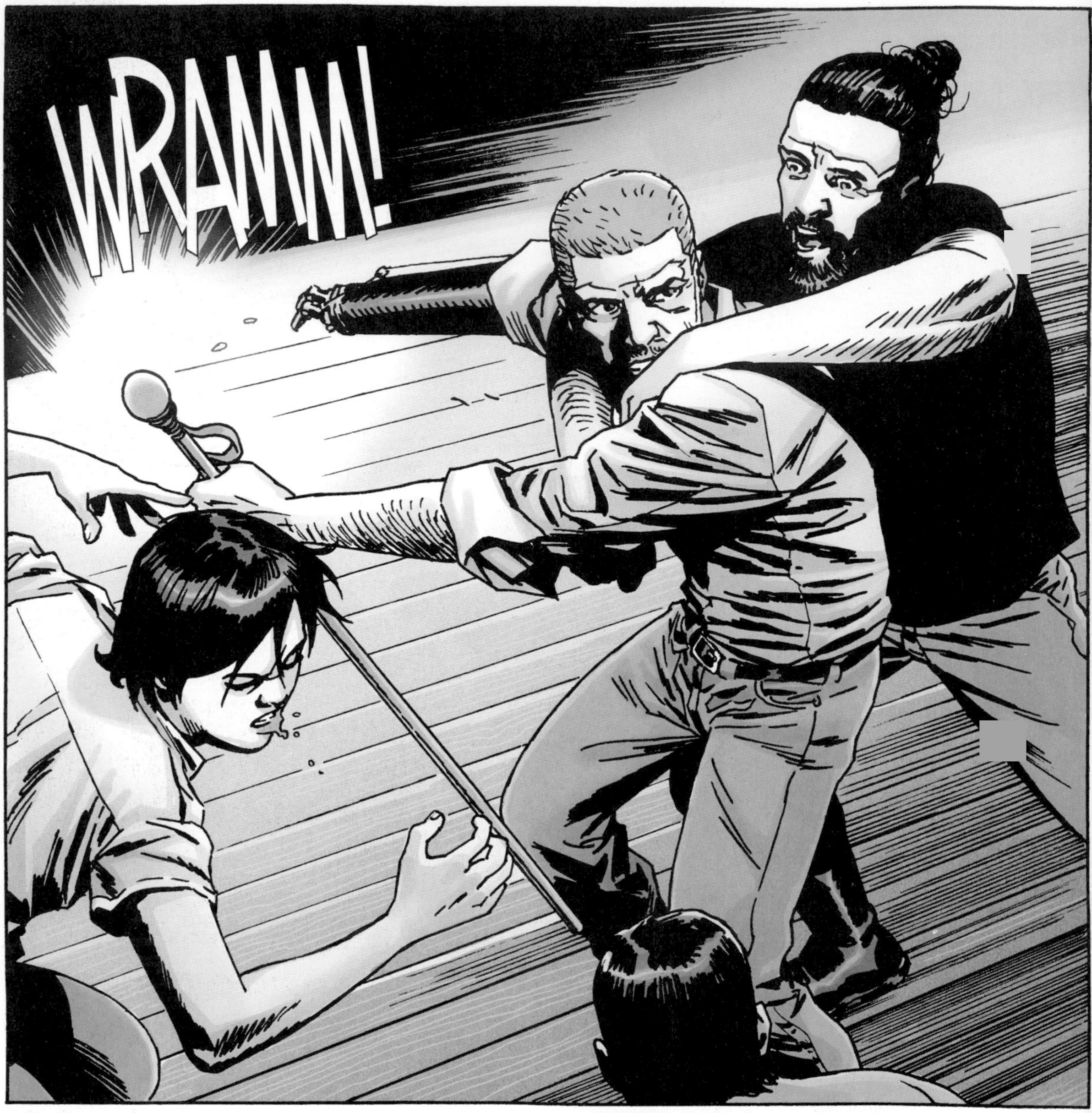
WRAMM!

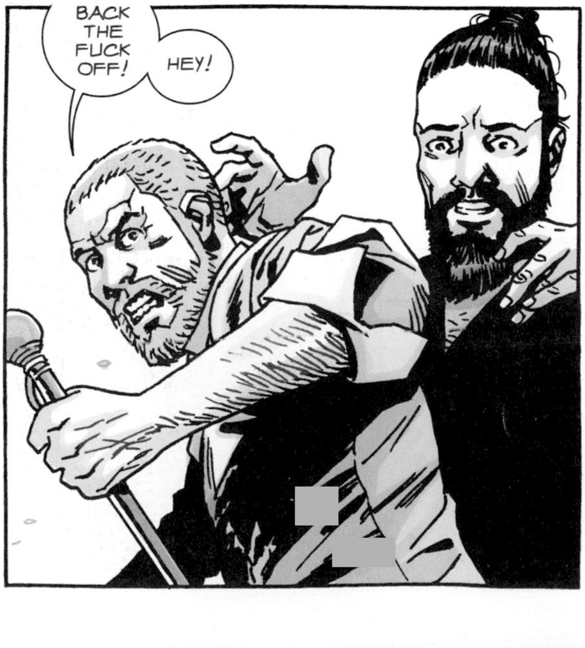
BACK THE FUCK OFF!
HEY!

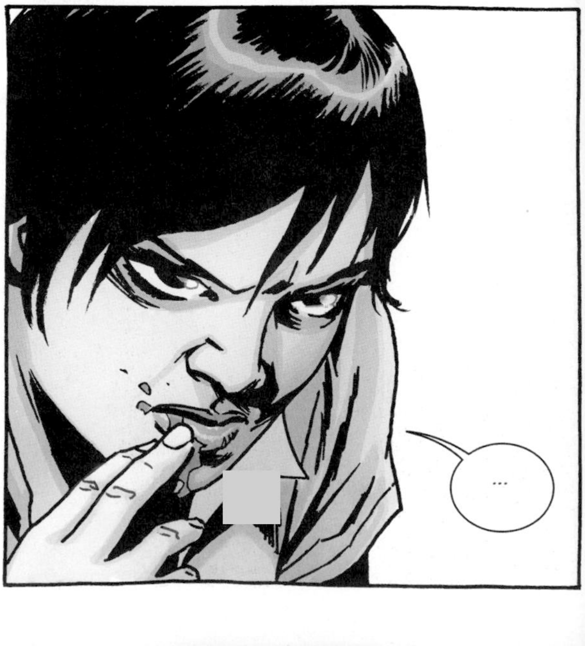
...

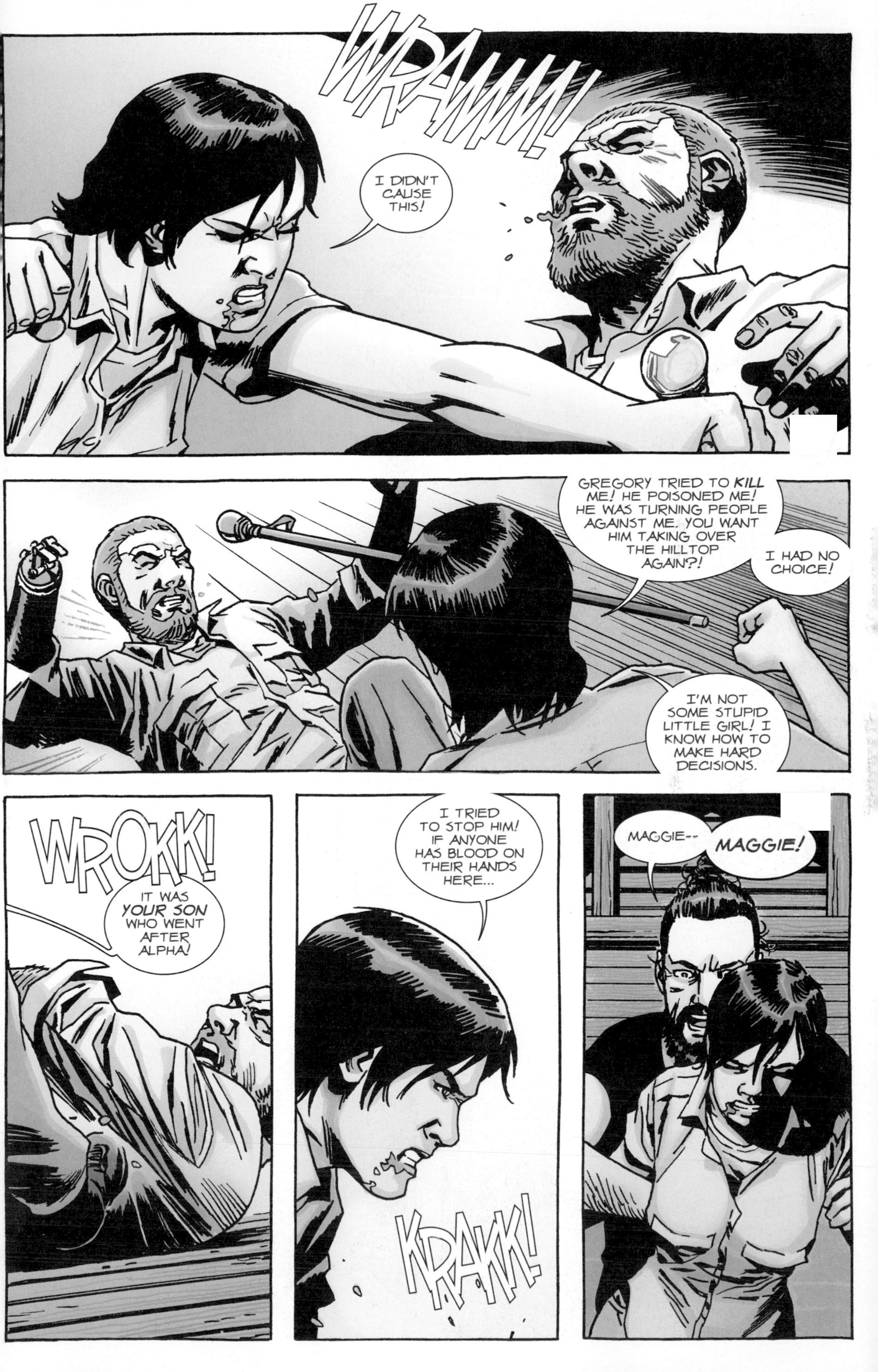
WRAMM!
I DIDN'T CAUSE THIS!
GREGORY TRIED TO KILL ME! HE POISONED ME! HE WAS TURNING PEOPLE AGAINST ME. YOU WANT HIM TAKING OVER THE HILLTOP AGAIN?!
I HAD NO CHOICE!
I'M NOT SOME STUPID LITTLE GIRL! I KNOW HOW TO MAKE HARD DECISIONS.
WROKK!
IT WAS YOUR SON WHO WENT AFTER ALPHA!
I TRIED TO STOP HIM! IF ANYONE HAS BLOOD ON THEIR HANDS HERE...
KRAKK!
MAGGIE--
MAGGIE!

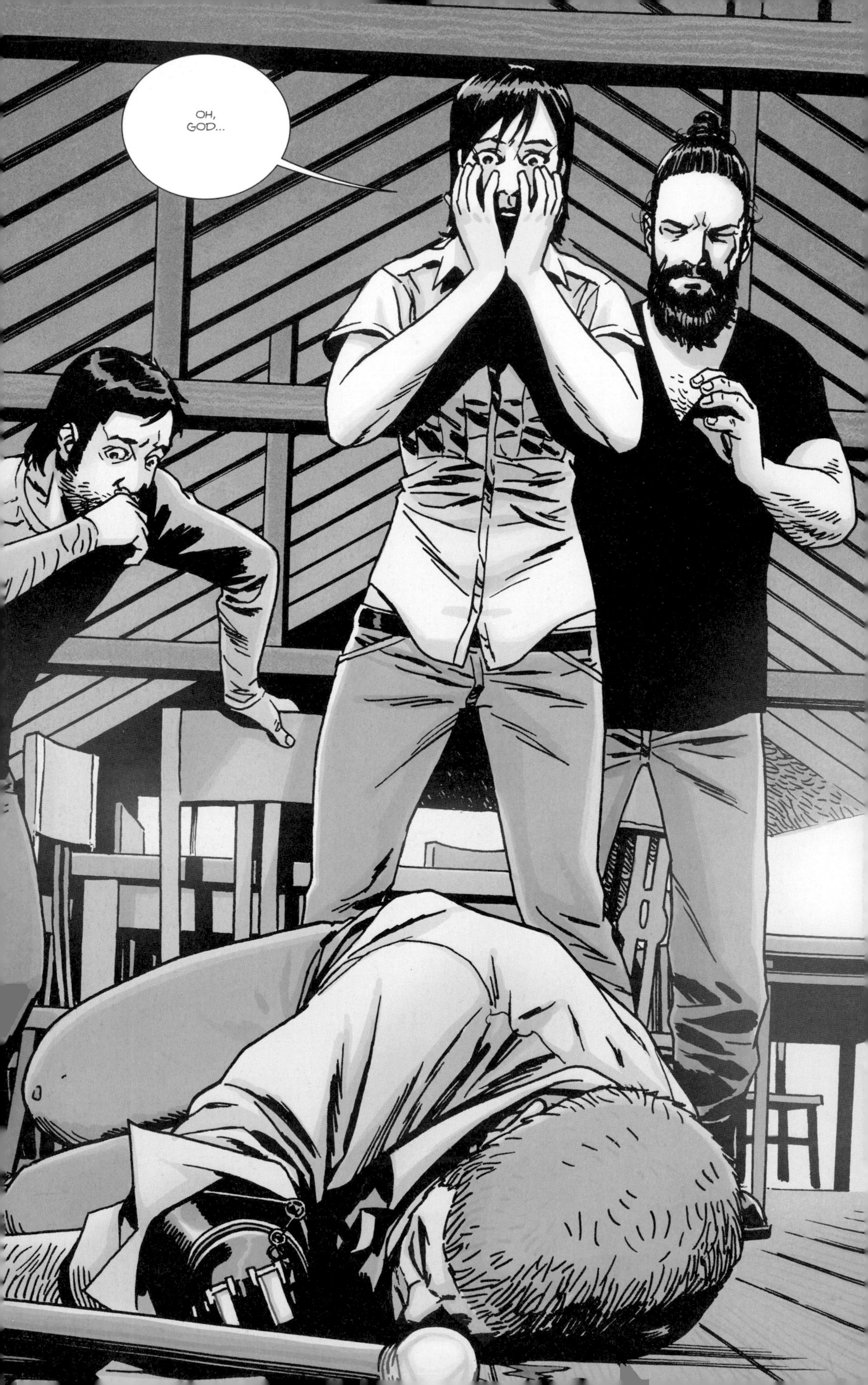
OH, GOD...

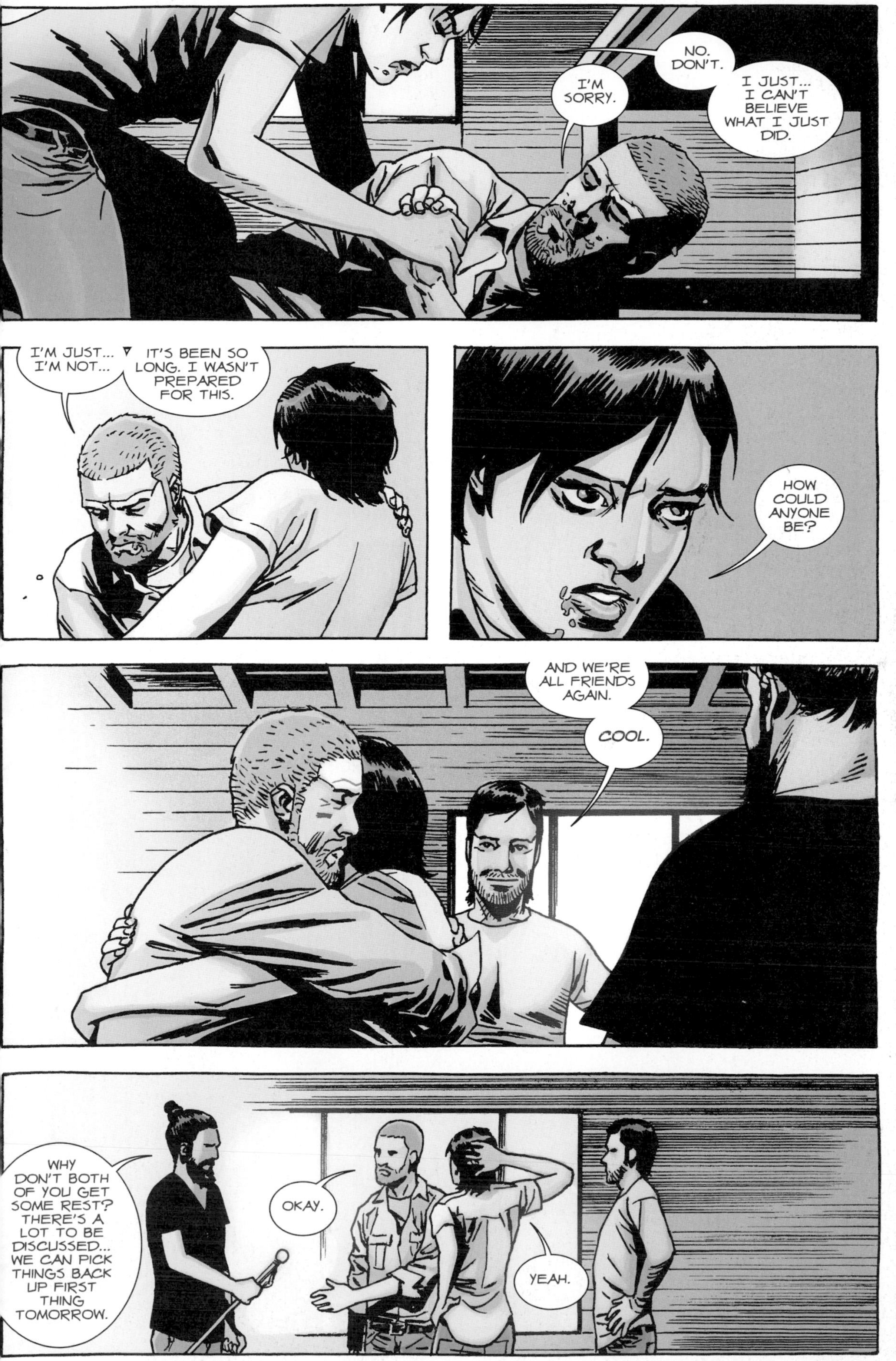
I'M SORRY.
NO. DON'T.
I JUST... I CAN'T BELIEVE WHAT I JUST DID.
I'M JUST... I'M NOT...
IT'S BEEN SO LONG. I WASN'T PREPARED FOR THIS.
HOW COULD ANYONE BE?
AND WE'RE ALL FRIENDS AGAIN.
COOL.
WHY DON'T BOTH OF YOU GET SOME REST? THERE'S A LOT TO BE DISCUSSED... WE CAN PICK THINGS BACK UP FIRST THING TOMORROW.
OKAY.
YEAH.

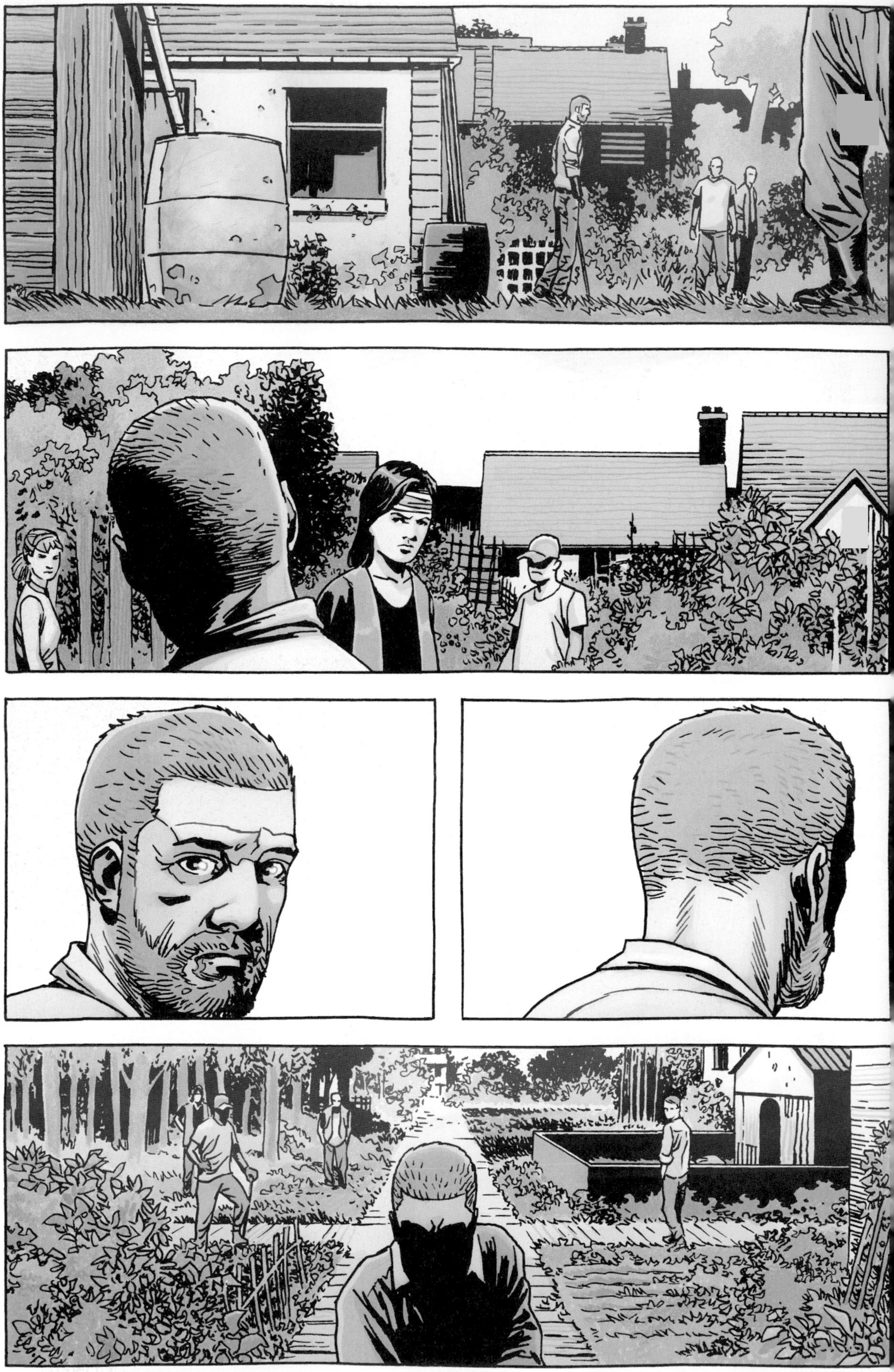

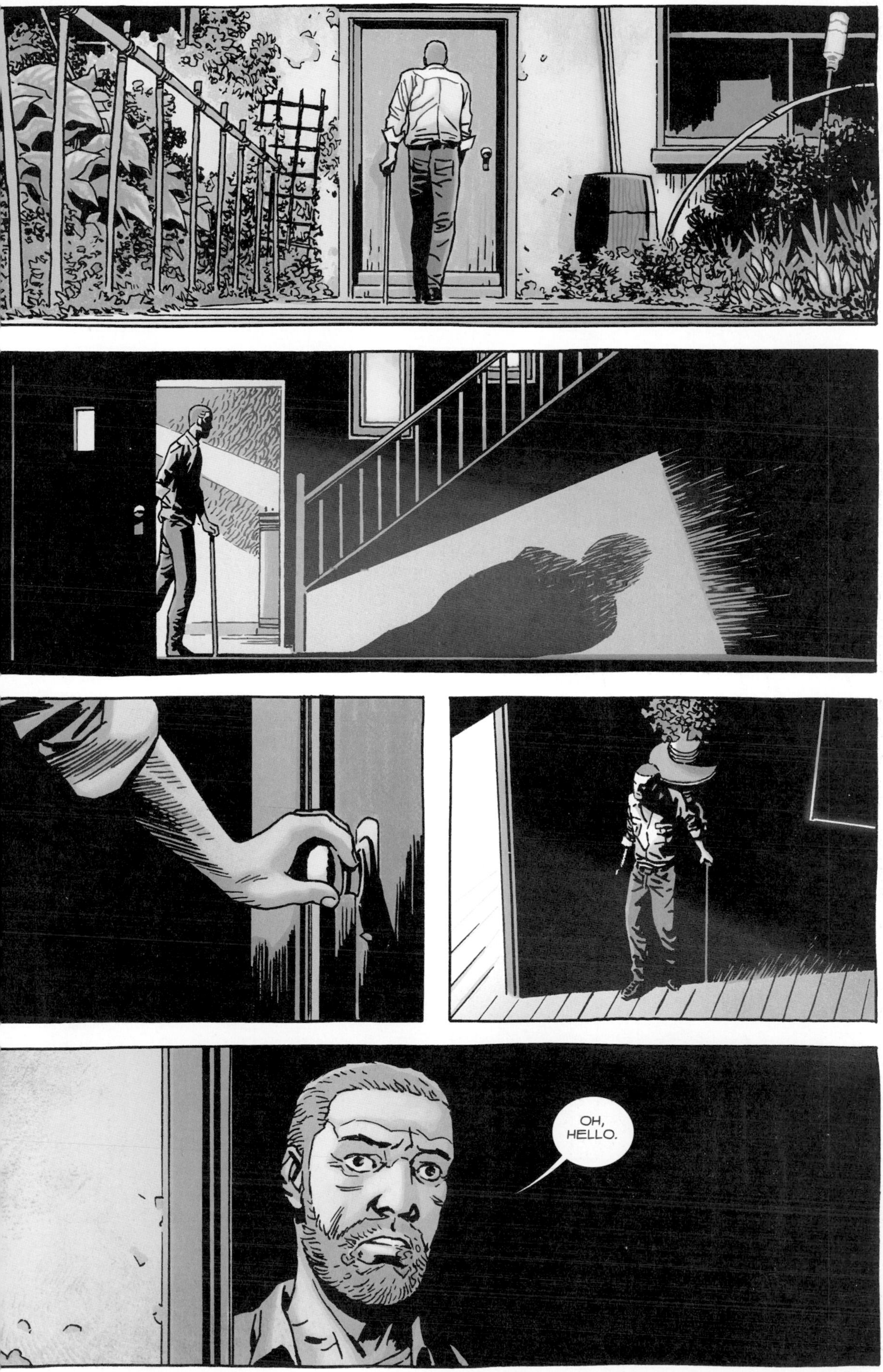
OH, HELLO.

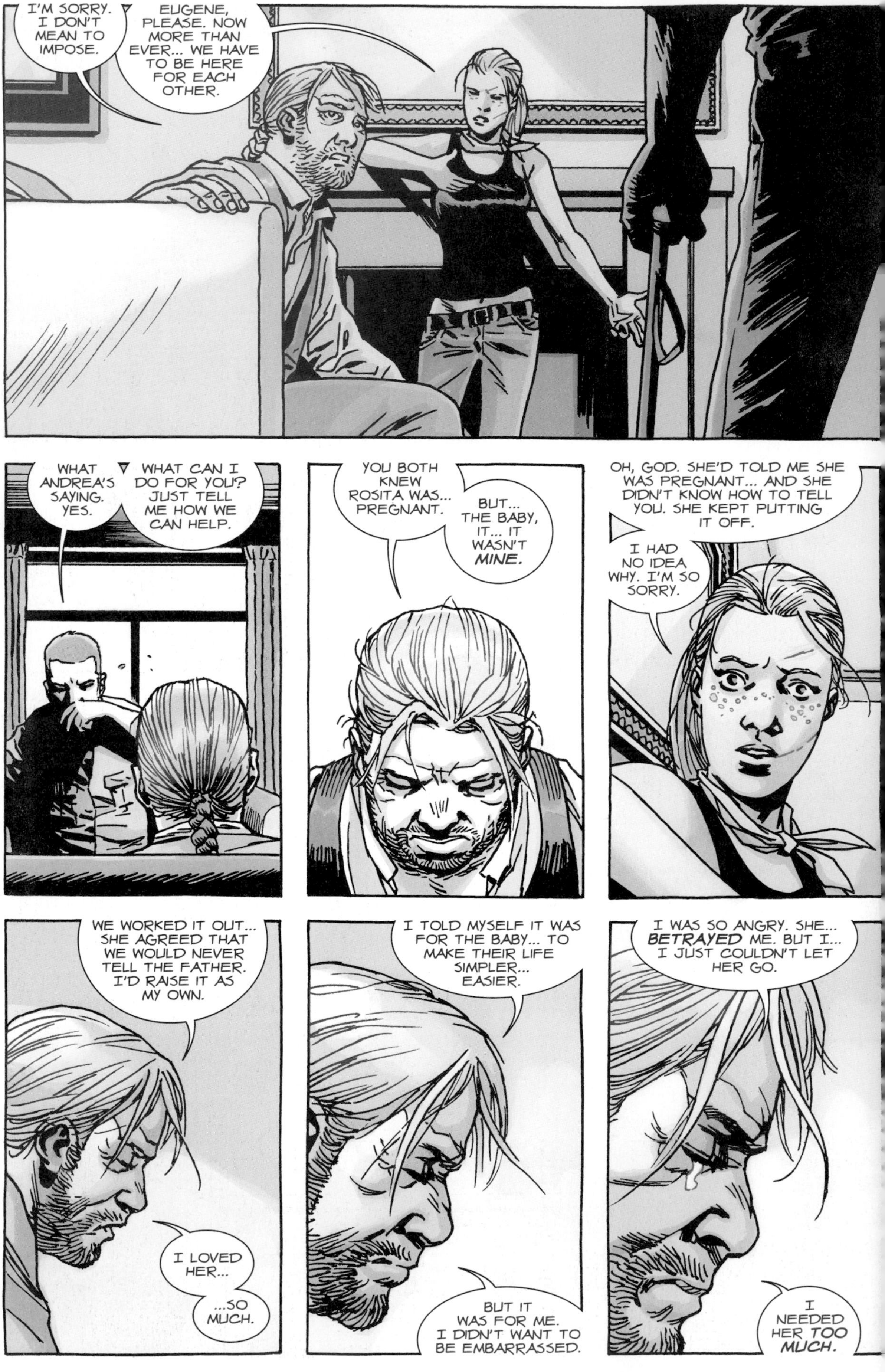
I'M SORRY. I DON'T MEAN TO IMPOSE.
EUGENE, PLEASE. NOW MORE THAN EVER... WE HAVE TO BE HERE FOR EACH OTHER.
WHAT ANDREA'S SAYING. YES.
WHAT CAN I DO FOR YOU? JUST TELL ME HOW WE CAN HELP.
YOU BOTH KNEW ROSITA WAS... PREGNANT.
BUT... THE BABY, IT... IT WASN'T MINE.
OH, GOD. SHE'D TOLD ME SHE WAS PREGNANT... AND SHE DIDN'T KNOW HOW TO TELL YOU. SHE KEPT PUTTING IT OFF.
I HAD NO IDEA WHY. I'M SO SORRY.
WE WORKED IT OUT... SHE AGREED THAT WE WOULD NEVER TELL THE FATHER. I'D RAISE IT AS MY OWN.
I LOVED HER...
...SO MUCH.
I TOLD MYSELF IT WAS FOR THE BABY... TO MAKE THEIR LIFE SIMPLER... EASIER.
BUT IT WAS FOR ME. I DIDN'T WANT TO BE EMBARRASSED.
I WAS SO ANGRY. SHE... BETRAYED ME. BUT I... I JUST COULDN'T LET HER GO.
I NEEDED HER TOO MUCH.

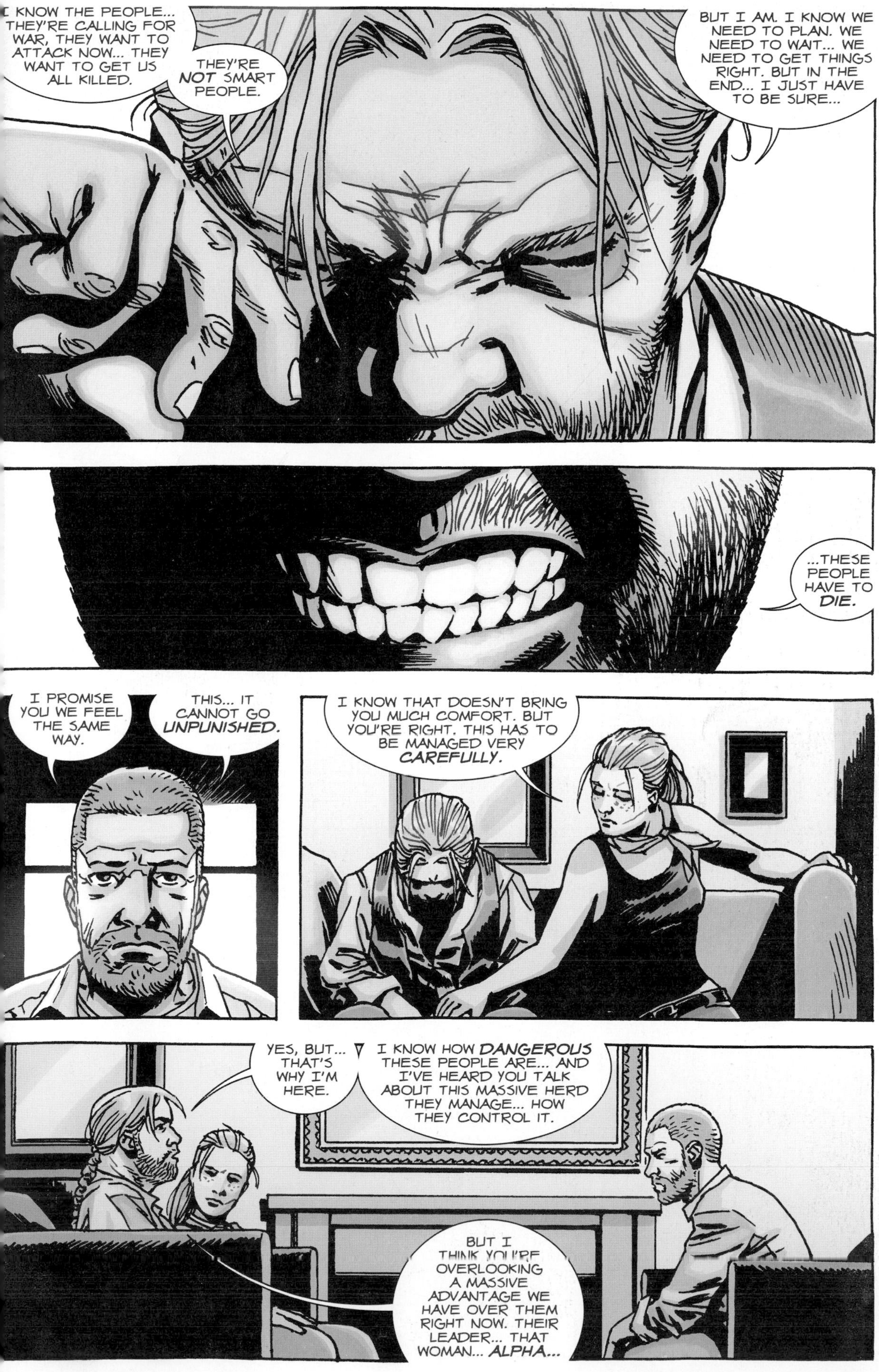
I KNOW THE PEOPLE... THEY'RE CALLING FOR WAR, THEY WANT TO ATTACK NOW... THEY WANT TO GET US ALL KILLED.
THEY'RE NOT SMART PEOPLE.
BUT I AM. I KNOW WE NEED TO PLAN. WE NEED TO WAIT... WE NEED TO GET THINGS RIGHT. BUT IN THE END... I JUST HAVE TO BE SURE...
...THESE PEOPLE HAVE TO DIE.
I PROMISE YOU WE FEEL THE SAME WAY.
THIS... IT CANNOT GO UNPUNISHED.
I KNOW THAT DOESN'T BRING YOU MUCH COMFORT. BUT YOU'RE RIGHT. THIS HAS TO BE MANAGED VERY CAREFULLY.
YES, BUT... THAT'S WHY I'M HERE.
I KNOW HOW DANGEROUS THESE PEOPLE ARE... AND I'VE HEARD YOU TALK ABOUT THIS MASSIVE HERD THEY MANAGE... HOW THEY CONTROL IT.
BUT I THINK YOU'RE OVERLOOKING A MASSIVE ADVANTAGE WE HAVE OVER THEM RIGHT NOW. THEIR LEADER... THAT WOMAN... ALPHA...

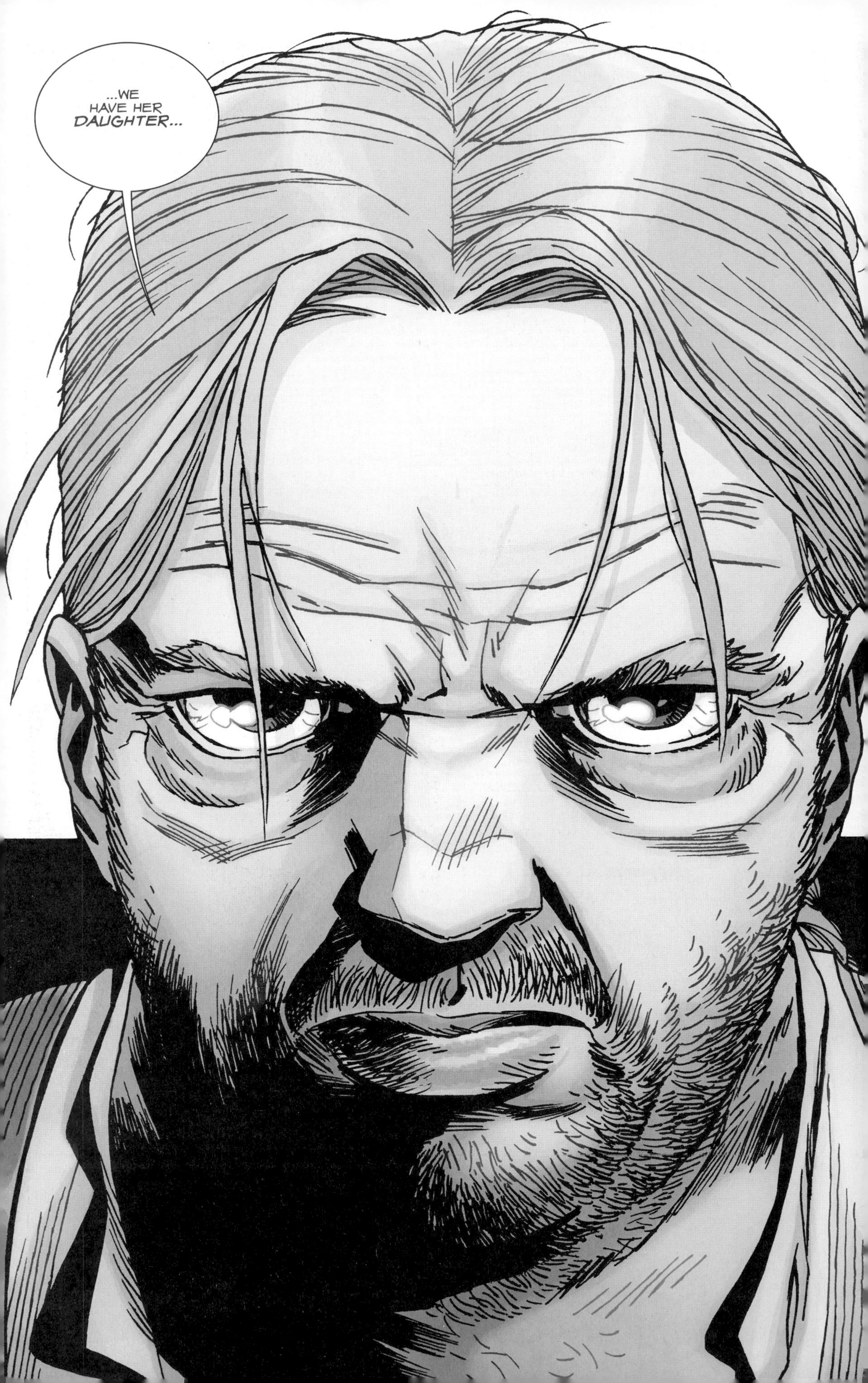
...WE HAVE HER DAUGHTER...

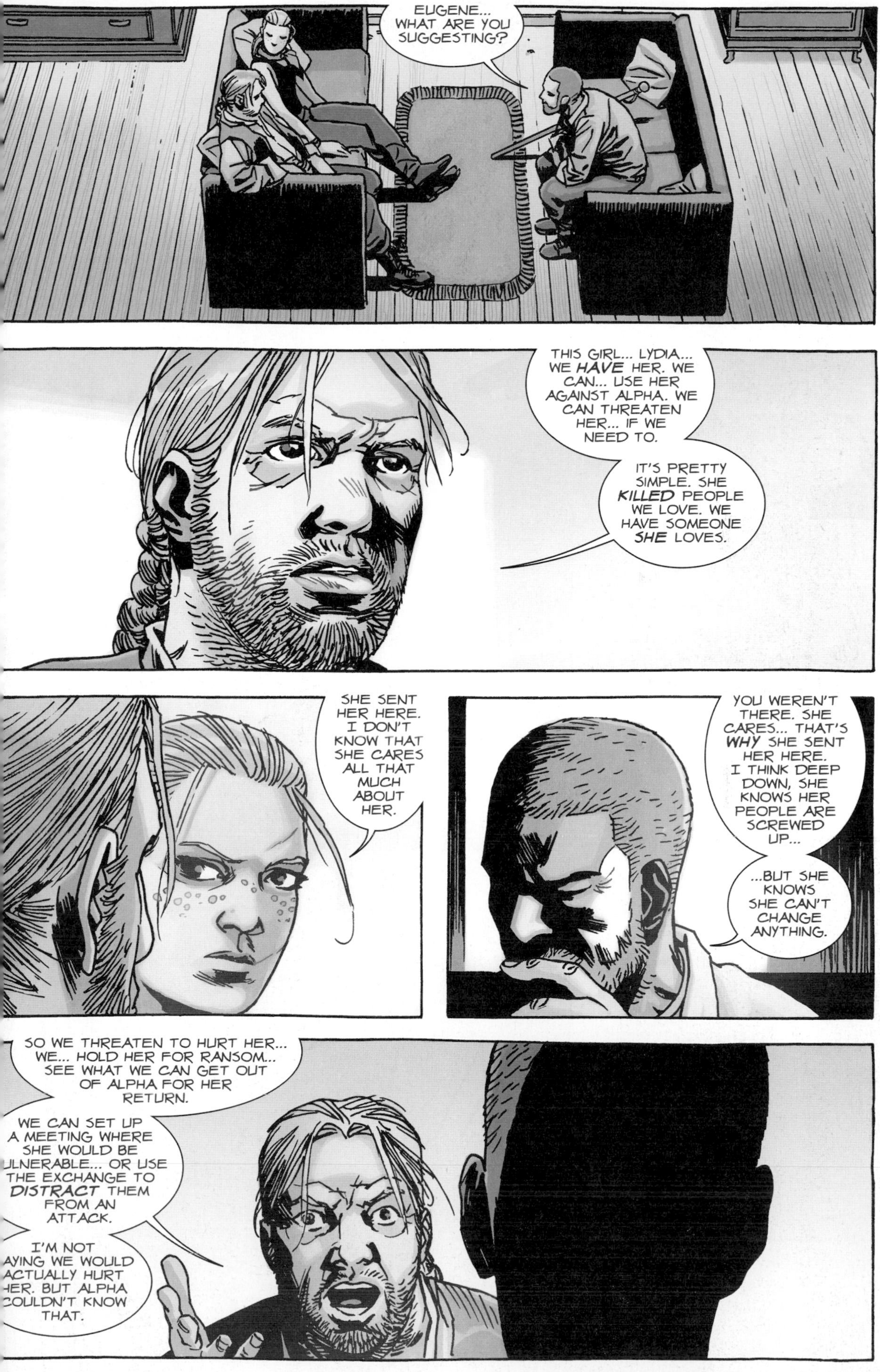
EUGENE... WHAT ARE YOU SUGGESTING?
THIS GIRL... LYDIA... WE *HAVE* HER. WE CAN... USE HER AGAINST ALPHA. WE CAN THREATEN HER... IF WE NEED TO.
IT'S PRETTY SIMPLE. SHE *KILLED* PEOPLE WE LOVE. WE HAVE SOMEONE *SHE* LOVES.
SHE SENT HER HERE. I DON'T KNOW THAT SHE CARES ALL THAT MUCH ABOUT HER.
YOU WEREN'T THERE. SHE CARES... THAT'S *WHY* SHE SENT HER HERE. I THINK DEEP DOWN, SHE KNOWS HER PEOPLE ARE SCREWED UP...
...BUT SHE KNOWS SHE CAN'T CHANGE ANYTHING.
SO WE THREATEN TO HURT HER... WE... HOLD HER FOR RANSOM... SEE WHAT WE CAN GET OUT OF ALPHA FOR HER RETURN.
WE CAN SET UP A MEETING WHERE SHE WOULD BE ULNERABLE... OR USE THE EXCHANGE TO *DISTRACT* THEM FROM AN ATTACK.
I'M NOT AYING WE WOULD CTUALLY HURT HER. BUT ALPHA OULDN'T KNOW THAT.

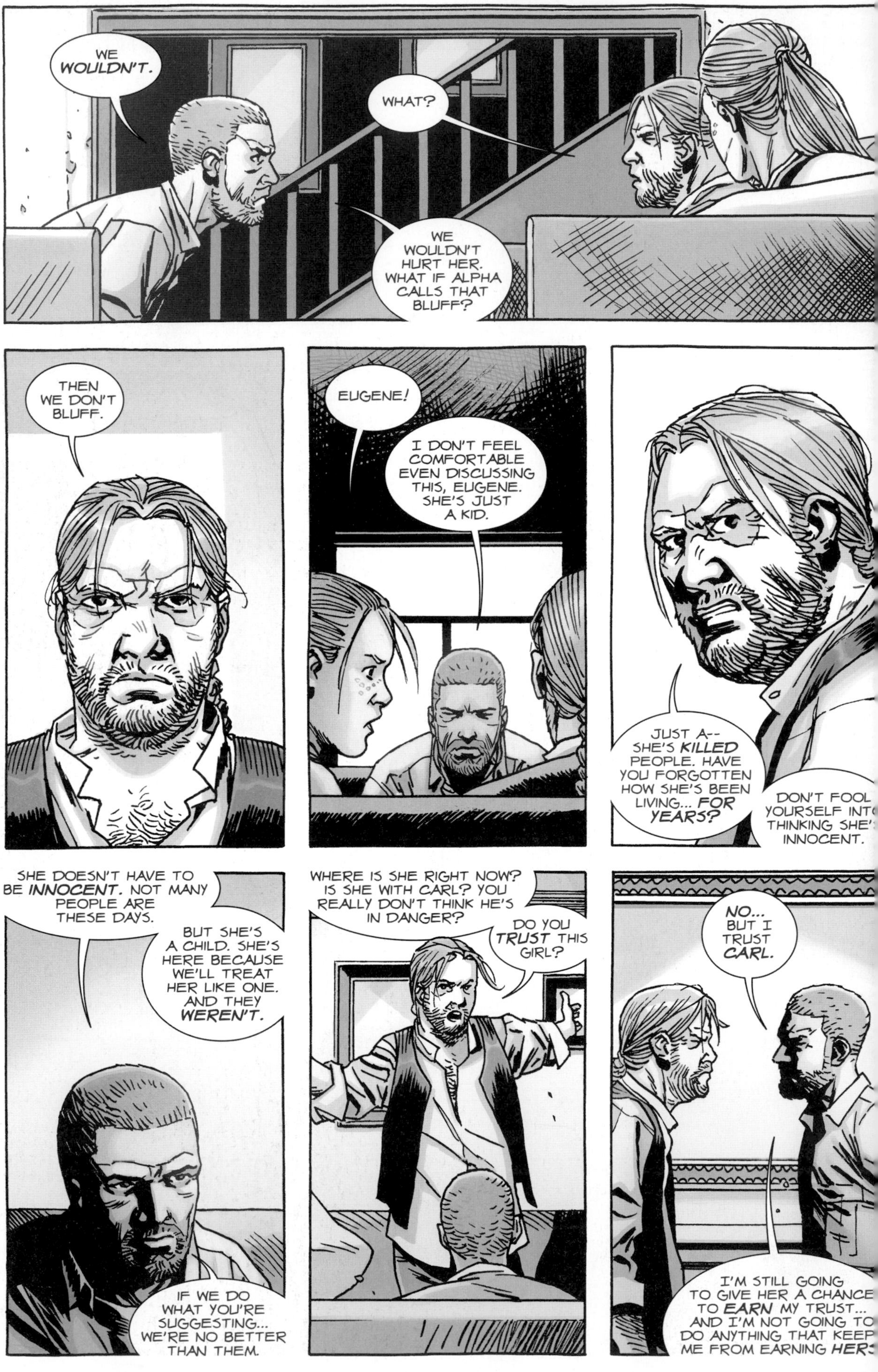

WE WOULDN'T.
WHAT?
WE WOULDN'T HURT HER. WHAT IF ALPHA CALLS THAT BLUFF?
THEN WE DON'T BLUFF.
EUGENE!
I DON'T FEEL COMFORTABLE EVEN DISCUSSING THIS, EUGENE. SHE'S JUST A KID.
JUST A-- SHE'S KILLED PEOPLE. HAVE YOU FORGOTTEN HOW SHE'S BEEN LIVING... FOR YEARS?
DON'T FOOL YOURSELF INTO THINKING SHE'S INNOCENT.
SHE DOESN'T HAVE TO BE INNOCENT. NOT MANY PEOPLE ARE THESE DAYS.
BUT SHE'S A CHILD. SHE'S HERE BECAUSE WE'LL TREAT HER LIKE ONE. AND THEY WEREN'T.
IF WE DO WHAT YOU'RE SUGGESTING... WE'RE NO BETTER THAN THEM.
WHERE IS SHE RIGHT NOW? IS SHE WITH CARL? YOU REALLY DON'T THINK HE'S IN DANGER?
DO YOU TRUST THIS GIRL?
NO... BUT I TRUST CARL.
I'M STILL GOING TO GIVE HER A CHANCE TO EARN MY TRUST... AND I'M NOT GOING TO DO ANYTHING THAT KEEPS ME FROM EARNING HERS

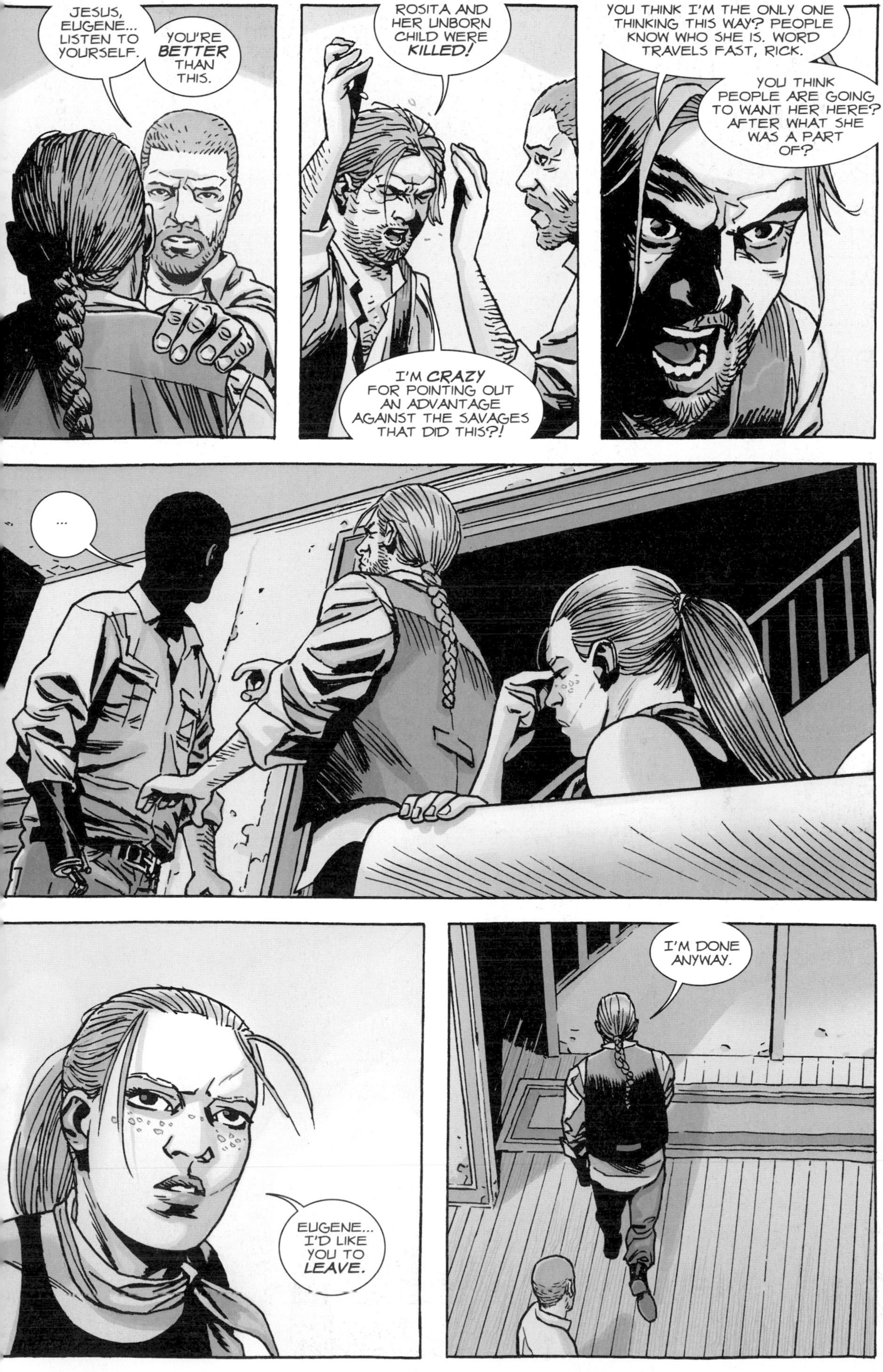
JESUS, EUGENE... LISTEN TO YOURSELF.
YOU'RE BETTER THAN THIS.
ROSITA AND HER UNBORN CHILD WERE KILLED!
I'M CRAZY FOR POINTING OUT AN ADVANTAGE AGAINST THE SAVAGES THAT DID THIS?!
YOU THINK I'M THE ONLY ONE THINKING THIS WAY? PEOPLE KNOW WHO SHE IS. WORD TRAVELS FAST, RICK.
YOU THINK PEOPLE ARE GOING TO WANT HER HERE? AFTER WHAT SHE WAS A PART OF?
...
EUGENE... I'D LIKE YOU TO LEAVE.
I'M DONE ANYWAY.

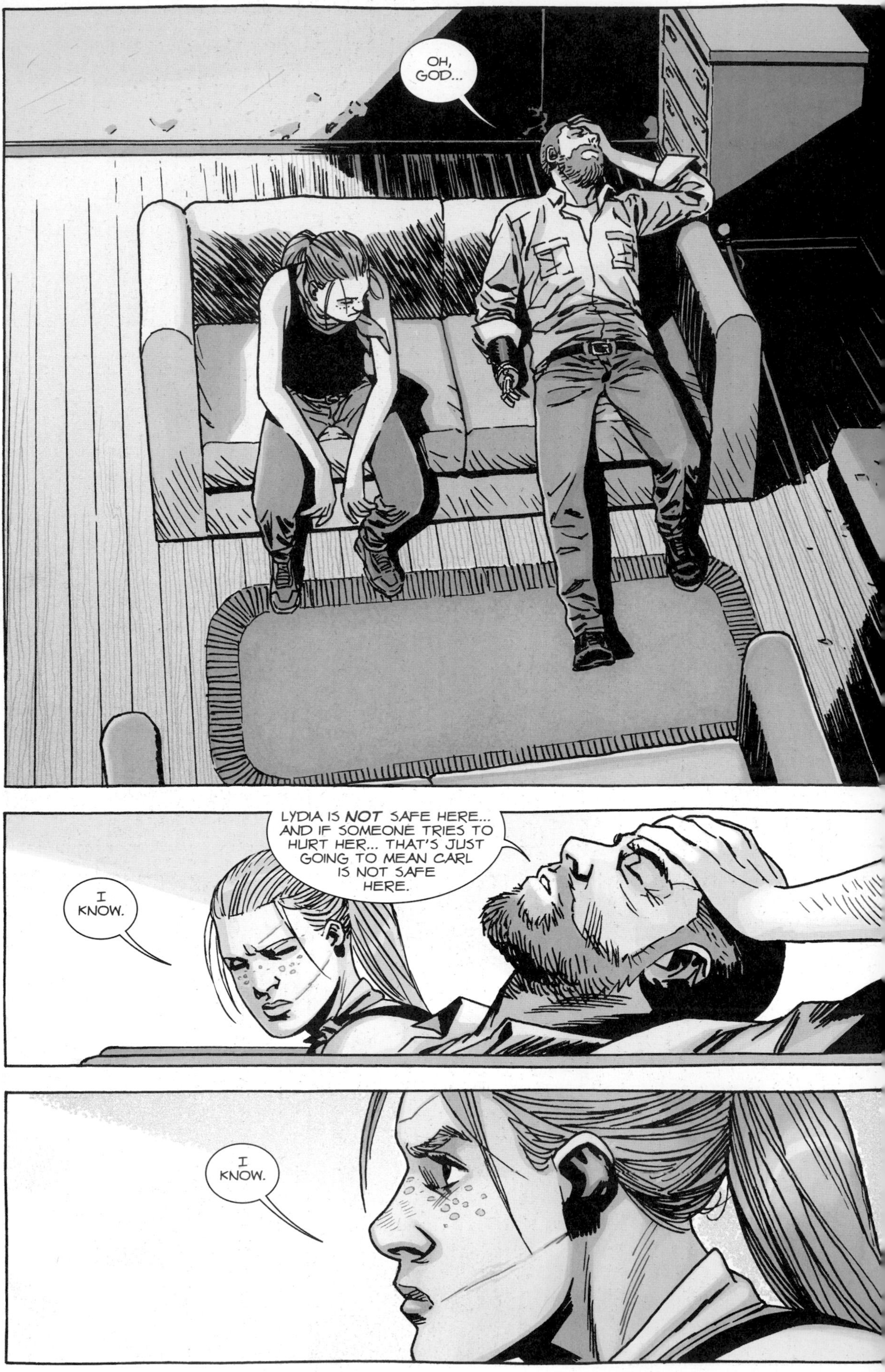
OH, GOD...
LYDIA IS NOT SAFE HERE... AND IF SOMEONE TRIES TO HURT HER... THAT'S JUST GOING TO MEAN CARL IS NOT SAFE HERE.
I KNOW.
I KNOW.

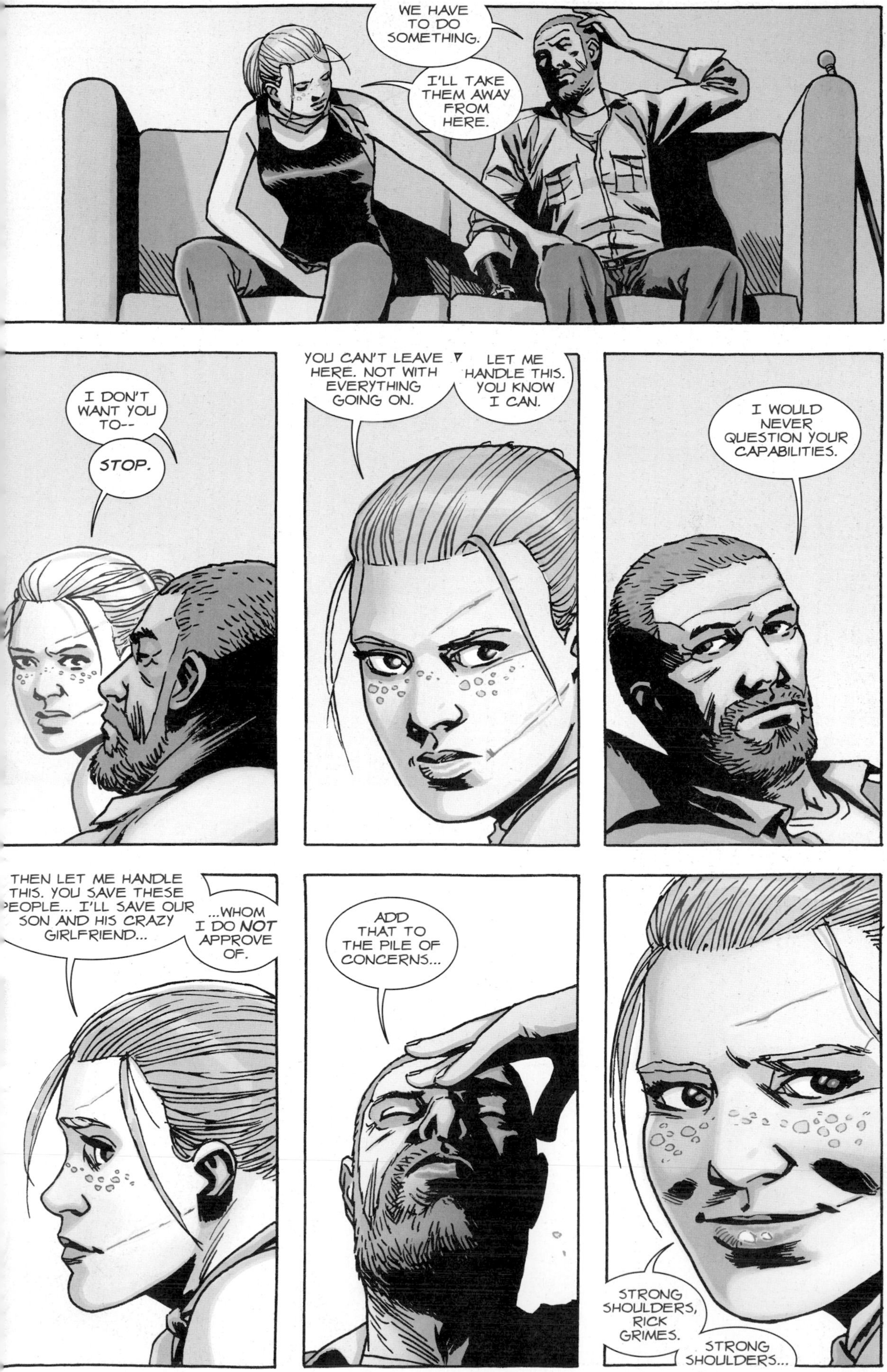
WE HAVE TO DO SOMETHING.
I'LL TAKE THEM AWAY FROM HERE.
I DON'T WANT YOU TO--
STOP.
YOU CAN'T LEAVE HERE. NOT WITH EVERYTHING GOING ON.
LET ME HANDLE THIS. YOU KNOW I CAN.
I WOULD NEVER QUESTION YOUR CAPABILITIES.
THEN LET ME HANDLE THIS. YOU SAVE THESE PEOPLE... I'LL SAVE OUR SON AND HIS CRAZY GIRLFRIEND...
...WHOM I DO NOT APPROVE OF.
ADD THAT TO THE PILE OF CONCERNS...
STRONG SHOULDERS, RICK GRIMES.
STRONG SHOULDERS...

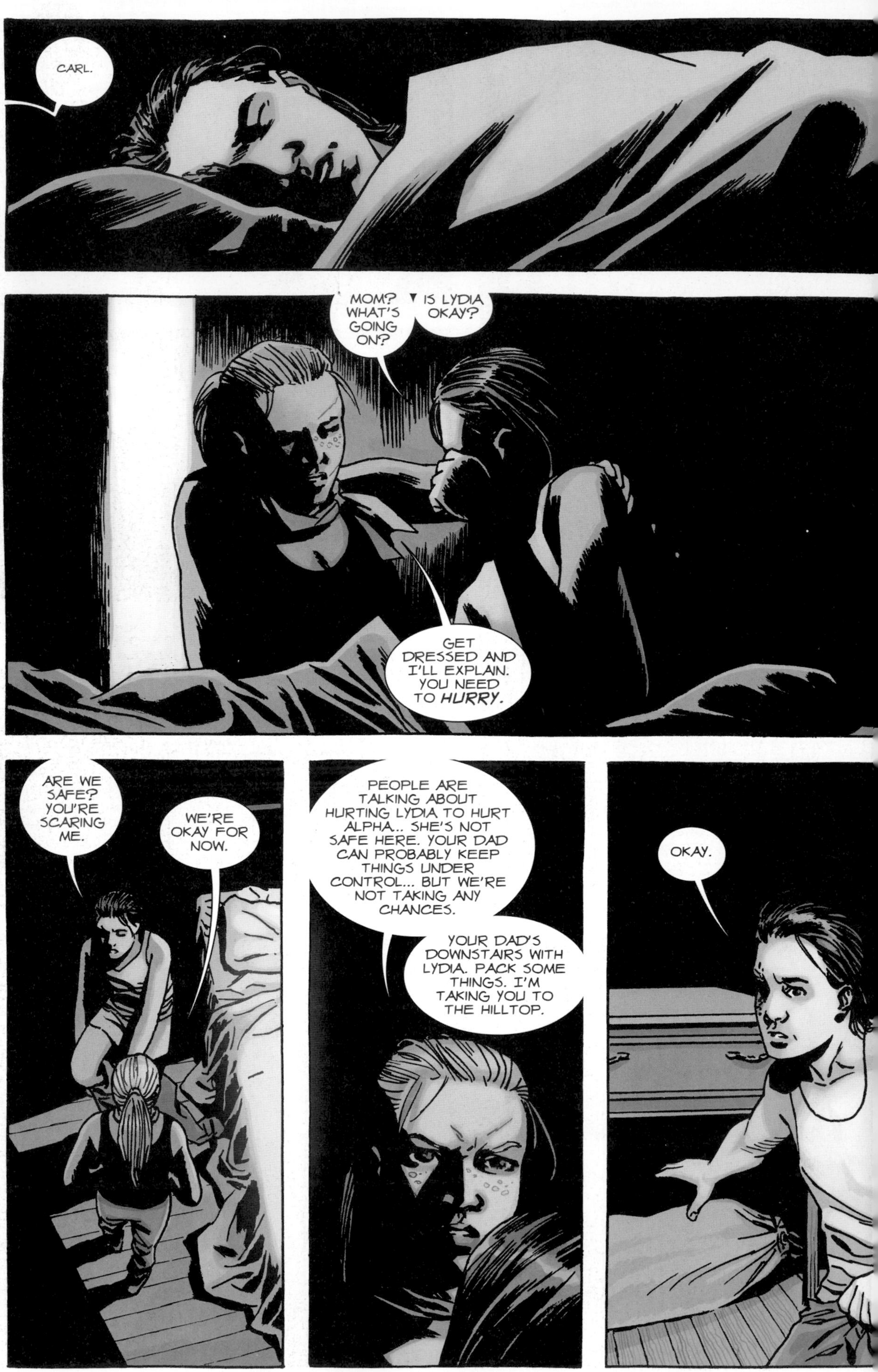
CARL.
MOM? WHAT'S GOING ON?
IS LYDIA OKAY?
GET DRESSED AND I'LL EXPLAIN. YOU NEED TO *HURRY.*
ARE WE SAFE? YOU'RE SCARING ME.
WE'RE OKAY FOR NOW.
PEOPLE ARE TALKING ABOUT HURTING LYDIA TO HURT ALPHA.. SHE'S NOT SAFE HERE. YOUR DAD CAN PROBABLY KEEP THINGS UNDER CONTROL... BUT WE'RE NOT TAKING ANY CHANCES.
YOUR DAD'S DOWNSTAIRS WITH LYDIA. PACK SOME THINGS. I'M TAKING YOU TO THE HILLTOP.
OKAY.

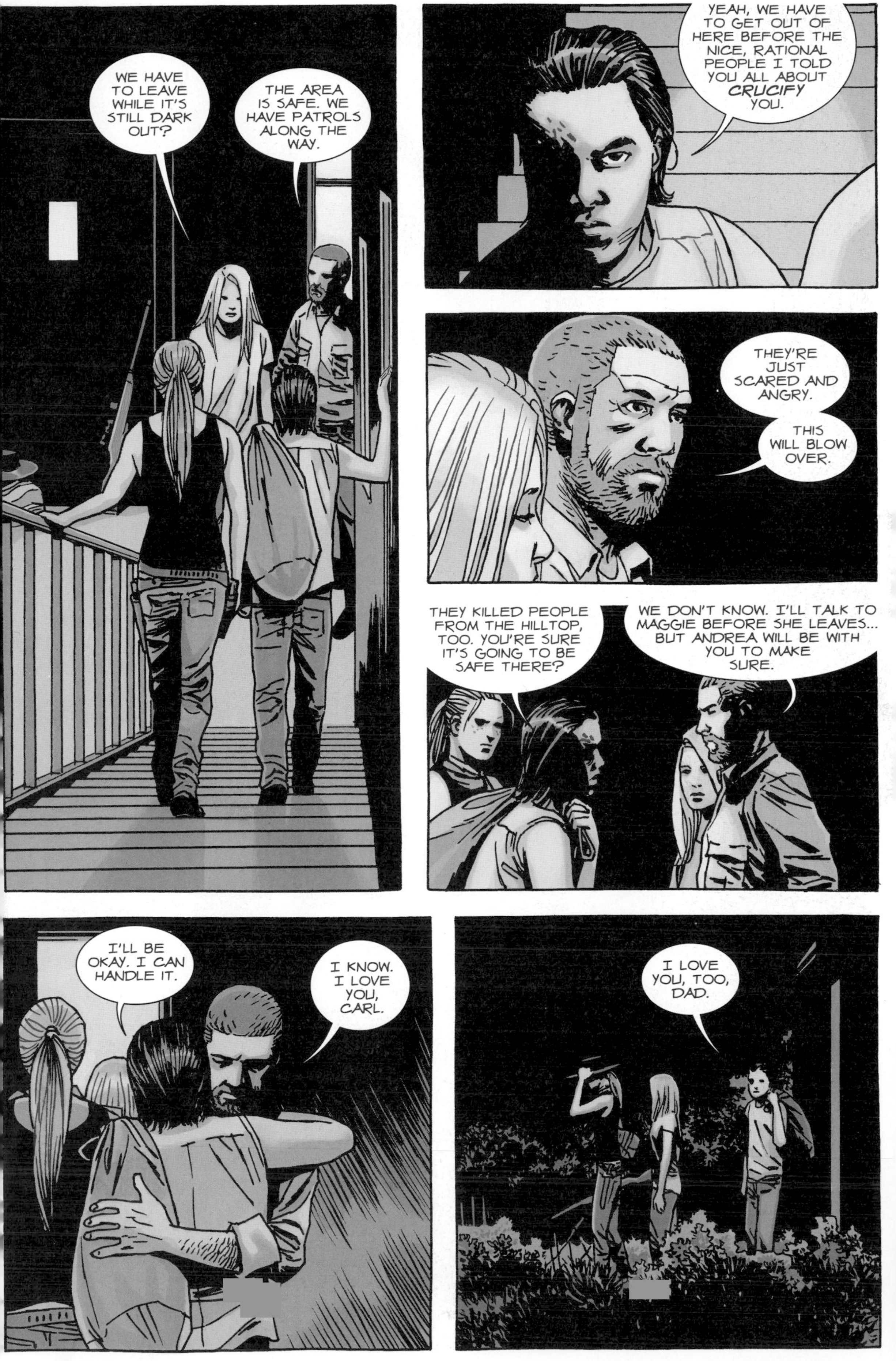
WE HAVE TO LEAVE WHILE IT'S STILL DARK OUT?
THE AREA IS SAFE. WE HAVE PATROLS ALONG THE WAY.
YEAH, WE HAVE TO GET OUT OF HERE BEFORE THE NICE, RATIONAL PEOPLE I TOLD YOU ALL ABOUT CRUCIFY YOU.
THEY'RE JUST SCARED AND ANGRY.
THIS WILL BLOW OVER.
THEY KILLED PEOPLE FROM THE HILLTOP, TOO. YOU'RE SURE IT'S GOING TO BE SAFE THERE?
WE DON'T KNOW. I'LL TALK TO MAGGIE BEFORE SHE LEAVES... BUT ANDREA WILL BE WITH YOU TO MAKE SURE.
I'LL BE OKAY. I CAN HANDLE IT.
I KNOW. I LOVE YOU, CARL.
I LOVE YOU, TOO, DAD.

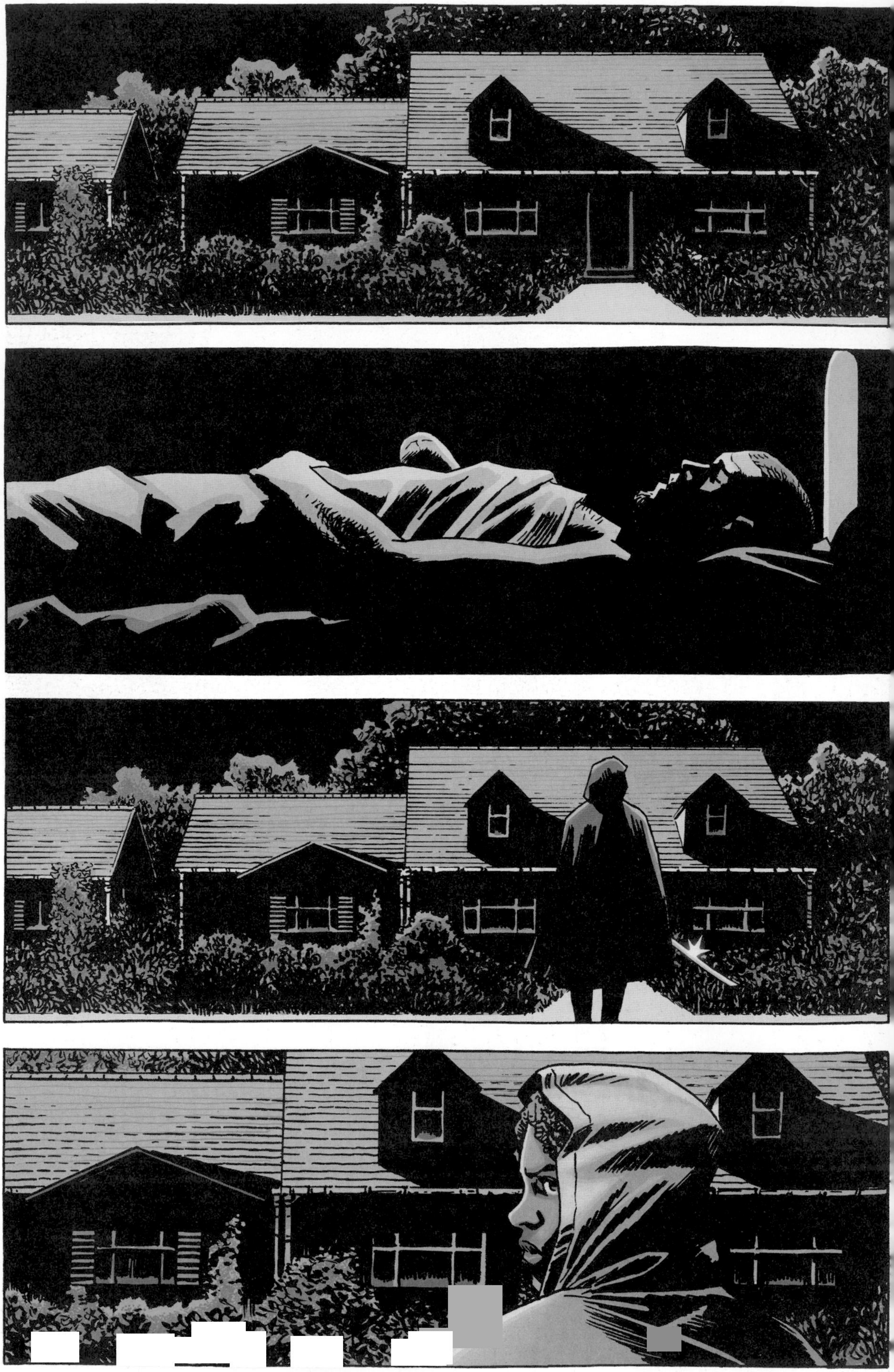

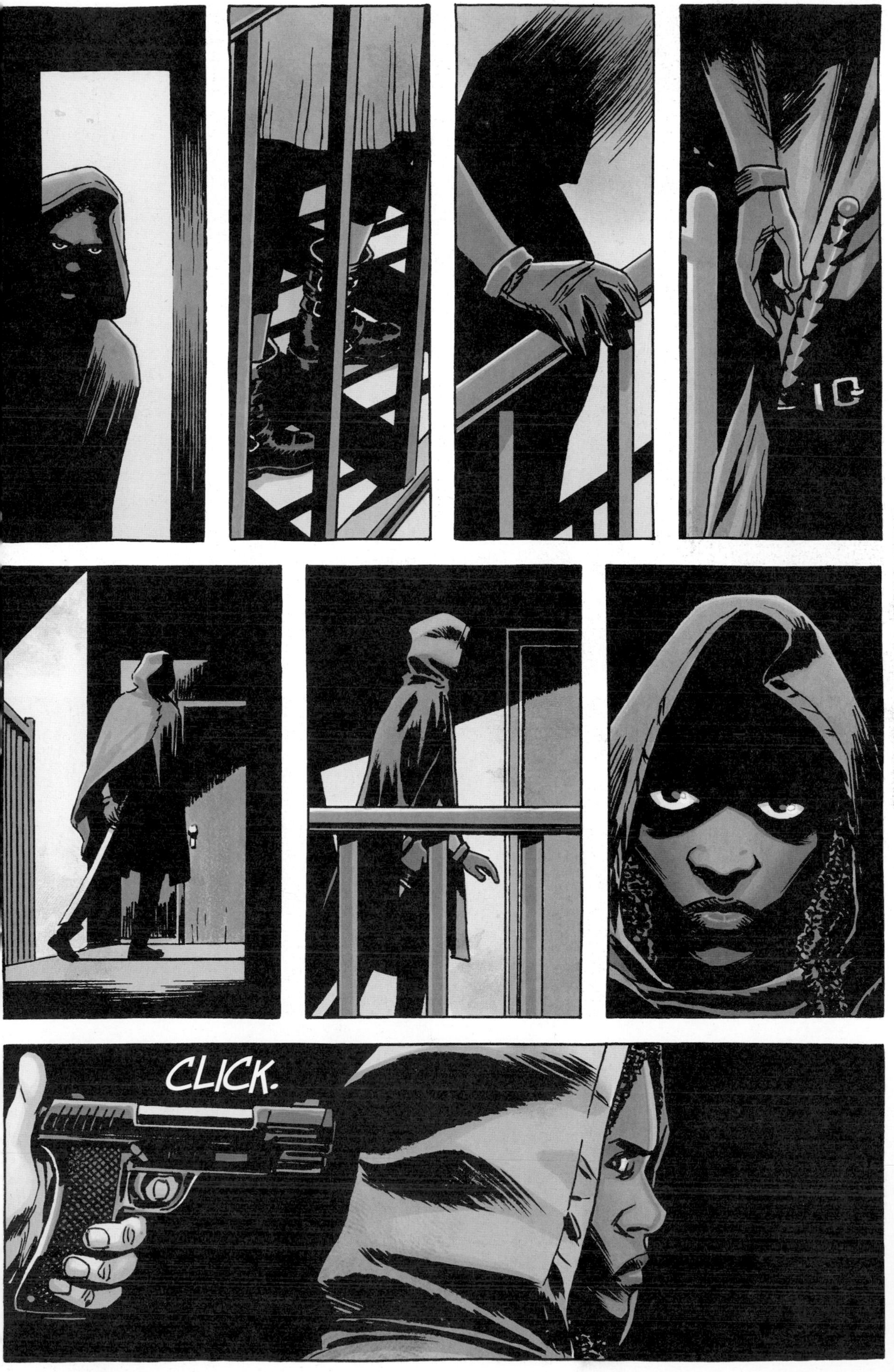
CLICK.

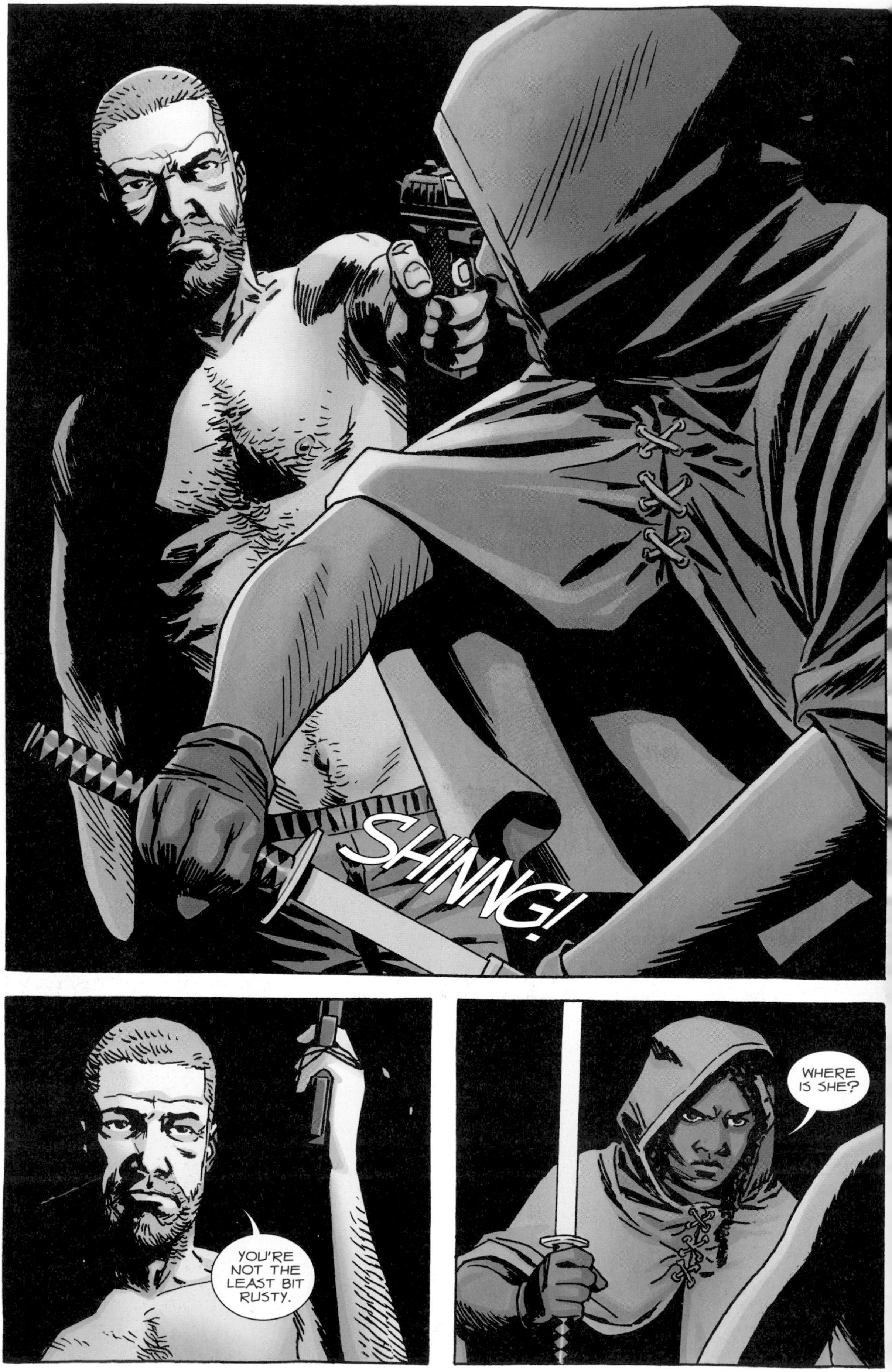
SHINNG!
YOU'RE NOT THE LEAST BIT RUSTY.
WHERE IS SHE?

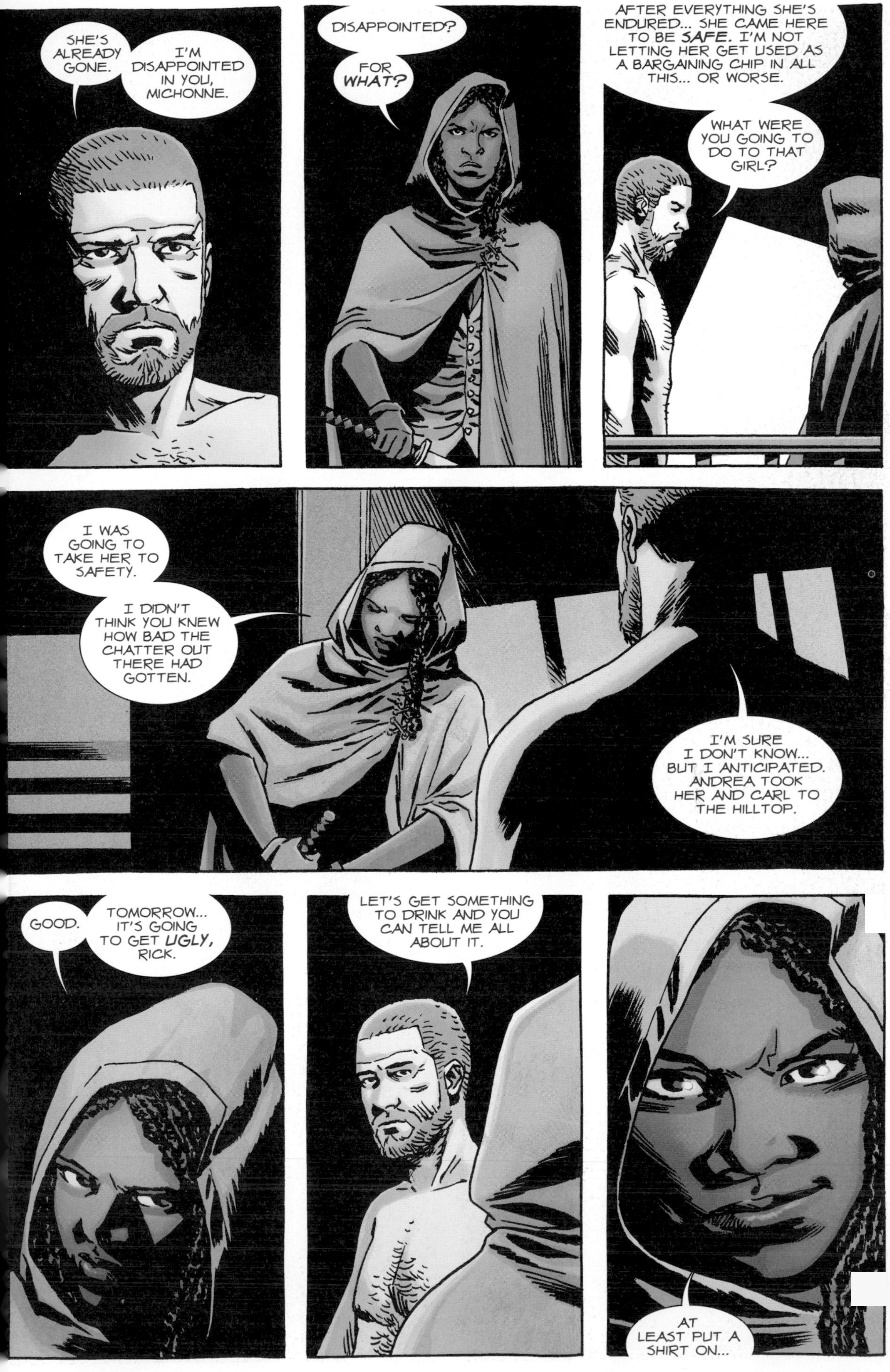
SHE'S ALREADY GONE.
I'M DISAPPOINTED IN YOU, MICHONNE.
DISAPPOINTED?
FOR WHAT?
AFTER EVERYTHING SHE'S ENDURED... SHE CAME HERE TO BE SAFE. I'M NOT LETTING HER GET USED AS A BARGAINING CHIP IN ALL THIS... OR WORSE.
WHAT WERE YOU GOING TO DO TO THAT GIRL?
I WAS GOING TO TAKE HER TO SAFETY.
I DIDN'T THINK YOU KNEW HOW BAD THE CHATTER OUT THERE HAD GOTTEN.
I'M SURE I DON'T KNOW... BUT I ANTICIPATED. ANDREA TOOK HER AND CARL TO THE HILLTOP.
GOOD.
TOMORROW... IT'S GOING TO GET UGLY, RICK.
LET'S GET SOMETHING TO DRINK AND YOU CAN TELL ME ALL ABOUT IT.
AT LEAST PUT A SHIRT ON...

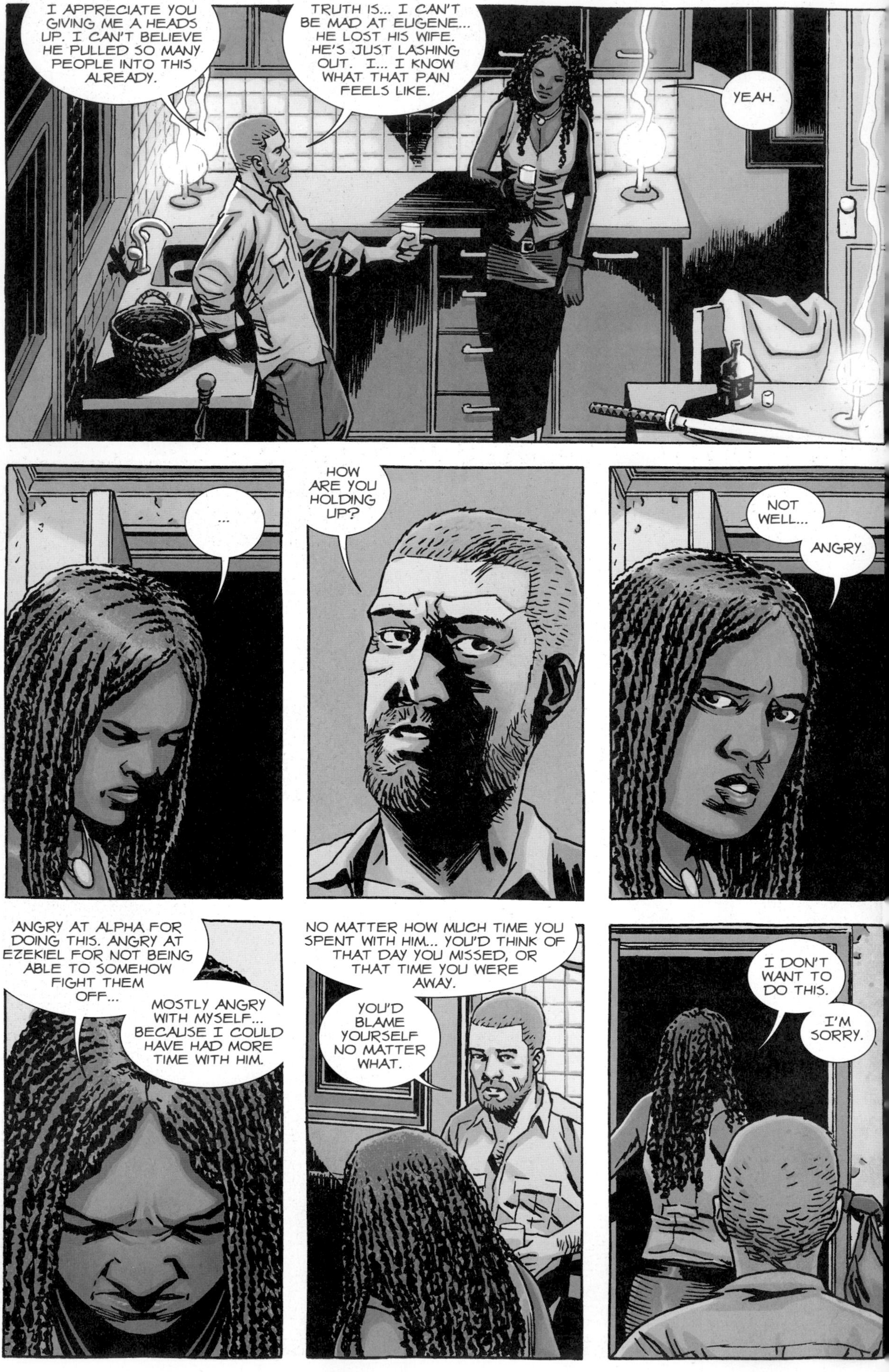
I APPRECIATE YOU GIVING ME A HEADS UP. I CAN'T BELIEVE HE PULLED SO MANY PEOPLE INTO THIS ALREADY.
TRUTH IS... I CAN'T BE MAD AT EUGENE... HE LOST HIS WIFE. HE'S JUST LASHING OUT. I... I KNOW WHAT THAT PAIN FEELS LIKE.
YEAH.
...
HOW ARE YOU HOLDING UP?
NOT WELL...
ANGRY.
ANGRY AT ALPHA FOR DOING THIS. ANGRY AT EZEKIEL FOR NOT BEING ABLE TO SOMEHOW FIGHT THEM OFF...
MOSTLY ANGRY WITH MYSELF... BECAUSE I COULD HAVE HAD MORE TIME WITH HIM.
NO MATTER HOW MUCH TIME YOU SPENT WITH HIM... YOU'D THINK OF THAT DAY YOU MISSED, OR THAT TIME YOU WERE AWAY.
YOU'D BLAME YOURSELF NO MATTER WHAT.
I DON'T WANT TO DO THIS.
I'M SORRY.

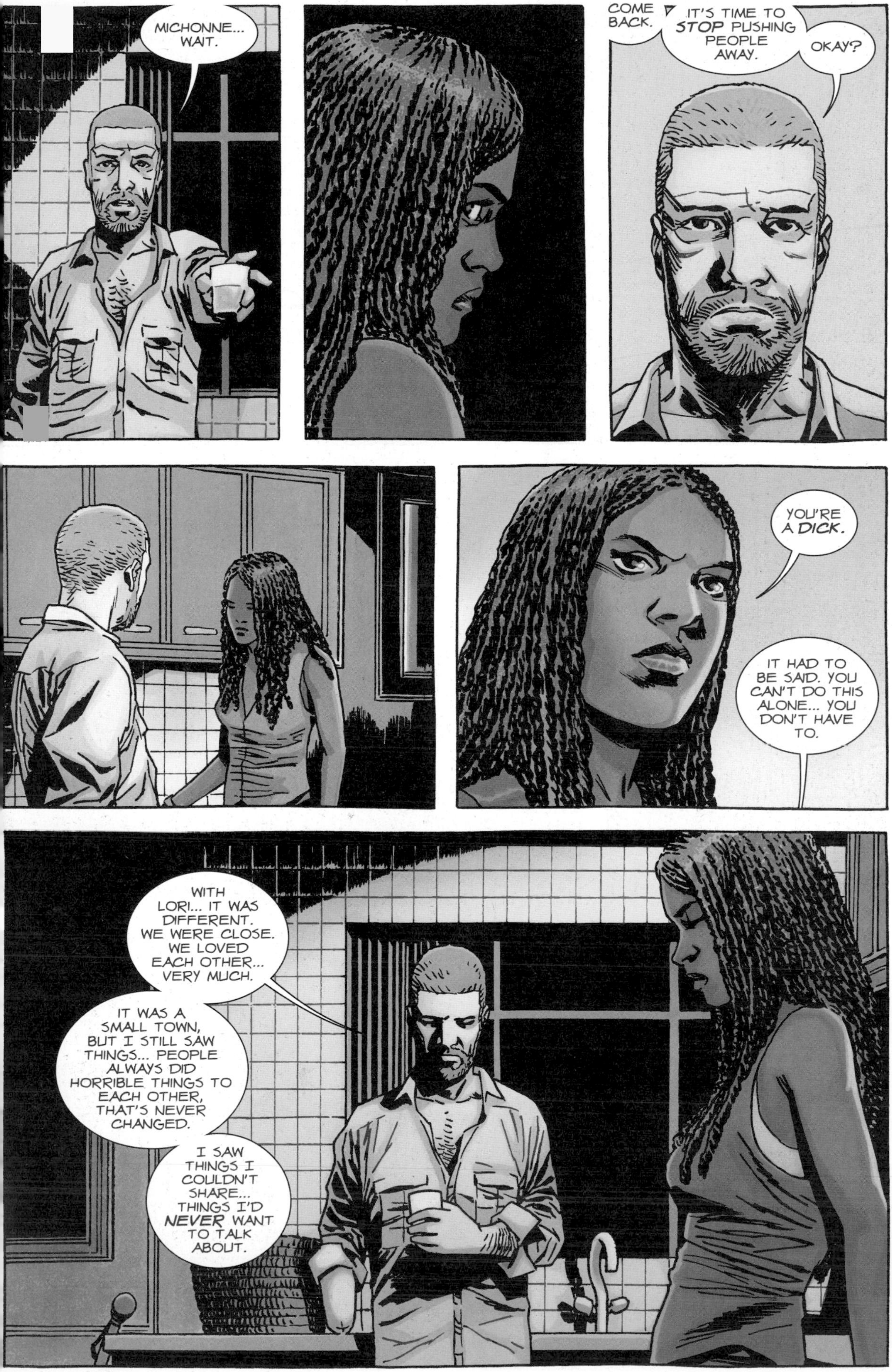
MICHONNE... WAIT.
COME BACK.
IT'S TIME TO STOP PUSHING PEOPLE AWAY.
OKAY?
YOU'RE A DICK.
IT HAD TO BE SAID. YOU CAN'T DO THIS ALONE... YOU DON'T HAVE TO.
WITH LORI... IT WAS DIFFERENT. WE WERE CLOSE. WE LOVED EACH OTHER... VERY MUCH.
IT WAS A SMALL TOWN, BUT I STILL SAW THINGS... PEOPLE ALWAYS DID HORRIBLE THINGS TO EACH OTHER, THAT'S NEVER CHANGED.
I SAW THINGS I COULDN'T SHARE... THINGS I'D NEVER WANT TO TALK ABOUT.

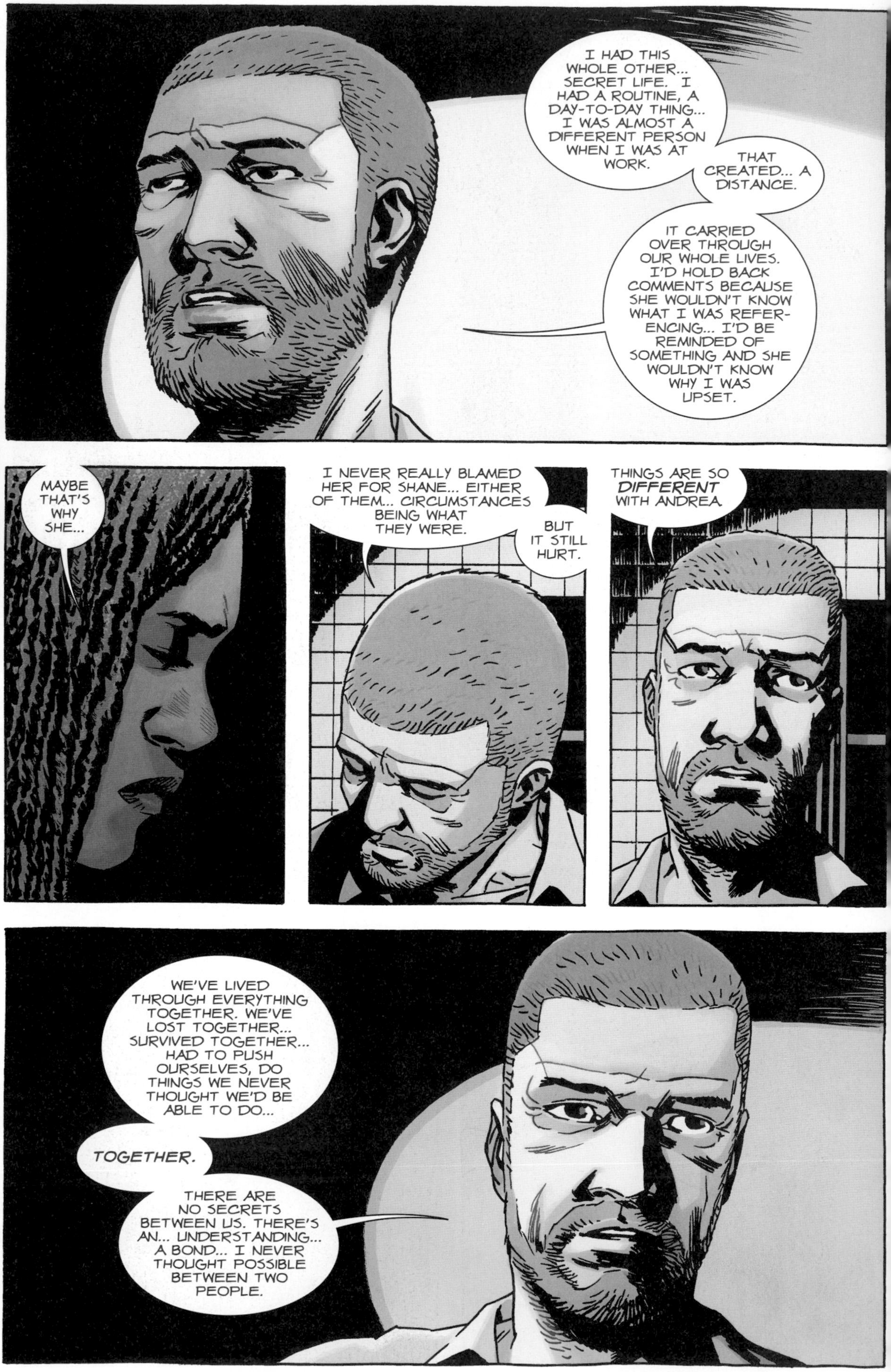
I HAD THIS WHOLE OTHER... SECRET LIFE. I HAD A ROUTINE, A DAY-TO-DAY THING... I WAS ALMOST A DIFFERENT PERSON WHEN I WAS AT WORK.
THAT CREATED... A DISTANCE.
IT CARRIED OVER THROUGH OUR WHOLE LIVES. I'D HOLD BACK COMMENTS BECAUSE SHE WOULDN'T KNOW WHAT I WAS REFERENCING... I'D BE REMINDED OF SOMETHING AND SHE WOULDN'T KNOW WHY I WAS UPSET.
MAYBE THAT'S WHY SHE...
I NEVER REALLY BLAMED HER FOR SHANE... EITHER OF THEM... CIRCUMSTANCES BEING WHAT THEY WERE.
BUT IT STILL HURT.
THINGS ARE SO *DIFFERENT* WITH ANDREA.
WE'VE LIVED THROUGH EVERYTHING TOGETHER. WE'VE LOST TOGETHER... SURVIVED TOGETHER... HAD TO PUSH OURSELVES, DO THINGS WE NEVER THOUGHT WE'D BE ABLE TO DO...
TOGETHER.
THERE ARE NO SECRETS BETWEEN US. THERE'S AN... UNDERSTANDING... A BOND... I NEVER THOUGHT POSSIBLE BETWEEN TWO PEOPLE.

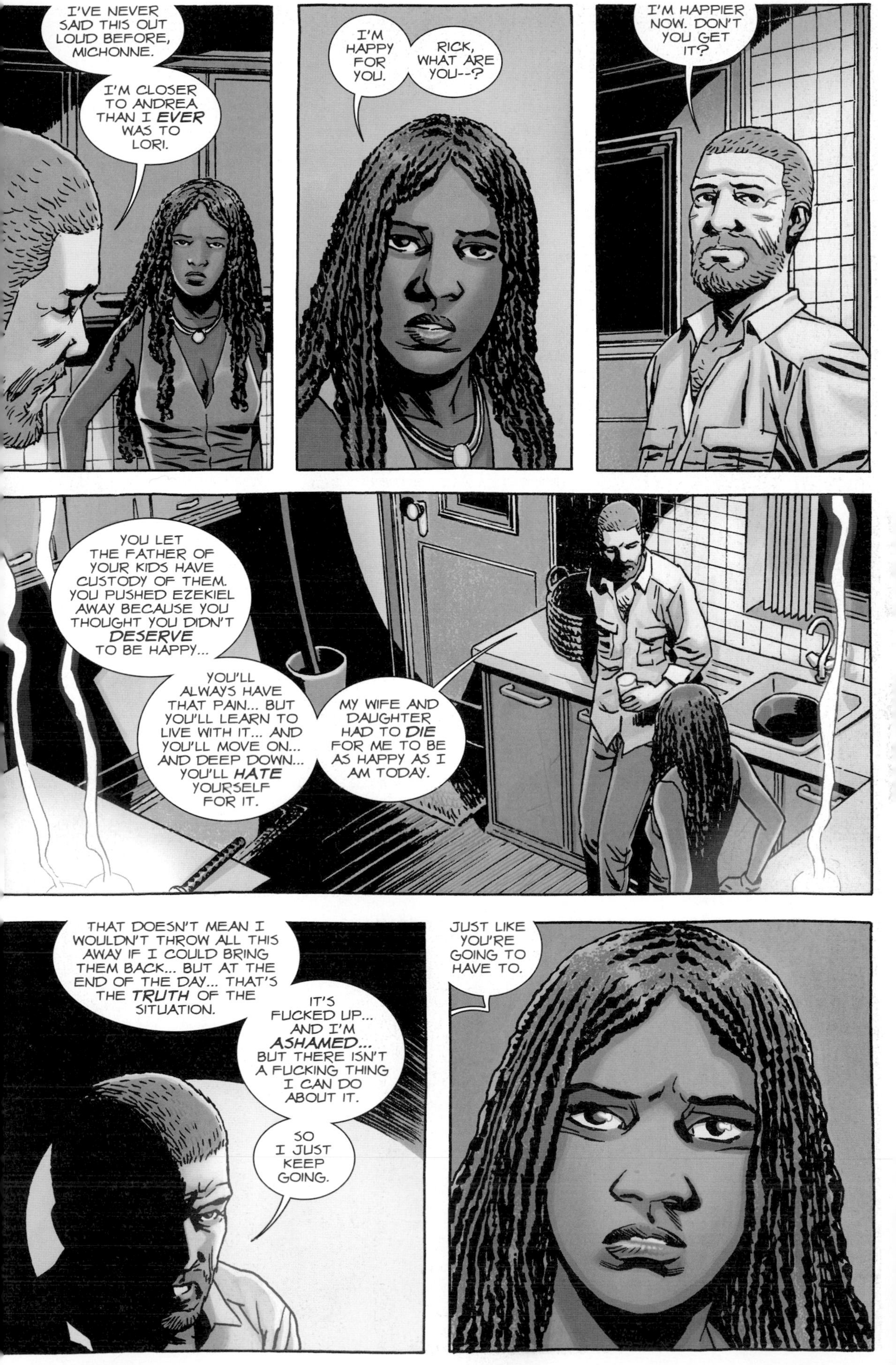
I'VE NEVER SAID THIS OUT LOUD BEFORE, MICHONNE.
I'M CLOSER TO ANDREA THAN I EVER WAS TO LORI.
I'M HAPPY FOR YOU.
RICK, WHAT ARE YOU--?
I'M HAPPIER NOW. DON'T YOU GET IT?
YOU LET THE FATHER OF YOUR KIDS HAVE CUSTODY OF THEM. YOU PUSHED EZEKIEL AWAY BECAUSE YOU THOUGHT YOU DIDN'T DESERVE TO BE HAPPY...
YOU'LL ALWAYS HAVE THAT PAIN... BUT YOU'LL LEARN TO LIVE WITH IT... AND YOU'LL MOVE ON... AND DEEP DOWN... YOU'LL HATE YOURSELF FOR IT.
MY WIFE AND DAUGHTER HAD TO DIE FOR ME TO BE AS HAPPY AS I AM TODAY.
THAT DOESN'T MEAN I WOULDN'T THROW ALL THIS AWAY IF I COULD BRING THEM BACK... BUT AT THE END OF THE DAY... THAT'S THE TRUTH OF THE SITUATION.
IT'S FUCKED UP... AND I'M ASHAMED... BUT THERE ISN'T A FUCKING THING I CAN DO ABOUT IT.
SO I JUST KEEP GOING.
JUST LIKE YOU'RE GOING TO HAVE TO.

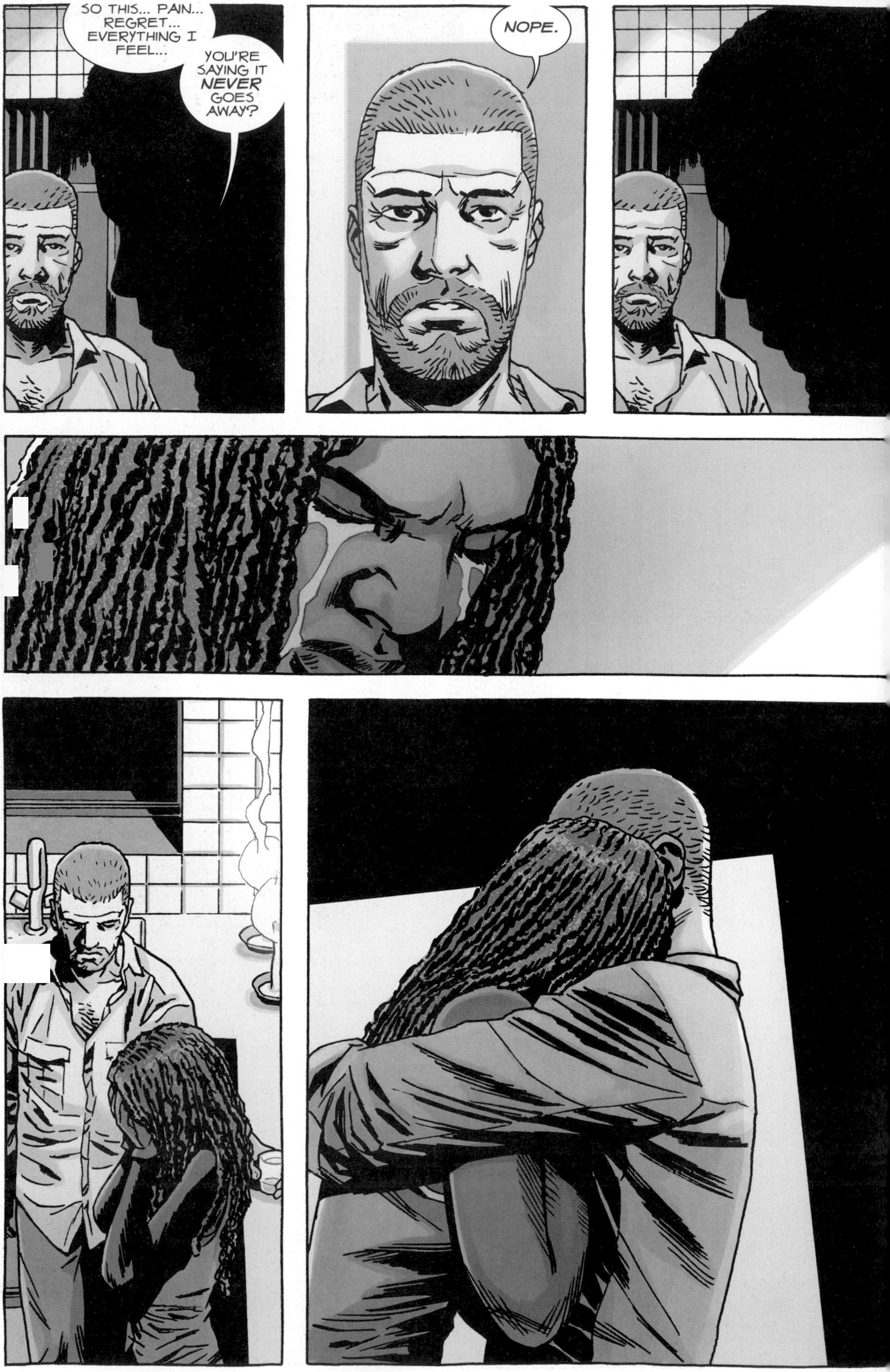
SO THIS... PAIN... REGRET... EVERYTHING I FEEL...
YOU'RE SAYING IT NEVER GOES AWAY?
NOPE.

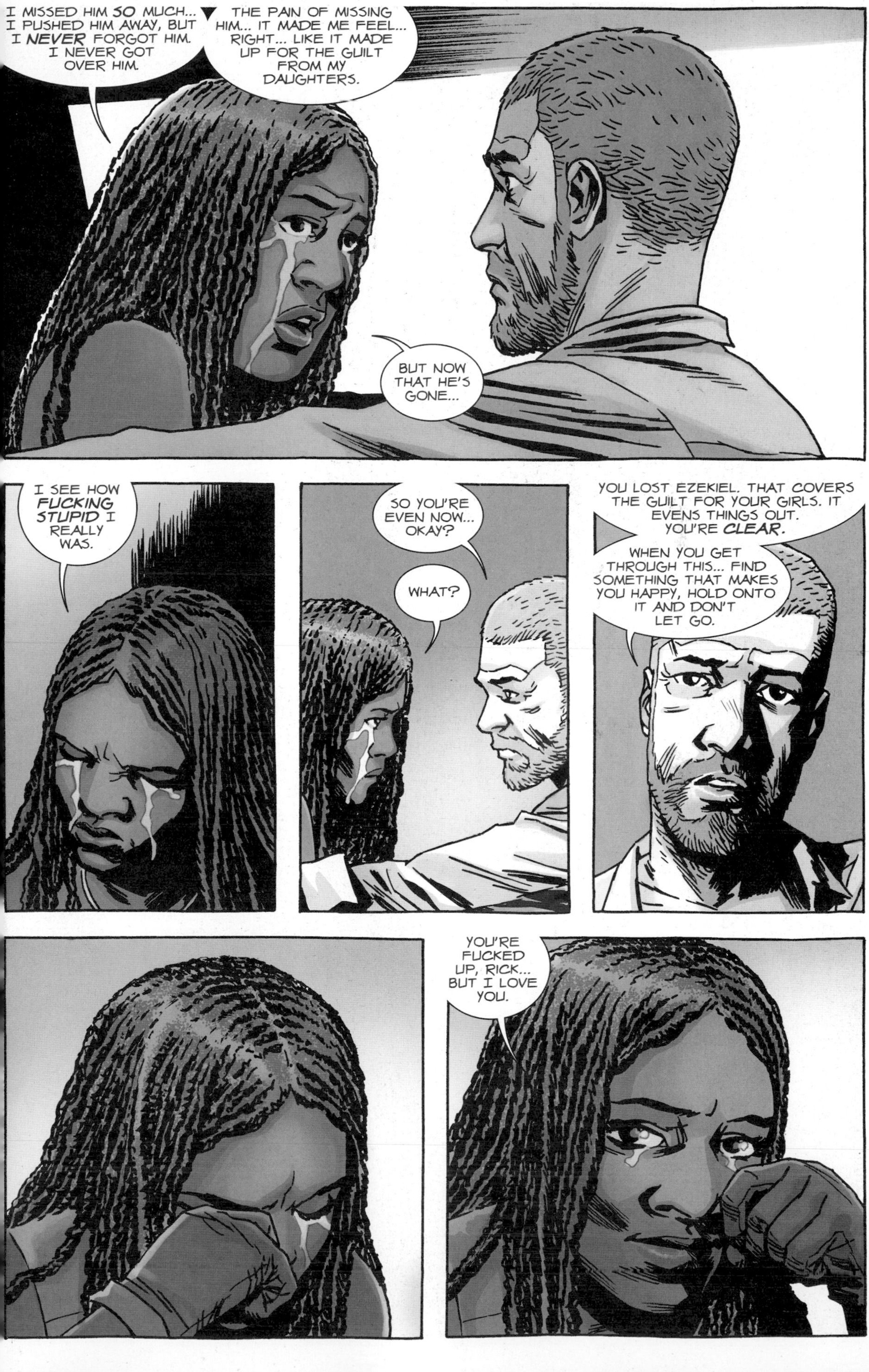
I MISSED HIM SO MUCH... I PUSHED HIM AWAY, BUT I NEVER FORGOT HIM. I NEVER GOT OVER HIM.
THE PAIN OF MISSING HIM... IT MADE ME FEEL... RIGHT... LIKE IT MADE UP FOR THE GUILT FROM MY DAUGHTERS.
BUT NOW THAT HE'S GONE...
I SEE HOW FUCKING STUPID I REALLY WAS.
SO YOU'RE EVEN NOW... OKAY?
WHAT?
YOU LOST EZEKIEL. THAT COVERS THE GUILT FOR YOUR GIRLS. IT EVENS THINGS OUT. YOU'RE CLEAR.
WHEN YOU GET THROUGH THIS... FIND SOMETHING THAT MAKES YOU HAPPY, HOLD ONTO IT AND DON'T LET GO.
YOU'RE FUCKED UP, RICK... BUT I LOVE YOU.

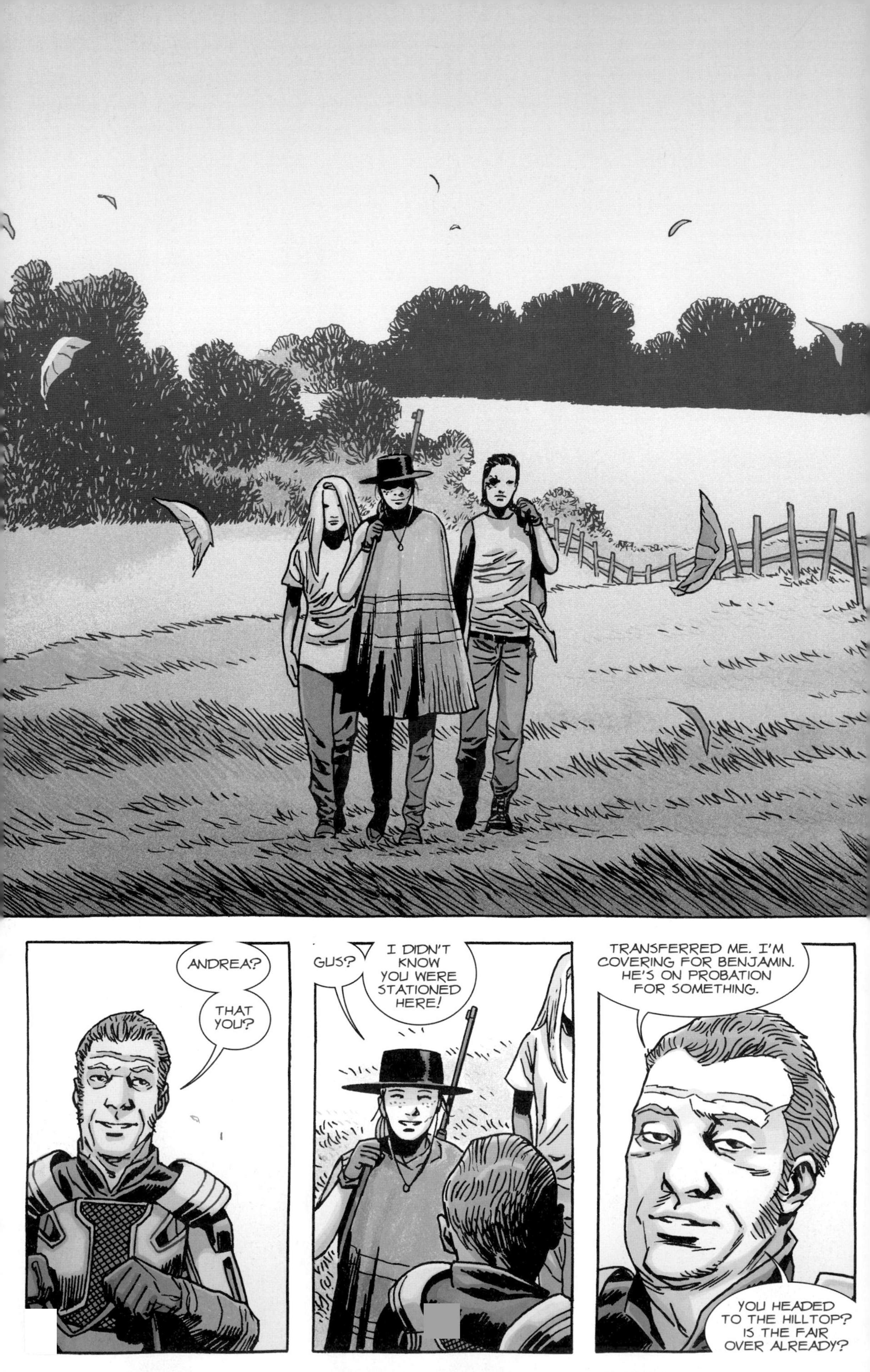

ANDREA?
THAT YOU?
GUS?
I DIDN'T KNOW YOU WERE STATIONED HERE!
TRANSFERRED ME. I'M COVERING FOR BENJAMIN. HE'S ON PROBATION FOR SOMETHING.
YOU HEADED TO THE HILLTOP? IS THE FAIR OVER ALREADY?

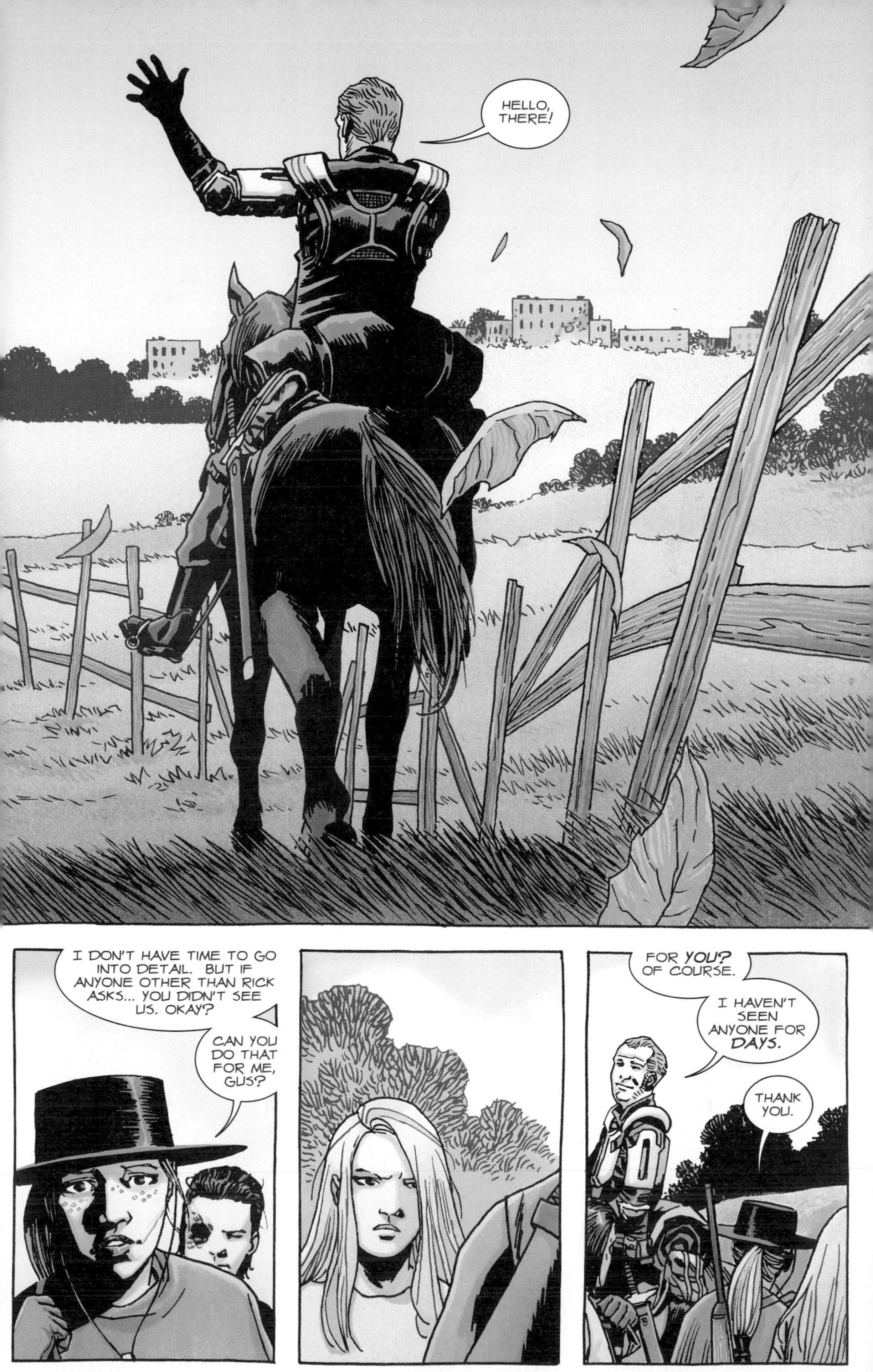
HELLO, THERE!
I DON'T HAVE TIME TO GO INTO DETAIL. BUT IF ANYONE OTHER THAN RICK ASKS... YOU DIDN'T SEE US. OKAY?
CAN YOU DO THAT FOR ME, GUS?
FOR *YOU?* OF COURSE.
I HAVEN'T SEEN ANYONE FOR *DAYS.*
THANK YOU.

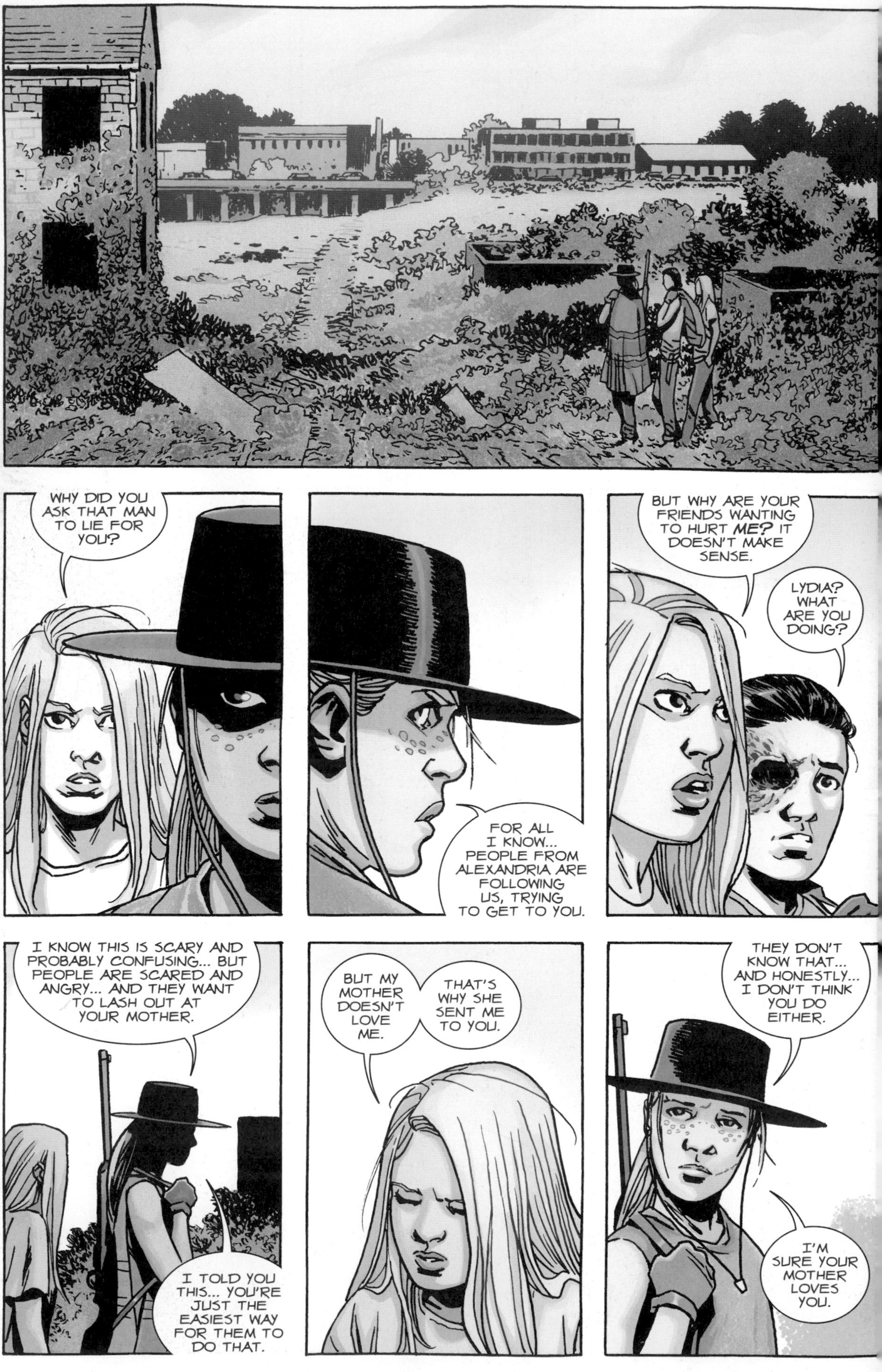

WHY DID YOU ASK THAT MAN TO LIE FOR YOU?
FOR ALL I KNOW... PEOPLE FROM ALEXANDRIA ARE FOLLOWING US, TRYING TO GET TO YOU.
BUT WHY ARE YOUR FRIENDS WANTING TO HURT **ME?** IT DOESN'T MAKE SENSE.
LYDIA? WHAT ARE YOU DOING?
I KNOW THIS IS SCARY AND PROBABLY CONFUSING... BUT PEOPLE ARE SCARED AND ANGRY... AND THEY WANT TO LASH OUT AT YOUR MOTHER.
I TOLD YOU THIS... YOU'RE JUST THE EASIEST WAY FOR THEM TO DO THAT.
BUT MY MOTHER DOESN'T LOVE ME.
THAT'S WHY SHE SENT ME TO YOU.
THEY DON'T KNOW THAT... AND HONESTLY... I DON'T THINK YOU DO EITHER.
I'M SURE YOUR MOTHER LOVES YOU.

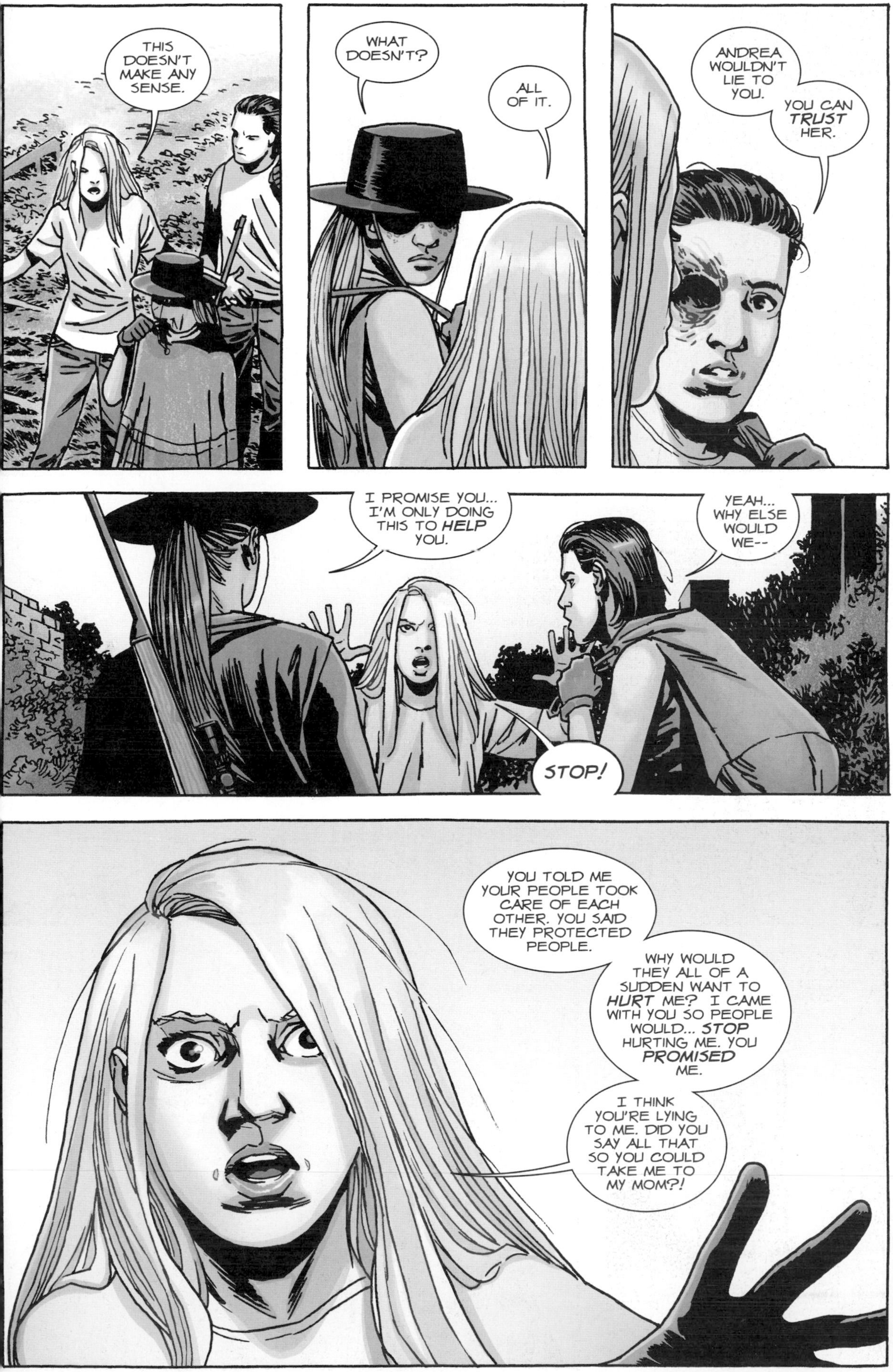

THIS DOESN'T MAKE ANY SENSE.
WHAT DOESN'T?
ALL OF IT.
ANDREA WOULDN'T LIE TO YOU.
YOU CAN TRUST HER.
I PROMISE YOU... I'M ONLY DOING THIS TO HELP YOU.
YEAH... WHY ELSE WOULD WE--
STOP!
YOU TOLD ME YOUR PEOPLE TOOK CARE OF EACH OTHER. YOU SAID THEY PROTECTED PEOPLE.
WHY WOULD THEY ALL OF A SUDDEN WANT TO HURT ME? I CAME WITH YOU SO PEOPLE WOULD... STOP HURTING ME. YOU PROMISED ME.
I THINK YOU'RE LYING TO ME. DID YOU SAY ALL THAT SO YOU COULD TAKE ME TO MY MOM?!

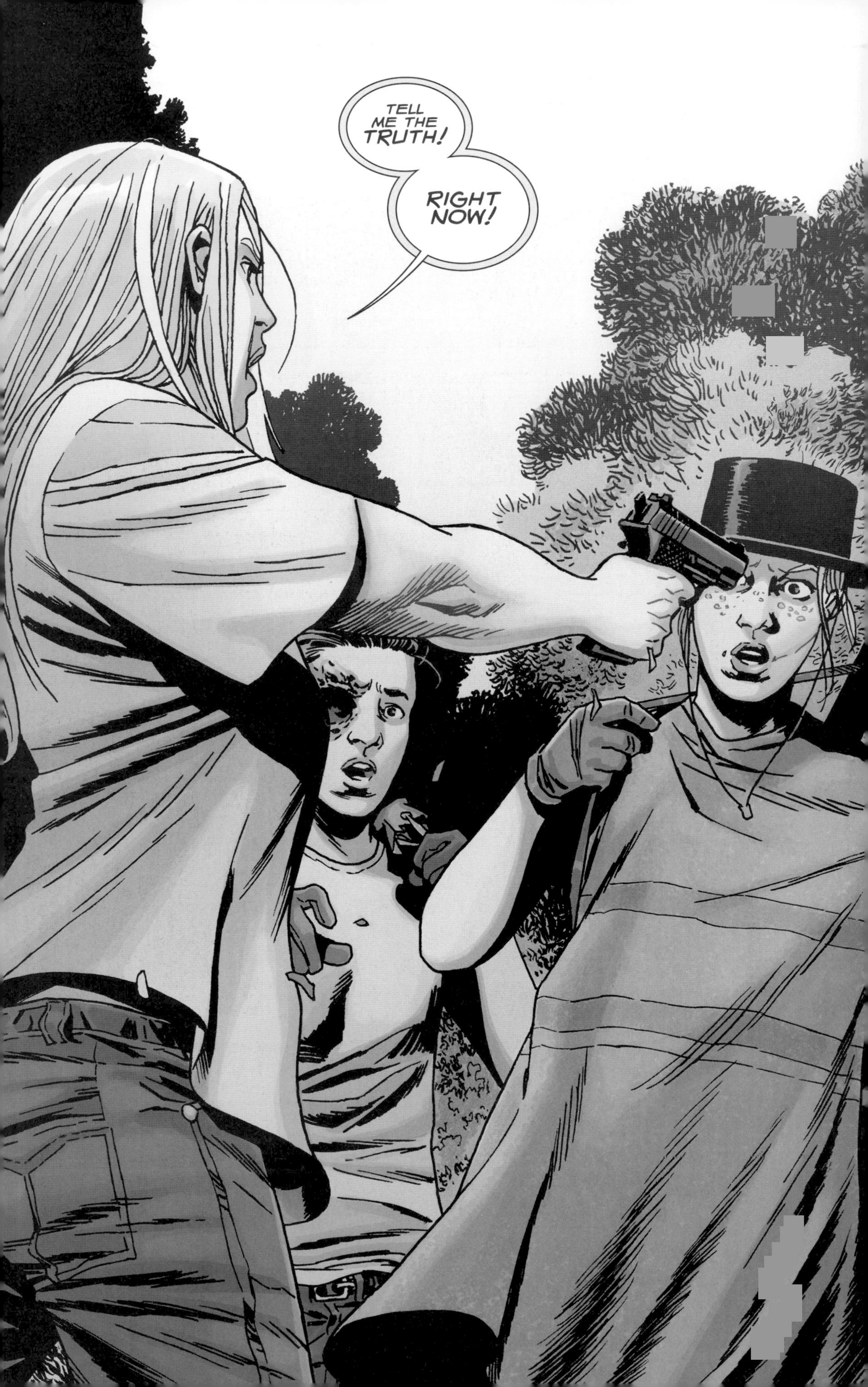
TELL ME THE TRUTH!
RIGHT NOW!

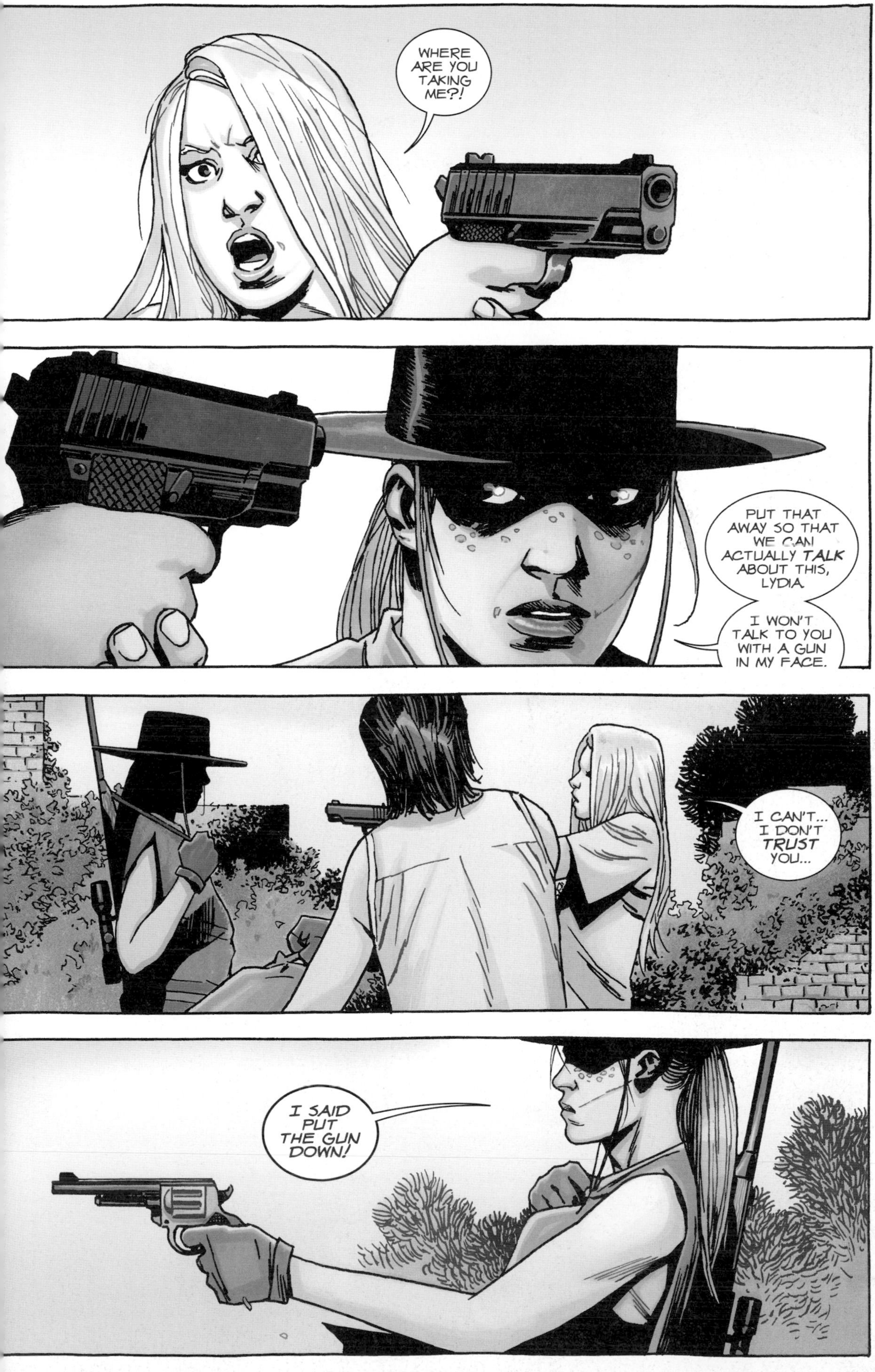
WHERE ARE YOU TAKING ME?!
PUT THAT AWAY SO THAT WE CAN ACTUALLY *TALK* ABOUT THIS, LYDIA.
I WON'T TALK TO YOU WITH A GUN IN MY FACE.
I CAN'T... I DON'T *TRUST* YOU...
I SAID PUT THE GUN DOWN!

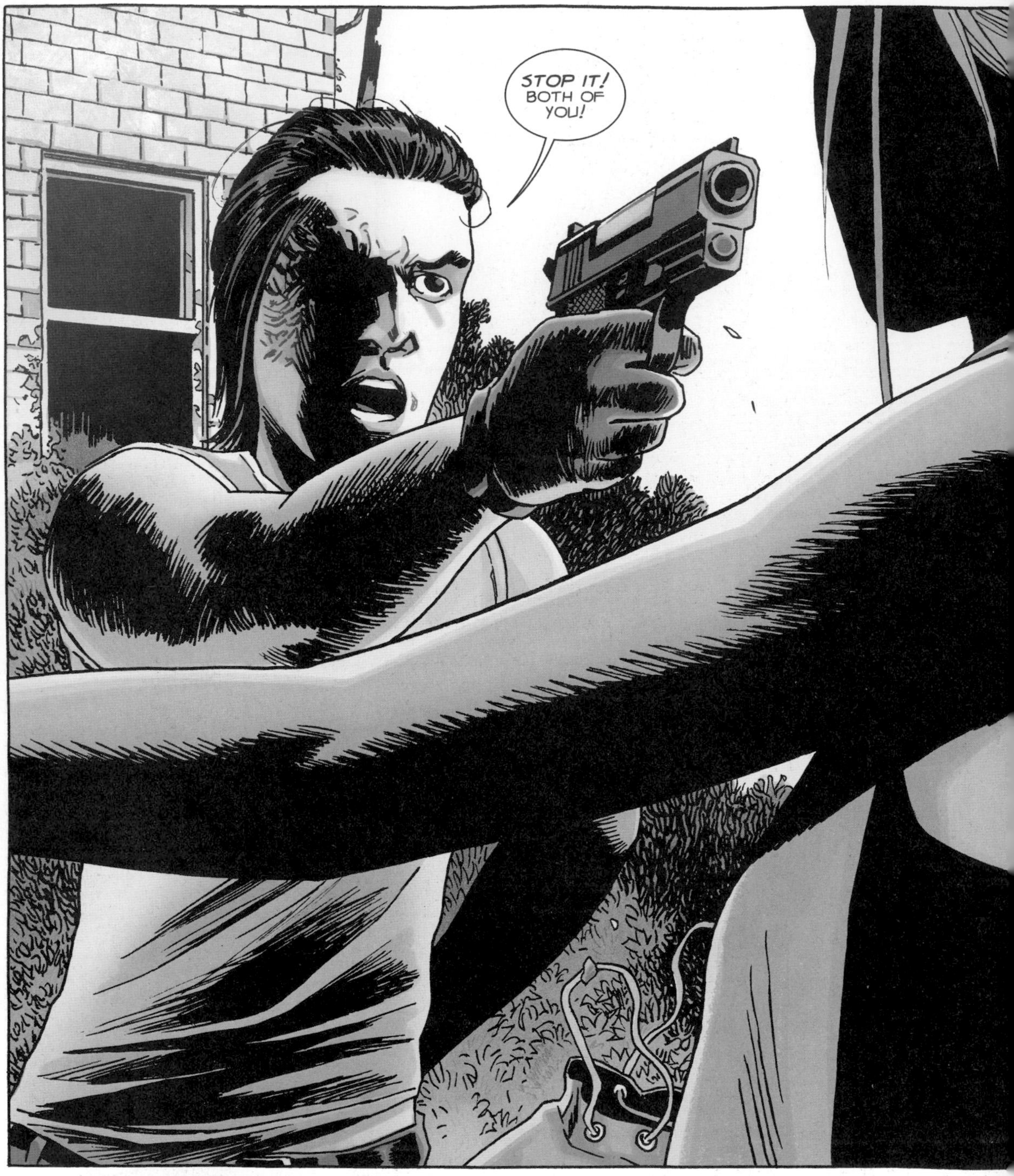
STOP IT! BOTH OF YOU!

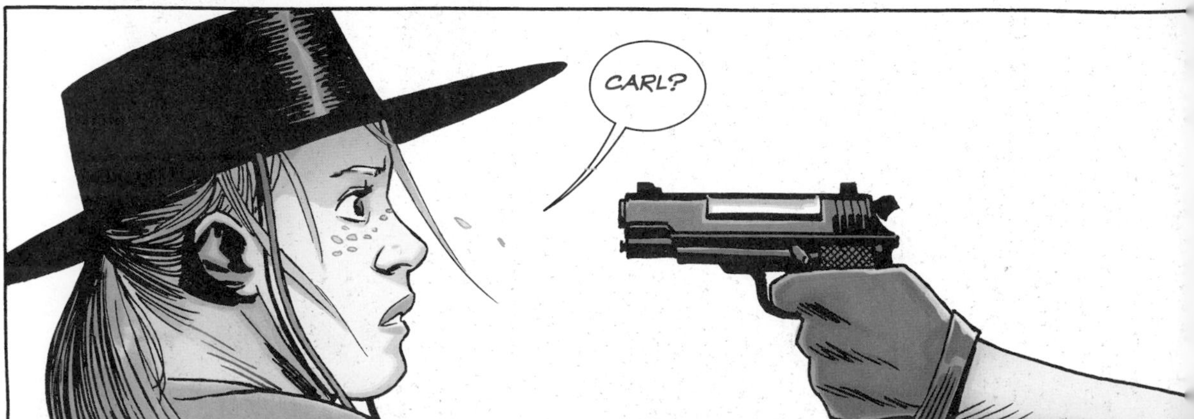
CARL?

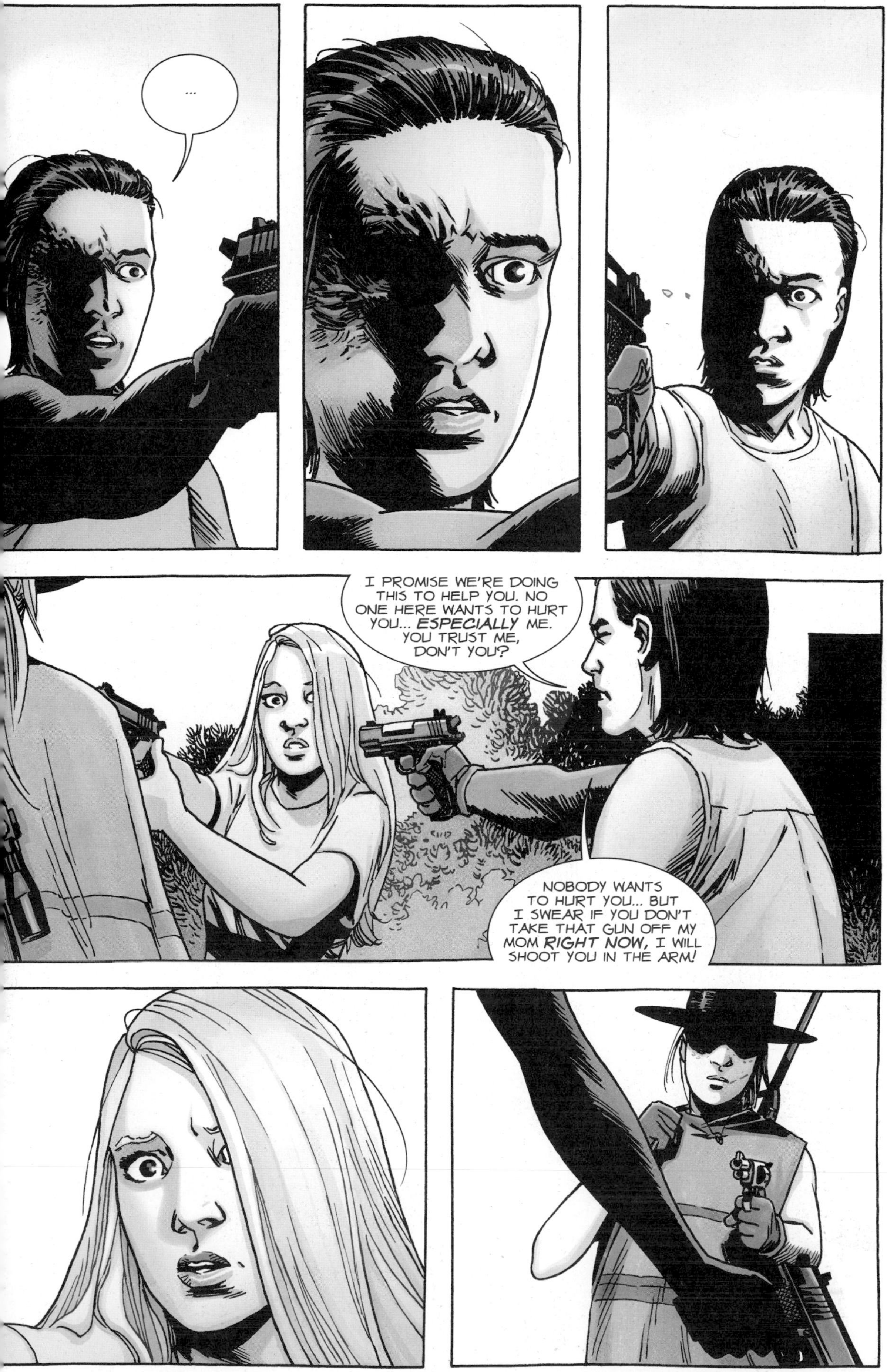
...
I PROMISE WE'RE DOING THIS TO HELP YOU. NO ONE HERE WANTS TO HURT YOU... *ESPECIALLY* ME. YOU TRUST ME, DON'T YOU?
NOBODY WANTS TO HURT YOU... BUT I SWEAR IF YOU DON'T TAKE THAT GUN OFF MY MOM *RIGHT NOW,* I WILL SHOOT YOU IN THE ARM!

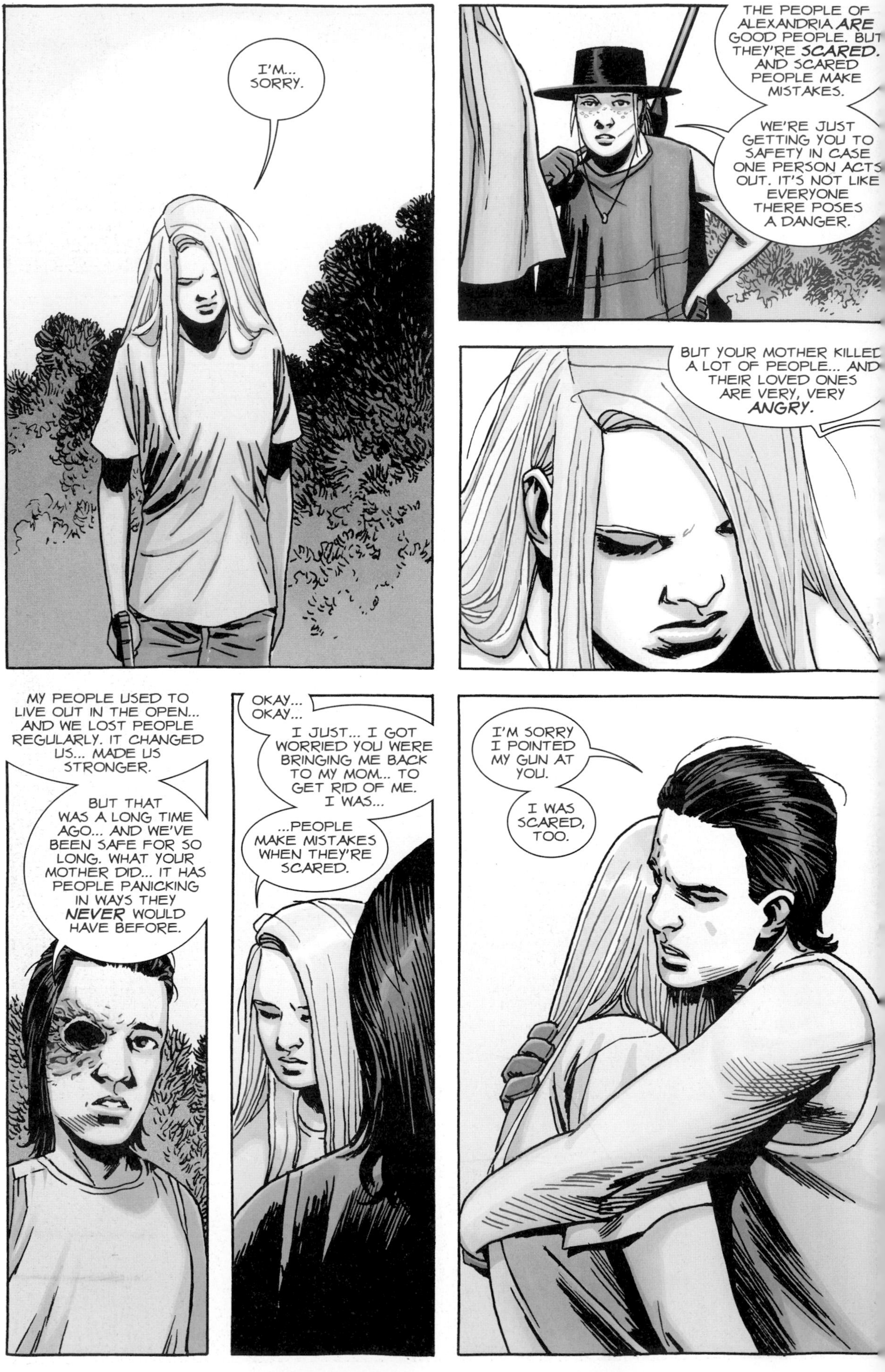
I'M... SORRY.
THE PEOPLE OF ALEXANDRIA ARE GOOD PEOPLE. BUT THEY'RE SCARED. AND SCARED PEOPLE MAKE MISTAKES.
WE'RE JUST GETTING YOU TO SAFETY IN CASE ONE PERSON ACTS OUT. IT'S NOT LIKE EVERYONE THERE POSES A DANGER.
BUT YOUR MOTHER KILLED A LOT OF PEOPLE... AND THEIR LOVED ONES ARE VERY, VERY ANGRY.
MY PEOPLE USED TO LIVE OUT IN THE OPEN... AND WE LOST PEOPLE REGULARLY. IT CHANGED US... MADE US STRONGER.
BUT THAT WAS A LONG TIME AGO... AND WE'VE BEEN SAFE FOR SO LONG. WHAT YOUR MOTHER DID... IT HAS PEOPLE PANICKING IN WAYS THEY NEVER WOULD HAVE BEFORE.
OKAY... OKAY...
I JUST... I GOT WORRIED YOU WERE BRINGING ME BACK TO MY MOM... TO GET RID OF ME. I WAS...
...PEOPLE MAKE MISTAKES WHEN THEY'RE SCARED.
I'M SORRY I POINTED MY GUN AT YOU.
I WAS SCARED, TOO.

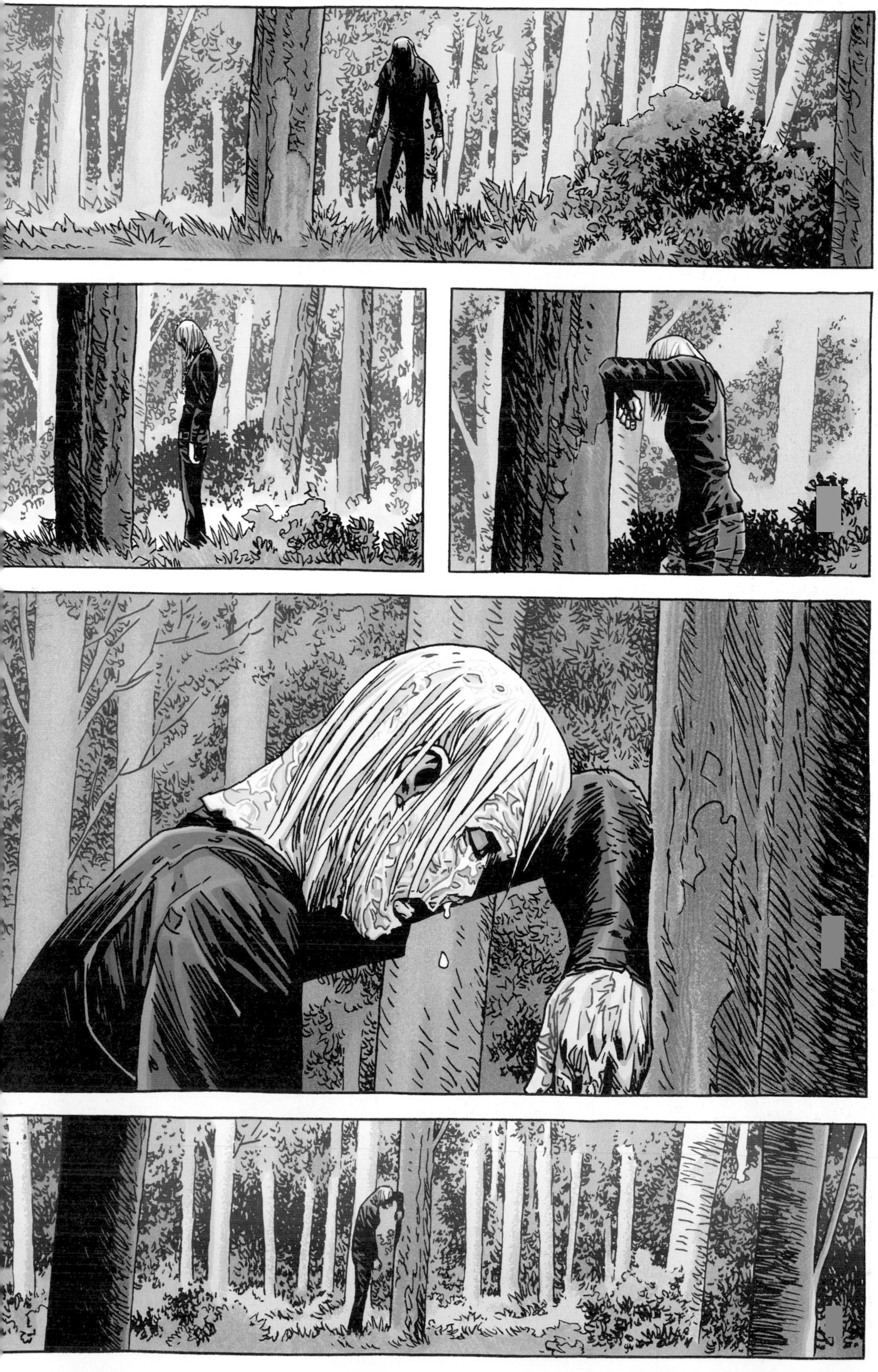

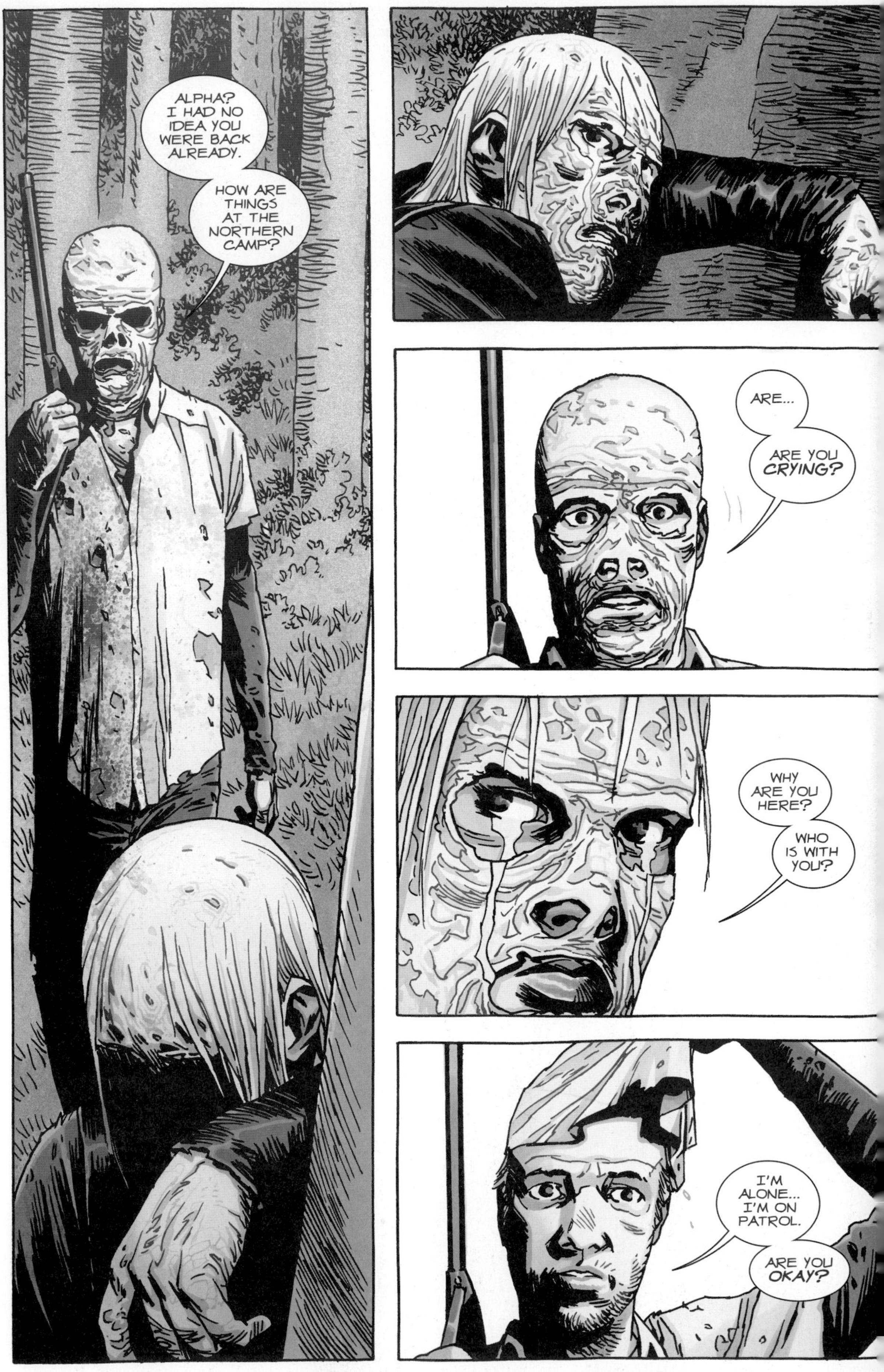
ALPHA? I HAD NO IDEA YOU WERE BACK ALREADY.
HOW ARE THINGS AT THE NORTHERN CAMP?
ARE...
ARE YOU CRYING?
WHY ARE YOU HERE?
WHO IS WITH YOU?
I'M ALONE... I'M ON PATROL.
ARE YOU OKAY?

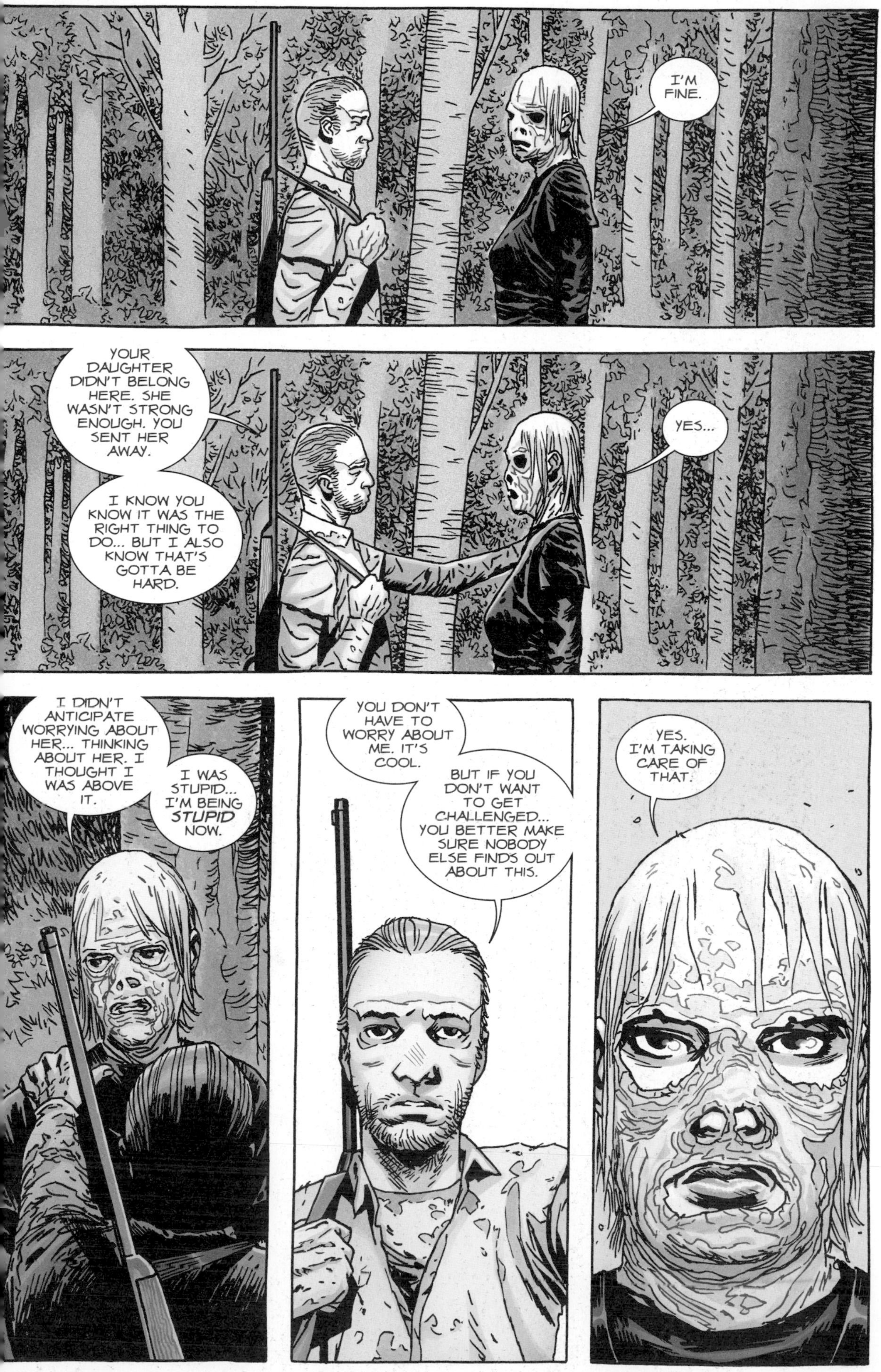
I'M FINE.
YOUR DAUGHTER DIDN'T BELONG HERE. SHE WASN'T STRONG ENOUGH. YOU SENT HER AWAY.
YES...
I KNOW YOU KNOW IT WAS THE RIGHT THING TO DO... BUT I ALSO KNOW THAT'S GOTTA BE HARD.
I DIDN'T ANTICIPATE WORRYING ABOUT HER... THINKING ABOUT HER. I THOUGHT I WAS ABOVE IT.
I WAS STUPID... I'M BEING *STUPID* NOW.
YOU DON'T HAVE TO WORRY ABOUT ME. IT'S COOL.
BUT IF YOU DON'T WANT TO GET CHALLENGED... YOU BETTER MAKE SURE NOBODY ELSE FINDS OUT ABOUT THIS.
YES. I'M TAKING CARE OF THAT.

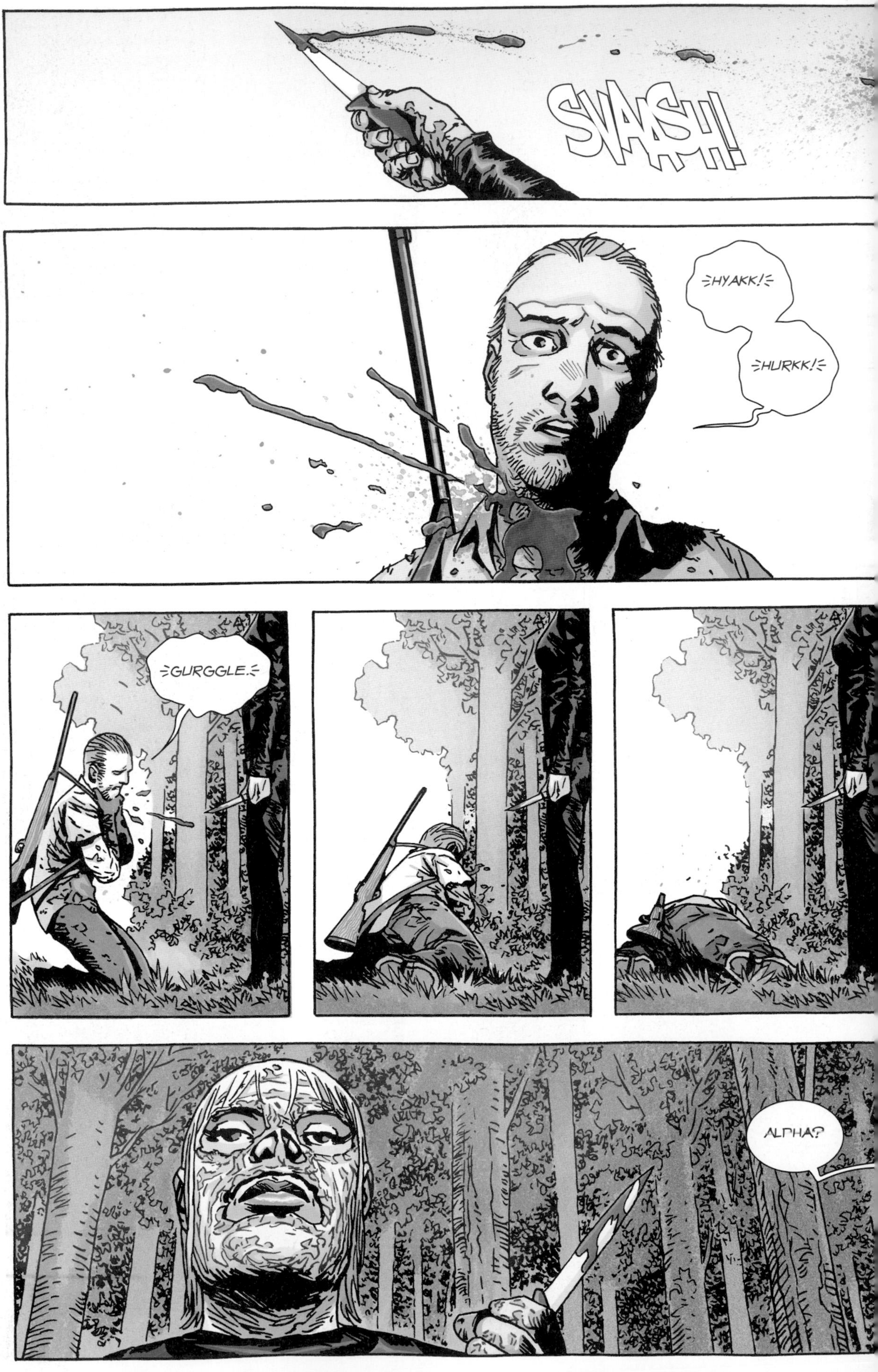
SVAASH!
HYAKK!
HURKK!
GURGGLE.
ALPHA?

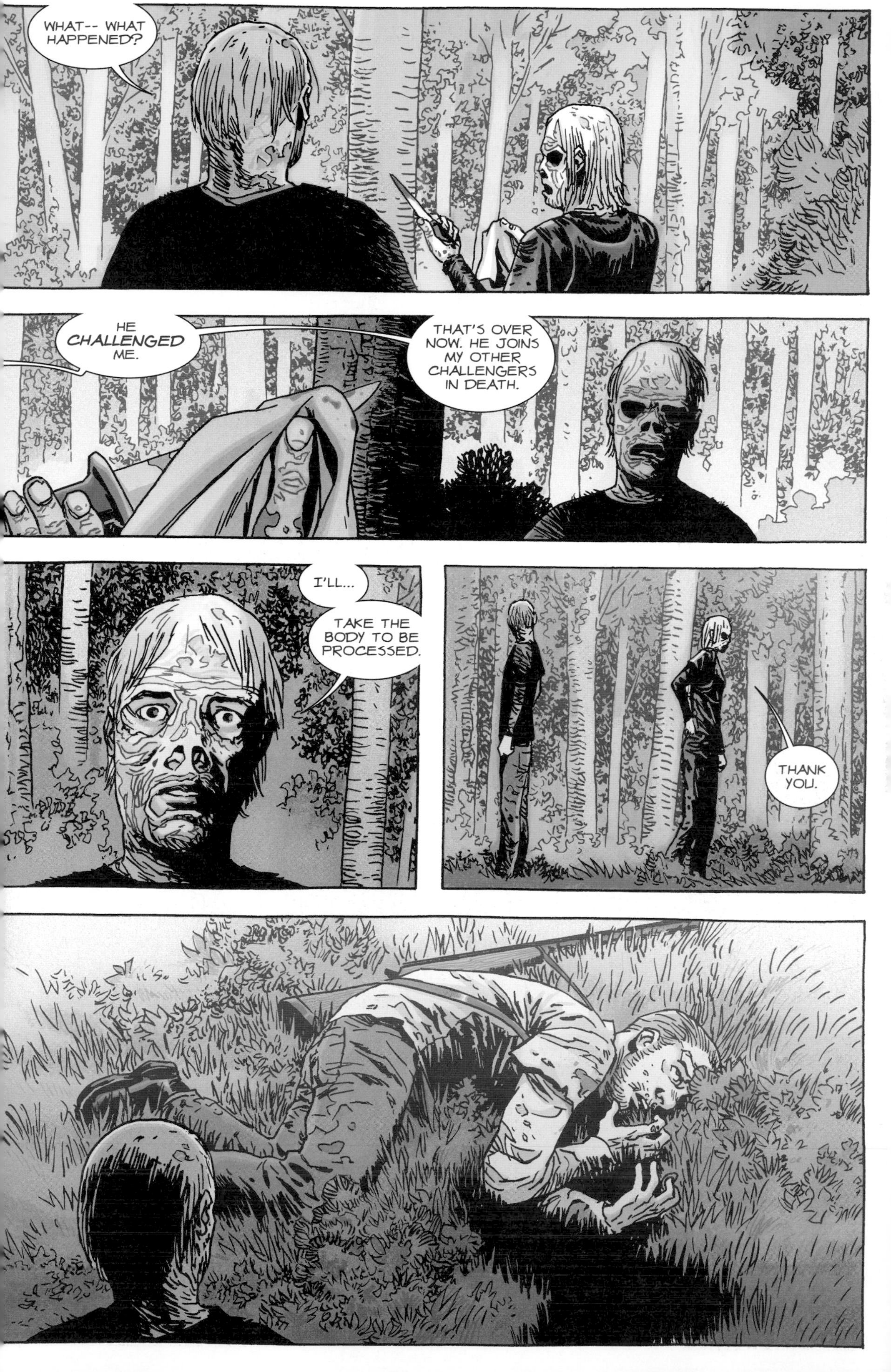
WHAT-- WHAT HAPPENED?
HE CHALLENGED ME.
THAT'S OVER NOW. HE JOINS MY OTHER CHALLENGERS IN DEATH.
I'LL...
TAKE THE BODY TO BE PROCESSED.
THANK YOU.

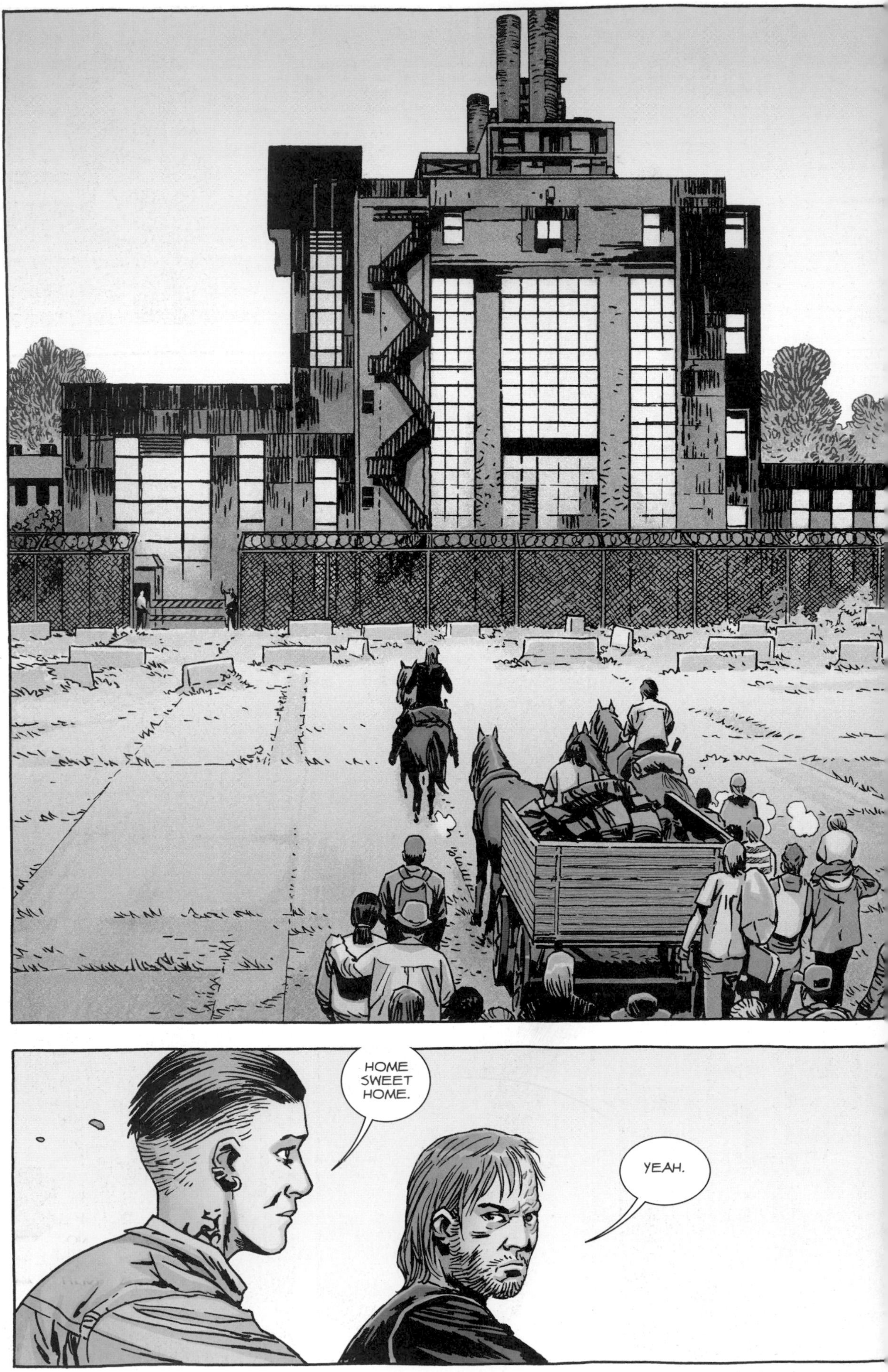
HOME SWEET HOME.
YEAH.

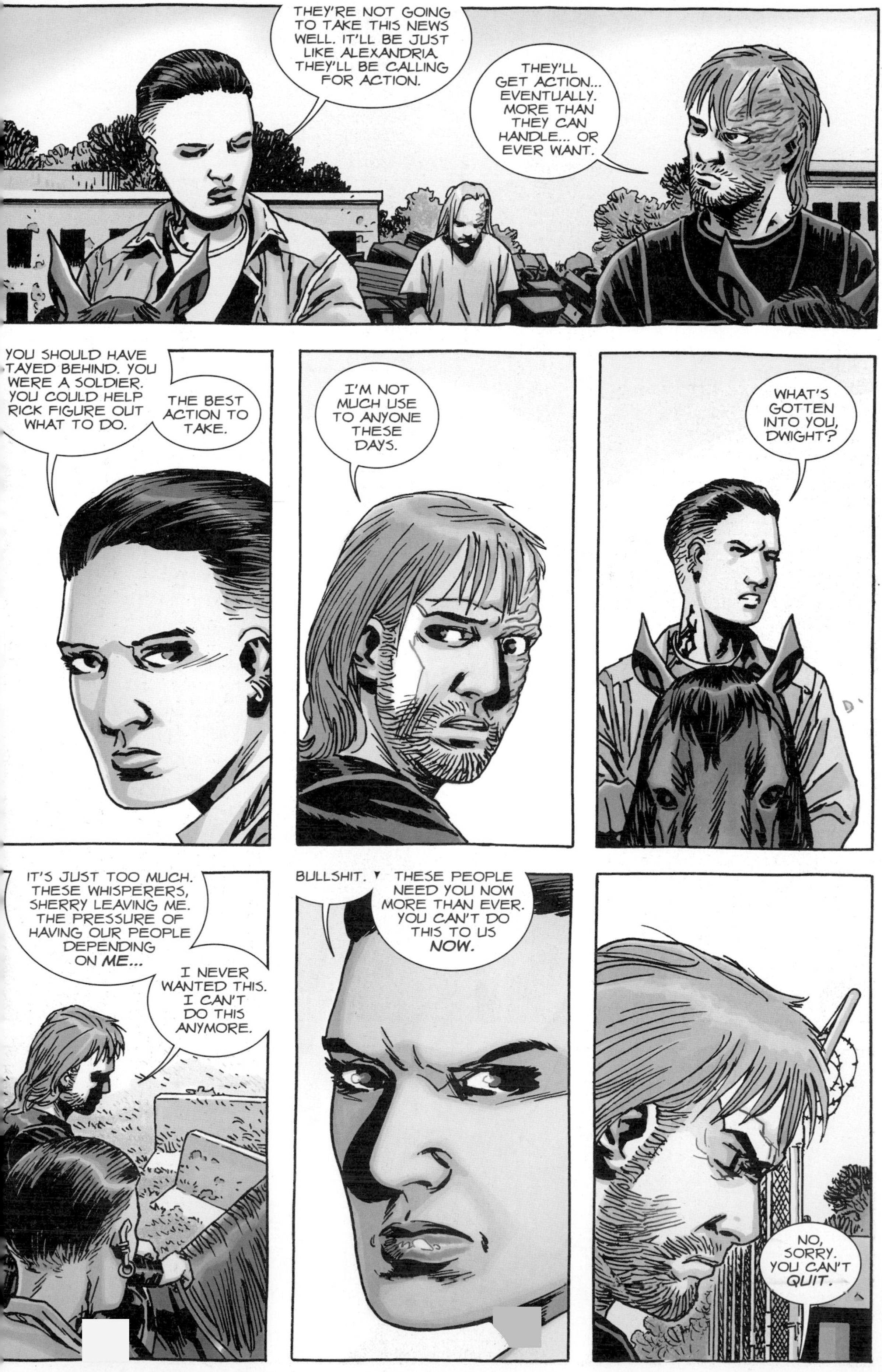

THEY'RE NOT GOING TO TAKE THIS NEWS WELL. IT'LL BE JUST LIKE ALEXANDRIA. THEY'LL BE CALLING FOR ACTION.
THEY'LL GET ACTION... EVENTUALLY. MORE THAN THEY CAN HANDLE... OR EVER WANT.
YOU SHOULD HAVE TAYED BEHIND. YOU WERE A SOLDIER. YOU COULD HELP RICK FIGURE OUT WHAT TO DO.
THE BEST ACTION TO TAKE.
I'M NOT MUCH USE TO ANYONE THESE DAYS.
WHAT'S GOTTEN INTO YOU, DWIGHT?
IT'S JUST TOO MUCH. THESE WHISPERERS, SHERRY LEAVING ME. THE PRESSURE OF HAVING OUR PEOPLE DEPENDING ON *ME*...
I NEVER WANTED THIS. I CAN'T DO THIS ANYMORE.
BULLSHIT.
THESE PEOPLE NEED YOU NOW MORE THAN EVER. YOU CAN'T DO THIS TO US *NOW*.
NO, SORRY. YOU CAN'T *QUIT*.

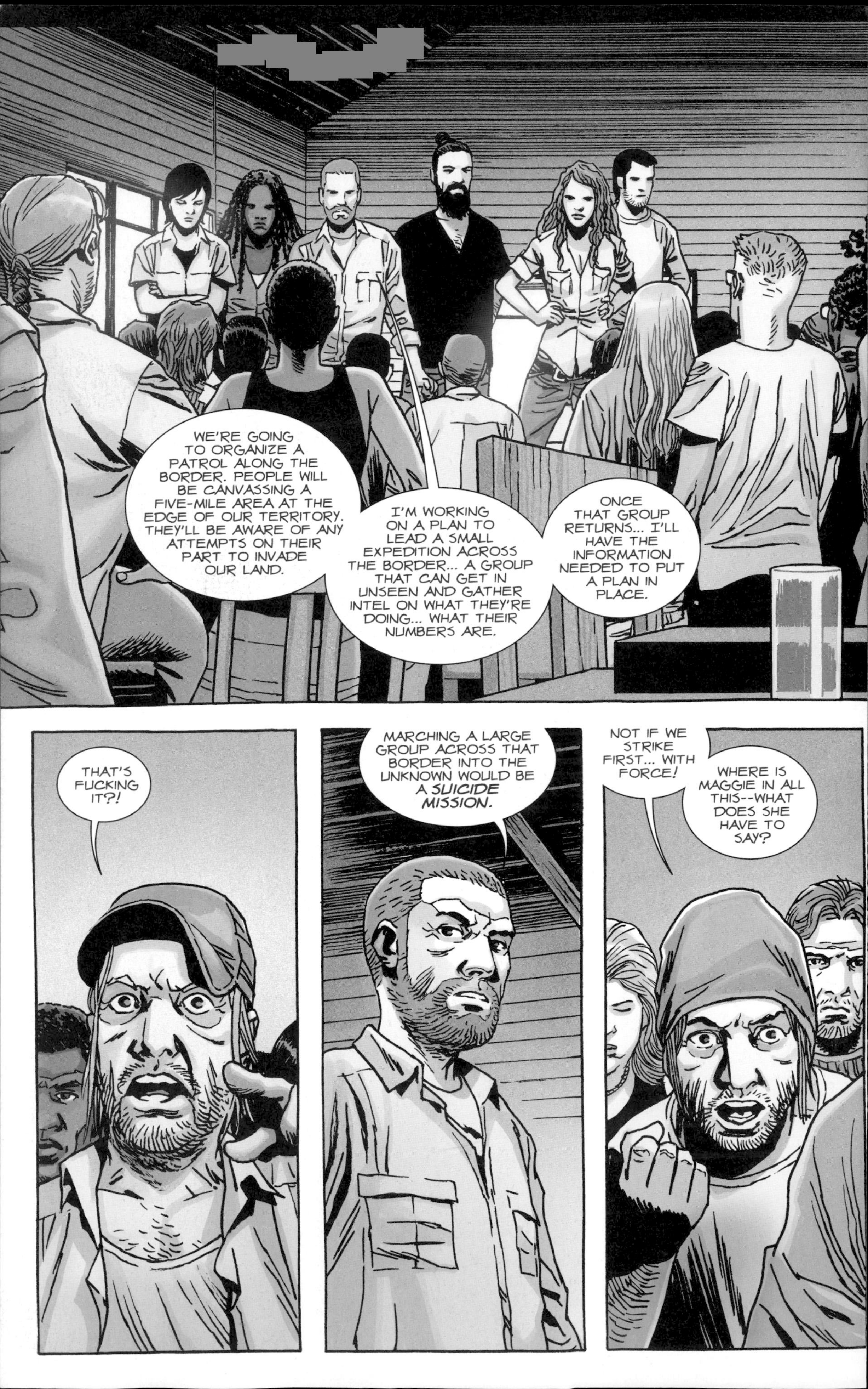
WE'RE GOING TO ORGANIZE A PATROL ALONG THE BORDER. PEOPLE WILL BE CANVASSING A FIVE-MILE AREA AT THE EDGE OF OUR TERRITORY. THEY'LL BE AWARE OF ANY ATTEMPTS ON THEIR PART TO INVADE OUR LAND.
I'M WORKING ON A PLAN TO LEAD A SMALL EXPEDITION ACROSS THE BORDER... A GROUP THAT CAN GET IN UNSEEN AND GATHER INTEL ON WHAT THEY'RE DOING... WHAT THEIR NUMBERS ARE.
ONCE THAT GROUP RETURNS... I'LL HAVE THE INFORMATION NEEDED TO PUT A PLAN IN PLACE.
THAT'S FUCKING IT?!
MARCHING A LARGE GROUP ACROSS THAT BORDER INTO THE UNKNOWN WOULD BE A *SUICIDE MISSION.*
NOT IF WE STRIKE FIRST... WITH FORCE!
WHERE IS MAGGIE IN ALL THIS--WHAT DOES SHE HAVE TO SAY?

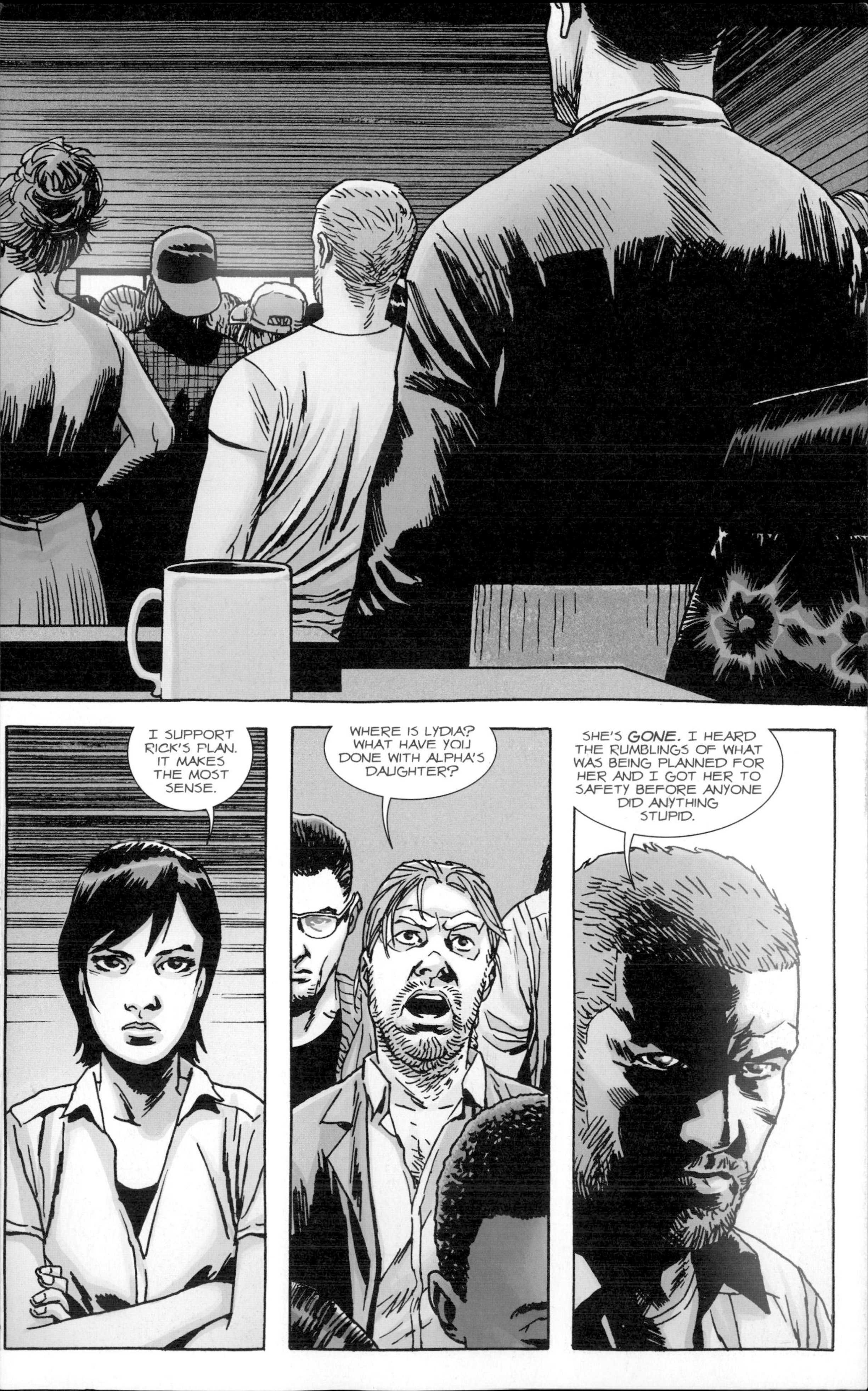
I SUPPORT RICK'S PLAN. IT MAKES THE MOST SENSE.
WHERE IS LYDIA? WHAT HAVE YOU DONE WITH ALPHA'S DAUGHTER?
SHE'S **GONE.** I HEARD THE RUMBLINGS OF WHAT WAS BEING PLANNED FOR HER AND I GOT HER TO SAFETY BEFORE ANYONE DID ANYTHING STUPID.

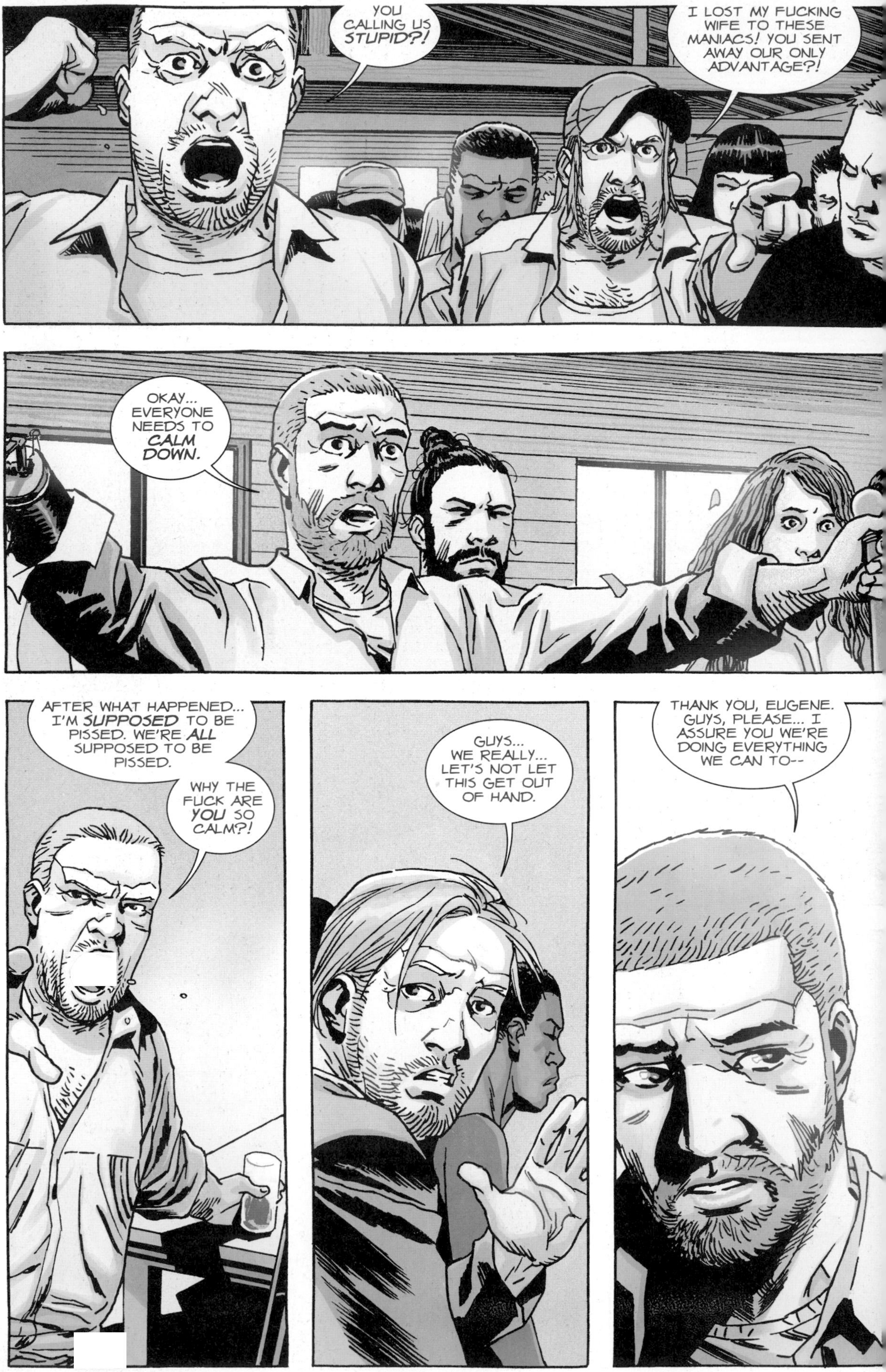
YOU CALLING US STUPID?!
I LOST MY FUCKING WIFE TO THESE MANIACS! YOU SENT AWAY OUR ONLY ADVANTAGE?!
OKAY... EVERYONE NEEDS TO CALM DOWN.
AFTER WHAT HAPPENED... I'M SUPPOSED TO BE PISSED. WE'RE ALL SUPPOSED TO BE PISSED.
WHY THE FUCK ARE YOU SO CALM?!
GUYS... WE REALLY... LET'S NOT LET THIS GET OUT OF HAND.
THANK YOU, EUGENE. GUYS, PLEASE... I ASSURE YOU WE'RE DOING EVERYTHING WE CAN TO--

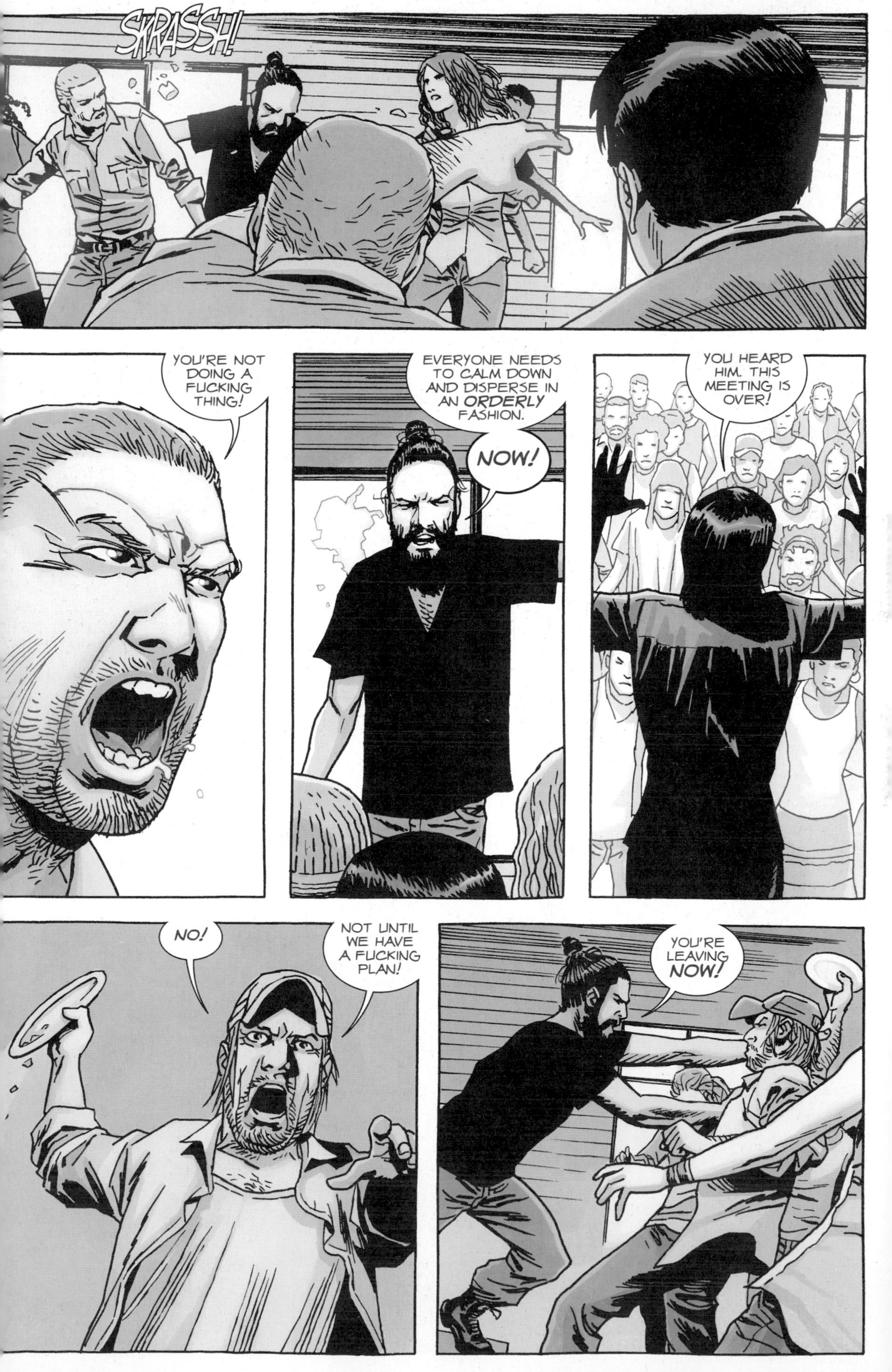
SKRASSH!
YOU'RE NOT DOING A FUCKING THING!
EVERYONE NEEDS TO CALM DOWN AND DISPERSE IN AN ORDERLY FASHION.
NOW!
YOU HEARD HIM. THIS MEETING IS OVER!
NO!
NOT UNTIL WE HAVE A FUCKING PLAN!
YOU'RE LEAVING NOW!

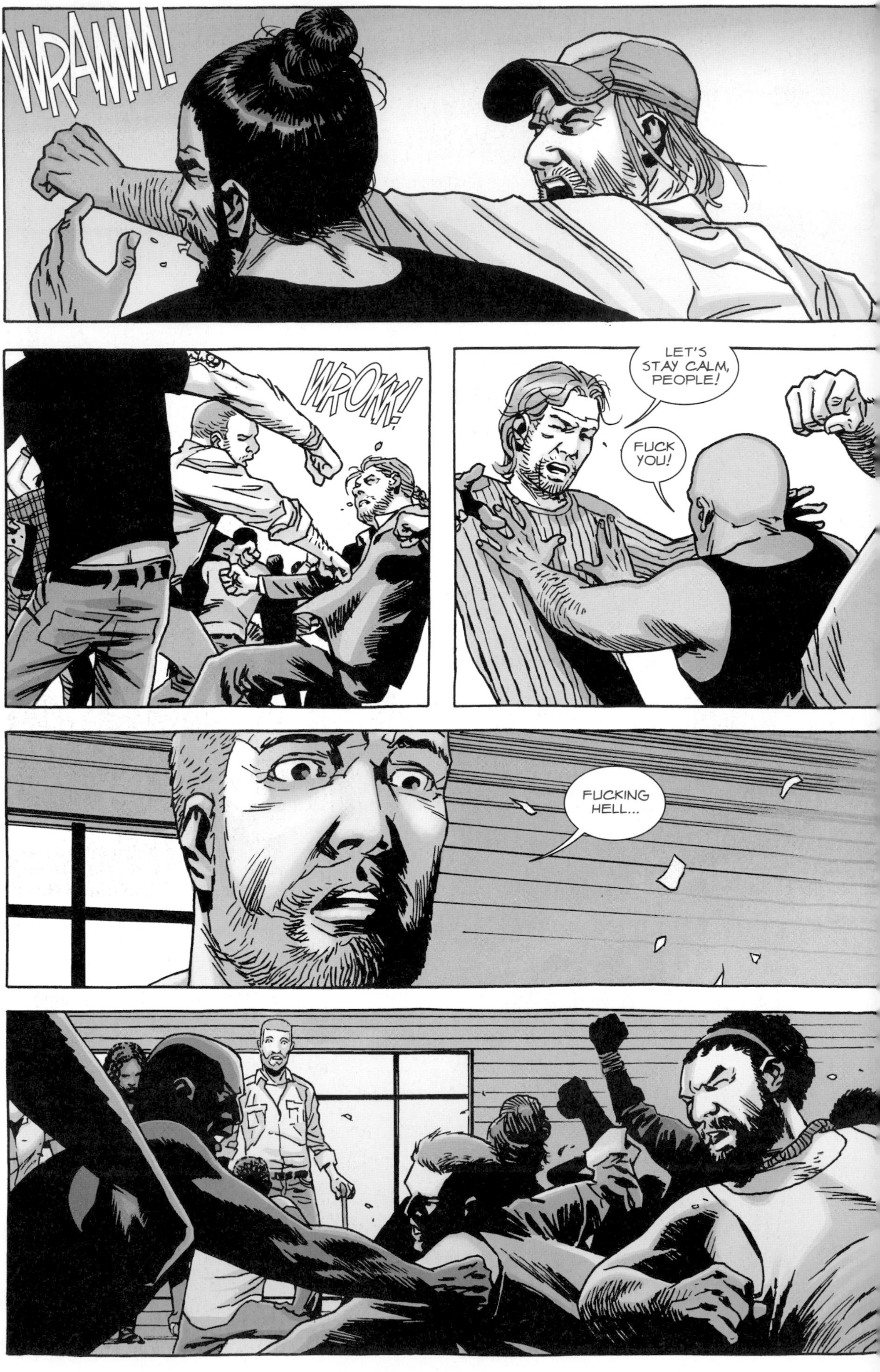
WRAMM!
WROKK!
LET'S STAY CALM, PEOPLE!
FUCK YOU!
FUCKING HELL...

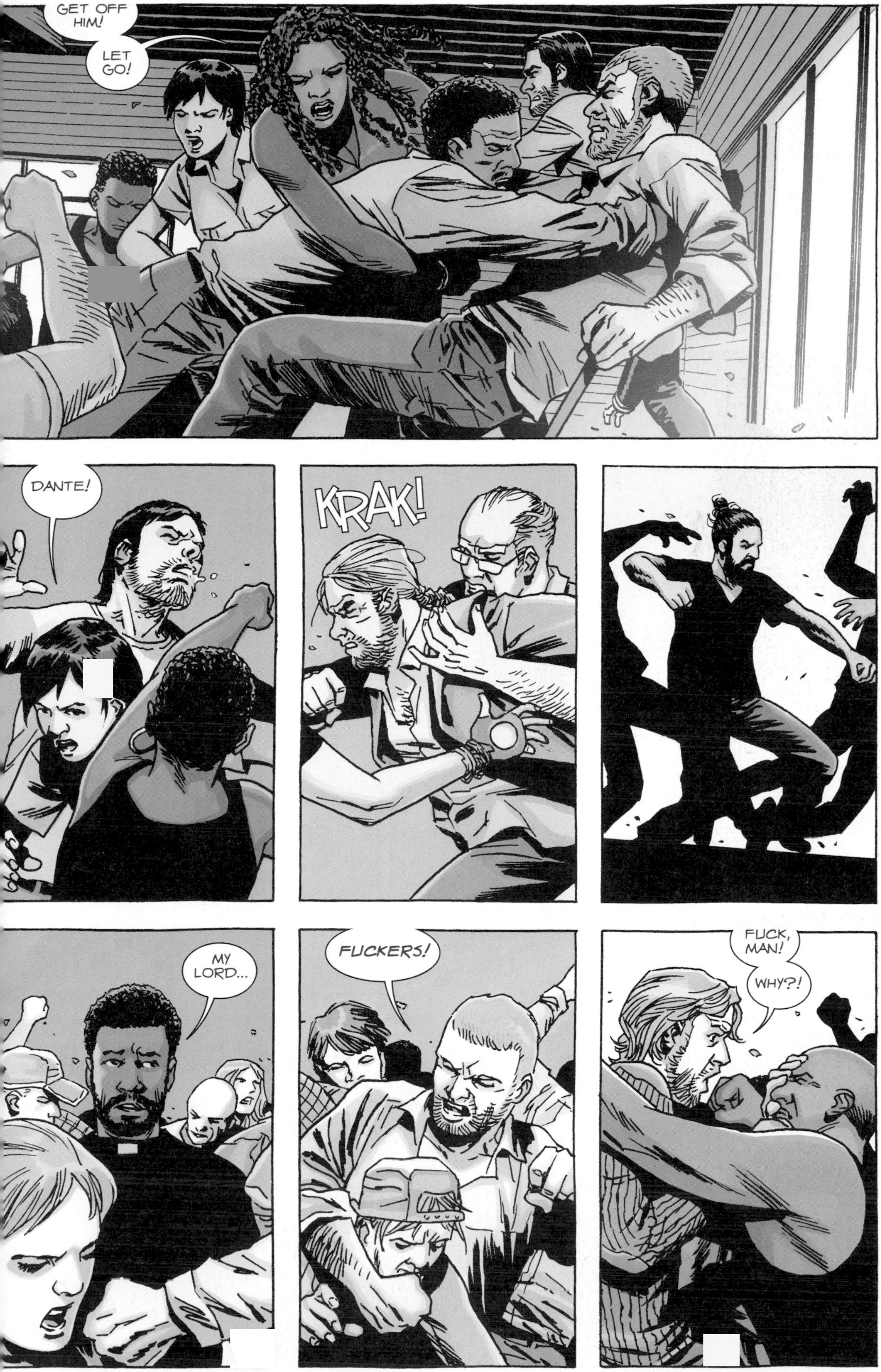
GET OFF HIM!
LET GO!
DANTE!
KRAK!
MY LORD...
FUCKERS!
FUCK, MAN!
WHY?!

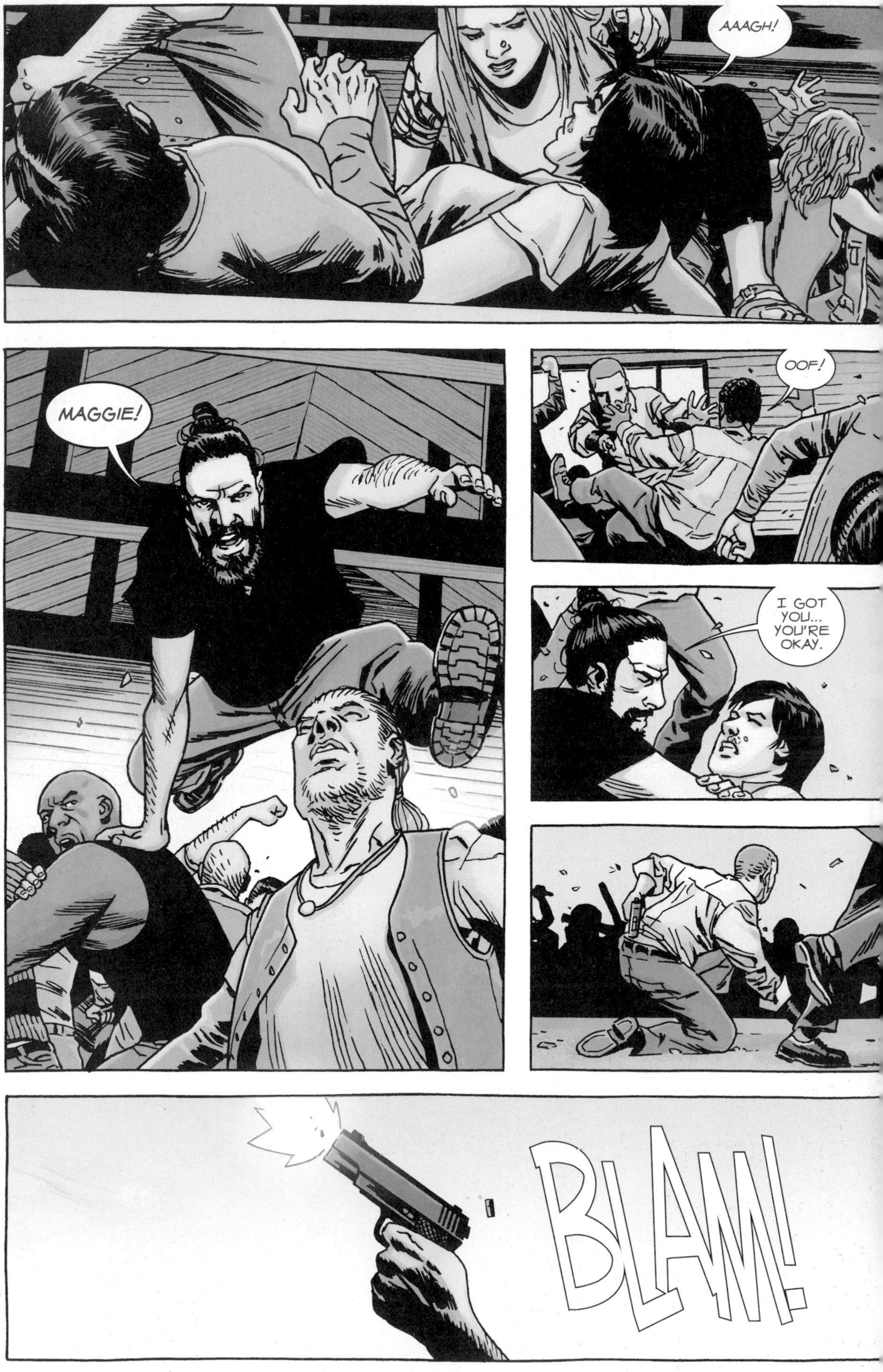
AAAGH!
MAGGIE!
OOF!
I GOT YOU... YOU'RE OKAY.
BLAM!

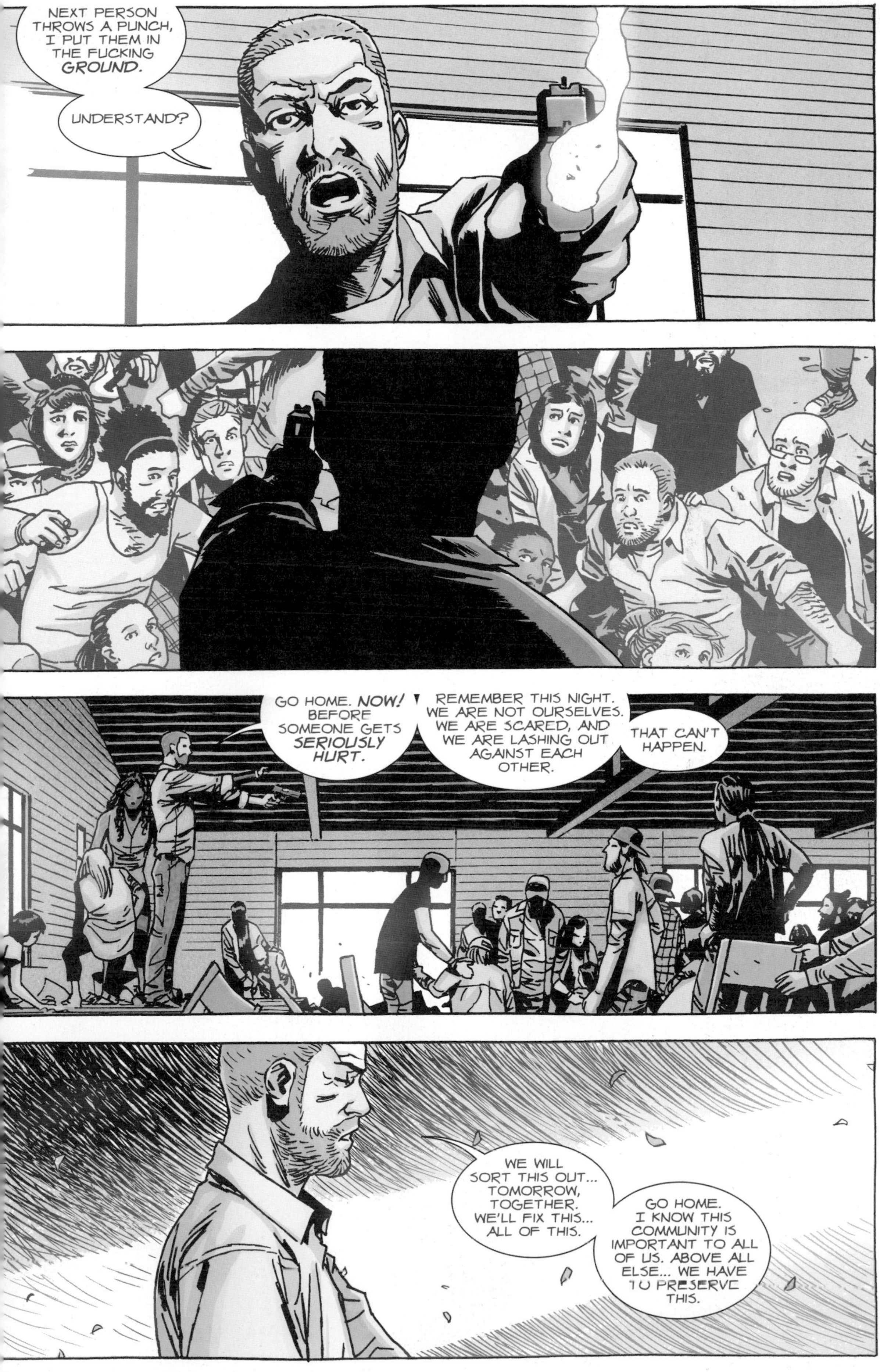
NEXT PERSON THROWS A PUNCH, I PUT THEM IN THE FUCKING GROUND.
UNDERSTAND?
GO HOME. NOW! BEFORE SOMEONE GETS SERIOUSLY HURT.
REMEMBER THIS NIGHT. WE ARE NOT OURSELVES. WE ARE SCARED, AND WE ARE LASHING OUT AGAINST EACH OTHER.
THAT CAN'T HAPPEN.
WE WILL SORT THIS OUT... TOMORROW, TOGETHER. WE'LL FIX THIS... ALL OF THIS.
GO HOME. I KNOW THIS COMMUNITY IS IMPORTANT TO ALL OF US. ABOVE ALL ELSE... WE HAVE TO PRESERVE THIS.

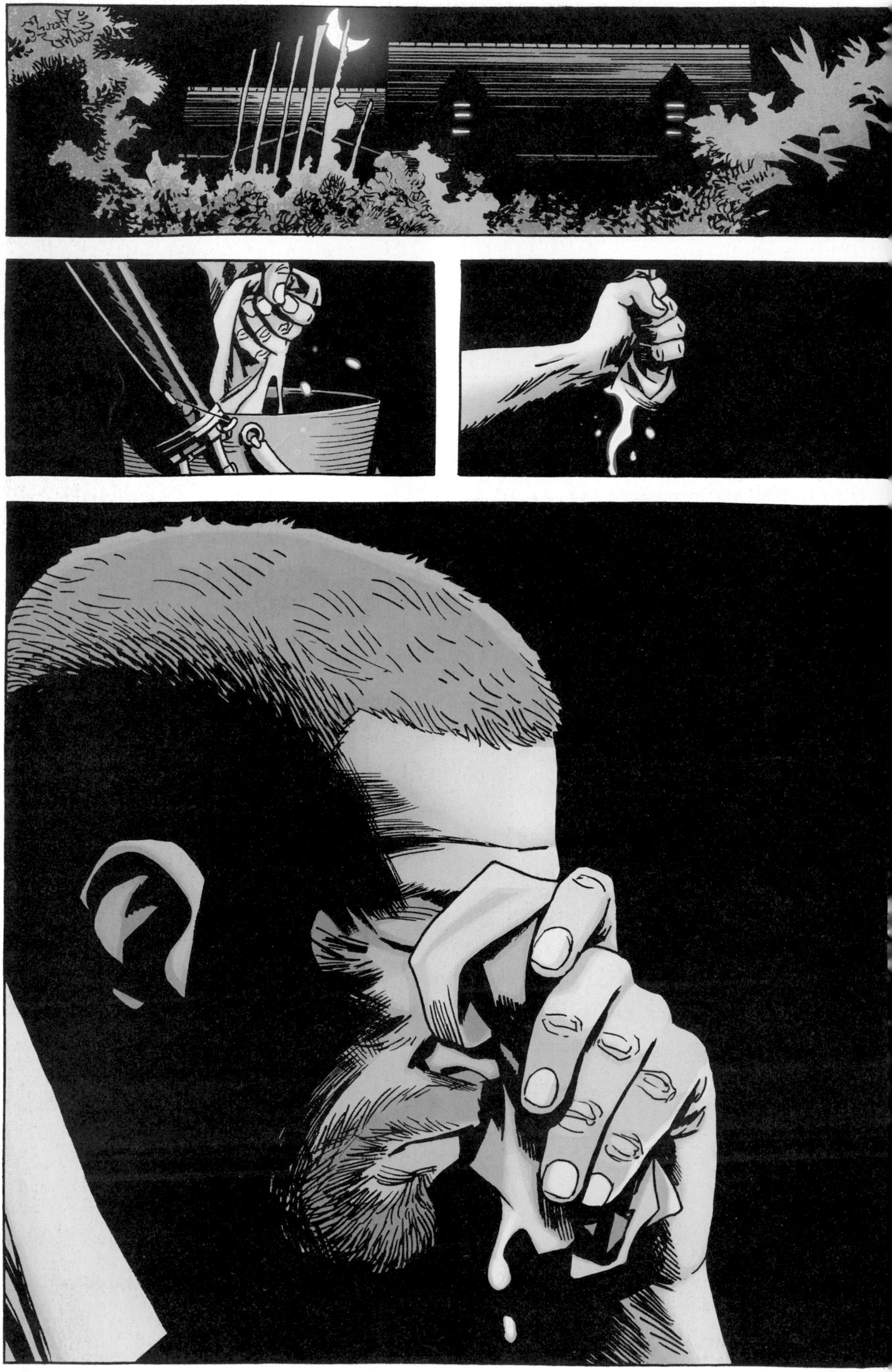

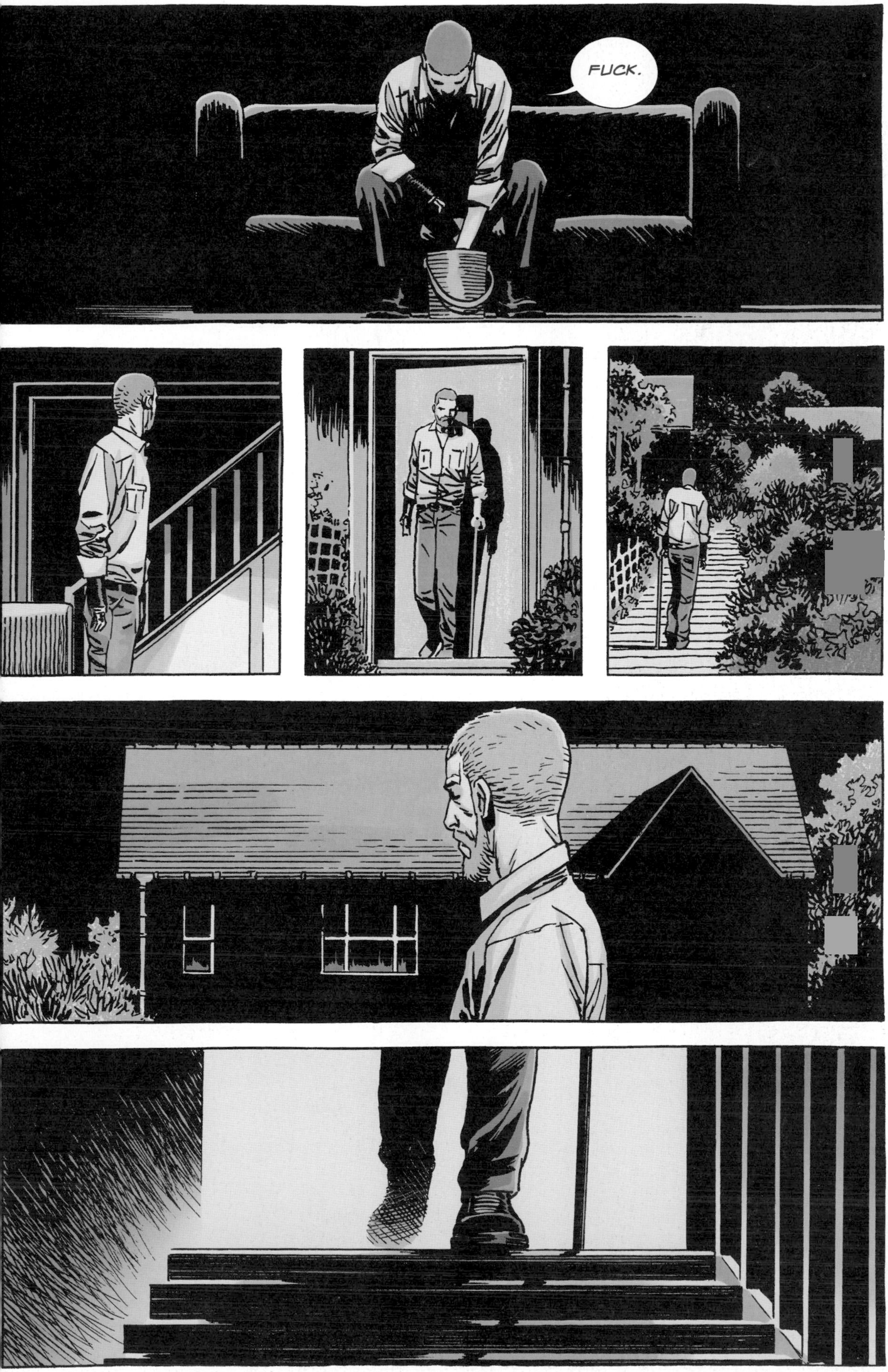
FUCK.

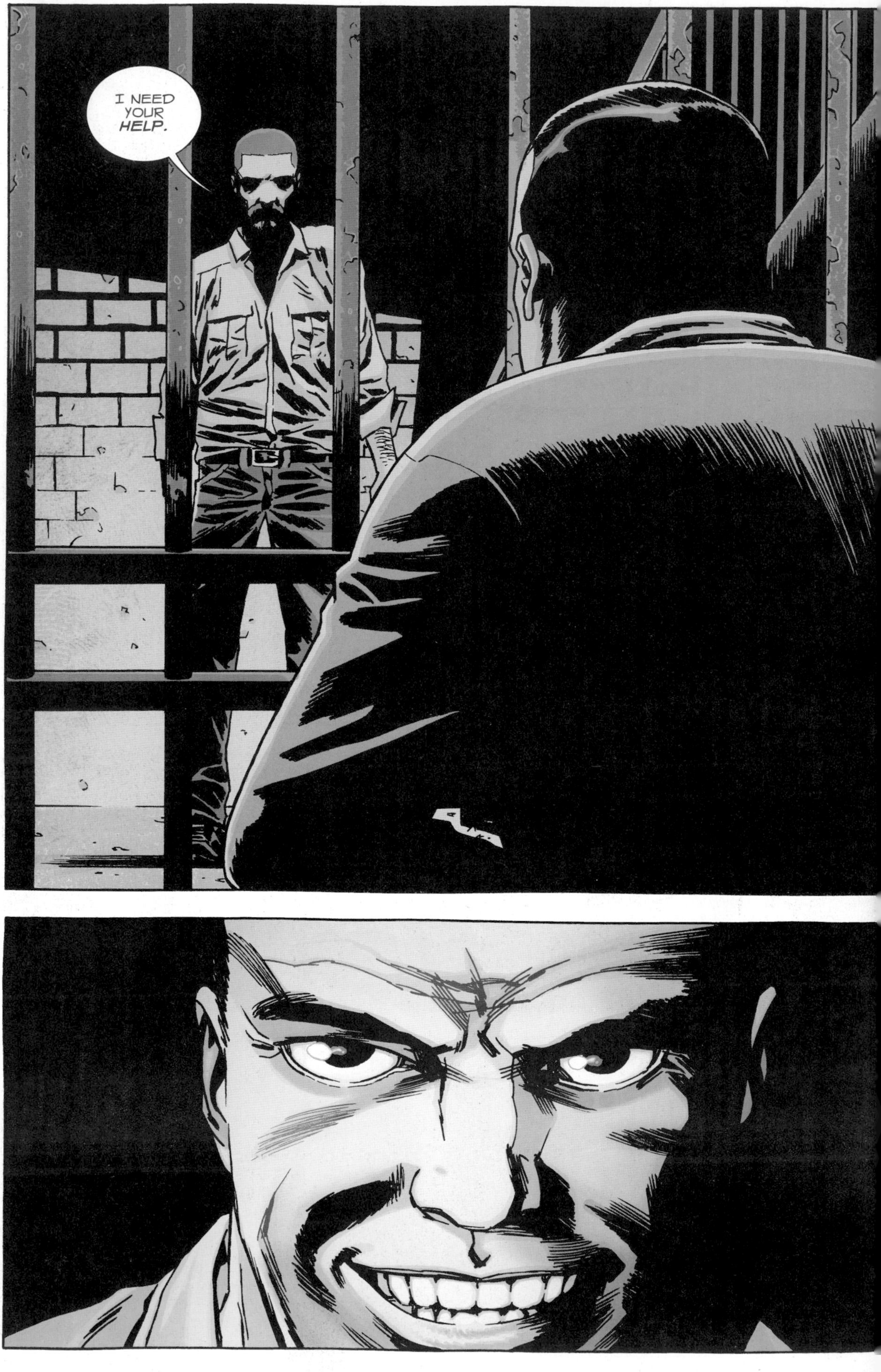
I NEED YOUR HELP.

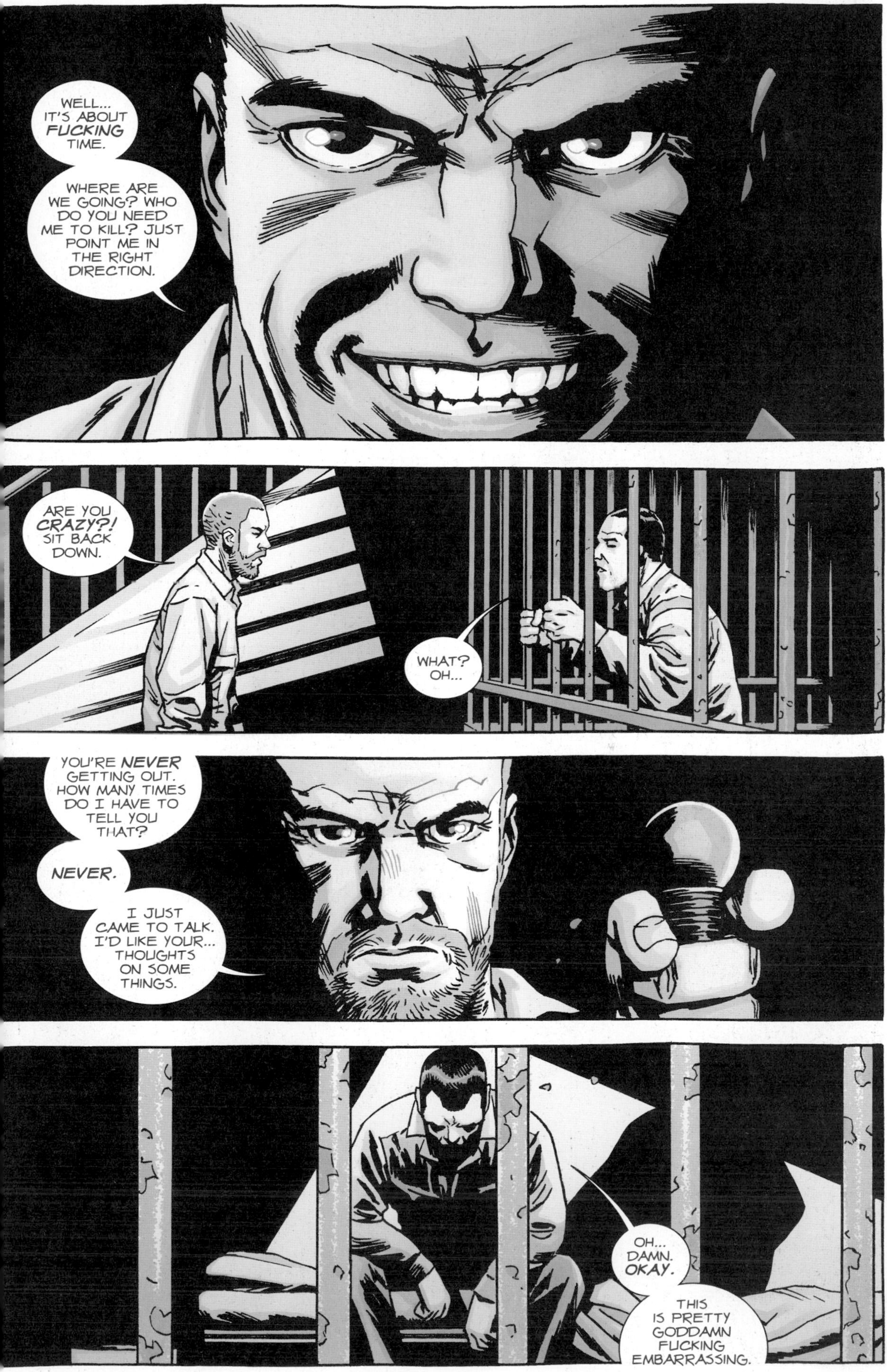
WELL... IT'S ABOUT FUCKING TIME.
WHERE ARE WE GOING? WHO DO YOU NEED ME TO KILL? JUST POINT ME IN THE RIGHT DIRECTION.
ARE YOU CRAZY?! SIT BACK DOWN.
WHAT? OH...
YOU'RE NEVER GETTING OUT. HOW MANY TIMES DO I HAVE TO TELL YOU THAT?
NEVER.
I JUST CAME TO TALK. I'D LIKE YOUR... THOUGHTS ON SOME THINGS.
OH... DAMN. OKAY.
THIS IS PRETTY GODDAMN FUCKING EMBARRASSING.

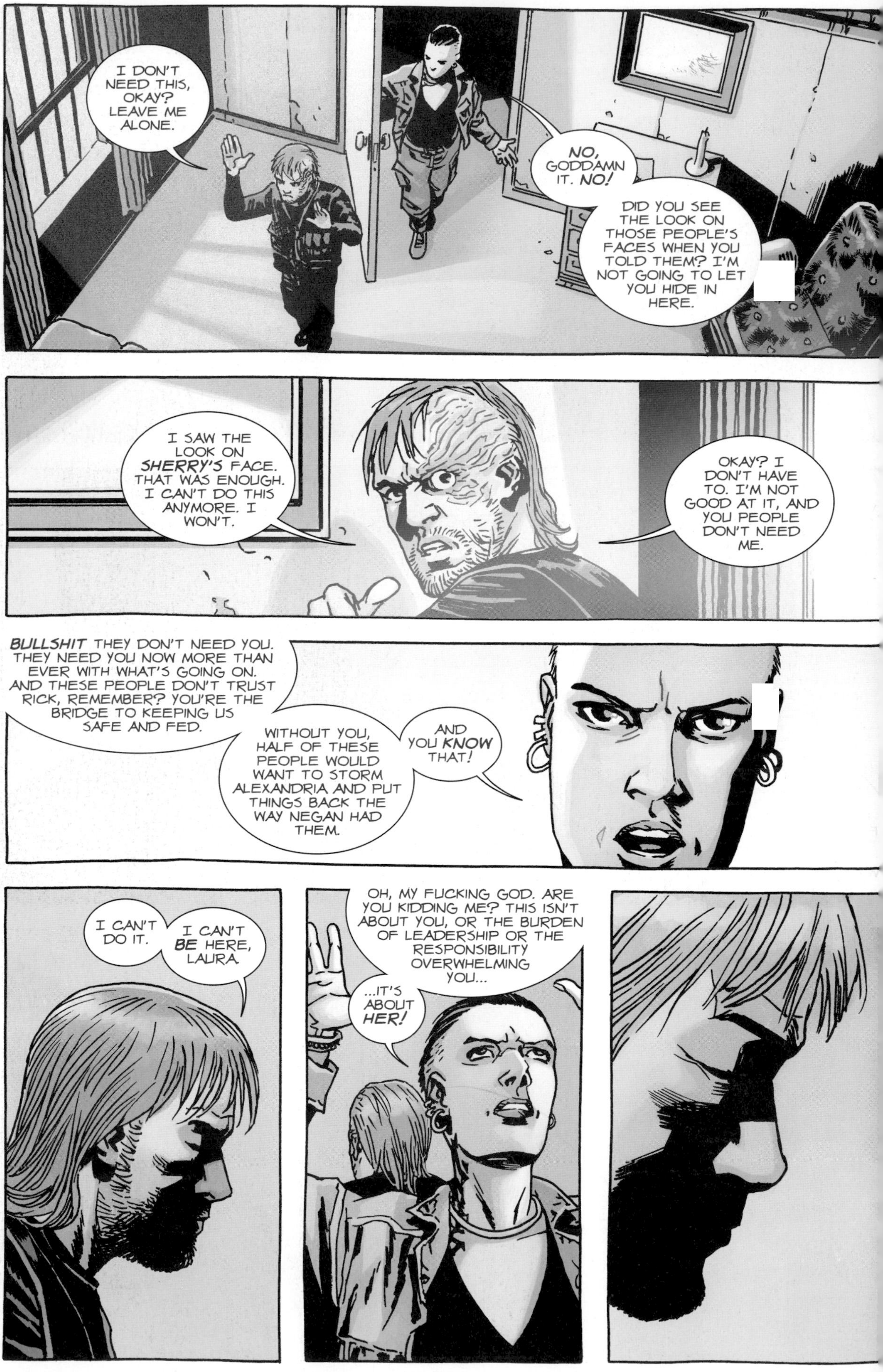
I DON'T NEED THIS, OKAY? LEAVE ME ALONE.
NO, GODDAMN IT. NO!
DID YOU SEE THE LOOK ON THOSE PEOPLE'S FACES WHEN YOU TOLD THEM? I'M NOT GOING TO LET YOU HIDE IN HERE.
I SAW THE LOOK ON SHERRY'S FACE. THAT WAS ENOUGH. I CAN'T DO THIS ANYMORE. I WON'T.
OKAY? I DON'T HAVE TO. I'M NOT GOOD AT IT, AND YOU PEOPLE DON'T NEED ME.
BULLSHIT THEY DON'T NEED YOU. THEY NEED YOU NOW MORE THAN EVER WITH WHAT'S GOING ON. AND THESE PEOPLE DON'T TRUST RICK, REMEMBER? YOU'RE THE BRIDGE TO KEEPING US SAFE AND FED.
WITHOUT YOU, HALF OF THESE PEOPLE WOULD WANT TO STORM ALEXANDRIA AND PUT THINGS BACK THE WAY NEGAN HAD THEM.
AND YOU KNOW THAT!
I CAN'T DO IT.
I CAN'T BE HERE, LAURA
OH, MY FUCKING GOD. ARE YOU KIDDING ME? THIS ISN'T ABOUT YOU, OR THE BURDEN OF LEADERSHIP OR THE RESPONSIBILITY OVERWHELMING YOU...
...IT'S ABOUT HER!

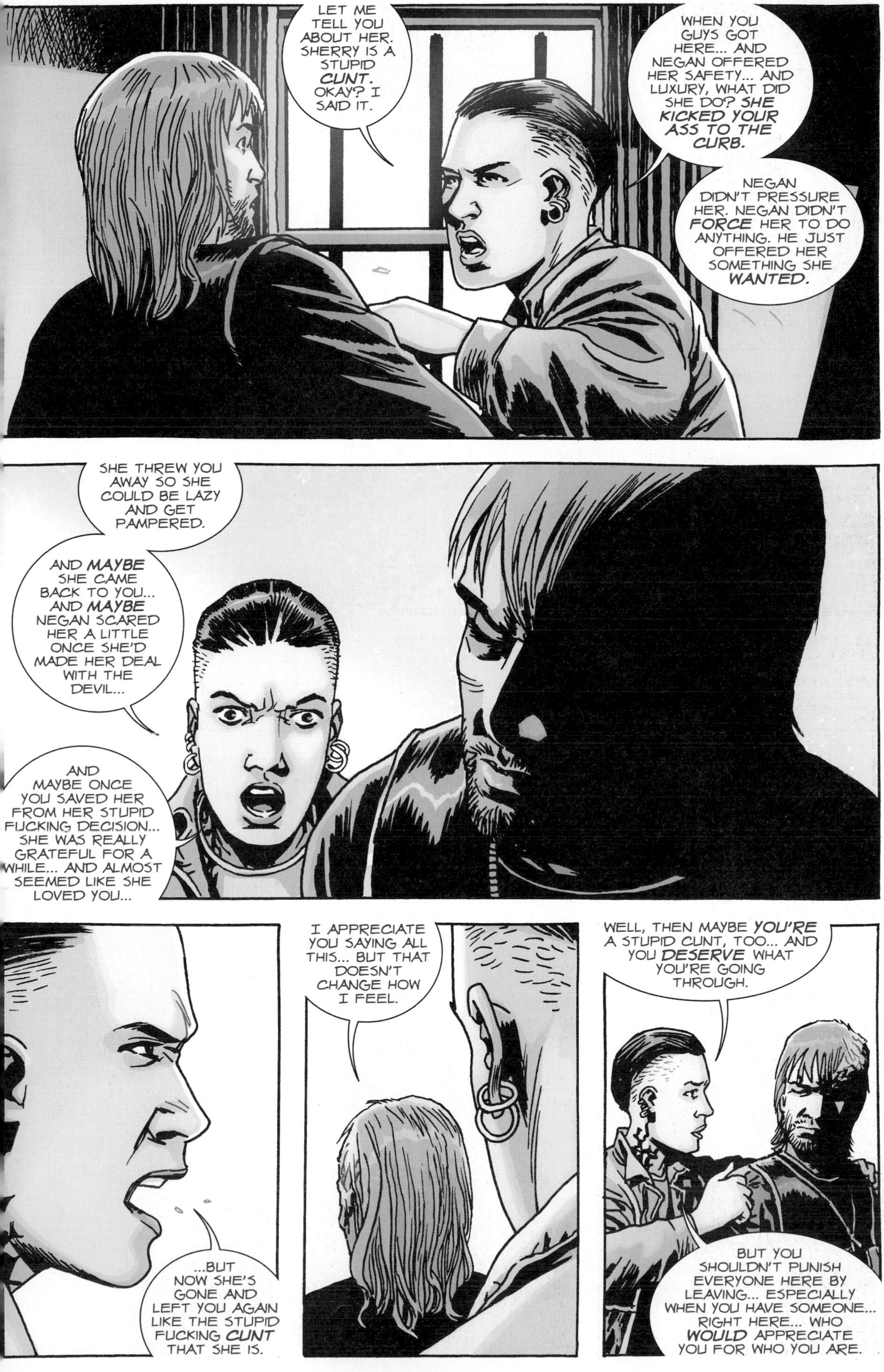

LET ME TELL YOU ABOUT HER. SHERRY IS A STUPID *CUNT*. OKAY? I SAID IT.
WHEN YOU GUYS GOT HERE... AND NEGAN OFFERED HER SAFETY... AND LUXURY, WHAT DID SHE DO? ***SHE KICKED YOUR ASS TO THE CURB.***
NEGAN DIDN'T PRESSURE HER. NEGAN DIDN'T *FORCE* HER TO DO ANYTHING. HE JUST OFFERED HER SOMETHING SHE ***WANTED.***
SHE THREW YOU AWAY SO SHE COULD BE LAZY AND GET PAMPERED.
AND ***MAYBE*** SHE CAME BACK TO YOU... AND ***MAYBE*** NEGAN SCARED HER A LITTLE ONCE SHE'D MADE HER DEAL WITH THE DEVIL...
AND MAYBE ONCE YOU SAVED HER FROM HER STUPID FUCKING DECISION... SHE WAS REALLY GRATEFUL FOR A WHILE... AND ALMOST SEEMED LIKE SHE LOVED YOU...
...BUT NOW SHE'S GONE AND LEFT YOU AGAIN LIKE THE STUPID FUCKING *CUNT* THAT SHE IS.
I APPRECIATE YOU SAYING ALL THIS... BUT THAT DOESN'T CHANGE HOW I FEEL.
WELL, THEN MAYBE ***YOU'RE*** A STUPID CUNT, TOO... AND YOU ***DESERVE*** WHAT YOU'RE GOING THROUGH.
BUT YOU SHOULDN'T PUNISH EVERYONE HERE BY LEAVING... ESPECIALLY WHEN YOU HAVE SOMEONE... RIGHT HERE... WHO ***WOULD*** APPRECIATE YOU FOR WHO YOU ARE.

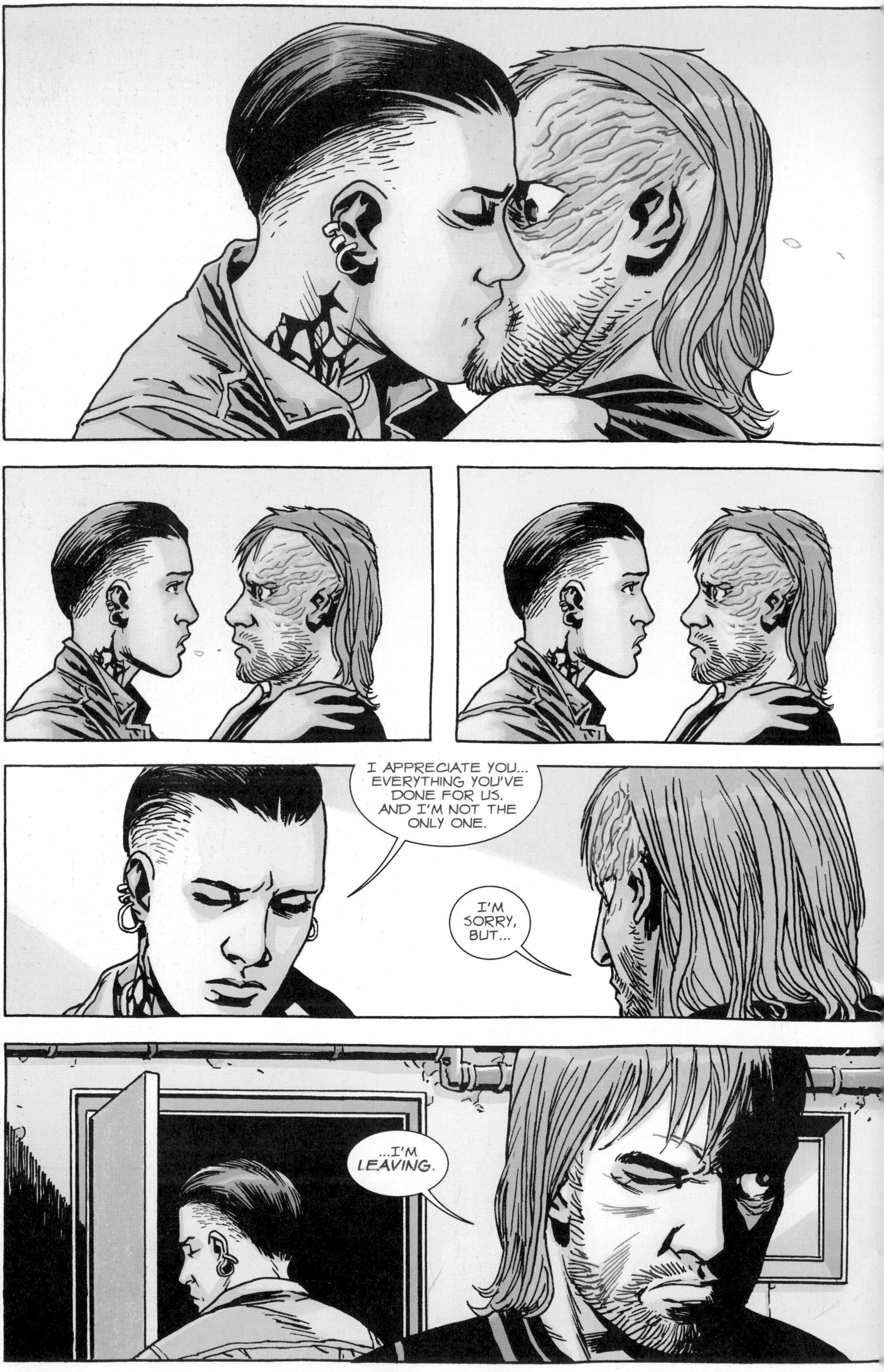
I APPRECIATE YOU... EVERYTHING YOU'VE DONE FOR US. AND I'M NOT THE ONLY ONE.
I'M SORRY, BUT...
...I'M *LEAVING*.

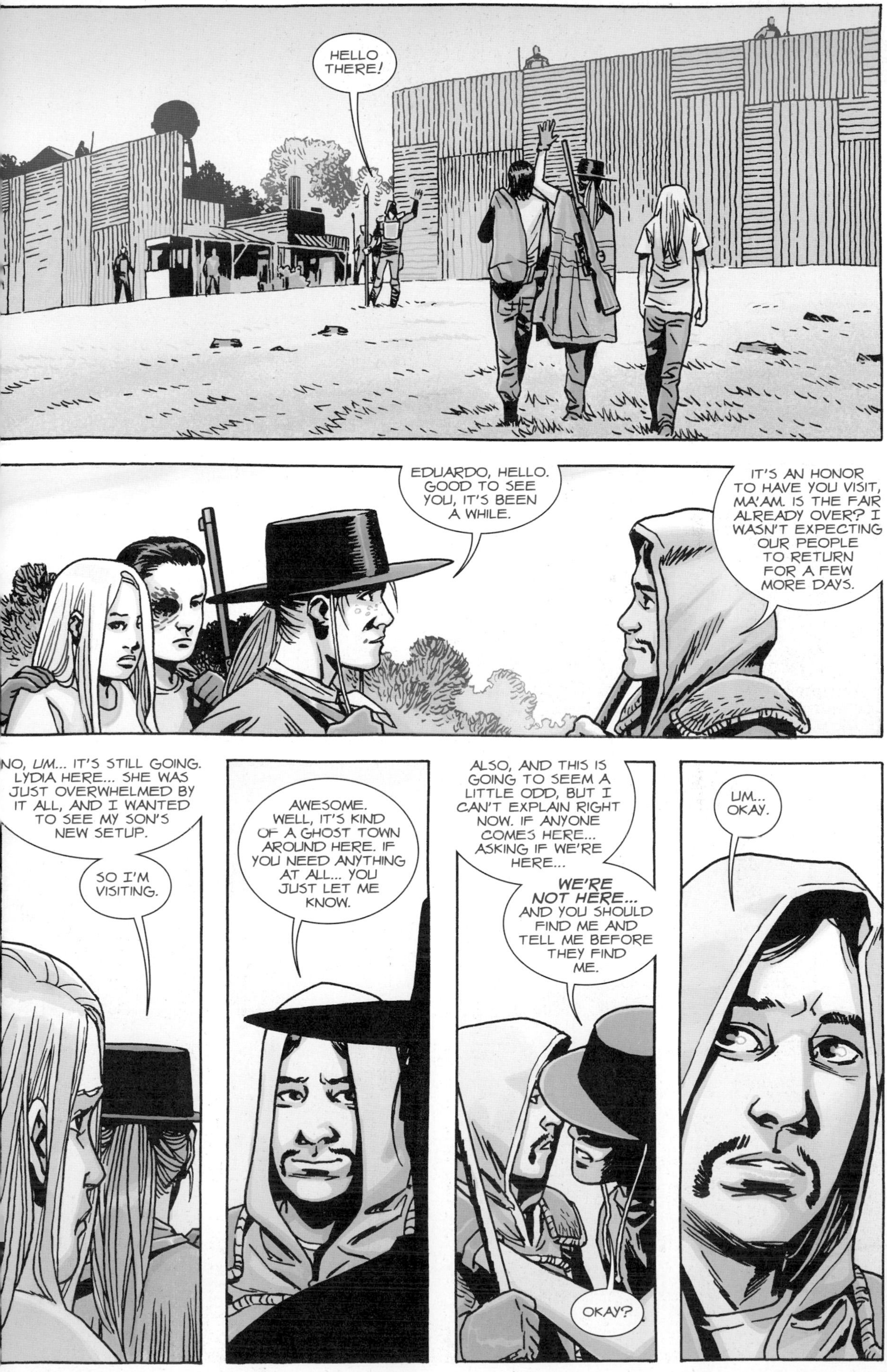
HELLO THERE!
EDUARDO, HELLO. GOOD TO SEE YOU, IT'S BEEN A WHILE.
IT'S AN HONOR TO HAVE YOU VISIT, MA'AM. IS THE FAIR ALREADY OVER? I WASN'T EXPECTING OUR PEOPLE TO RETURN FOR A FEW MORE DAYS.
NO, *UM*... IT'S STILL GOING. LYDIA HERE... SHE WAS JUST OVERWHELMED BY IT ALL, AND I WANTED TO SEE MY SON'S NEW SETUP.
SO I'M VISITING.
AWESOME. WELL, IT'S KIND OF A GHOST TOWN AROUND HERE. IF YOU NEED ANYTHING AT ALL... YOU JUST LET ME KNOW.
ALSO, AND THIS IS GOING TO SEEM A LITTLE ODD, BUT I CAN'T EXPLAIN RIGHT NOW. IF ANYONE COMES HERE... ASKING IF WE'RE HERE...
WE'RE NOT HERE... AND YOU SHOULD FIND ME AND TELL ME BEFORE THEY FIND ME.
OKAY?
UM... OKAY.

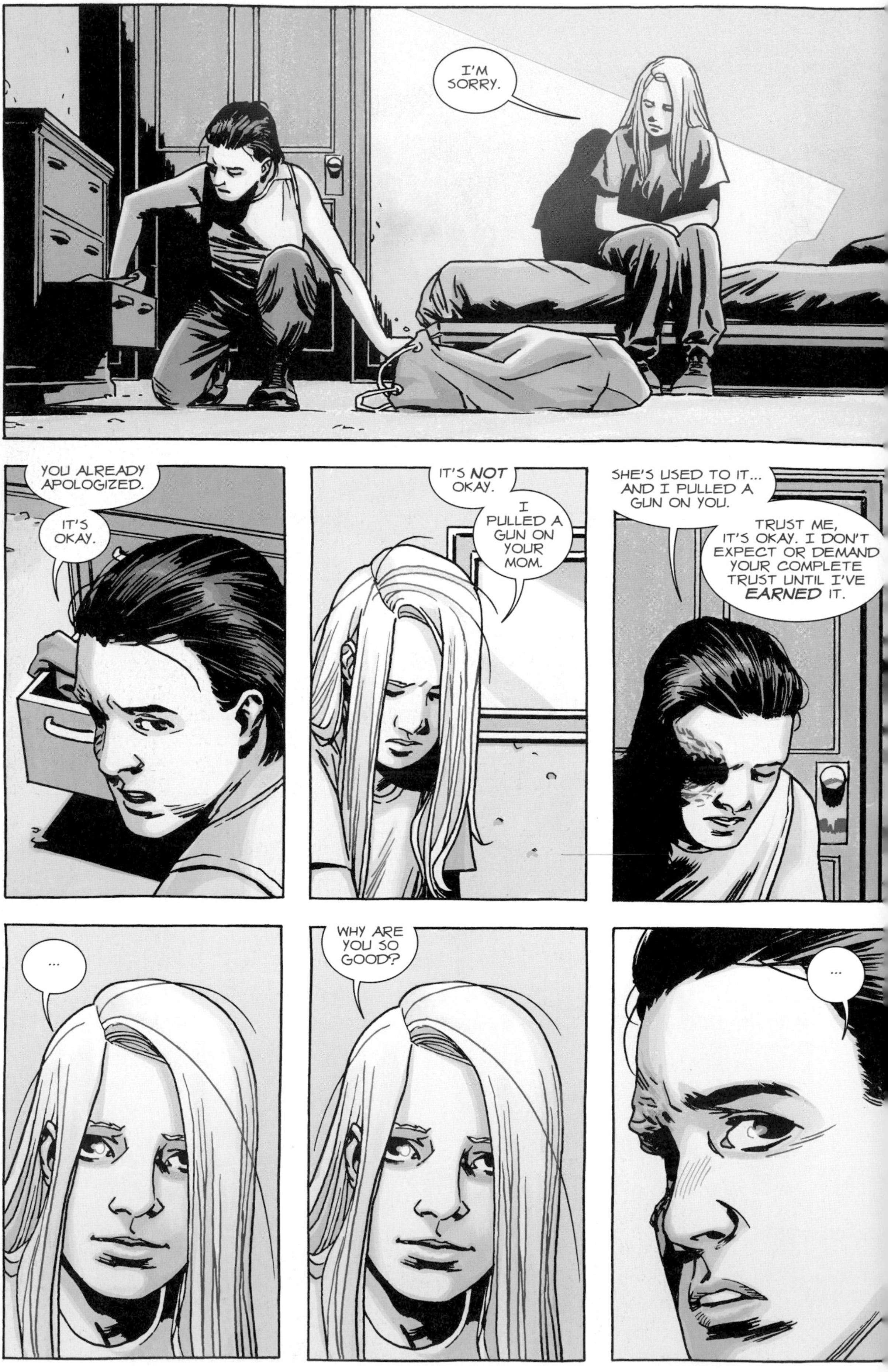
I'M SORRY.
YOU ALREADY APOLOGIZED.
IT'S OKAY.
IT'S *NOT* OKAY.
I PULLED A GUN ON YOUR MOM.
SHE'S USED TO IT... AND I PULLED A GUN ON YOU.
TRUST ME, IT'S OKAY. I DON'T EXPECT OR DEMAND YOUR COMPLETE TRUST UNTIL I'VE *EARNED* IT.
...
WHY ARE YOU SO GOOD?
...

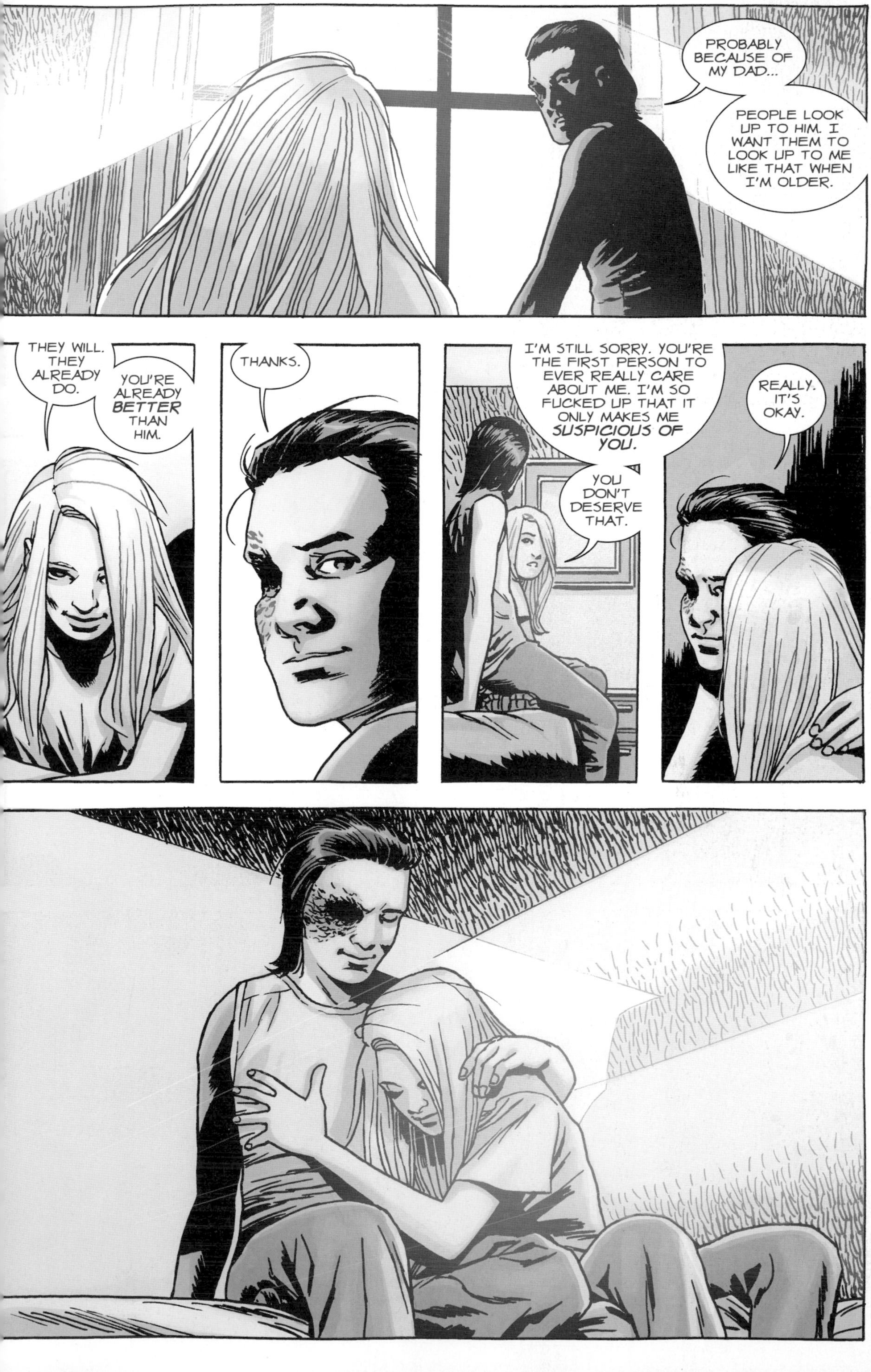
PROBABLY BECAUSE OF MY DAD...
PEOPLE LOOK UP TO HIM. I WANT THEM TO LOOK UP TO ME LIKE THAT WHEN I'M OLDER.
THEY WILL. THEY ALREADY DO.
YOU'RE ALREADY BETTER THAN HIM.
THANKS.
I'M STILL SORRY. YOU'RE THE FIRST PERSON TO EVER REALLY CARE ABOUT ME. I'M SO FUCKED UP THAT IT ONLY MAKES ME SUSPICIOUS OF YOU.
YOU DON'T DESERVE THAT.
REALLY. IT'S OKAY.

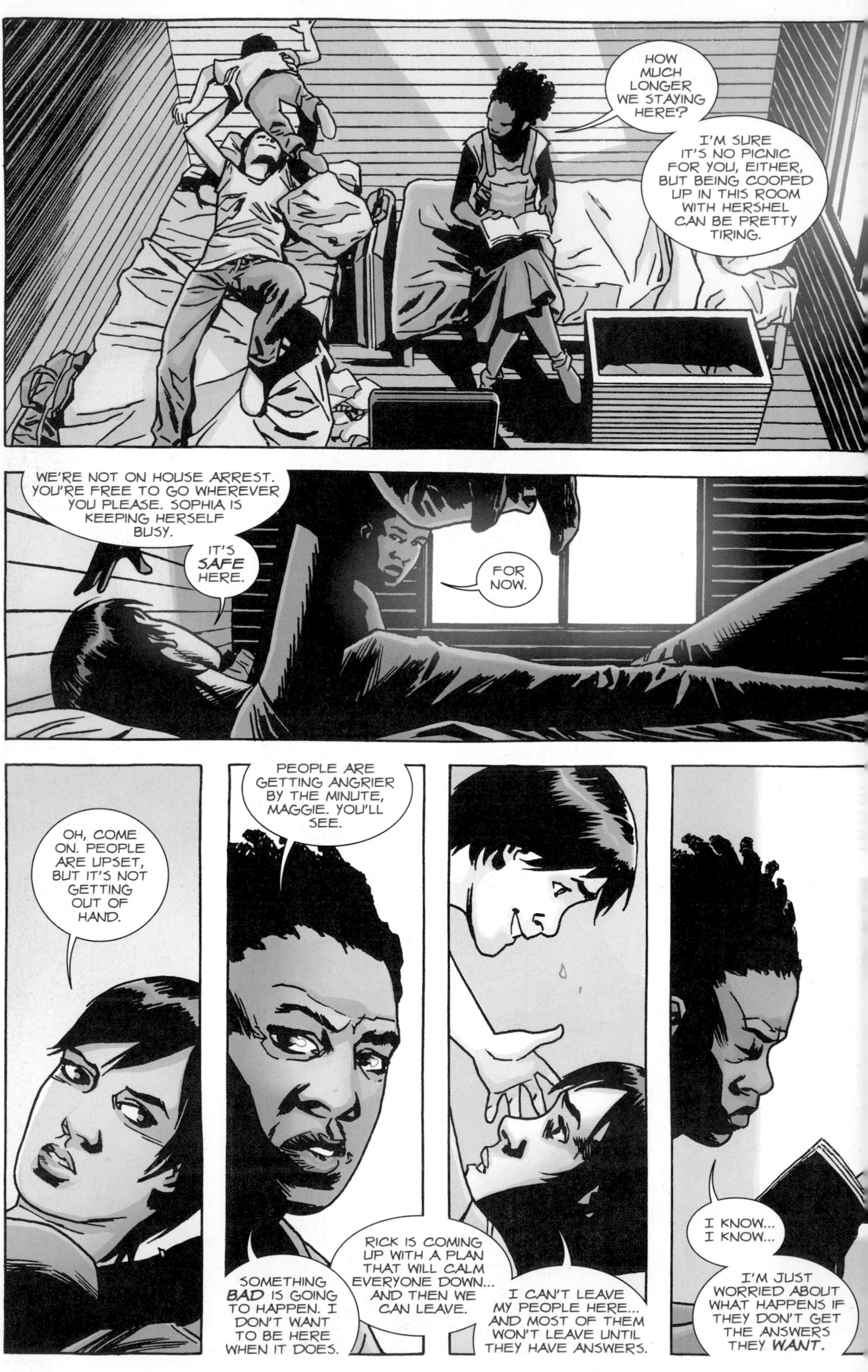
HOW MUCH LONGER WE STAYING HERE?
I'M SURE IT'S NO PICNIC FOR YOU, EITHER, BUT BEING COOPED UP IN THIS ROOM WITH HERSHEL CAN BE PRETTY TIRING.
WE'RE NOT ON HOUSE ARREST. YOU'RE FREE TO GO WHEREVER YOU PLEASE. SOPHIA IS KEEPING HERSELF BUSY.
IT'S SAFE HERE.
FOR NOW.
OH, COME ON. PEOPLE ARE UPSET, BUT IT'S NOT GETTING OUT OF HAND.
PEOPLE ARE GETTING ANGRIER BY THE MINUTE, MAGGIE. YOU'LL SEE.
SOMETHING BAD IS GOING TO HAPPEN. I DON'T WANT TO BE HERE WHEN IT DOES.
RICK IS COMING UP WITH A PLAN THAT WILL CALM EVERYONE DOWN... AND THEN WE CAN LEAVE.
I CAN'T LEAVE MY PEOPLE HERE... AND MOST OF THEM WON'T LEAVE UNTIL THEY HAVE ANSWERS.
I KNOW... I KNOW...
I'M JUST WORRIED ABOUT WHAT HAPPENS IF THEY DON'T GET THE ANSWERS THEY WANT.

SKEEEEE.

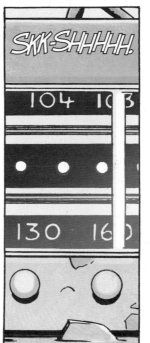

SKK-SHHHHH.

104 103

130 160

SHHH-

KLICK.

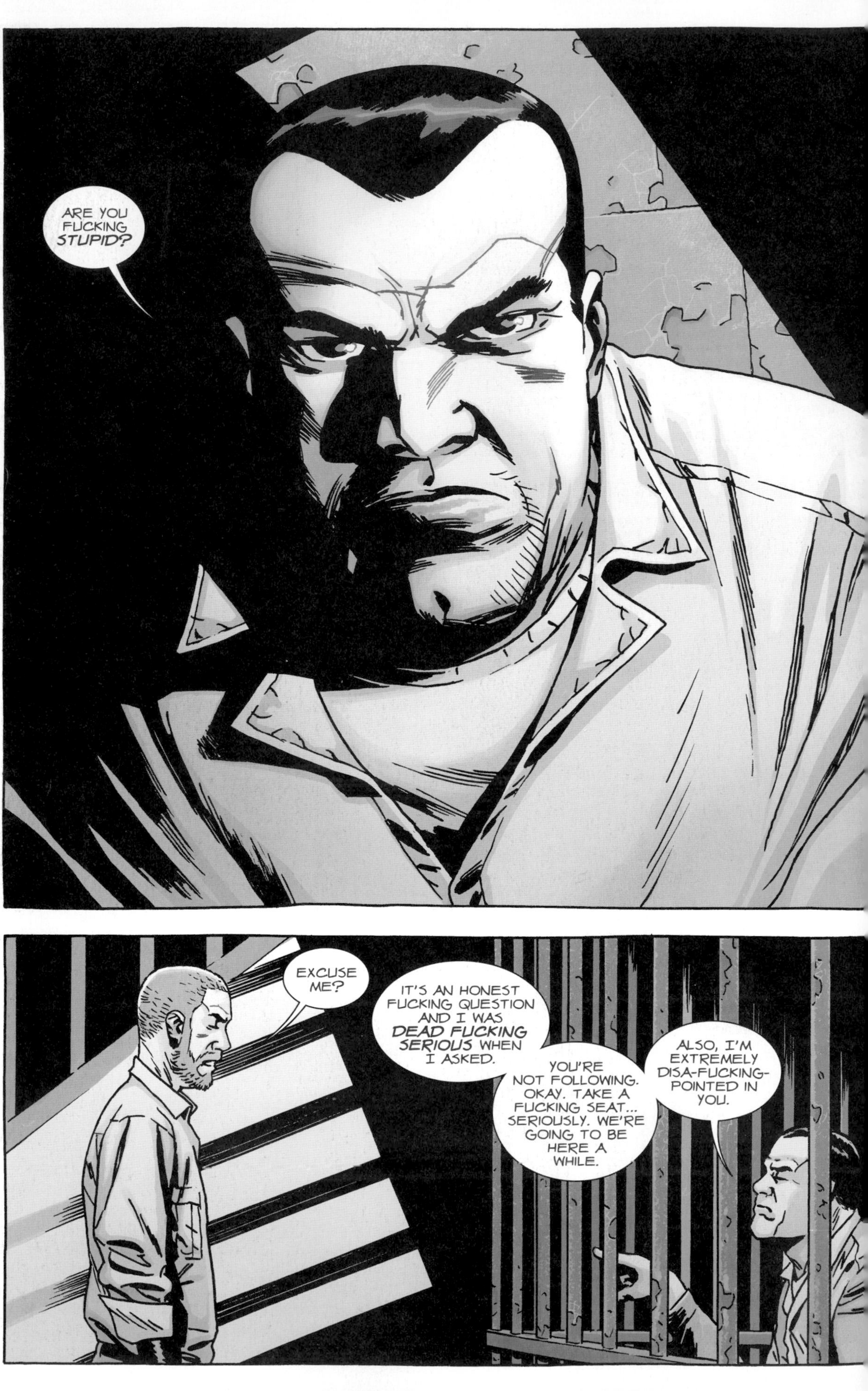
ARE YOU FUCKING STUPID?
EXCUSE ME?
IT'S AN HONEST FUCKING QUESTION AND I WAS DEAD FUCKING SERIOUS WHEN I ASKED.
YOU'RE NOT FOLLOWING. OKAY. TAKE A FUCKING SEAT... SERIOUSLY. WE'RE GOING TO BE HERE A WHILE.
ALSO, I'M EXTREMELY DISA-FUCKING-POINTED IN YOU.

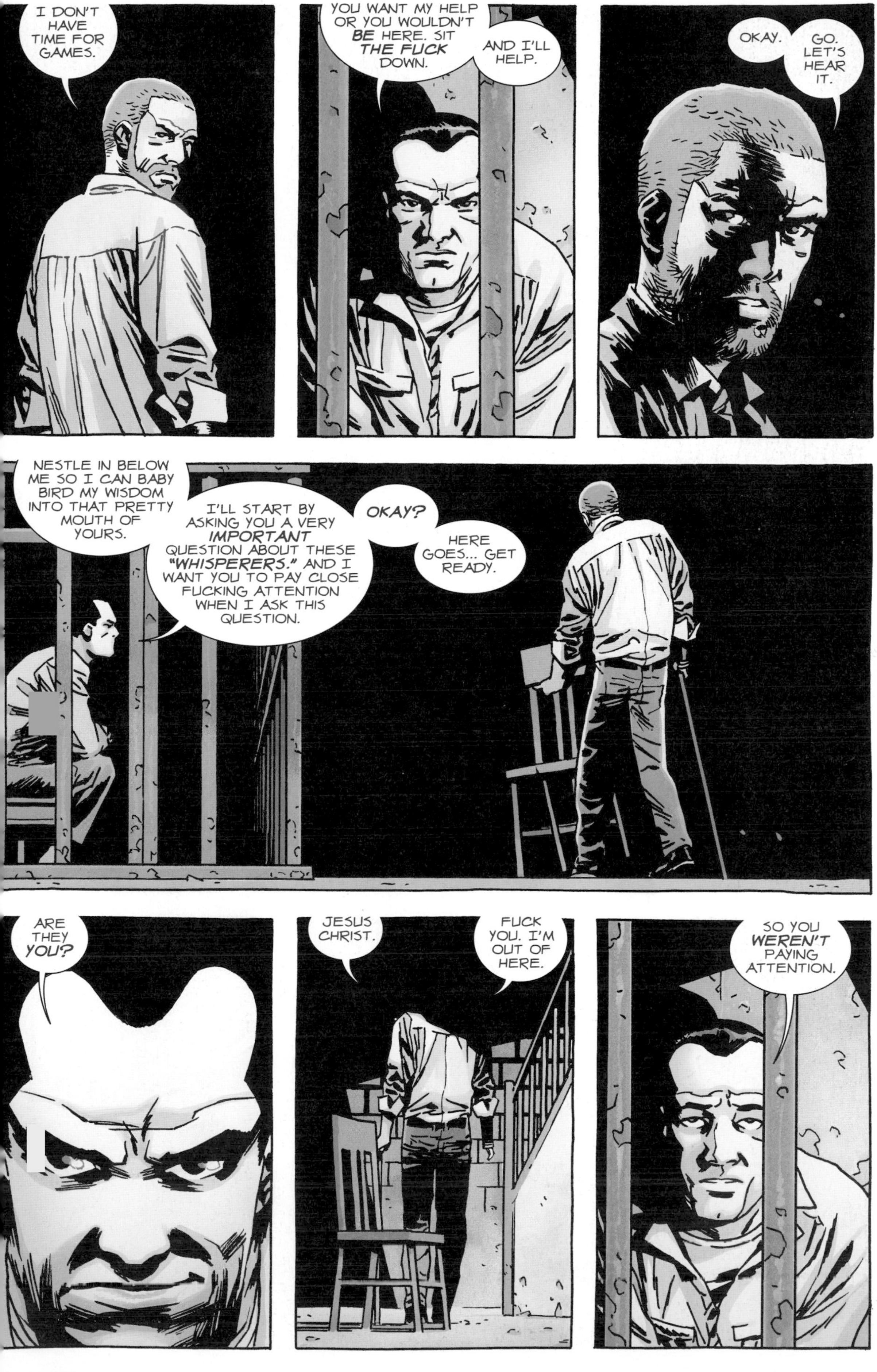
I DON'T HAVE TIME FOR GAMES.
YOU WANT MY HELP OR YOU WOULDN'T *BE* HERE. SIT *THE FUCK* DOWN.
AND I'LL HELP.
OKAY.
GO. LET'S HEAR IT.
NESTLE IN BELOW ME SO I CAN BABY BIRD MY WISDOM INTO THAT PRETTY MOUTH OF YOURS.
I'LL START BY ASKING YOU A VERY *IMPORTANT* QUESTION ABOUT THESE *"WHISPERERS."* AND I WANT YOU TO PAY CLOSE FUCKING ATTENTION WHEN I ASK THIS QUESTION.
OKAY?
HERE GOES... GET READY.
ARE THEY *YOU?*
JESUS CHRIST.
FUCK YOU. I'M OUT OF HERE.
SO YOU *WEREN'T* PAYING ATTENTION.

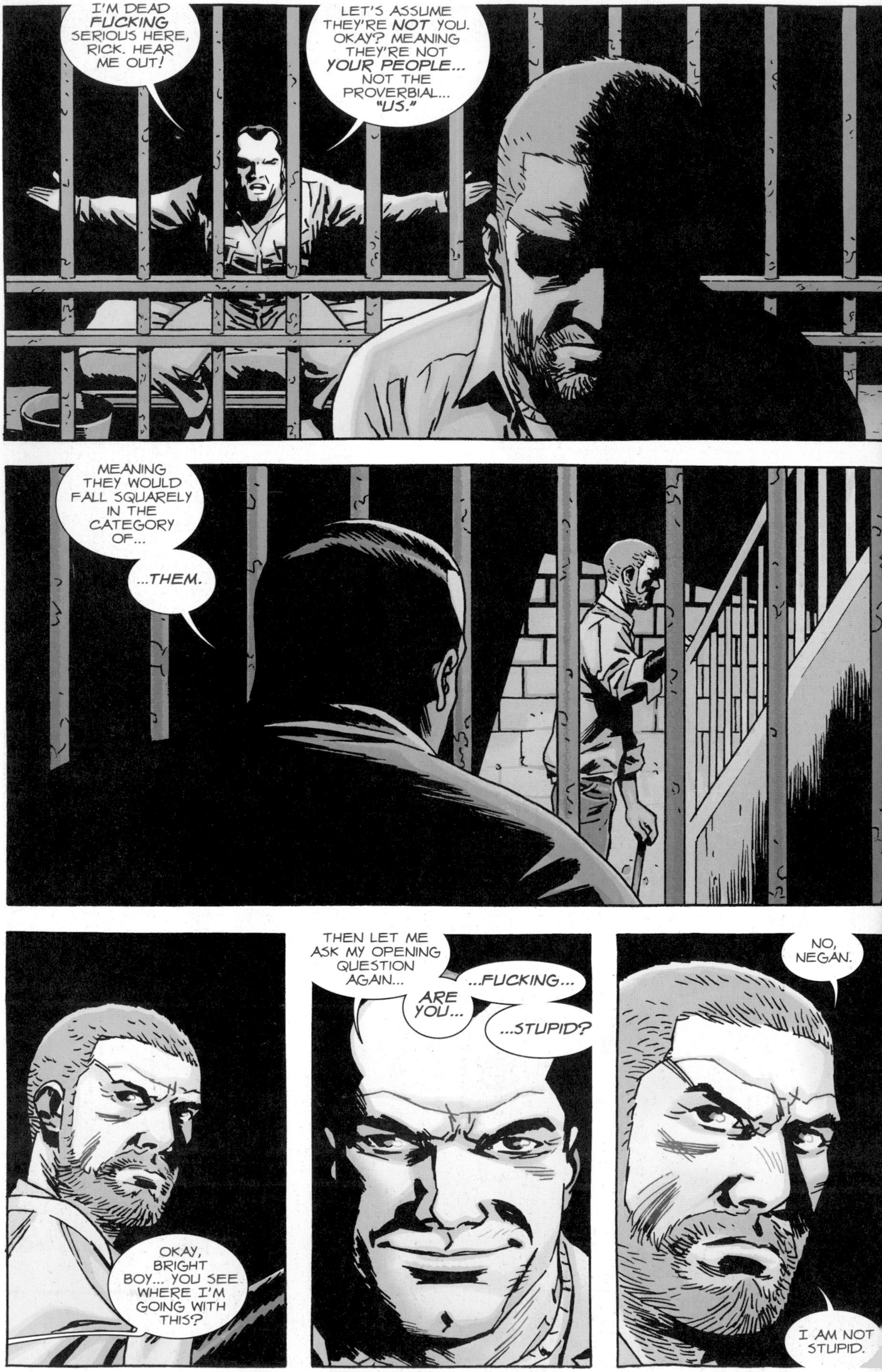
I'M DEAD FUCKING SERIOUS HERE, RICK. HEAR ME OUT!
LET'S ASSUME THEY'RE NOT YOU. OKAY? MEANING THEY'RE NOT YOUR PEOPLE... NOT THE PROVERBIAL... "US."
MEANING THEY WOULD FALL SQUARELY IN THE CATEGORY OF...
...THEM.
OKAY, BRIGHT BOY... YOU SEE WHERE I'M GOING WITH THIS?
THEN LET ME ASK MY OPENING QUESTION AGAIN...
ARE YOU...
...FUCKING...
...STUPID?
NO, NEGAN.
I AM NOT STUPID.

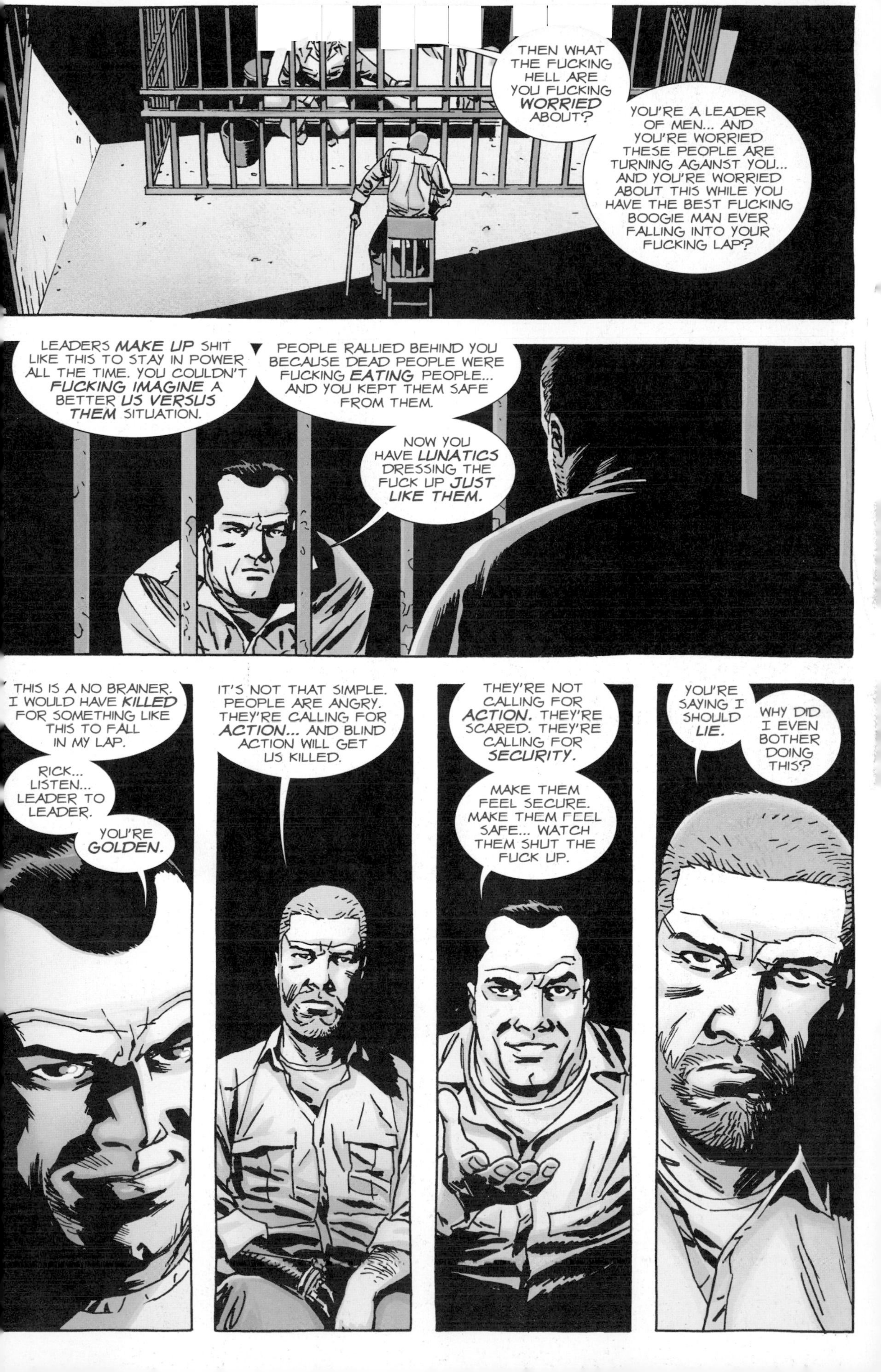
THEN WHAT THE FUCKING HELL ARE YOU FUCKING WORRIED ABOUT?
YOU'RE A LEADER OF MEN... AND YOU'RE WORRIED THESE PEOPLE ARE TURNING AGAINST YOU... AND YOU'RE WORRIED ABOUT THIS WHILE YOU HAVE THE BEST FUCKING BOOGIE MAN EVER FALLING INTO YOUR FUCKING LAP?
LEADERS MAKE UP SHIT LIKE THIS TO STAY IN POWER ALL THE TIME. YOU COULDN'T FUCKING IMAGINE A BETTER US VERSUS THEM SITUATION.
PEOPLE RALLIED BEHIND YOU BECAUSE DEAD PEOPLE WERE FUCKING EATING PEOPLE... AND YOU KEPT THEM SAFE FROM THEM.
NOW YOU HAVE LUNATICS DRESSING THE FUCK UP JUST LIKE THEM.
THIS IS A NO BRAINER. I WOULD HAVE KILLED FOR SOMETHING LIKE THIS TO FALL IN MY LAP.
RICK... LISTEN... LEADER TO LEADER.
YOU'RE GOLDEN.
IT'S NOT THAT SIMPLE. PEOPLE ARE ANGRY. THEY'RE CALLING FOR ACTION... AND BLIND ACTION WILL GET US KILLED.
THEY'RE NOT CALLING FOR ACTION. THEY'RE SCARED. THEY'RE CALLING FOR SECURITY.
MAKE THEM FEEL SECURE. MAKE THEM FEEL SAFE... WATCH THEM SHUT THE FUCK UP.
YOU'RE SAYING I SHOULD LIE.
WHY DID I EVEN BOTHER DOING THIS?

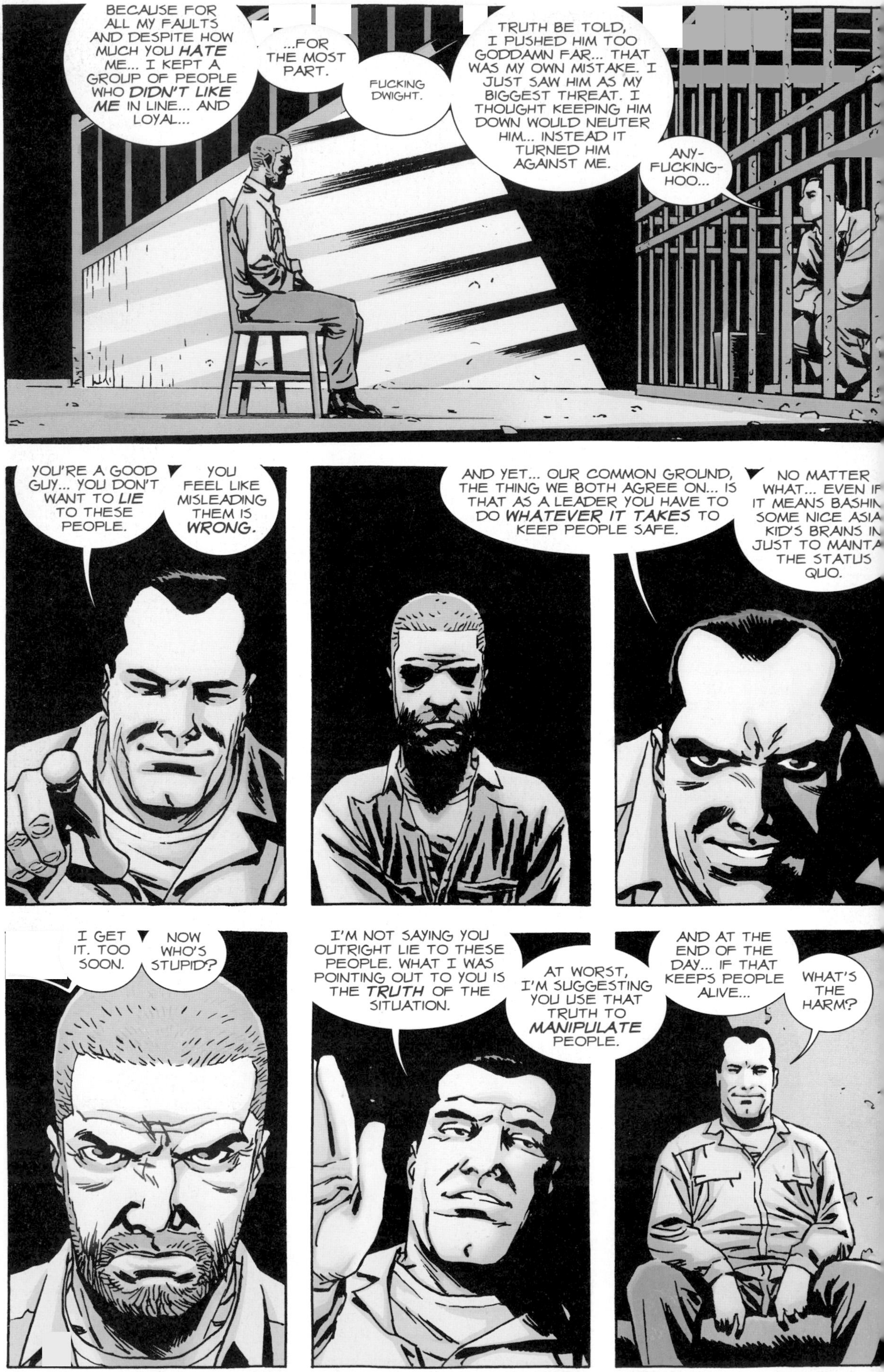
BECAUSE FOR ALL MY FAULTS AND DESPITE HOW MUCH YOU HATE ME... I KEPT A GROUP OF PEOPLE WHO DIDN'T LIKE ME IN LINE... AND LOYAL...
...FOR THE MOST PART.
FUCKING DWIGHT.
TRUTH BE TOLD, I PUSHED HIM TOO GODDAMN FAR... THAT WAS MY OWN MISTAKE. I JUST SAW HIM AS MY BIGGEST THREAT. I THOUGHT KEEPING HIM DOWN WOULD NEUTER HIM... INSTEAD IT TURNED HIM AGAINST ME.
ANY-FUCKING-HOO...
YOU'RE A GOOD GUY... YOU DON'T WANT TO LIE TO THESE PEOPLE.
YOU FEEL LIKE MISLEADING THEM IS WRONG.
AND YET... OUR COMMON GROUND, THE THING WE BOTH AGREE ON... IS THAT AS A LEADER YOU HAVE TO DO WHATEVER IT TAKES TO KEEP PEOPLE SAFE.
NO MATTER WHAT... EVEN IF IT MEANS BASHIN SOME NICE ASIA KID'S BRAINS IN JUST TO MAINTA THE STATUS QUO.
I GET IT. TOO SOON.
NOW WHO'S STUPID?
I'M NOT SAYING YOU OUTRIGHT LIE TO THESE PEOPLE. WHAT I WAS POINTING OUT TO YOU IS THE TRUTH OF THE SITUATION.
AT WORST, I'M SUGGESTING YOU USE THAT TRUTH TO MANIPULATE PEOPLE.
AND AT THE END OF THE DAY... IF THAT KEEPS PEOPLE ALIVE...
WHAT'S THE HARM?

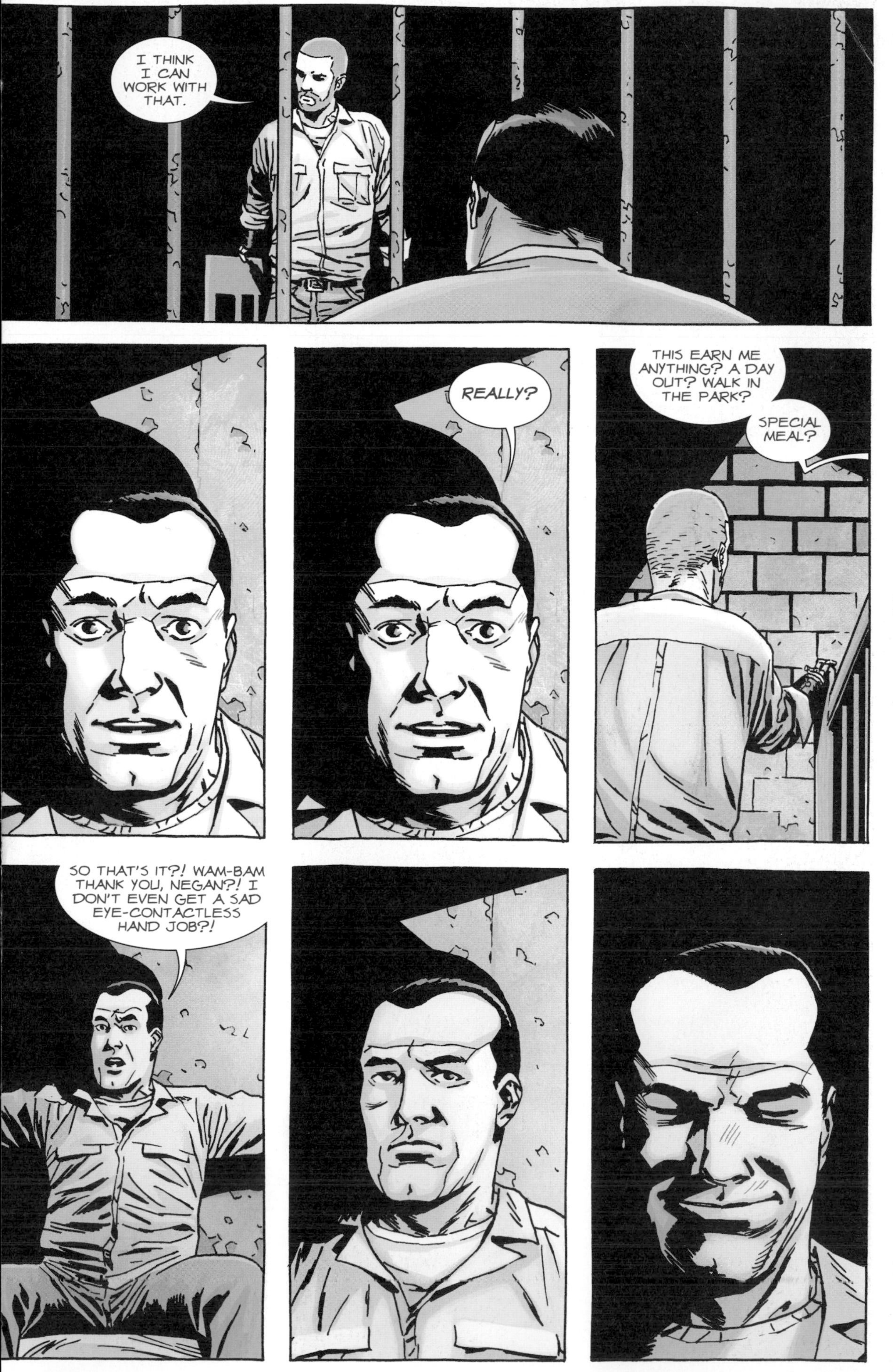
I THINK I CAN WORK WITH THAT.
REALLY?
THIS EARN ME ANYTHING? A DAY OUT? WALK IN THE PARK?
SPECIAL MEAL?
SO THAT'S IT?! WAM-BAM THANK YOU, NEGAN?! I DON'T EVEN GET A SAD EYE-CONTACTLESS HAND JOB?!

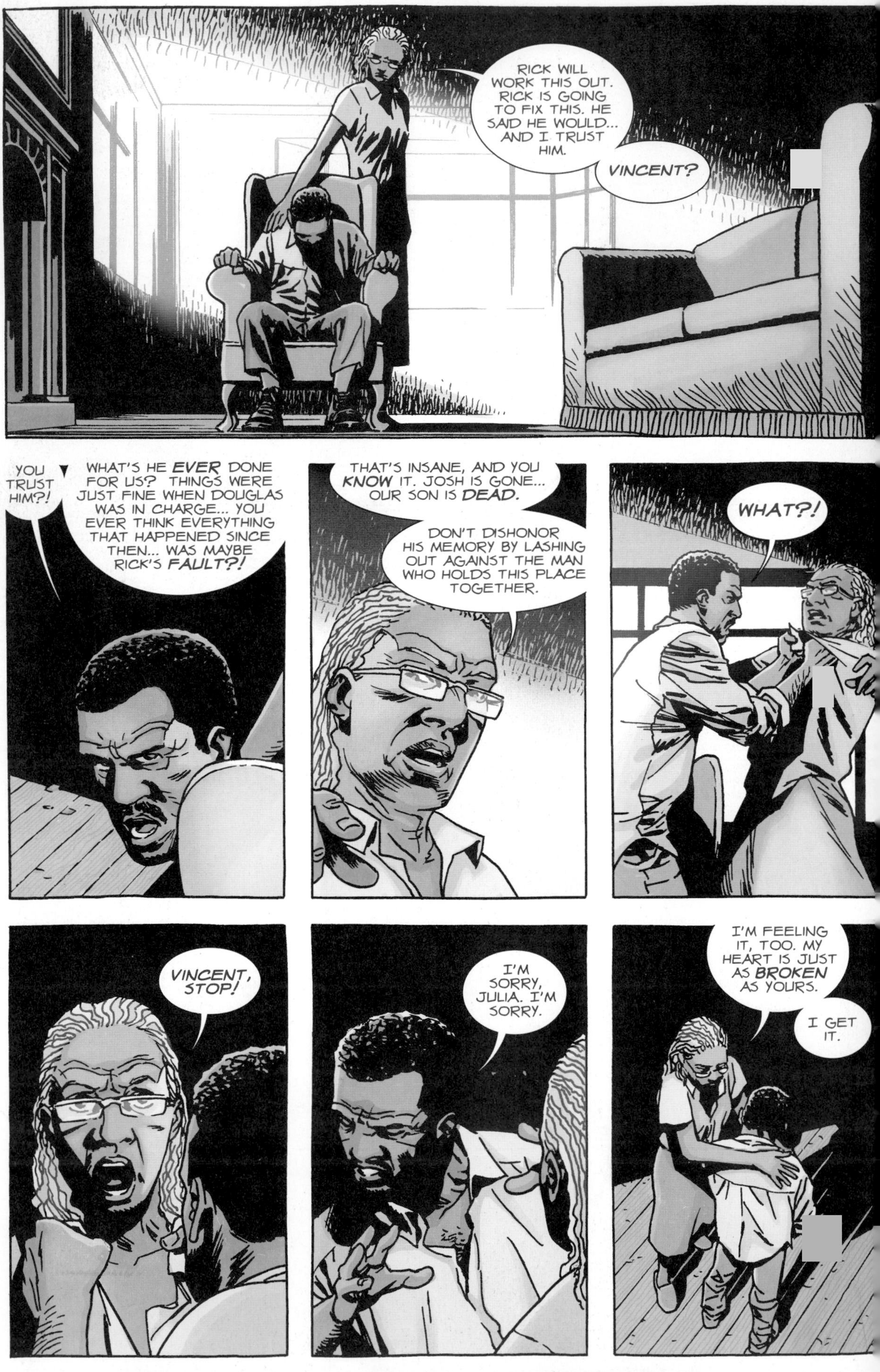
RICK WILL WORK THIS OUT. RICK IS GOING TO FIX THIS. HE SAID HE WOULD... AND I TRUST HIM.
VINCENT?
YOU TRUST HIM?!
WHAT'S HE EVER DONE FOR US? THINGS WERE JUST FINE WHEN DOUGLAS WAS IN CHARGE... YOU EVER THINK EVERYTHING THAT HAPPENED SINCE THEN... WAS MAYBE RICK'S FAULT?!
THAT'S INSANE, AND YOU KNOW IT. JOSH IS GONE... OUR SON IS DEAD.
DON'T DISHONOR HIS MEMORY BY LASHING OUT AGAINST THE MAN WHO HOLDS THIS PLACE TOGETHER.
WHAT?!
VINCENT, STOP!
I'M SORRY, JULIA. I'M SORRY.
I'M FEELING IT, TOO. MY HEART IS JUST AS BROKEN AS YOURS.
I GET IT.

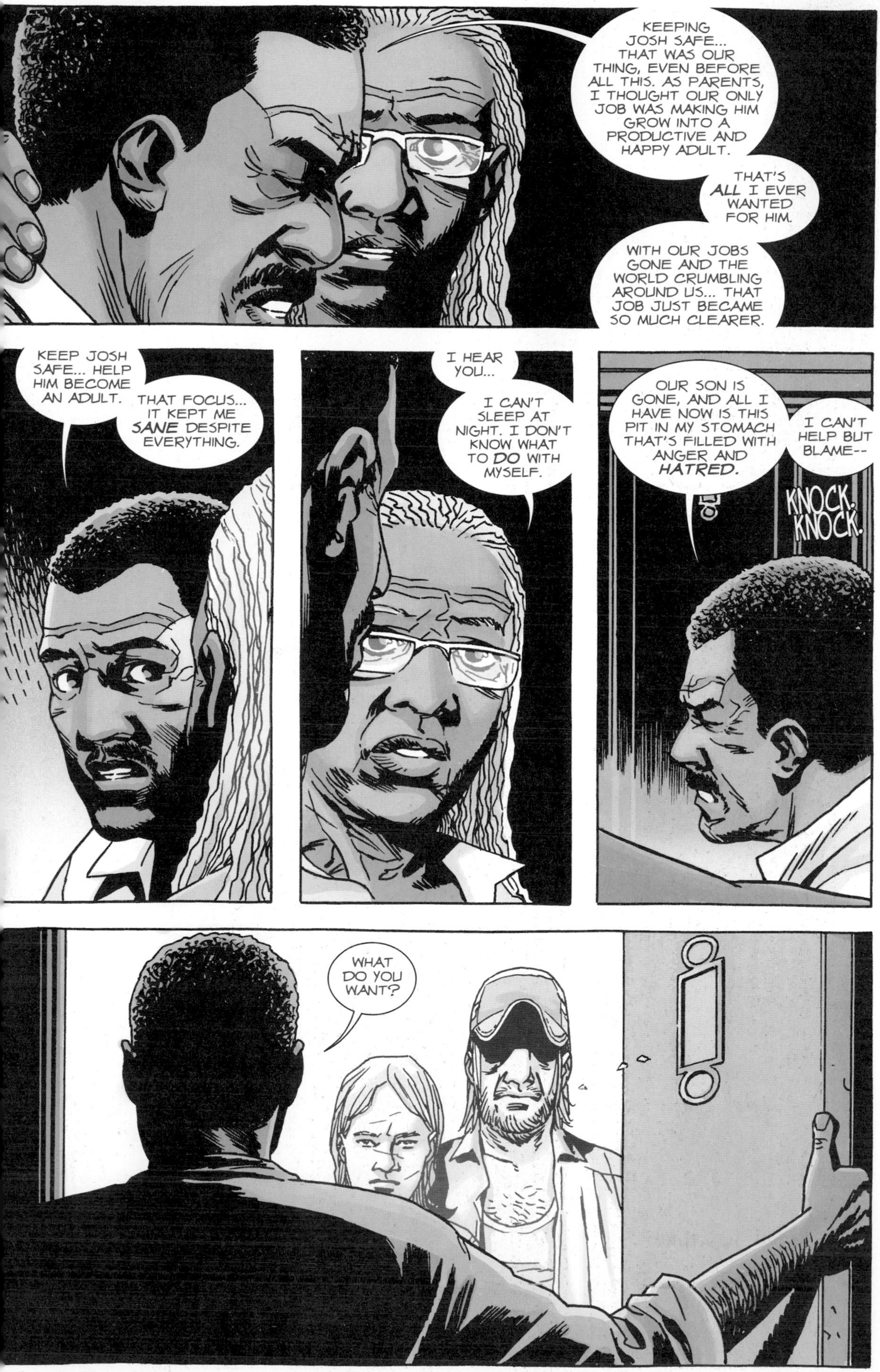

KEEPING JOSH SAFE... THAT WAS OUR THING, EVEN BEFORE ALL THIS. AS PARENTS, I THOUGHT OUR ONLY JOB WAS MAKING HIM GROW INTO A PRODUCTIVE AND HAPPY ADULT.
THAT'S ALL I EVER WANTED FOR HIM.
WITH OUR JOBS GONE AND THE WORLD CRUMBLING AROUND US... THAT JOB JUST BECAME SO MUCH CLEARER.
KEEP JOSH SAFE... HELP HIM BECOME AN ADULT.
THAT FOCUS... IT KEPT ME SANE DESPITE EVERYTHING.
I HEAR YOU...
I CAN'T SLEEP AT NIGHT. I DON'T KNOW WHAT TO DO WITH MYSELF.
OUR SON IS GONE, AND ALL I HAVE NOW IS THIS PIT IN MY STOMACH THAT'S FILLED WITH ANGER AND HATRED.
I CAN'T HELP BUT BLAME--
KNOCK. KNOCK.
WHAT DO YOU WANT?

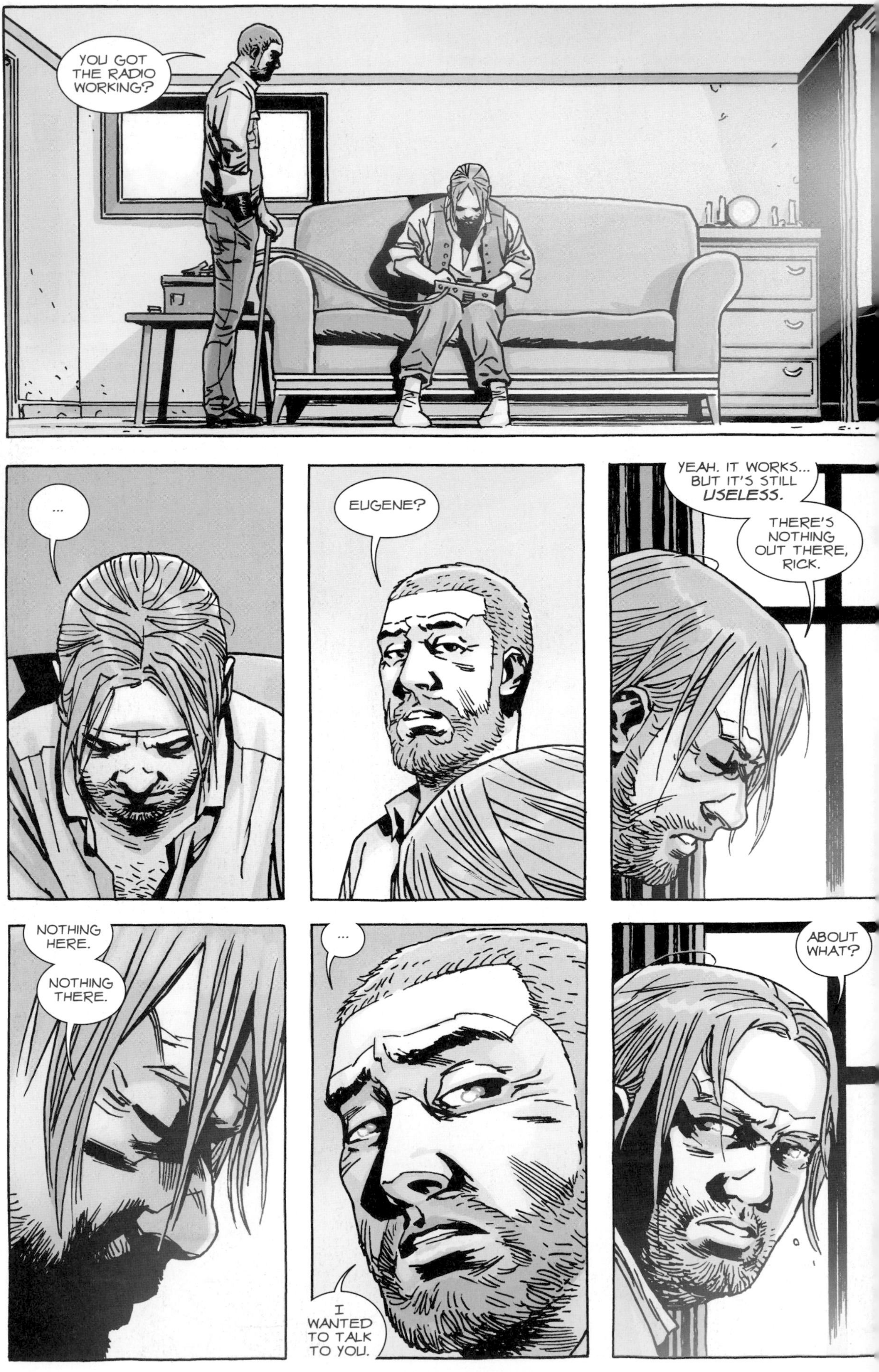
YOU GOT THE RADIO WORKING?
...
EUGENE?
YEAH. IT WORKS... BUT IT'S STILL *USELESS.*
THERE'S NOTHING OUT THERE, RICK.
NOTHING HERE.
NOTHING THERE.
...
I WANTED TO TALK TO YOU.
ABOUT WHAT?

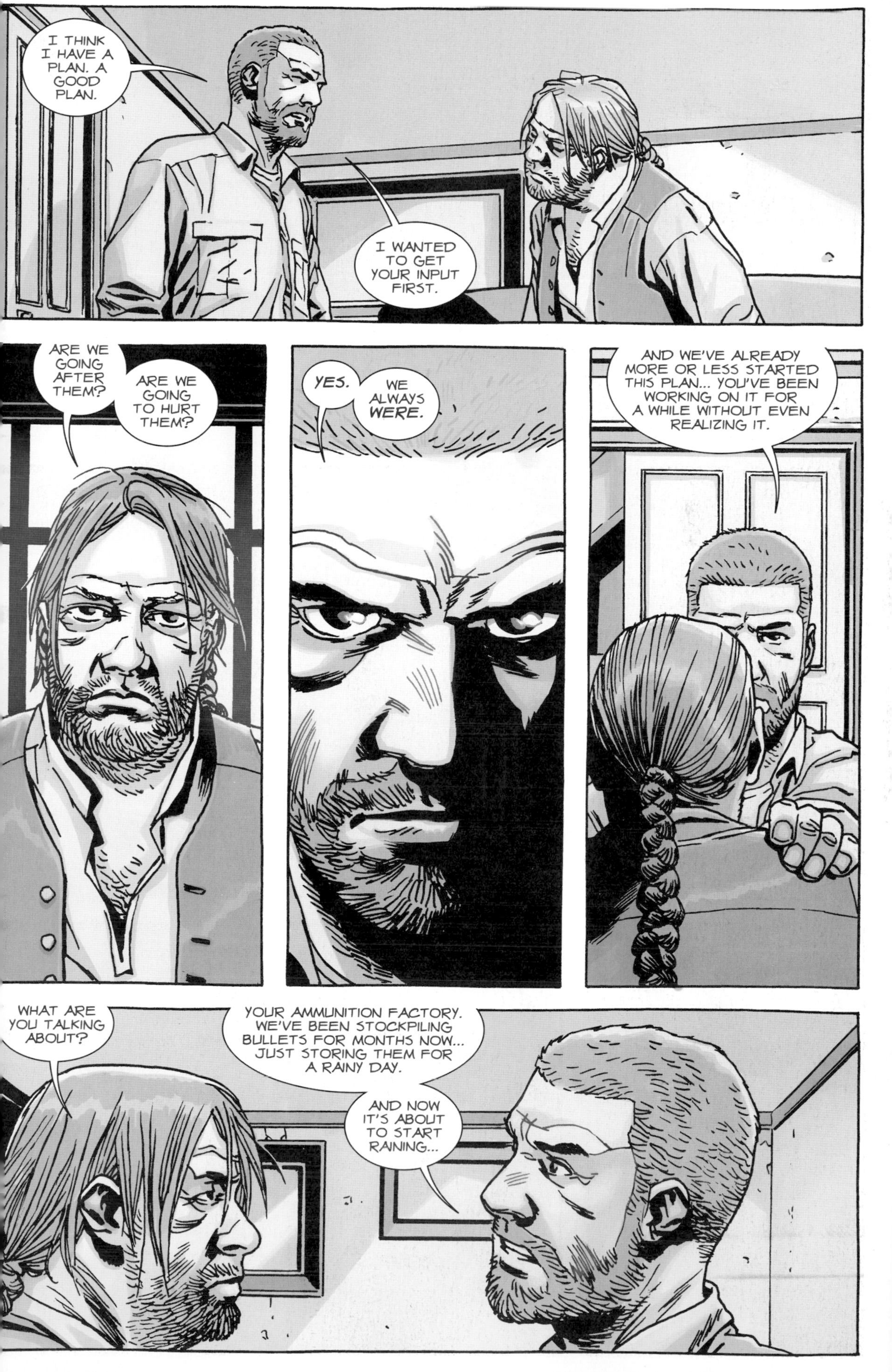
I THINK I HAVE A PLAN. A GOOD PLAN.
I WANTED TO GET YOUR INPUT FIRST.
ARE WE GOING AFTER THEM?
ARE WE GOING TO HURT THEM?
YES.
WE ALWAYS WERE.
AND WE'VE ALREADY MORE OR LESS STARTED THIS PLAN... YOU'VE BEEN WORKING ON IT FOR A WHILE WITHOUT EVEN REALIZING IT.
WHAT ARE YOU TALKING ABOUT?
YOUR AMMUNITION FACTORY. WE'VE BEEN STOCKPILING BULLETS FOR MONTHS NOW... JUST STORING THEM FOR A RAINY DAY.
AND NOW IT'S ABOUT TO START RAINING...

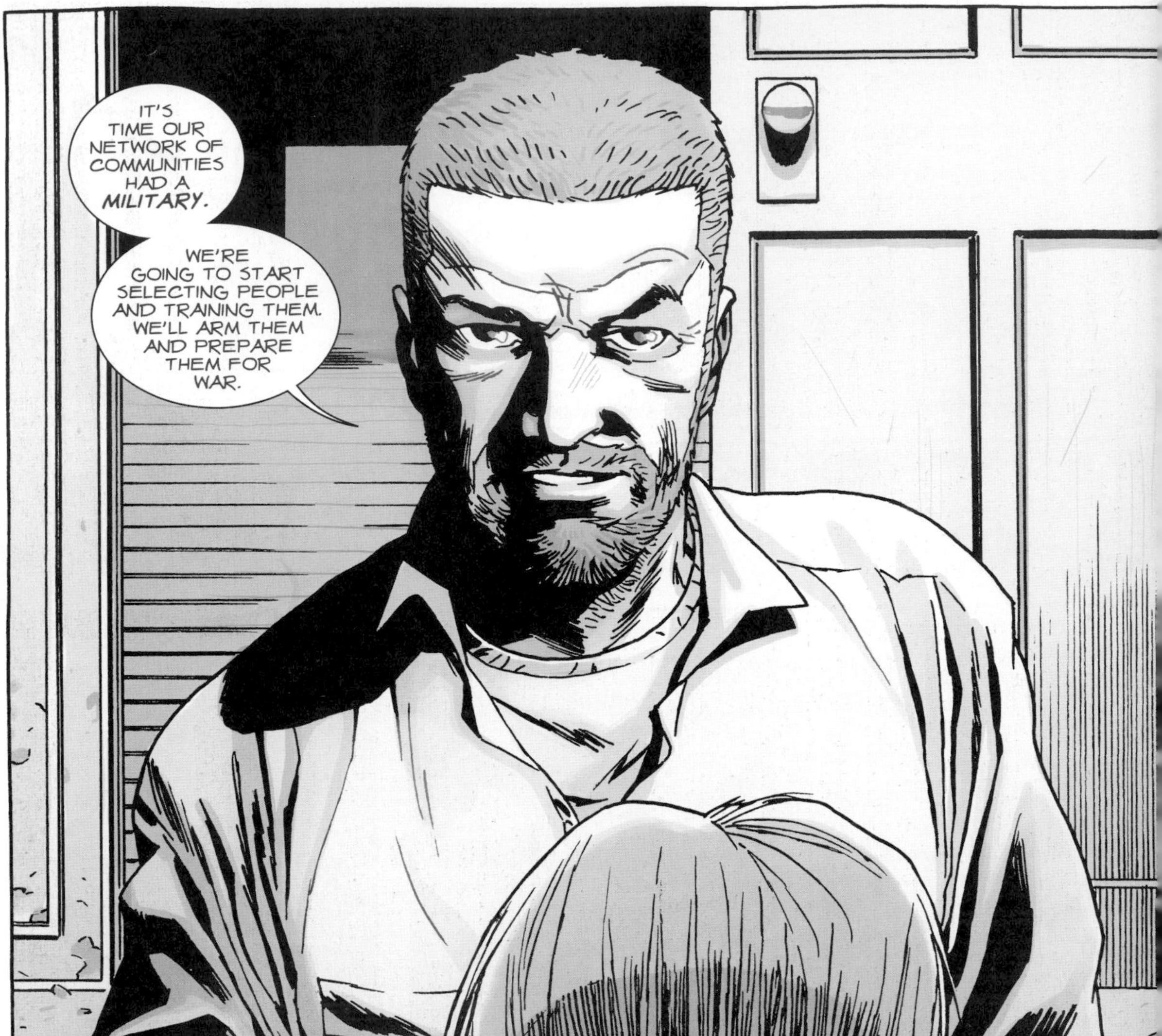
IT'S TIME OUR NETWORK OF COMMUNITIES HAD A MILITARY.
WE'RE GOING TO START SELECTING PEOPLE AND TRAINING THEM. WE'LL ARM THEM AND PREPARE THEM FOR WAR.

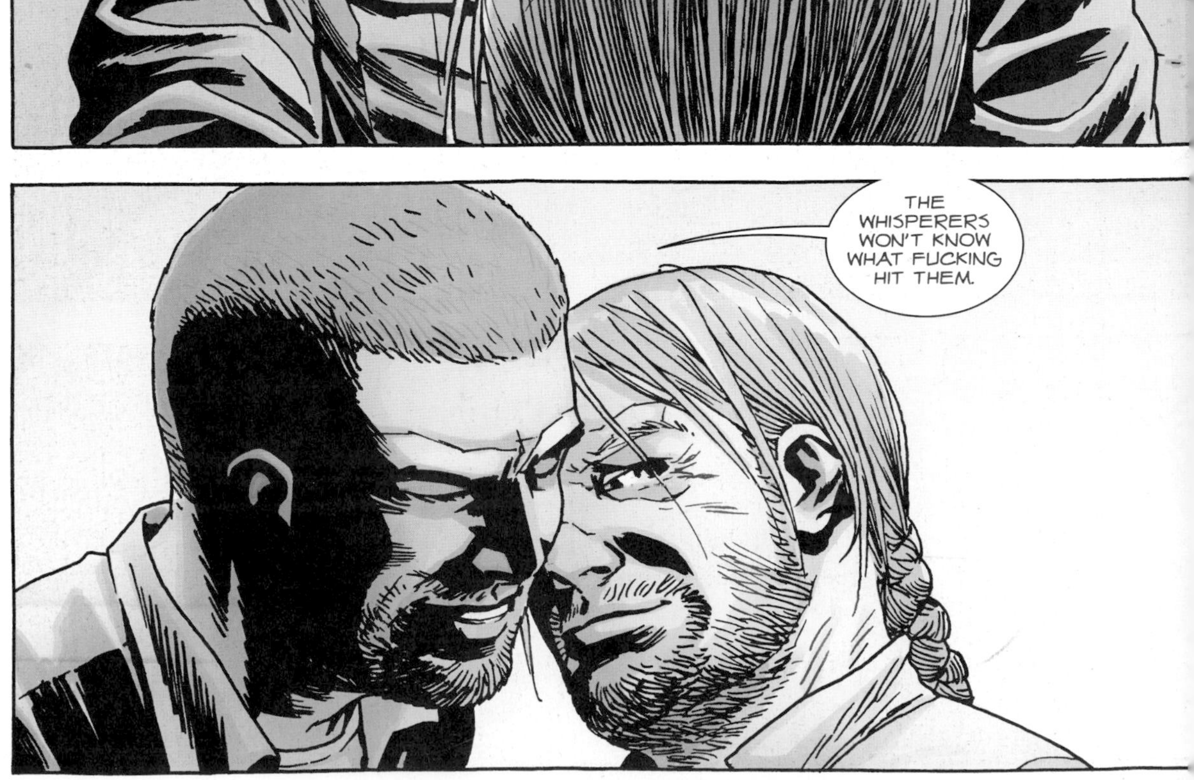
THE WHISPERERS WON'T KNOW WHAT FUCKING HIT THEM.

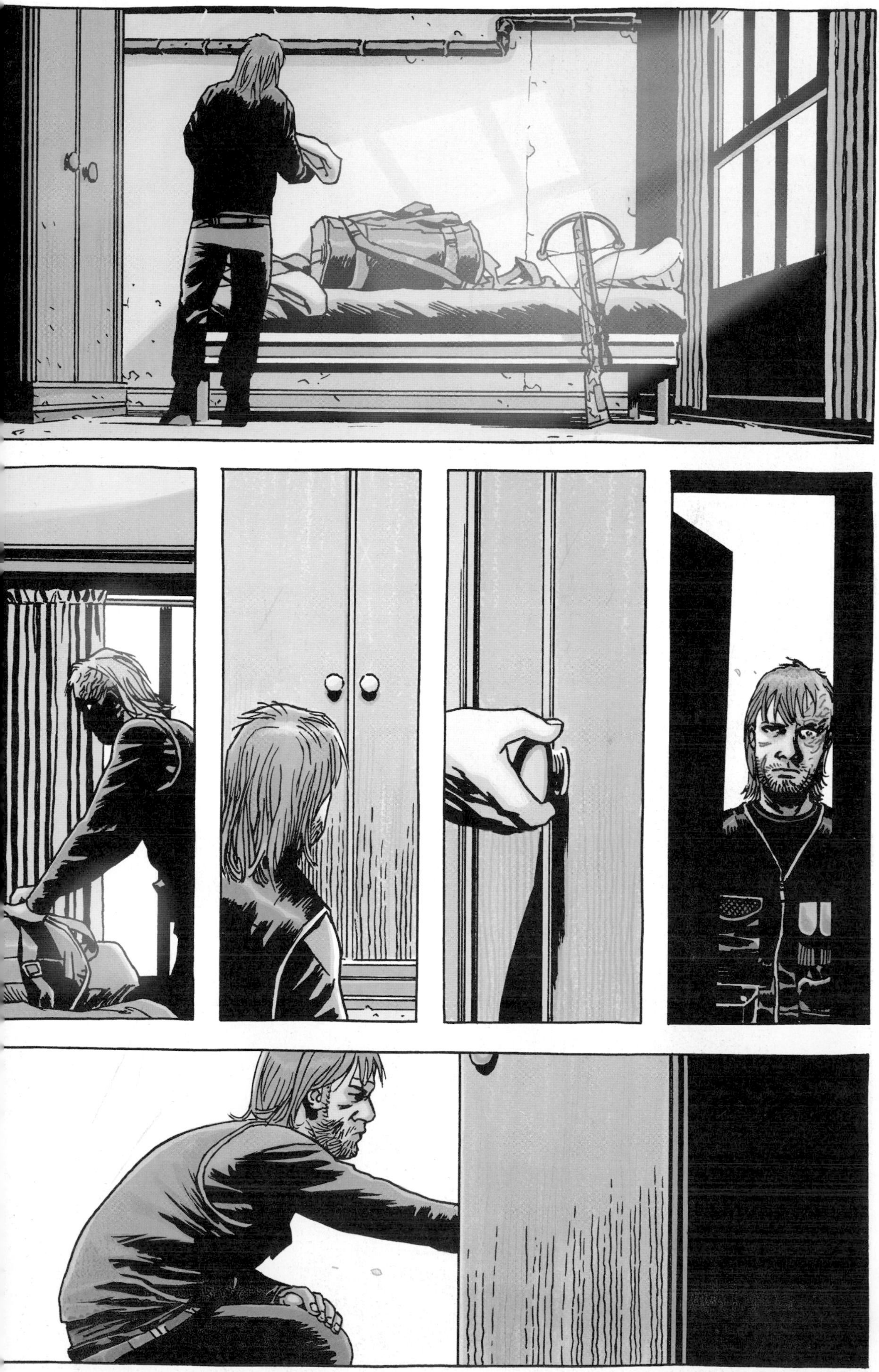

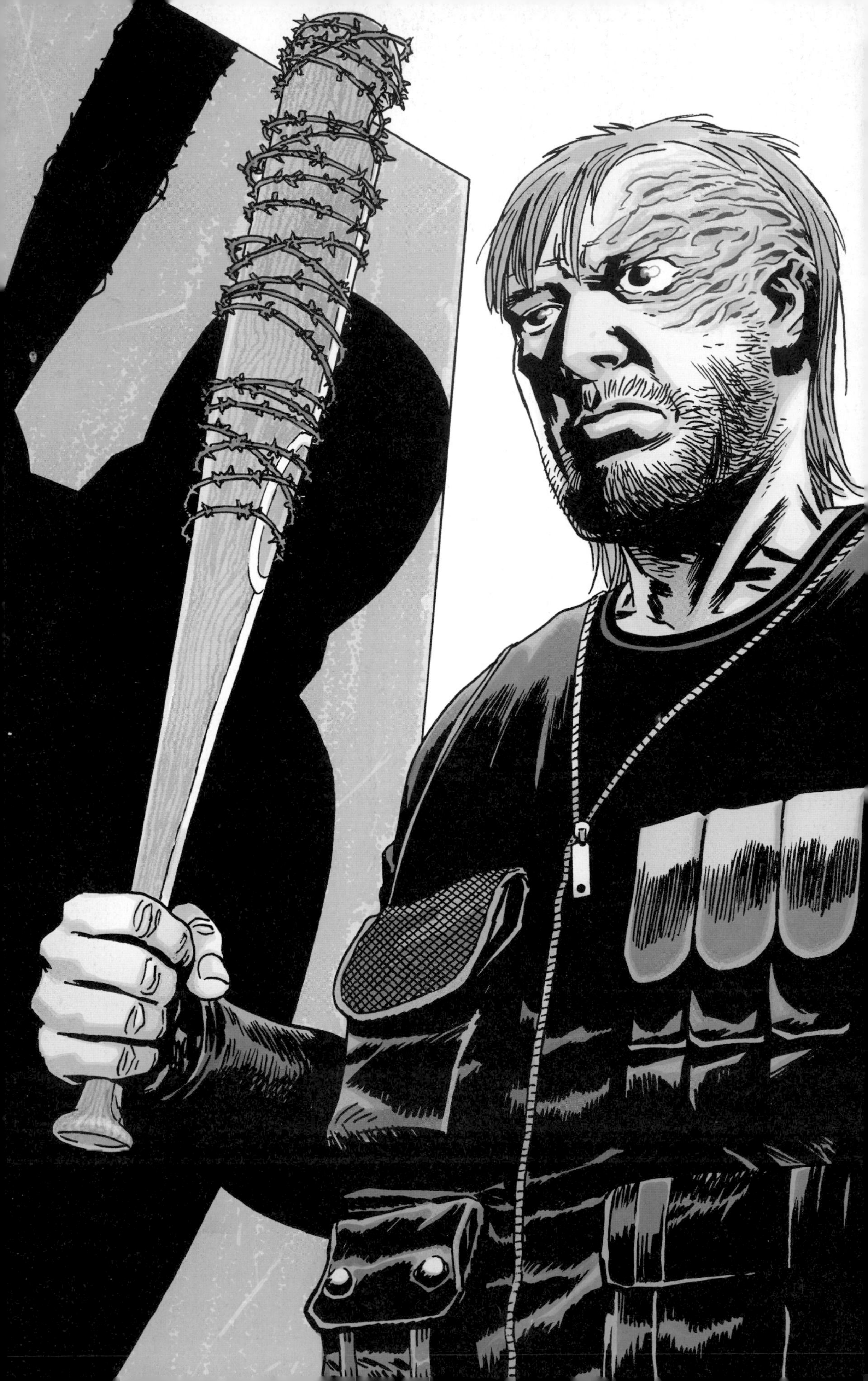

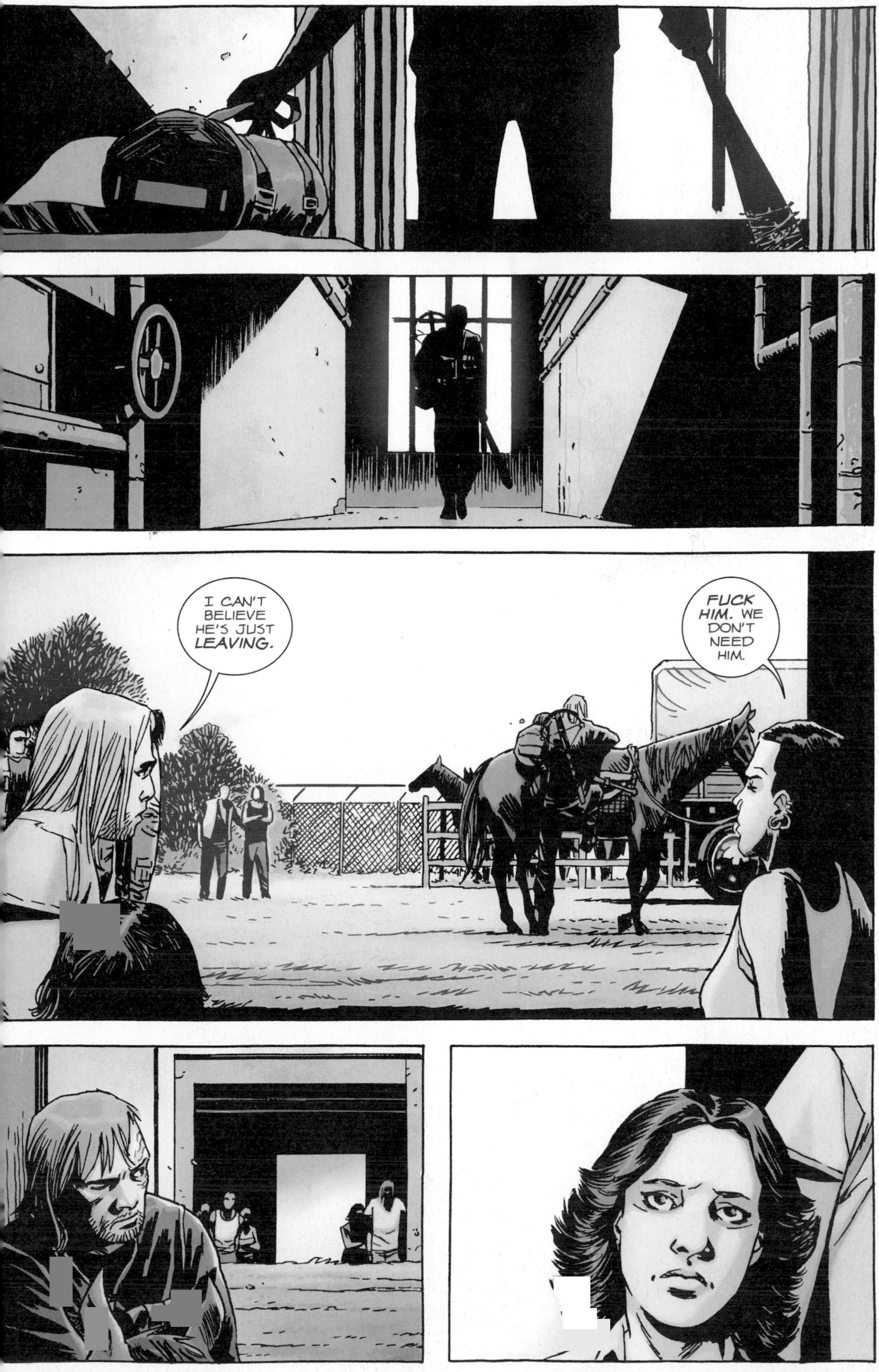
I CAN'T BELIEVE HE'S JUST LEAVING.
FUCK HIM. WE DON'T NEED HIM.

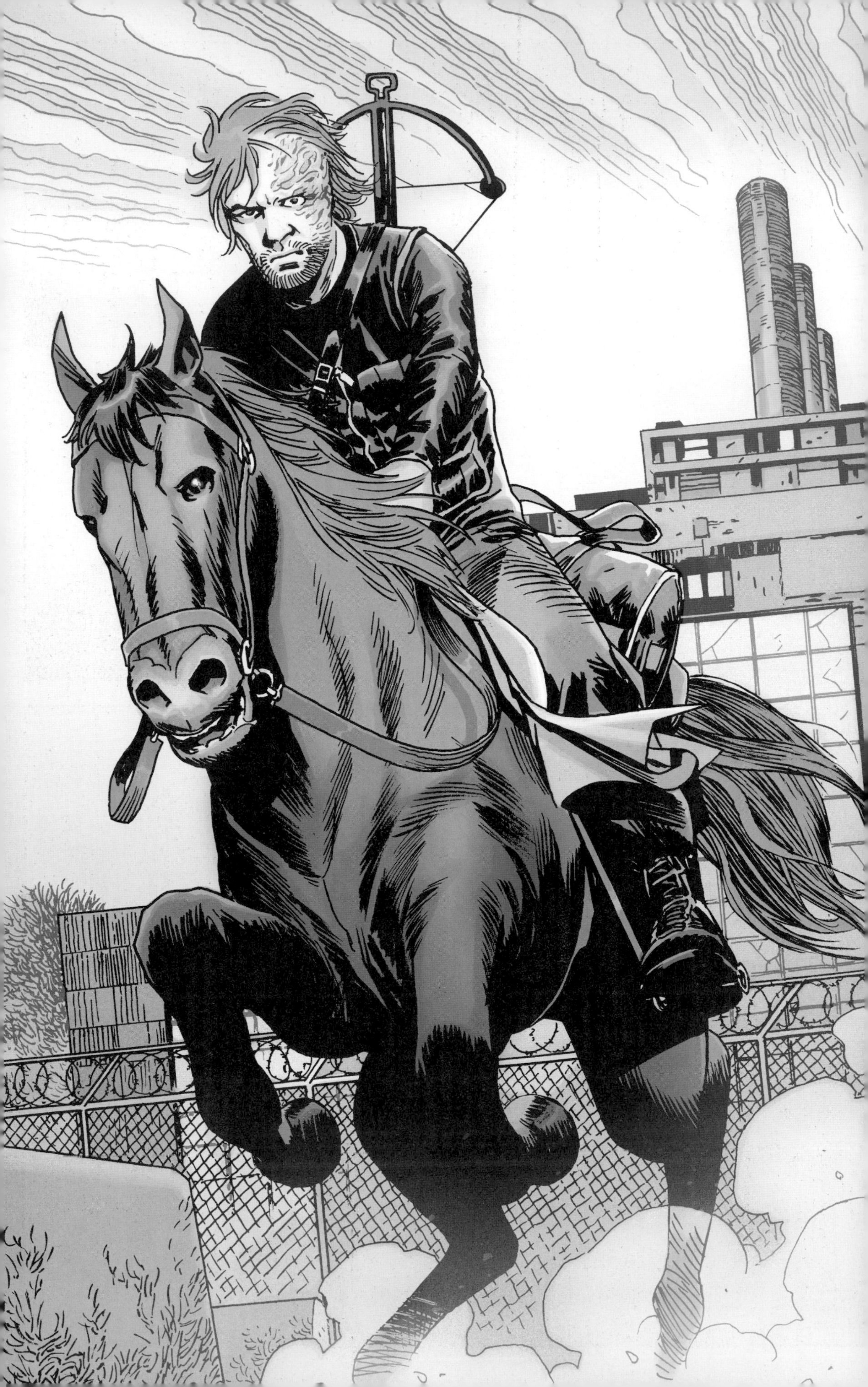

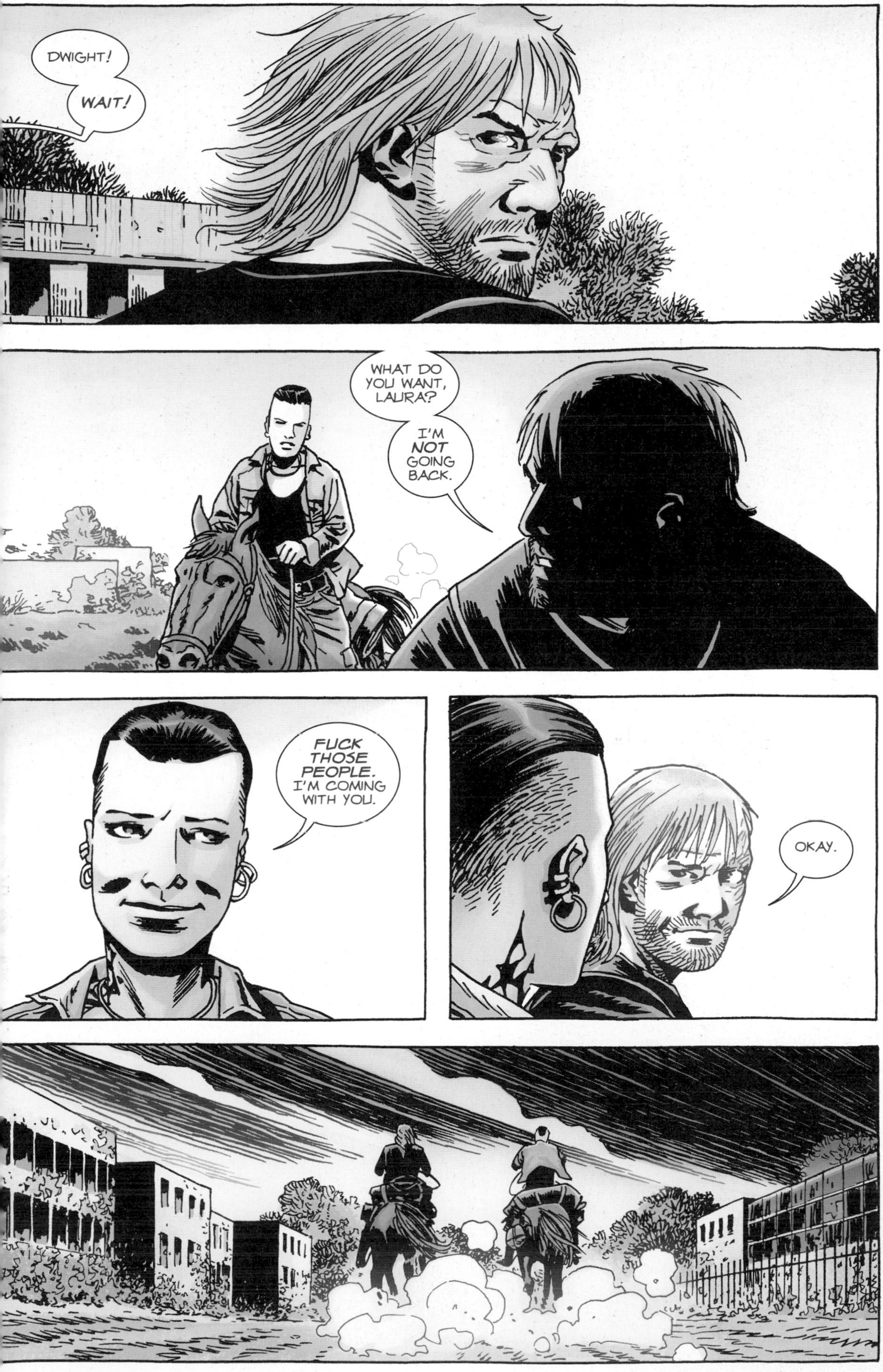
DWIGHT!
WAIT!
WHAT DO YOU WANT, LAURA?
I'M NOT GOING BACK.
FUCK THOSE PEOPLE. I'M COMING WITH YOU.
OKAY.

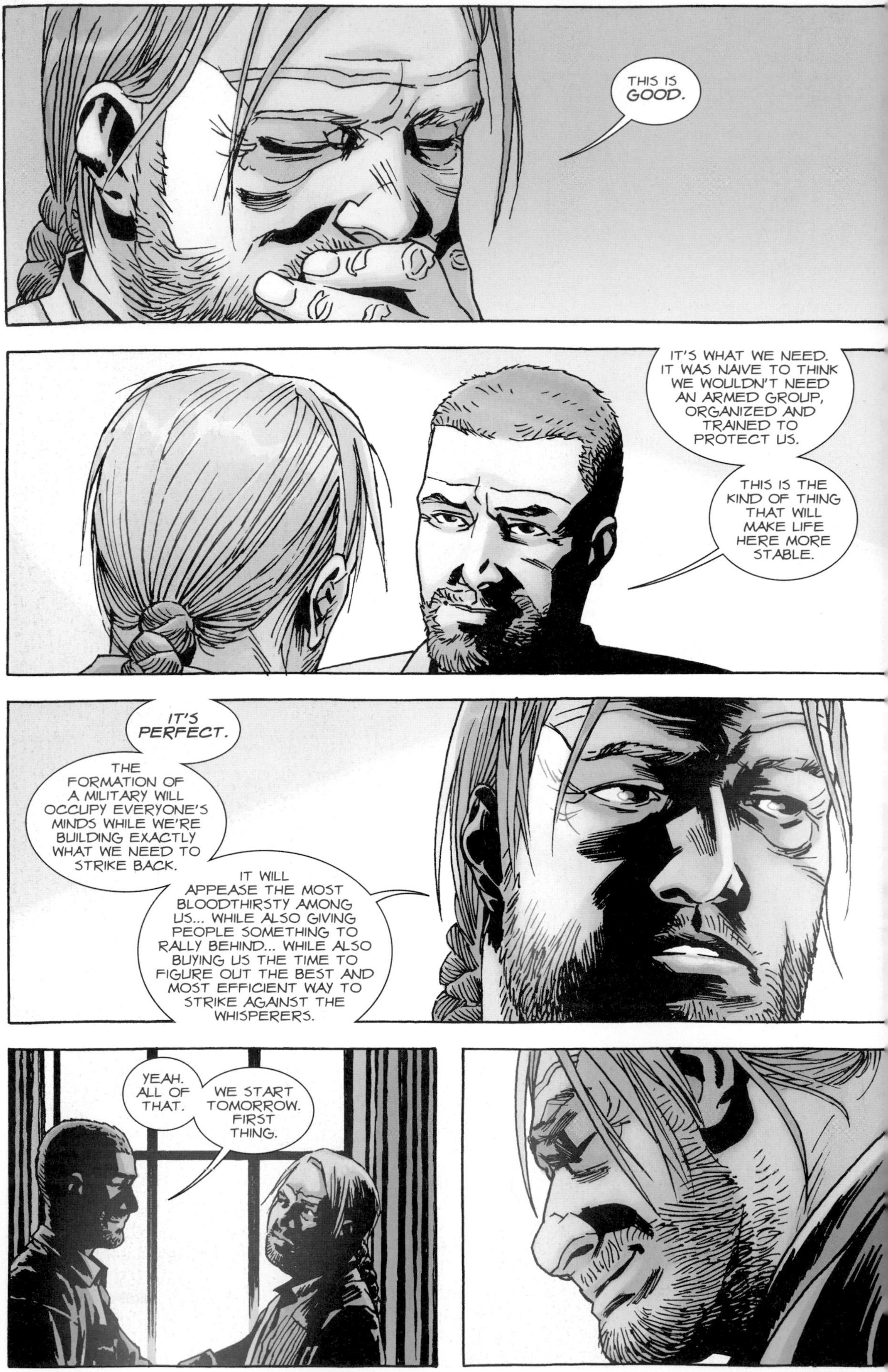
THIS IS GOOD.
IT'S WHAT WE NEED. IT WAS NAIVE TO THINK WE WOULDN'T NEED AN ARMED GROUP, ORGANIZED AND TRAINED TO PROTECT US.
THIS IS THE KIND OF THING THAT WILL MAKE LIFE HERE MORE STABLE.
IT'S PERFECT.
THE FORMATION OF A MILITARY WILL OCCUPY EVERYONE'S MINDS WHILE WE'RE BUILDING EXACTLY WHAT WE NEED TO STRIKE BACK.
IT WILL APPEASE THE MOST BLOODTHIRSTY AMONG US... WHILE ALSO GIVING PEOPLE SOMETHING TO RALLY BEHIND... WHILE ALSO BUYING US THE TIME TO FIGURE OUT THE BEST AND MOST EFFICIENT WAY TO STRIKE AGAINST THE WHISPERERS.
YEAH. ALL OF THAT.
WE START TOMORROW. FIRST THING.

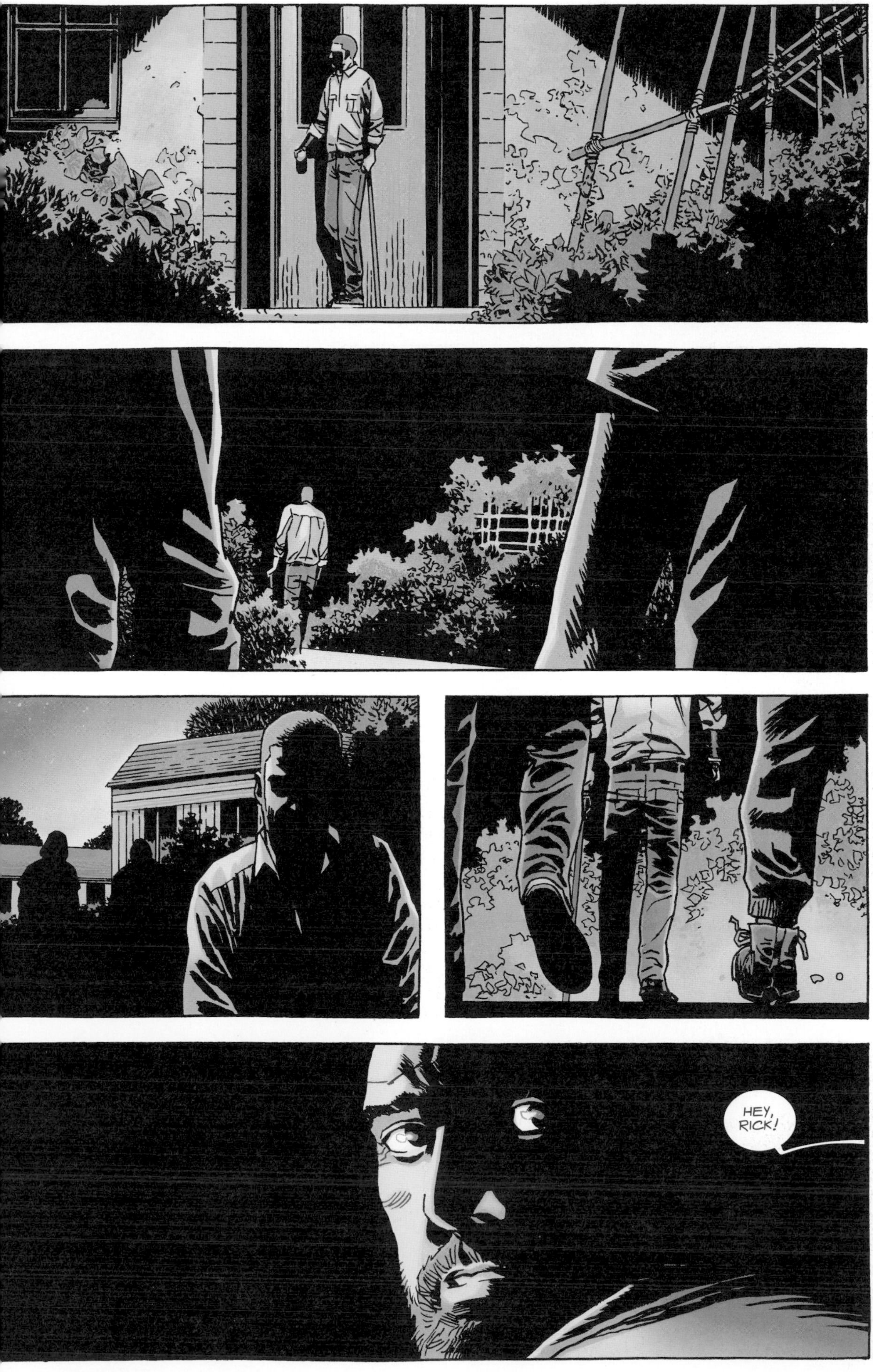
HEY, RICK!

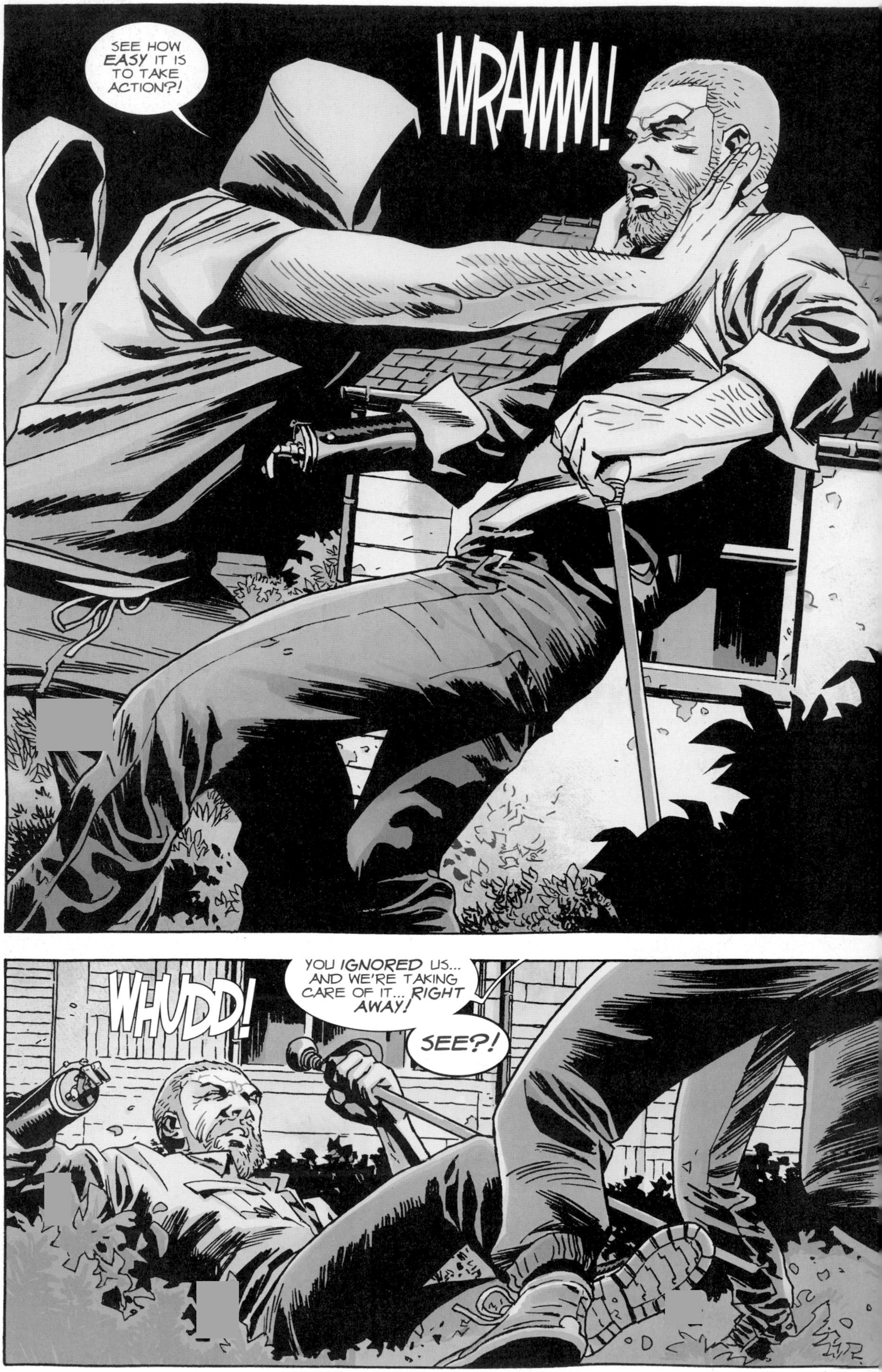
SEE HOW *EASY* IT IS TO TAKE ACTION?!
WRAMM!
WHUDD!
YOU *IGNORED* US... AND WE'RE TAKING CARE OF IT... *RIGHT AWAY!*
SEE?!

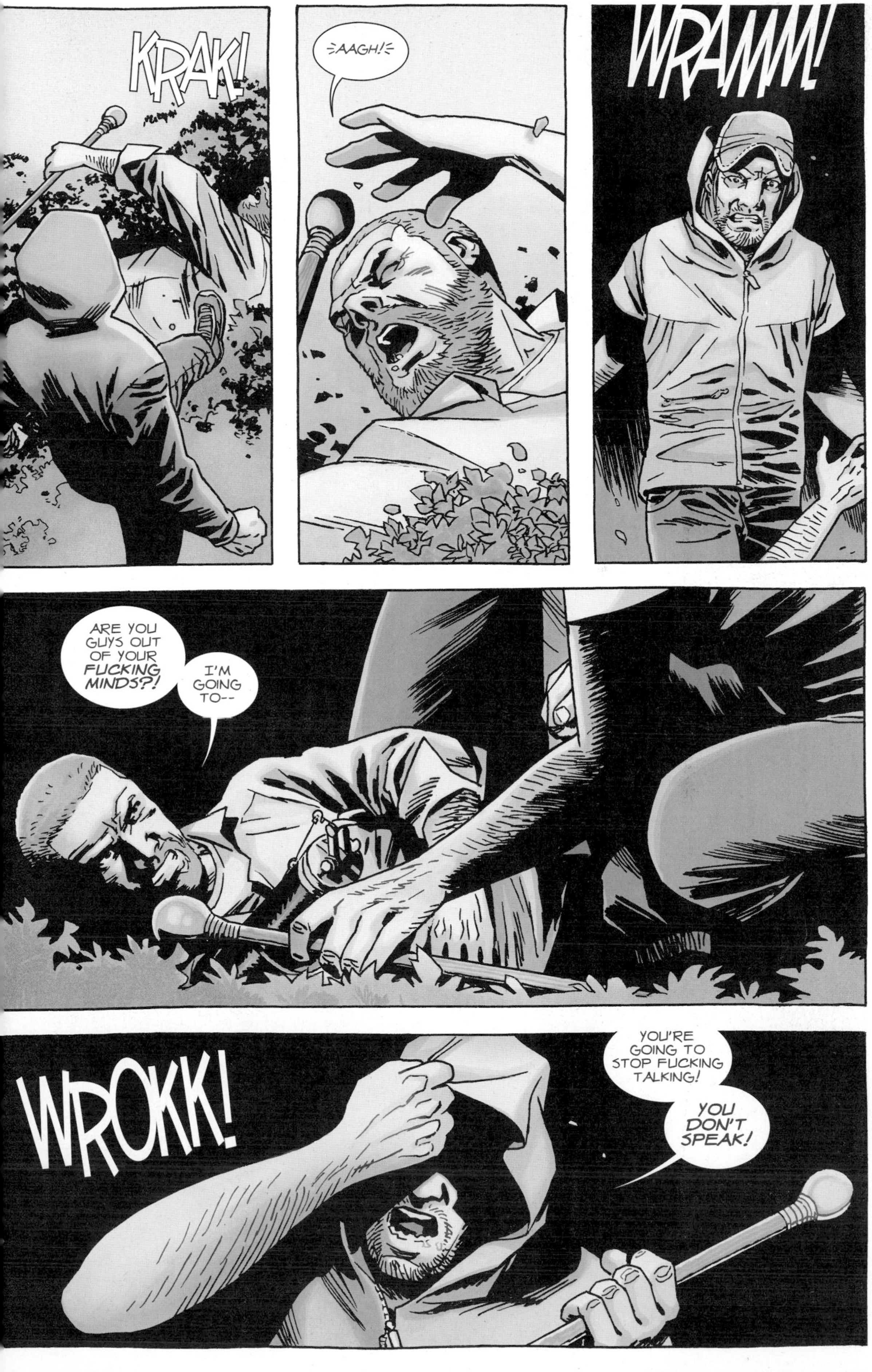
KRAK!
AAGH!
WRAMM!
ARE YOU GUYS OUT OF YOUR FUCKING MINDS?!
I'M GOING TO--
WROKK!
YOU'RE GOING TO STOP FUCKING TALKING!
YOU DON'T SPEAK!

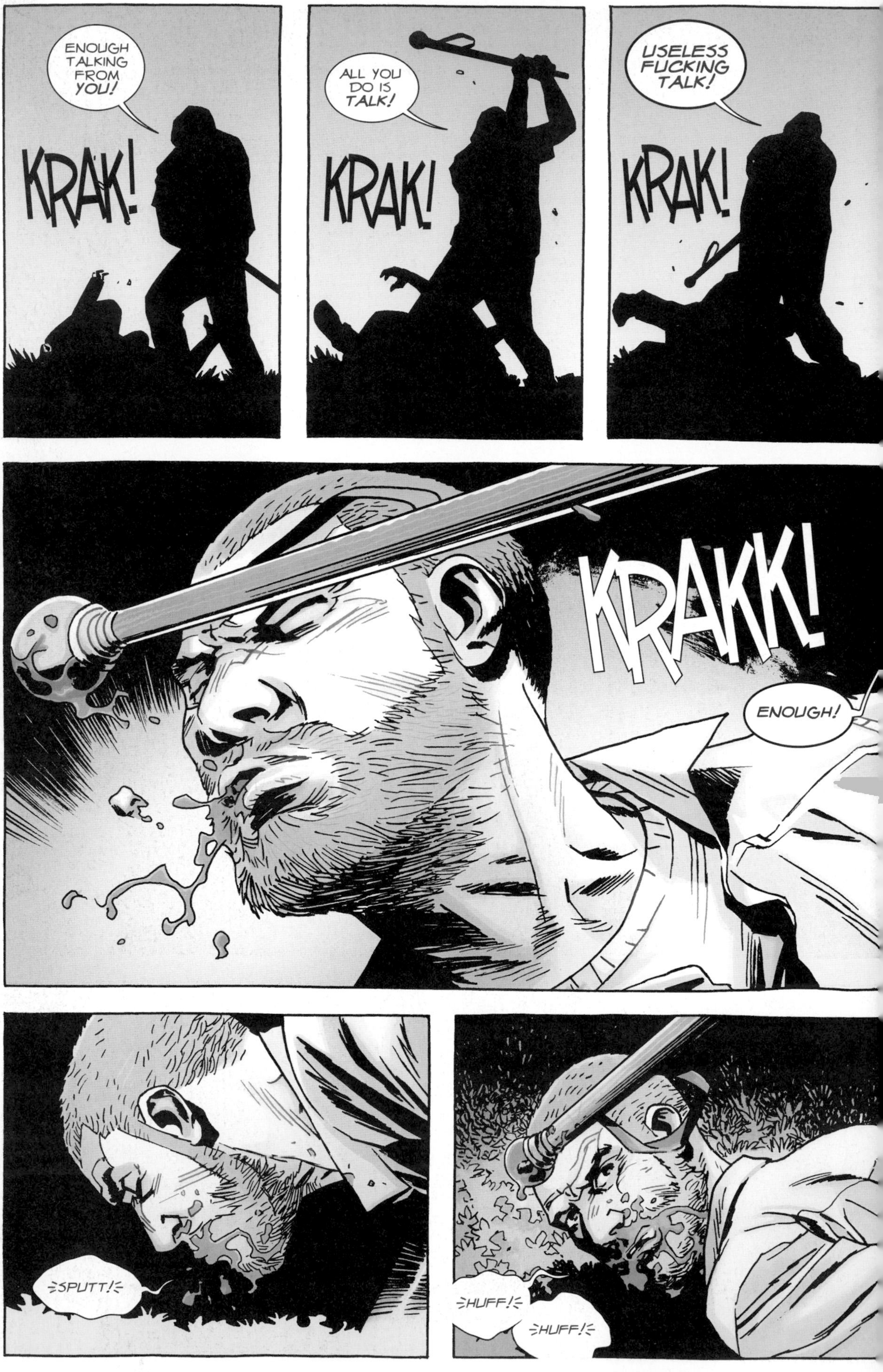
ENOUGH TALKING FROM YOU!
KRAK!
ALL YOU DO IS TALK!
KRAK!
USELESS FUCKING TALK!
KRAK!
KRAKK!
ENOUGH!
SPUTT!
HUFF!
HUFF!

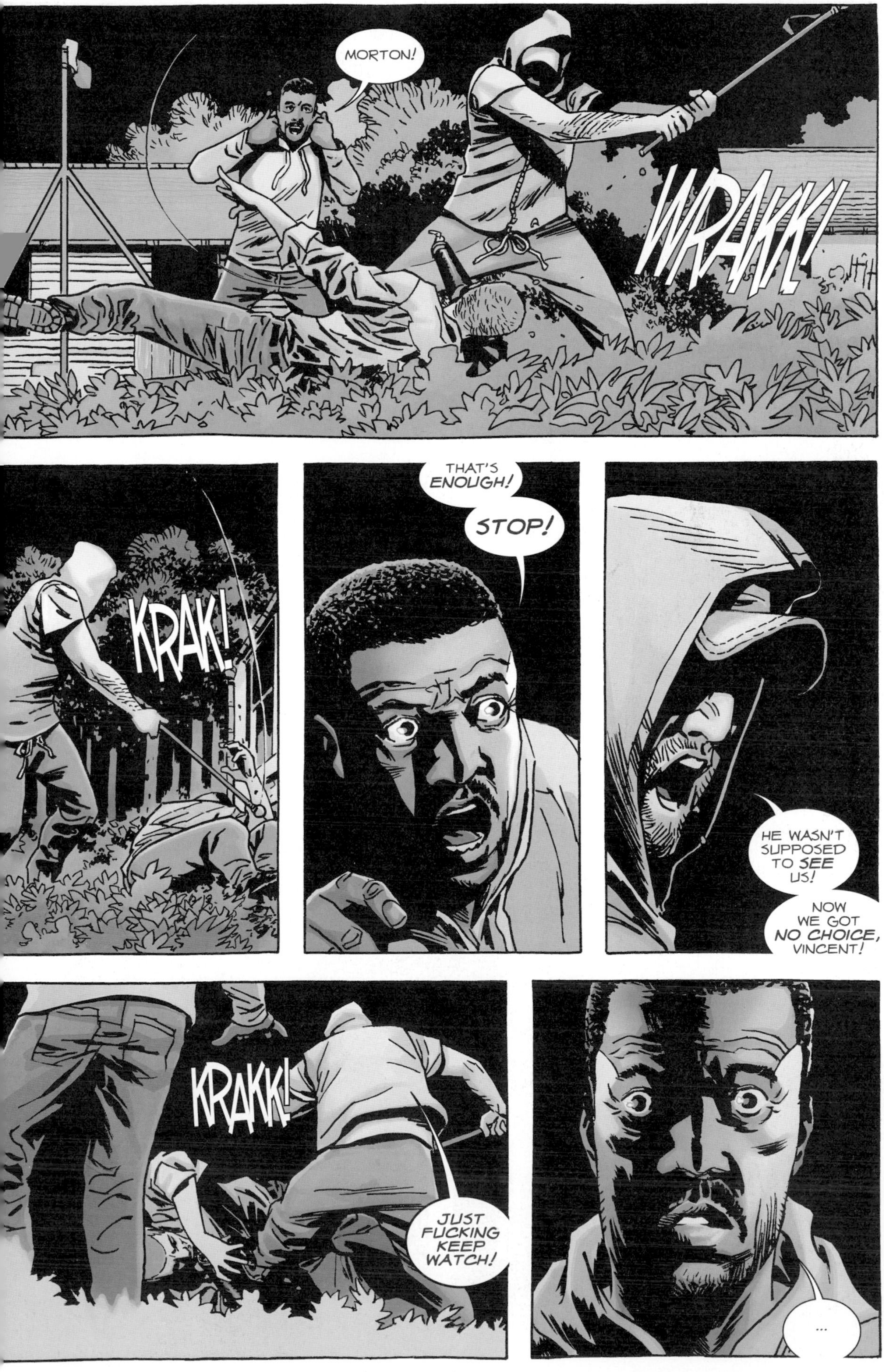
MORTON!
WRAKK!
KRAK!
THAT'S ENOUGH!
STOP!
HE WASN'T SUPPOSED TO SEE US!
NOW WE GOT NO CHOICE, VINCENT!
KRAKK!
JUST FUCKING KEEP WATCH!
...

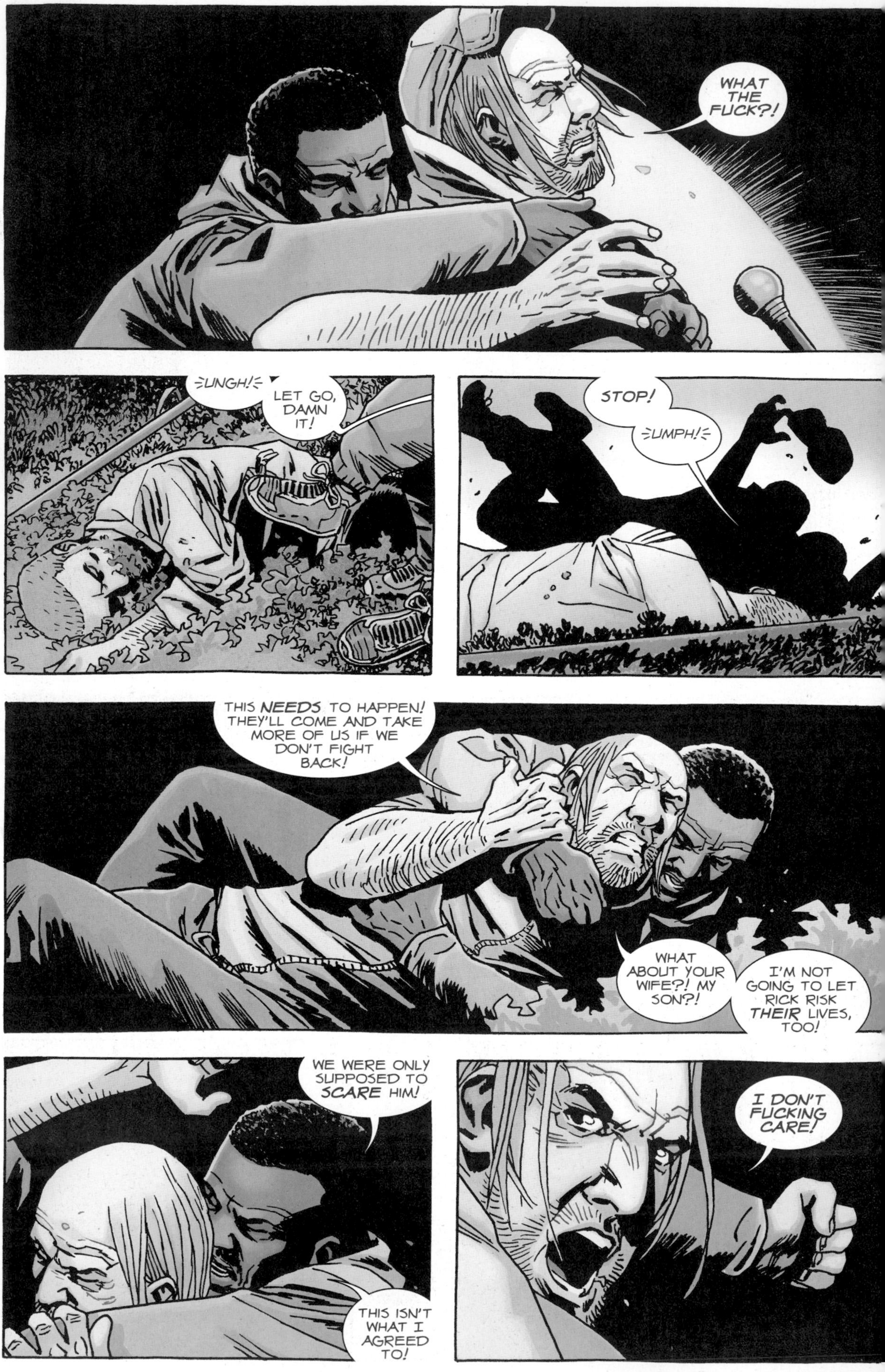
WHAT THE FUCK?!
UNGH!
LET GO, DAMN IT!
STOP!
UMPH!
THIS NEEDS TO HAPPEN! THEY'LL COME AND TAKE MORE OF US IF WE DON'T FIGHT BACK!
WHAT ABOUT YOUR WIFE?! MY SON?!
I'M NOT GOING TO LET RICK RISK THEIR LIVES, TOO!
WE WERE ONLY SUPPOSED TO SCARE HIM!
THIS ISN'T WHAT I AGREED TO!
I DON'T FUCKING CARE!

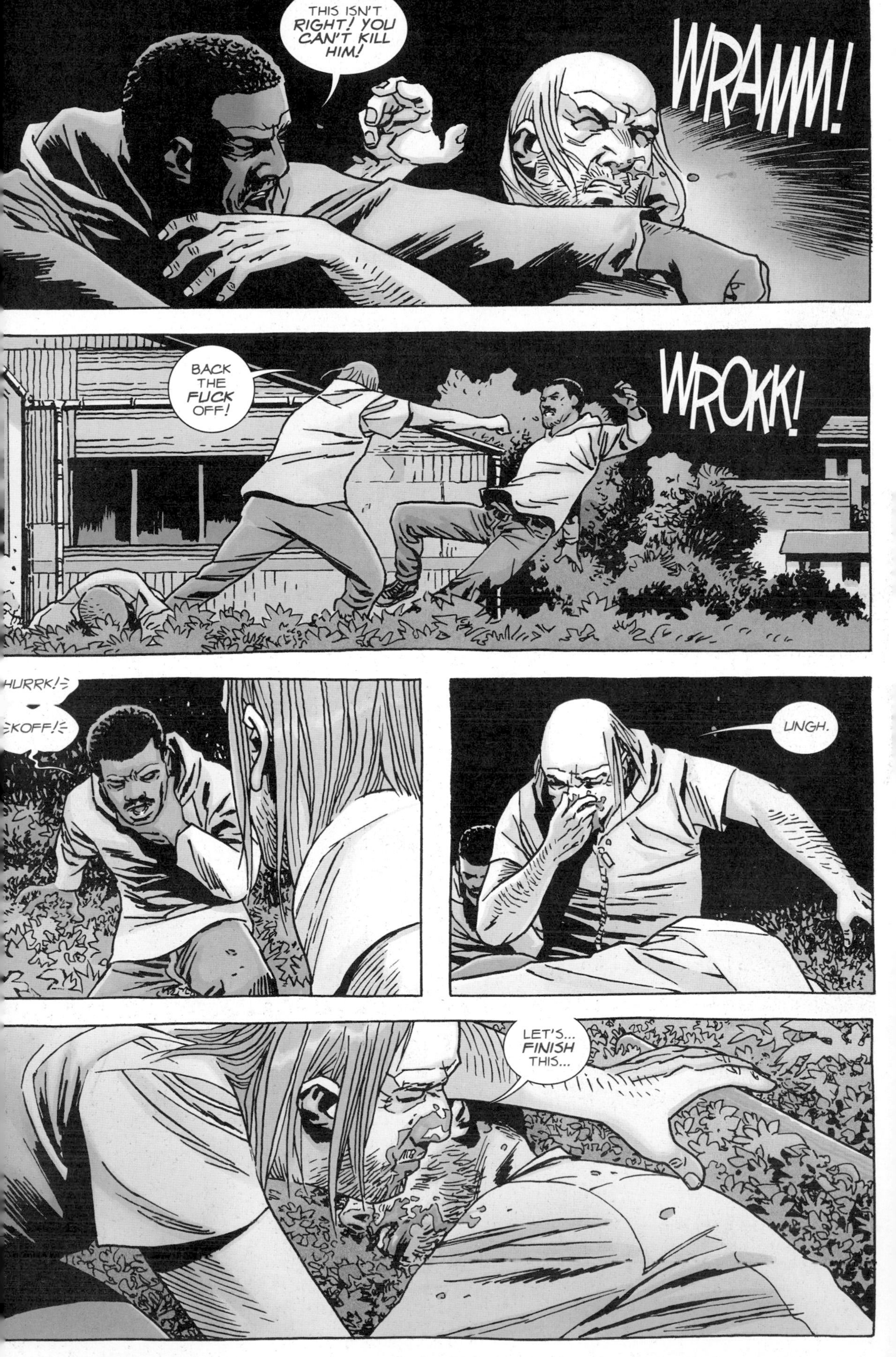
THIS ISN'T RIGHT! YOU CAN'T KILL HIM!
WRAMM!
BACK THE FUCK OFF!
WROKK!
HURRK!
KOFF!
UNGH.
LET'S... FINISH THIS...

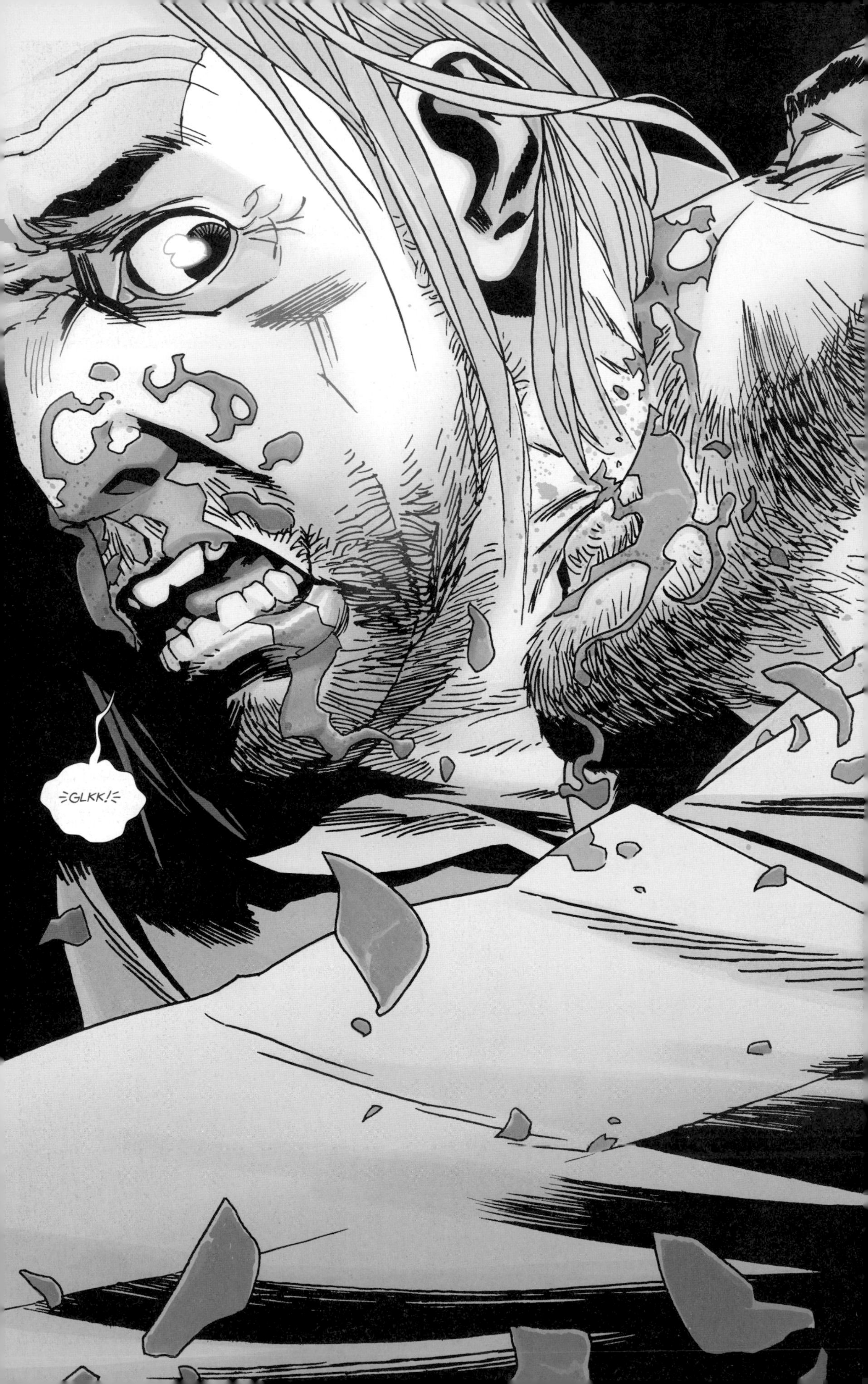
GLKK!

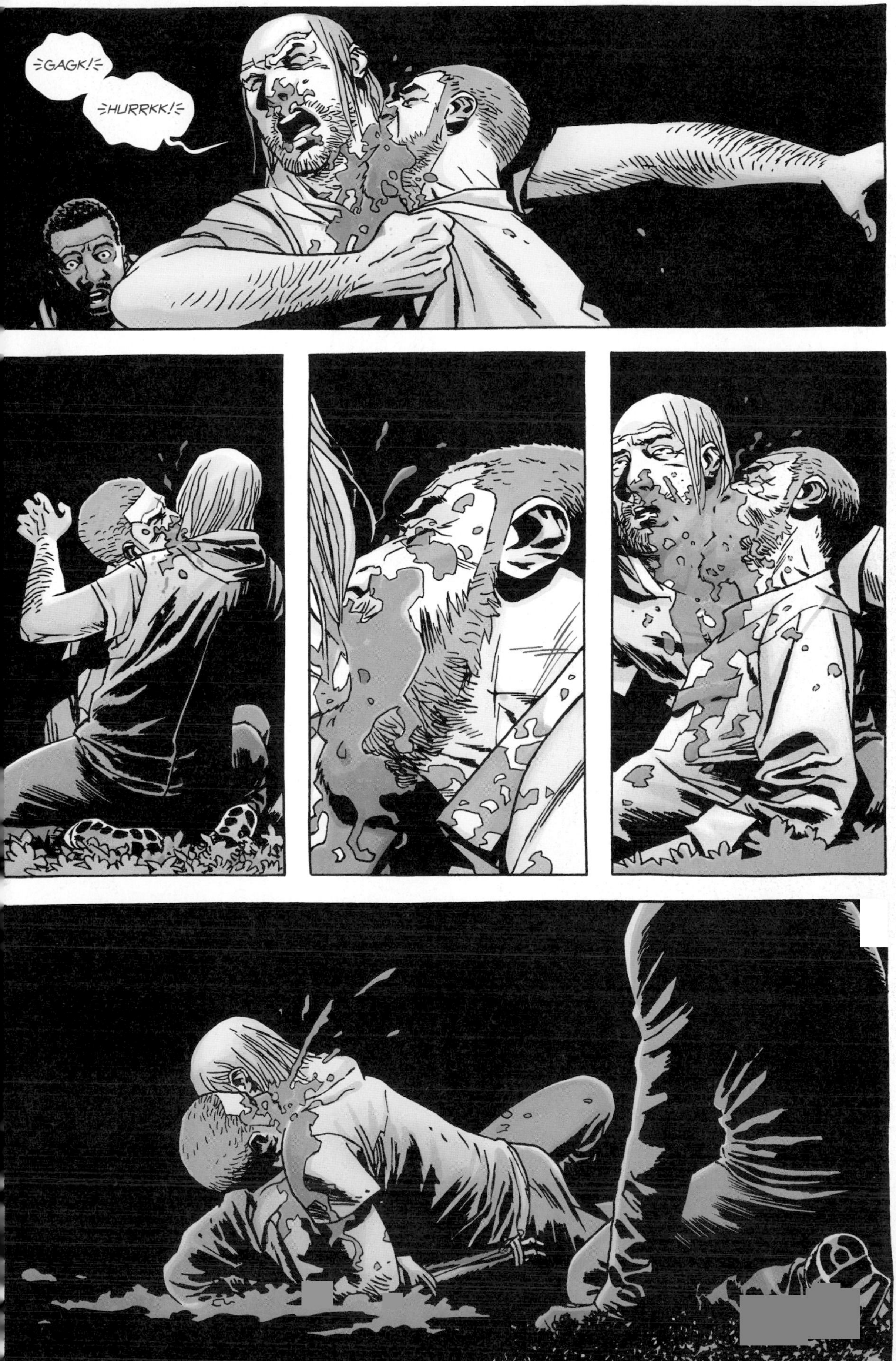
GAGK!
HURRKK!

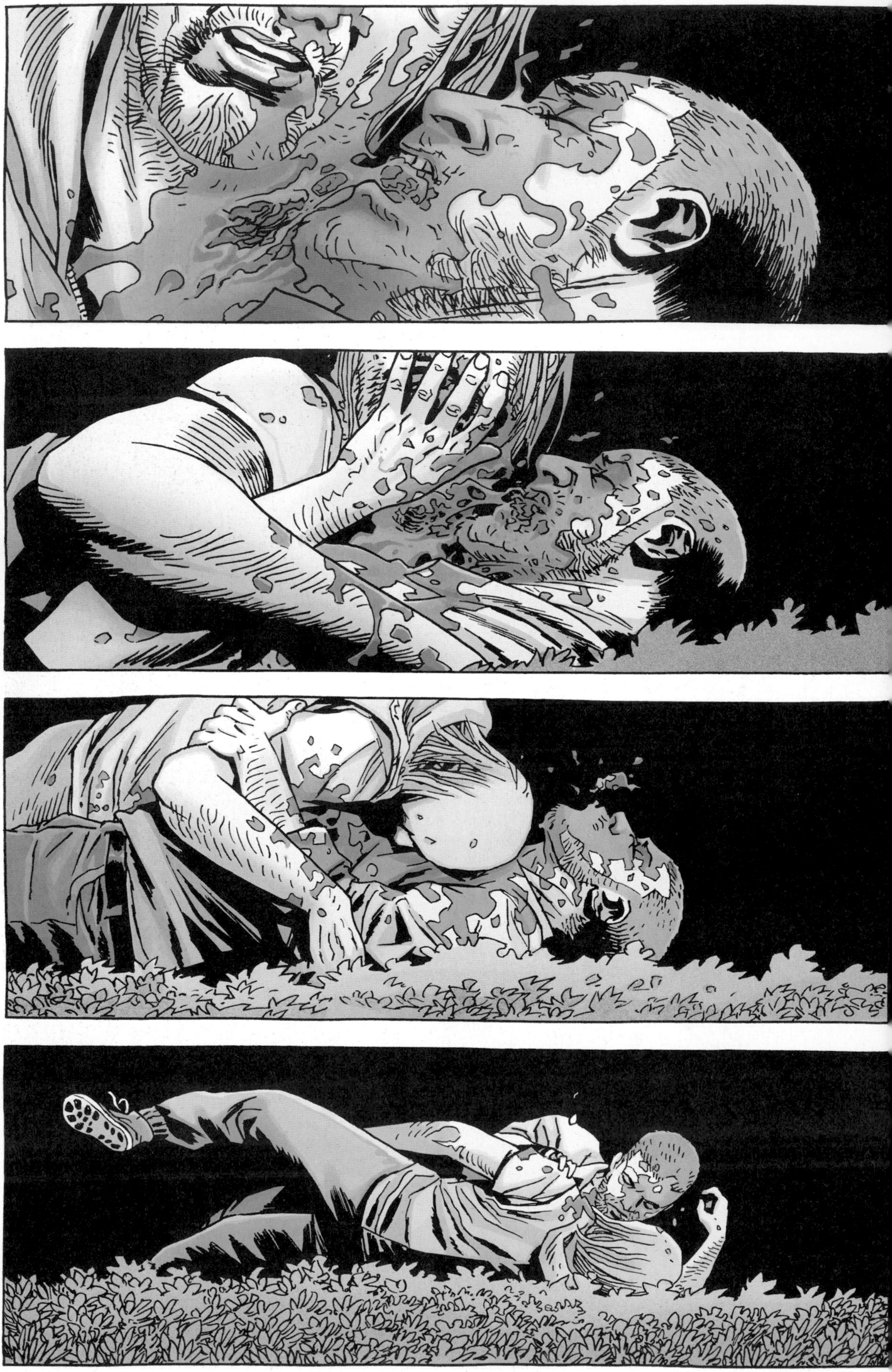

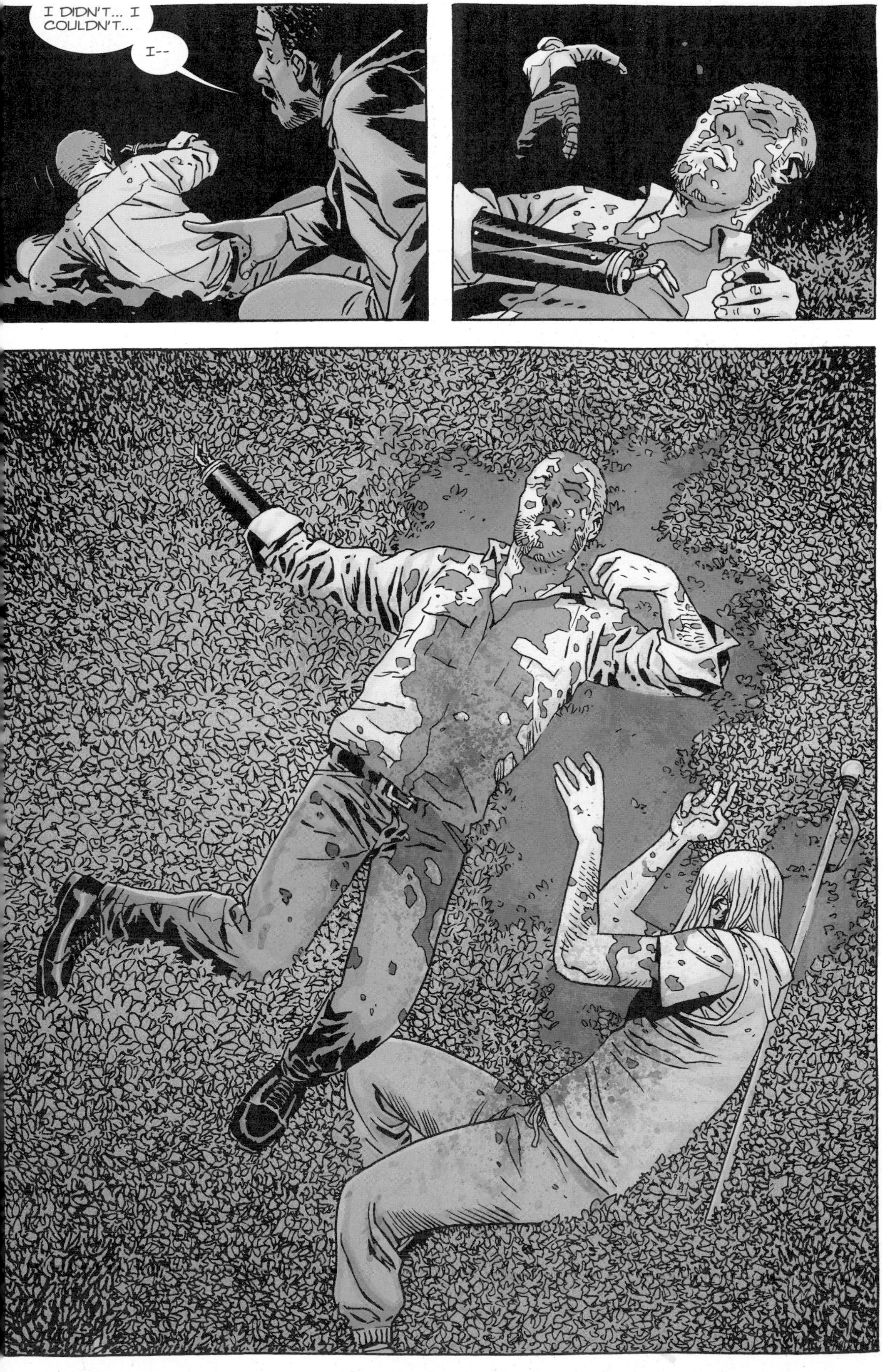
I DIDN'T... I COULDN'T...
I--

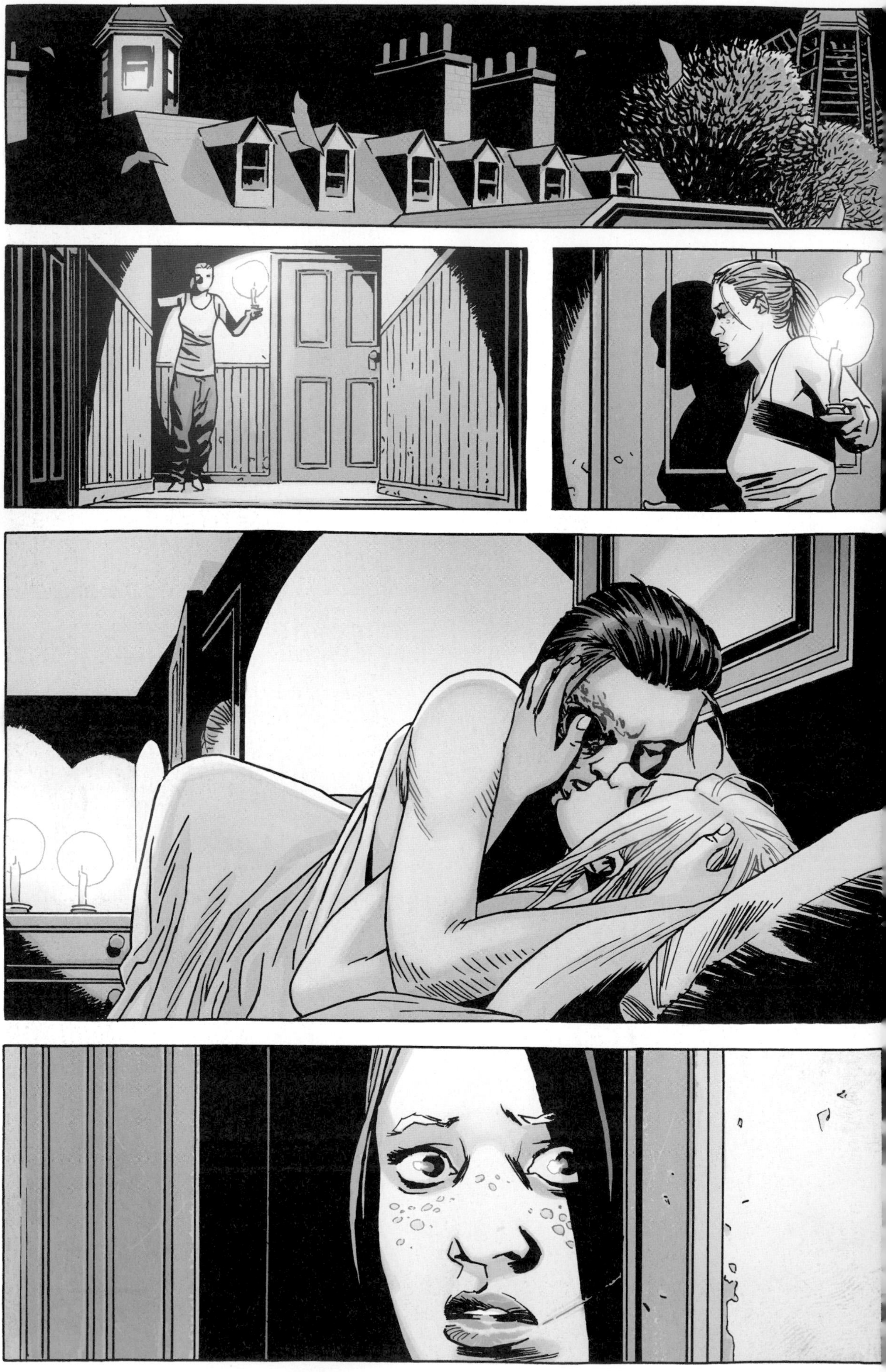

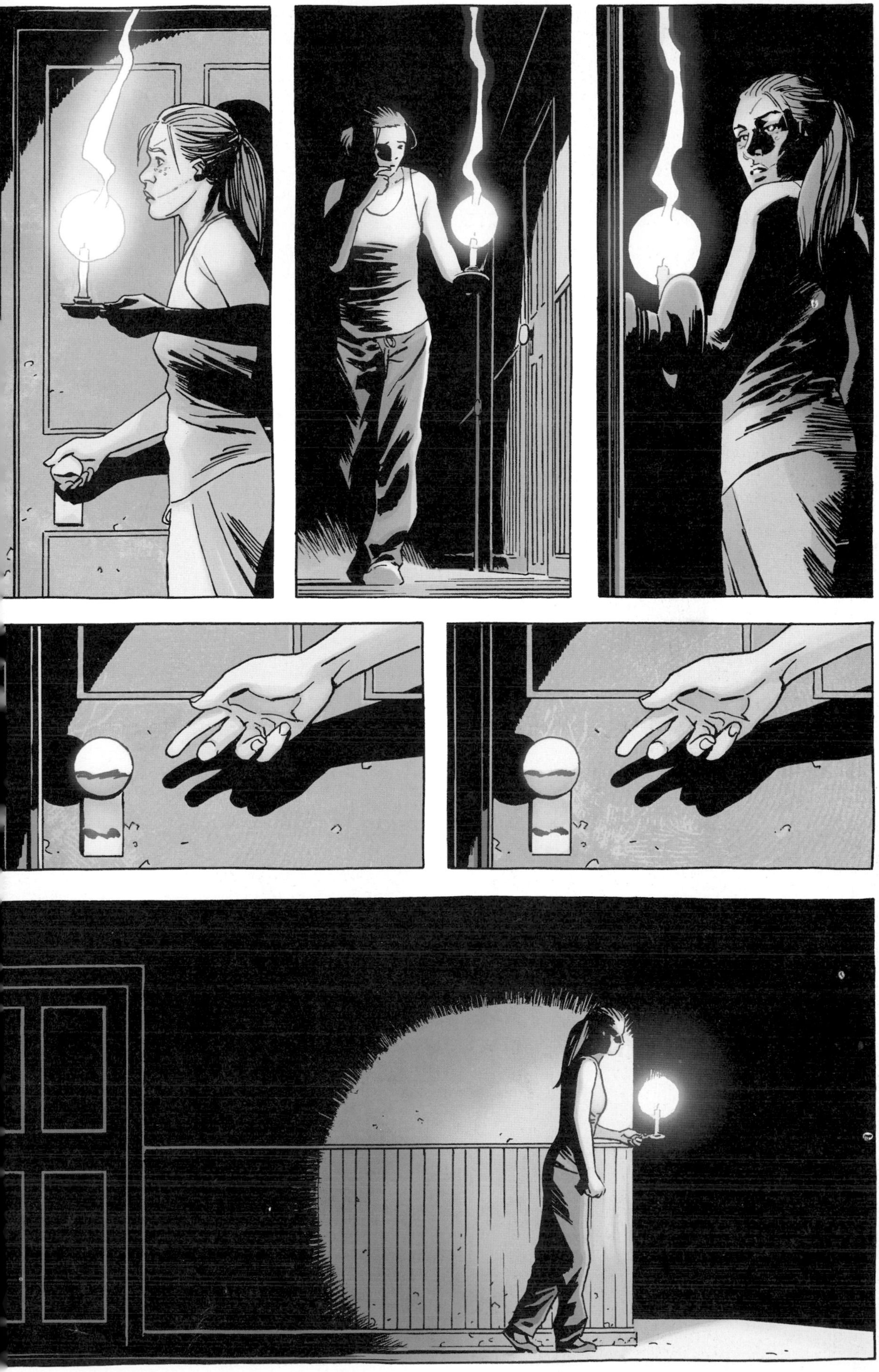

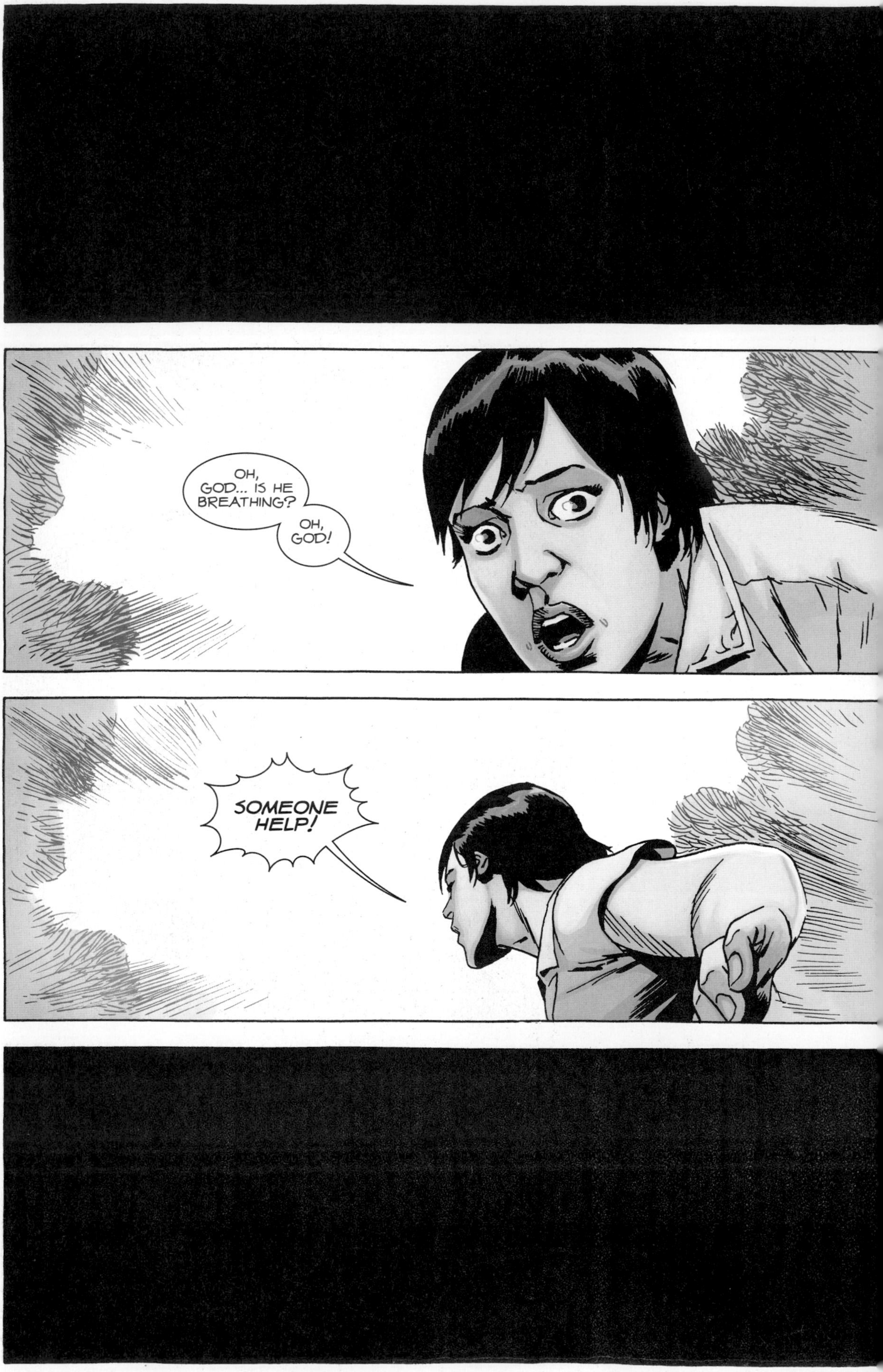
OH, GOD... IS HE BREATHING?
OH, GOD!
SOMEONE HELP!

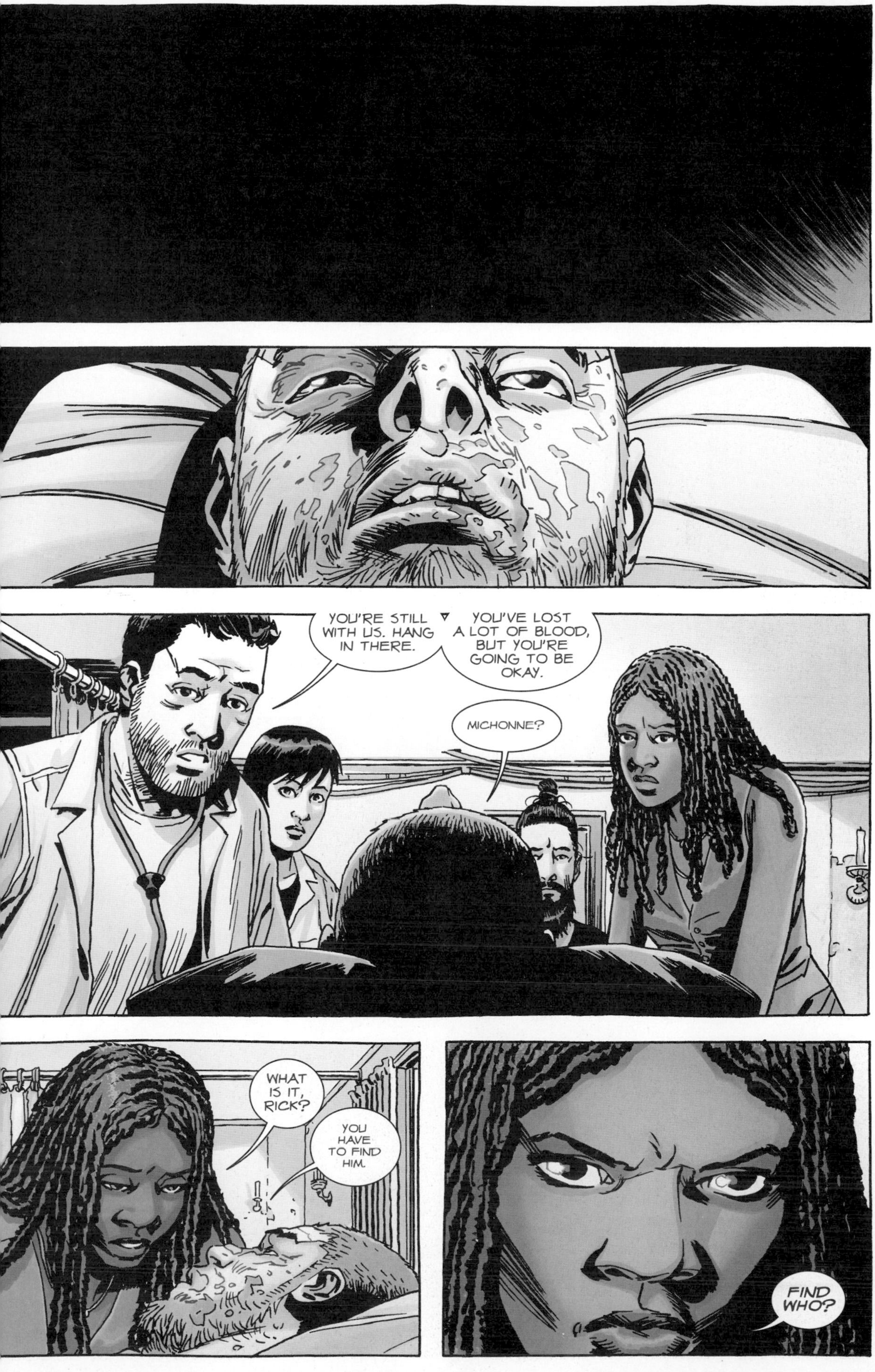

YOU'RE STILL WITH US. HANG IN THERE.
YOU'VE LOST A LOT OF BLOOD, BUT YOU'RE GOING TO BE OKAY.
MICHONNE?
WHAT IS IT, RICK?
YOU HAVE TO FIND HIM.
FIND WHO?

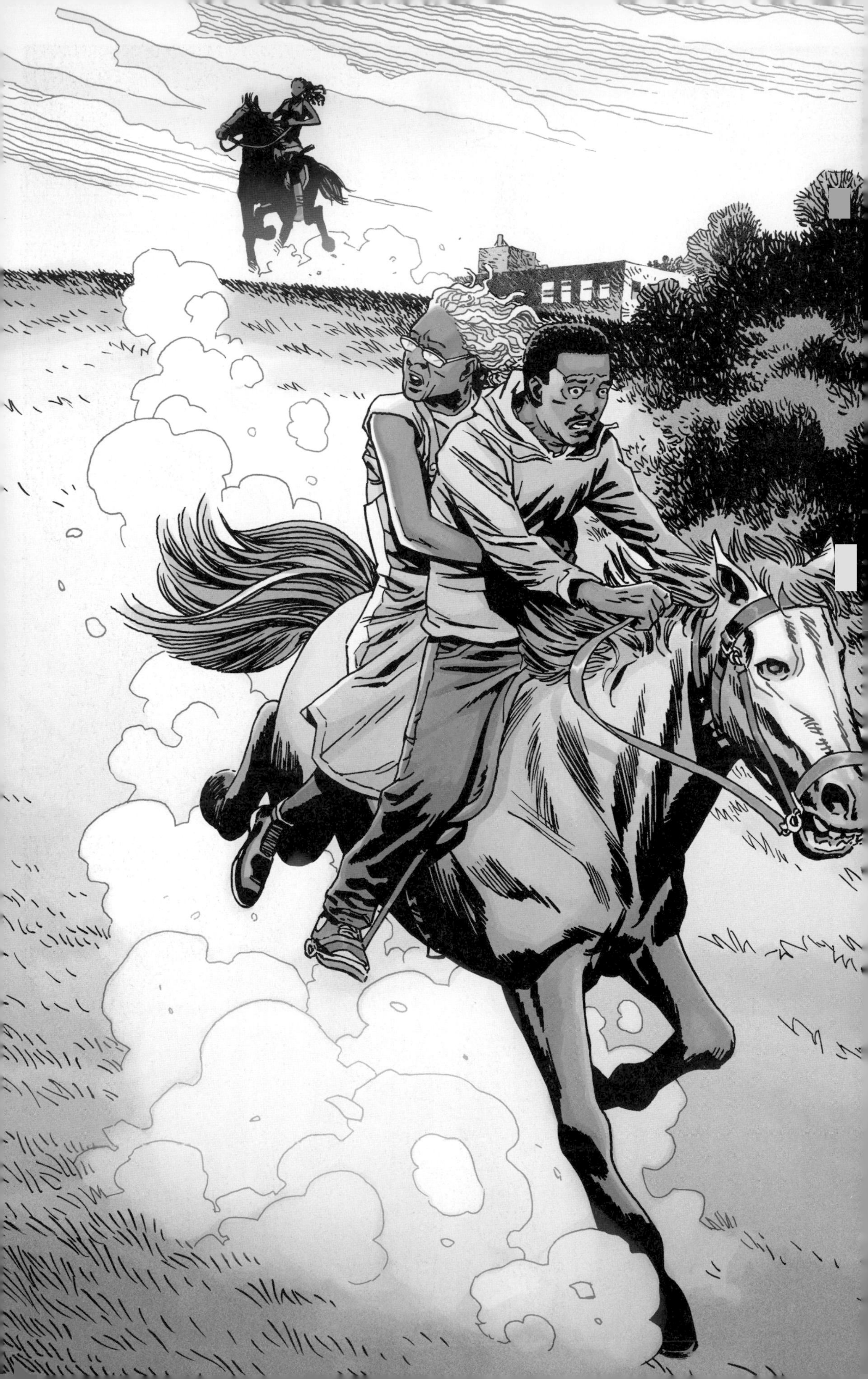

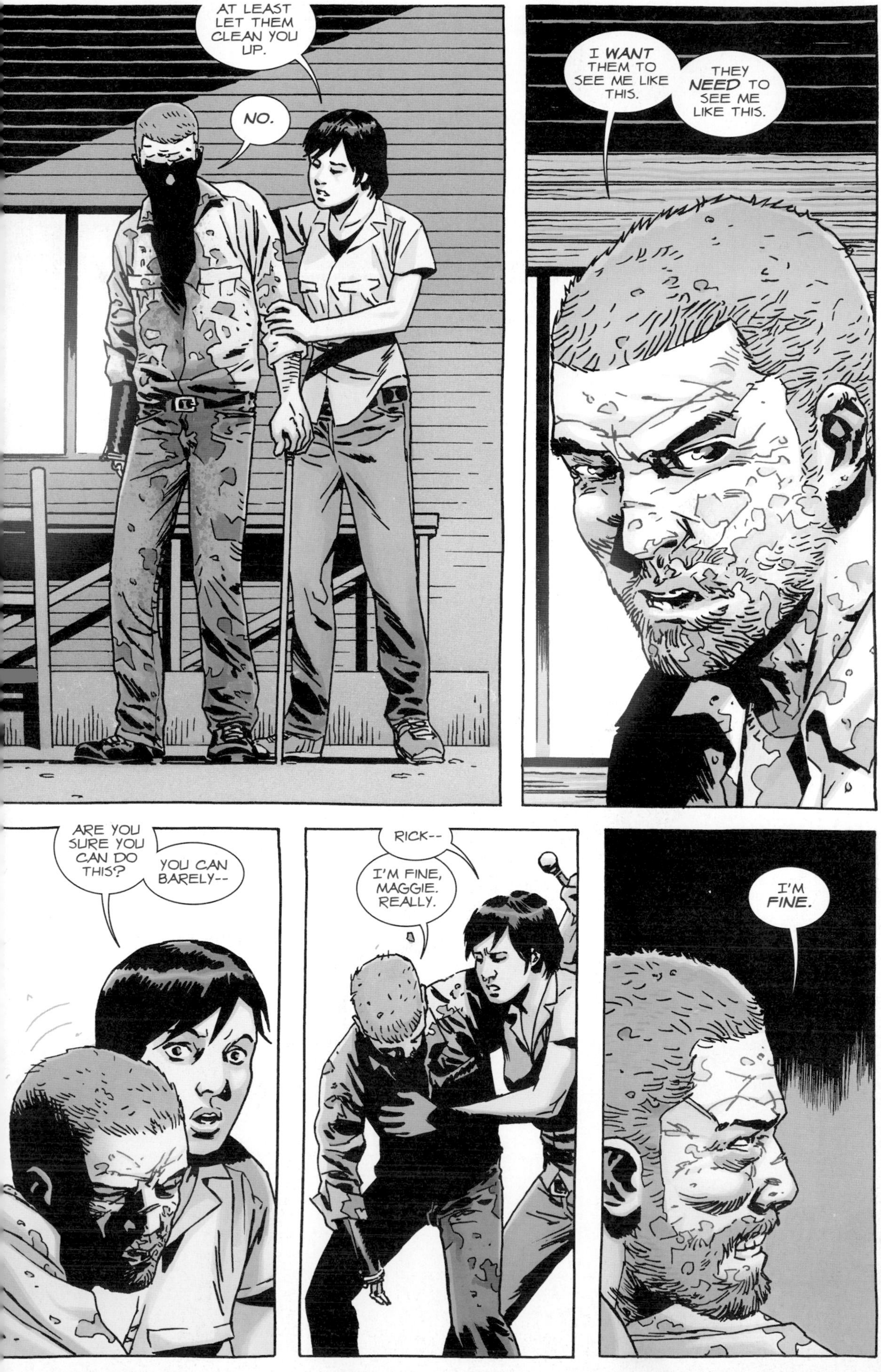

AT LEAST LET THEM CLEAN YOU UP.
NO.
I *WANT* THEM TO SEE ME LIKE THIS.
THEY *NEED* TO SEE ME LIKE THIS.
ARE YOU SURE YOU CAN DO THIS?
YOU CAN BARELY--
RICK--
I'M FINE, MAGGIE. REALLY.
I'M *FINE.*

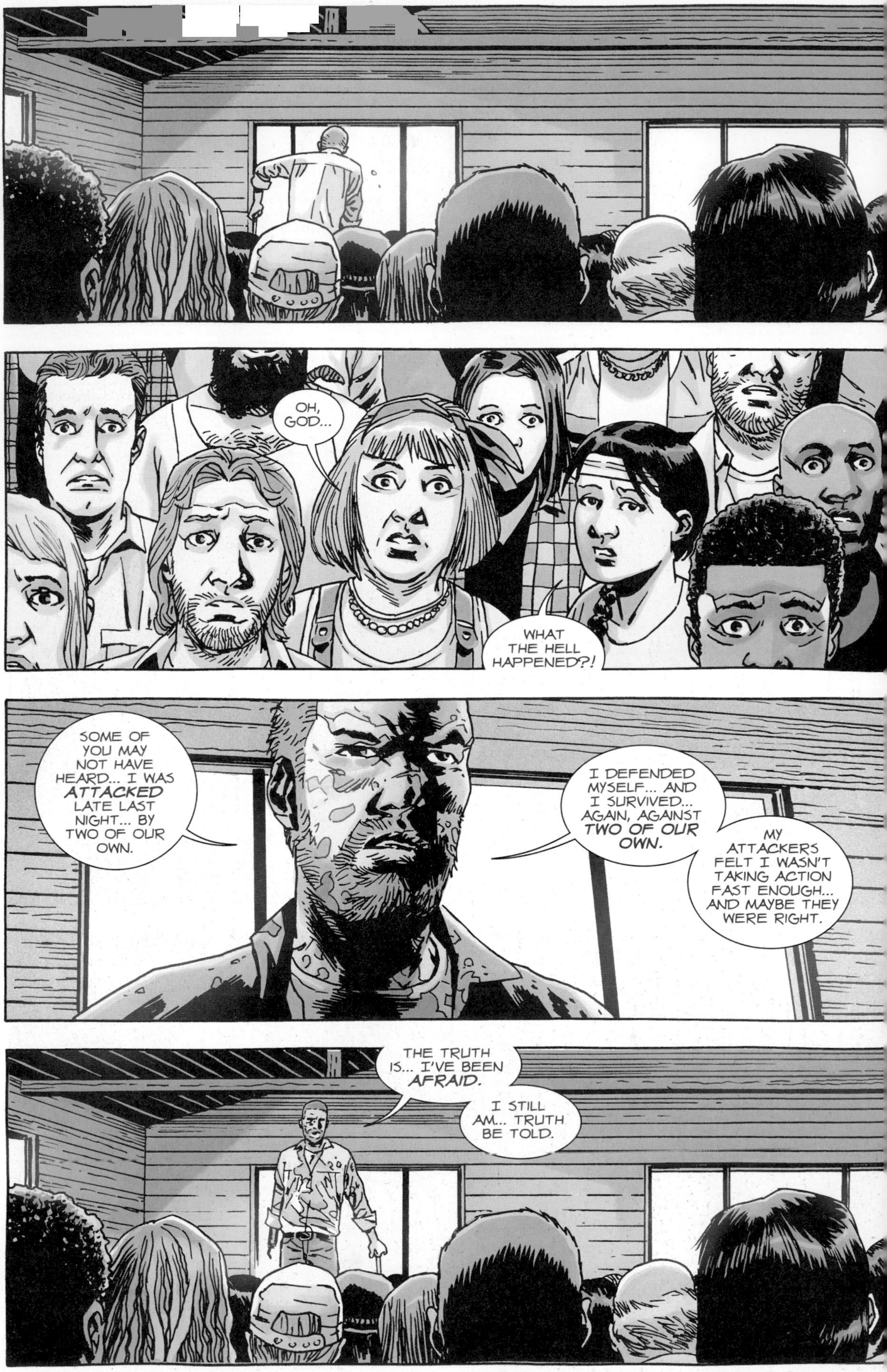
OH, GOD...
WHAT THE HELL HAPPENED?!
SOME OF YOU MAY NOT HAVE HEARD... I WAS ATTACKED LATE LAST NIGHT... BY TWO OF OUR OWN.
I DEFENDED MYSELF... AND I SURVIVED... AGAIN, AGAINST TWO OF OUR OWN.
MY ATTACKERS FELT I WASN'T TAKING ACTION FAST ENOUGH... AND MAYBE THEY WERE RIGHT.
THE TRUTH IS... I'VE BEEN AFRAID.
I STILL AM... TRUTH BE TOLD.

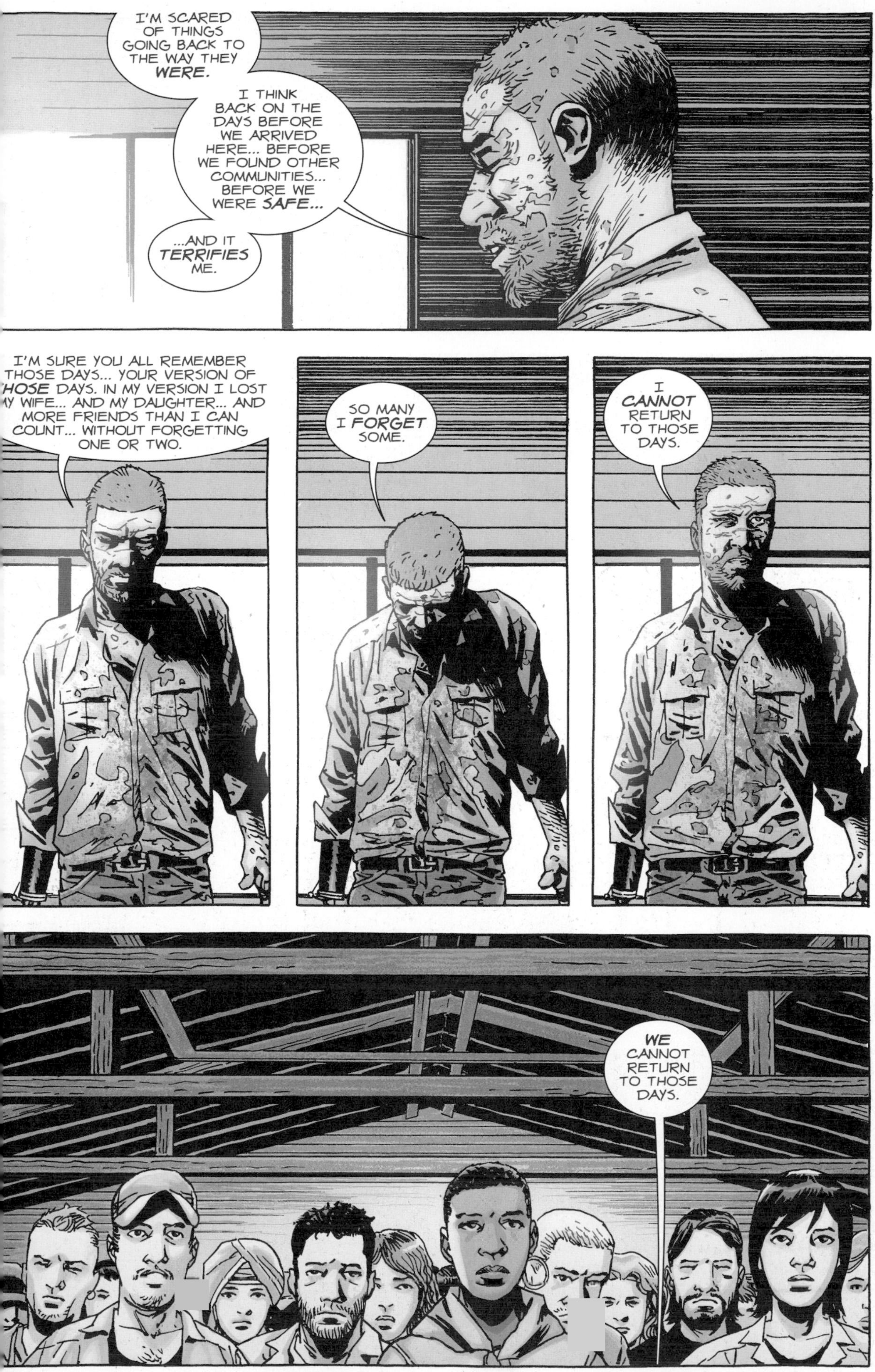
I'M SCARED OF THINGS GOING BACK TO THE WAY THEY WERE.
I THINK BACK ON THE DAYS BEFORE WE ARRIVED HERE... BEFORE WE FOUND OTHER COMMUNITIES... BEFORE WE WERE SAFE...
...AND IT TERRIFIES ME.
I'M SURE YOU ALL REMEMBER THOSE DAYS... YOUR VERSION OF THOSE DAYS. IN MY VERSION I LOST MY WIFE... AND MY DAUGHTER... AND MORE FRIENDS THAN I CAN COUNT... WITHOUT FORGETTING ONE OR TWO.
SO MANY I FORGET SOME.
I CANNOT RETURN TO THOSE DAYS.
WE CANNOT RETURN TO THOSE DAYS.

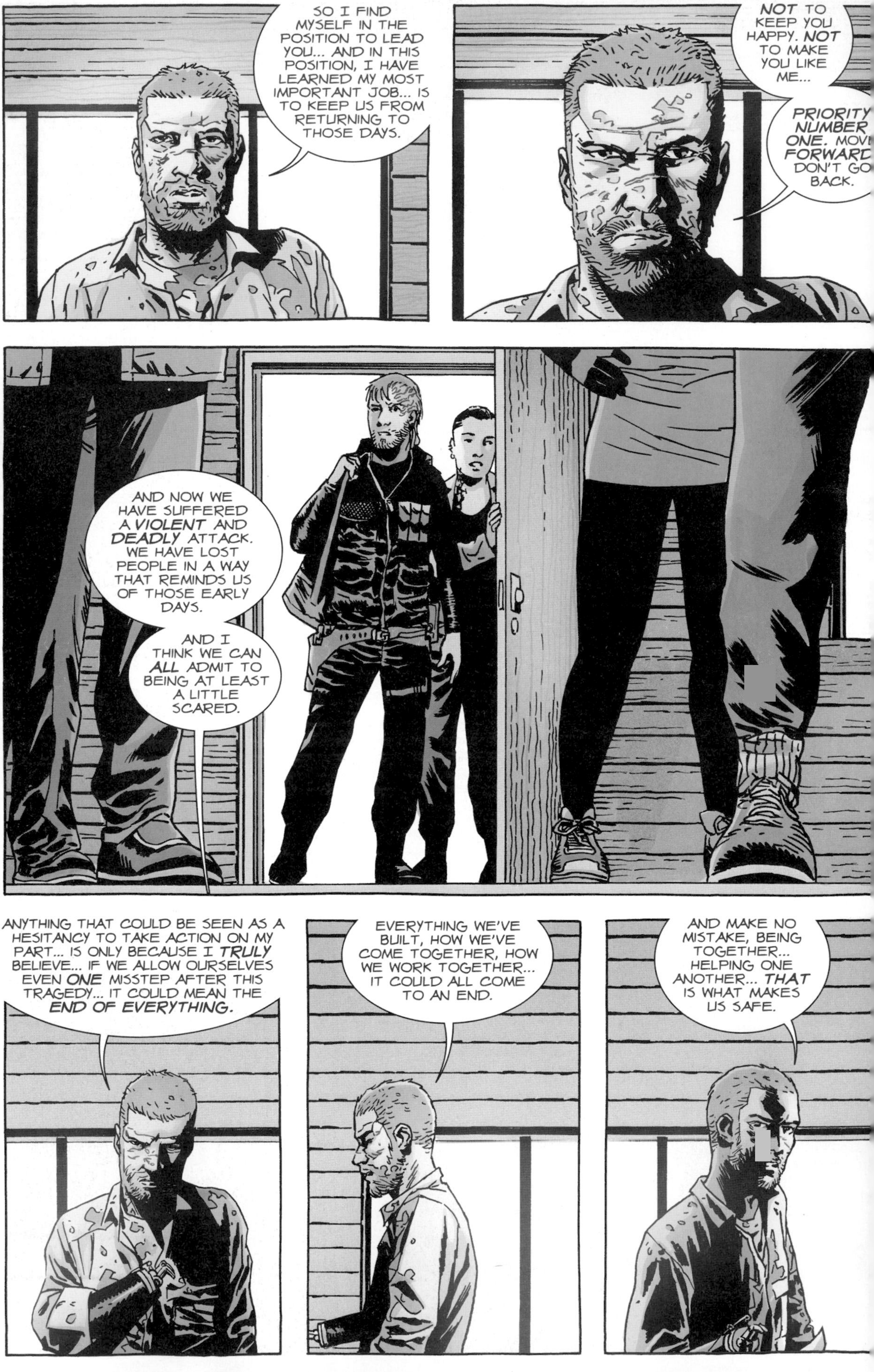

SO I FIND MYSELF IN THE POSITION TO LEAD YOU... AND IN THIS POSITION, I HAVE LEARNED MY MOST IMPORTANT JOB... IS TO KEEP US FROM RETURNING TO THOSE DAYS.
NOT TO KEEP YOU HAPPY. NOT TO MAKE YOU LIKE ME...
PRIORITY NUMBER ONE. MOV FORWARD DON'T GO BACK.
AND NOW WE HAVE SUFFERED A VIOLENT AND DEADLY ATTACK. WE HAVE LOST PEOPLE IN A WAY THAT REMINDS US OF THOSE EARLY DAYS.
AND I THINK WE CAN ALL ADMIT TO BEING AT LEAST A LITTLE SCARED.
ANYTHING THAT COULD BE SEEN AS A HESITANCY TO TAKE ACTION ON MY PART... IS ONLY BECAUSE I TRULY BELIEVE... IF WE ALLOW OURSELVES EVEN ONE MISSTEP AFTER THIS TRAGEDY... IT COULD MEAN THE END OF EVERYTHING.
EVERYTHING WE'VE BUILT, HOW WE'VE COME TOGETHER, HOW WE WORK TOGETHER... IT COULD ALL COME TO AN END.
AND MAKE NO MISTAKE, BEING TOGETHER... HELPING ONE ANOTHER... THAT IS WHAT MAKES US SAFE.

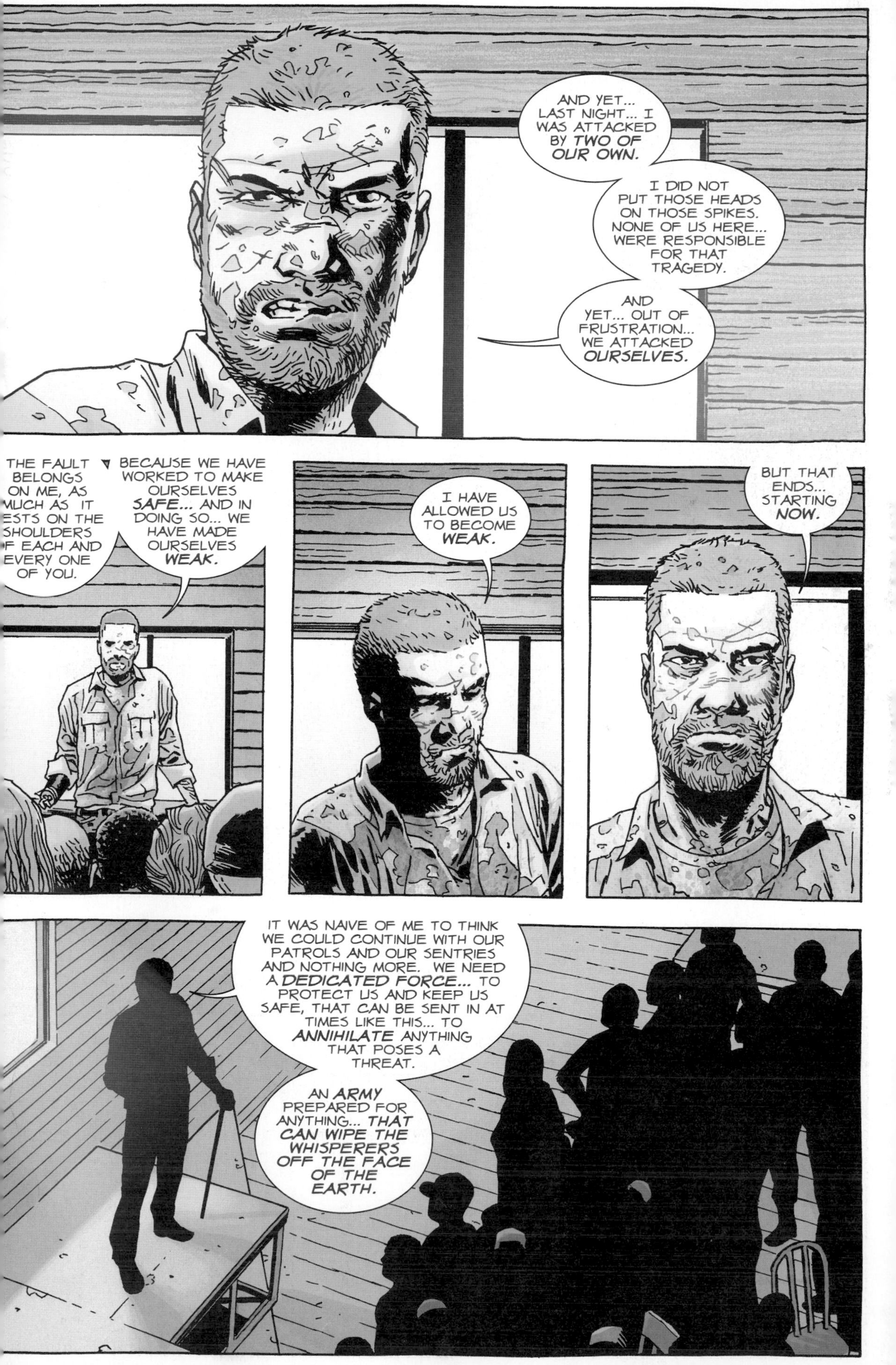

AND YET... LAST NIGHT... I WAS ATTACKED BY TWO OF OUR OWN.
I DID NOT PUT THOSE HEADS ON THOSE SPIKES. NONE OF US HERE... WERE RESPONSIBLE FOR THAT TRAGEDY.
AND YET... OUT OF FRUSTRATION... WE ATTACKED OURSELVES.
THE FAULT BELONGS ON ME, AS MUCH AS IT ESTS ON THE SHOULDERS F EACH AND EVERY ONE OF YOU.
BECAUSE WE HAVE WORKED TO MAKE OURSELVES SAFE... AND IN DOING SO... WE HAVE MADE OURSELVES WEAK.
I HAVE ALLOWED US TO BECOME WEAK.
BUT THAT ENDS... STARTING NOW.
IT WAS NAIVE OF ME TO THINK WE COULD CONTINUE WITH OUR PATROLS AND OUR SENTRIES AND NOTHING MORE. WE NEED A DEDICATED FORCE... TO PROTECT US AND KEEP US SAFE, THAT CAN BE SENT IN AT TIMES LIKE THIS... TO ANNIHILATE ANYTHING THAT POSES A THREAT.
AN ARMY PREPARED FOR ANYTHING... THAT CAN WIPE THE WHISPERERS OFF THE FACE OF THE EARTH.

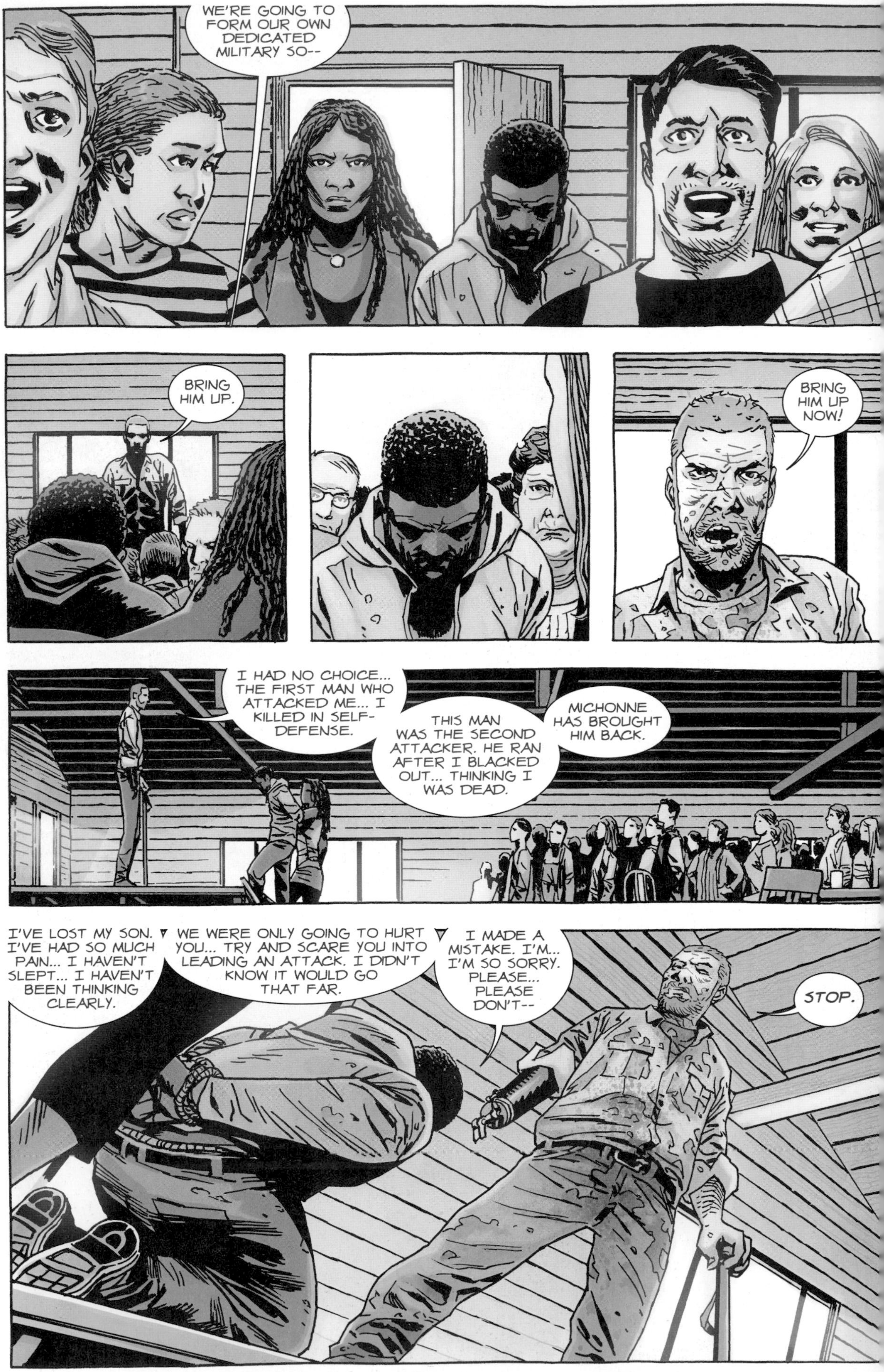
WE'RE GOING TO FORM OUR OWN DEDICATED MILITARY SO--
BRING HIM UP.
BRING HIM UP NOW!
I HAD NO CHOICE... THE FIRST MAN WHO ATTACKED ME... I KILLED IN SELF-DEFENSE.
THIS MAN WAS THE SECOND ATTACKER. HE RAN AFTER I BLACKED OUT... THINKING I WAS DEAD.
MICHONNE HAS BROUGHT HIM BACK.
I'VE LOST MY SON. I'VE HAD SO MUCH PAIN... I HAVEN'T SLEPT... I HAVEN'T BEEN THINKING CLEARLY.
WE WERE ONLY GOING TO HURT YOU... TRY AND SCARE YOU INTO LEADING AN ATTACK. I DIDN'T KNOW IT WOULD GO THAT FAR.
I MADE A MISTAKE. I'M... I'M SO SORRY. PLEASE... PLEASE DON'T--
STOP.

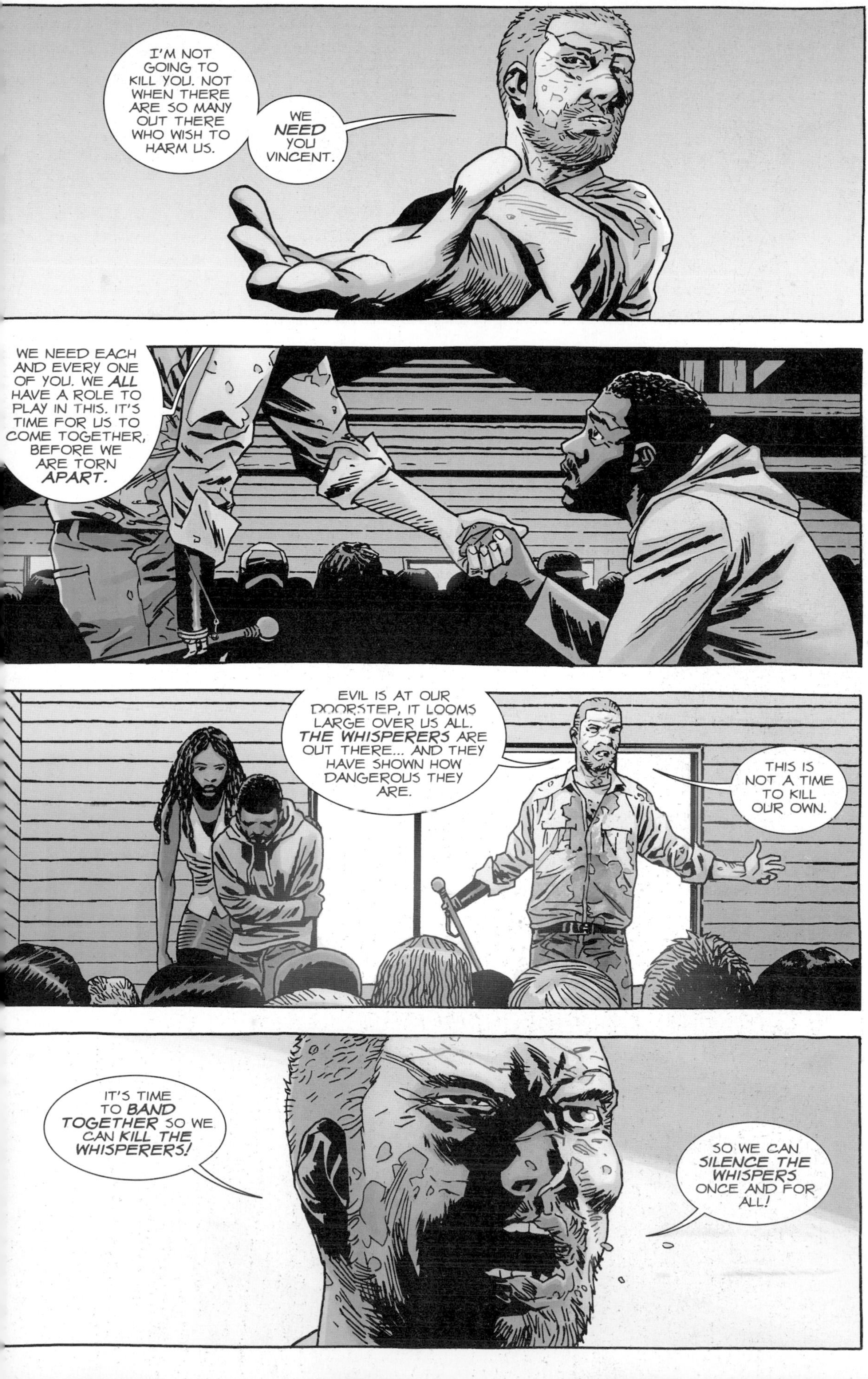

I'M NOT GOING TO KILL YOU. NOT WHEN THERE ARE SO MANY OUT THERE WHO WISH TO HARM US.
WE NEED YOU VINCENT.
WE NEED EACH AND EVERY ONE OF YOU. WE ALL HAVE A ROLE TO PLAY IN THIS. IT'S TIME FOR US TO COME TOGETHER, BEFORE WE ARE TORN APART.
EVIL IS AT OUR DOORSTEP, IT LOOMS LARGE OVER US ALL. THE WHISPERERS ARE OUT THERE... AND THEY HAVE SHOWN HOW DANGEROUS THEY ARE.
THIS IS NOT A TIME TO KILL OUR OWN.
IT'S TIME TO BAND TOGETHER SO WE CAN KILL THE WHISPERERS!
SO WE CAN SILENCE THE WHISPERS ONCE AND FOR ALL!

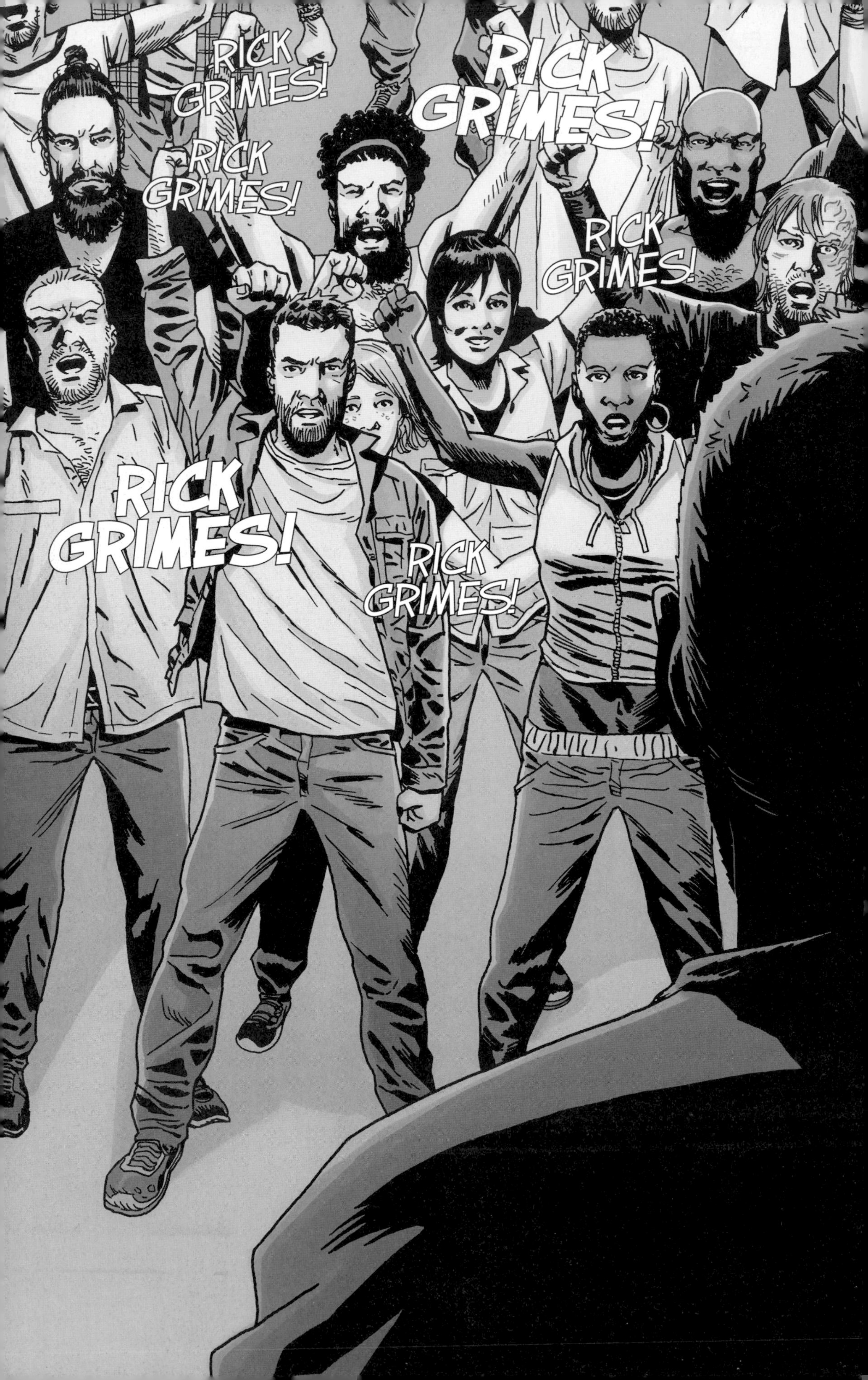
RICK GRIMES!
RICK GRIMES!
RICK GRIMES!
RICK GRIMES!
RICK GRIMES!
RICK GRIMES!

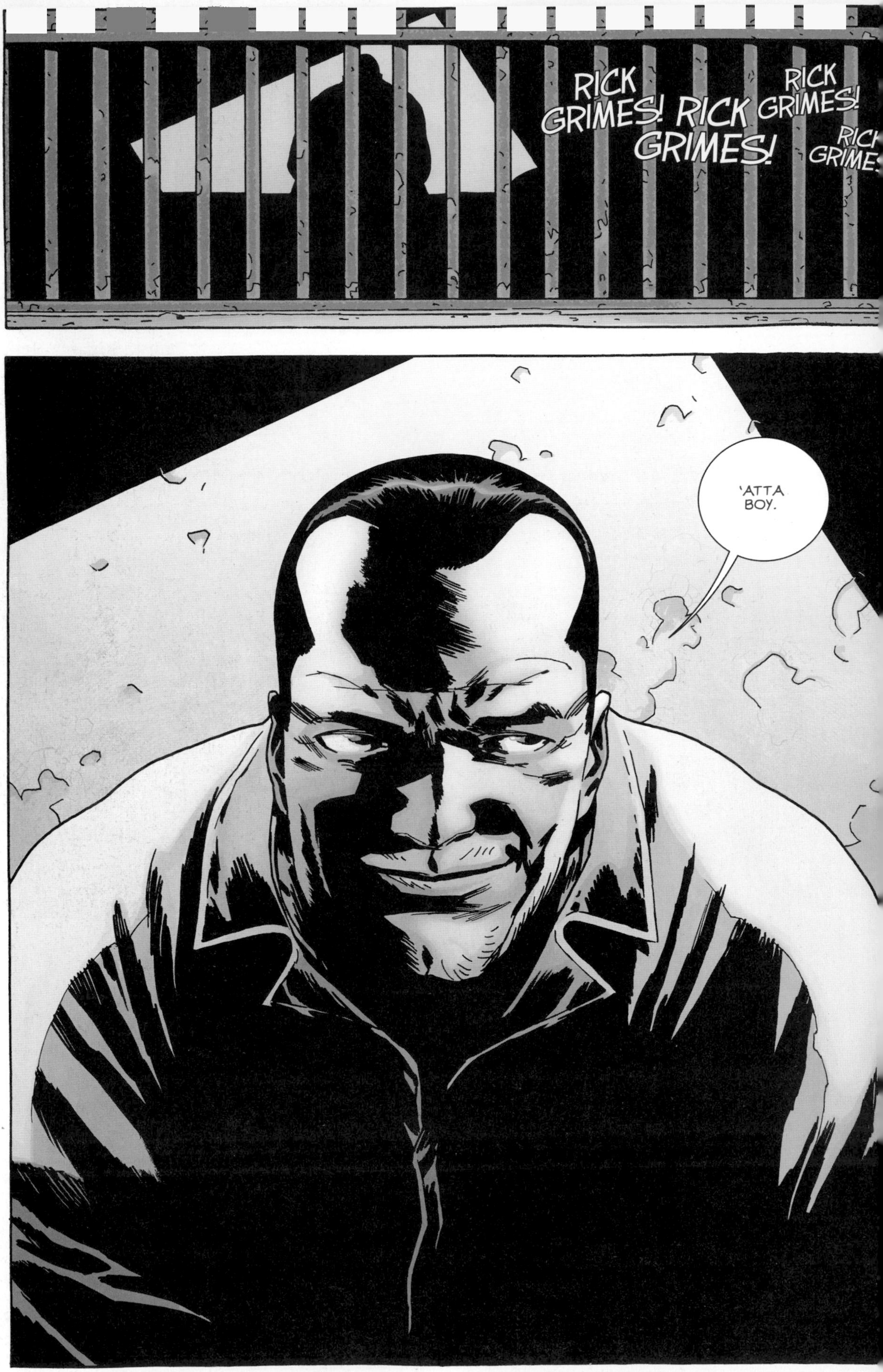
RICK GRIMES! RICK GRIMES! RICK GRIMES!
'ATTA BOY.

TO BE CONTINUED...

for more tales from ROBERT KIRKMAN and SKYBOUND

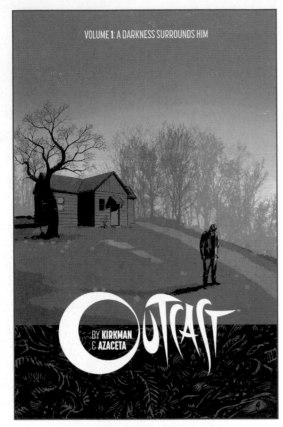

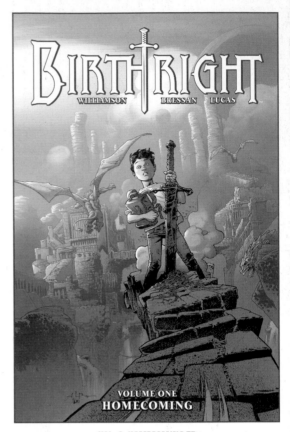

VOL. 1: A DARKNESS SURROUNDS HIM TP
ISBN: 978-1-63215-053-0
$9.99

VOL. 2: A VAST AND UNENDING RUIN TP
ISBN: 978-1-63215-448-4
$14.99

VOL. 1: HOMECOMING TP
ISBN: 978-1-63215-231-2
$9.99

VOL. 2: CALL TO ADVENTURE TP
ISBN: 978-1-63215-446-0
$12.99

VOL. 1: FIRST GENERATION TP
ISBN: 978-1-60706-683-5
$12.99

VOL. 2: SECOND GENERATION TP
ISBN: 978-1-60706-830-3
$12.99

VOL. 3: THIRD GENERATION TP
ISBN: 978-1-60706-939-3
$12.99

VOL. 4: FOURTH GENERATION TP
ISBN: 978-1-63215-036-3
$12.99

VOL. 1: HAUNTED HEIST TP
ISBN: 978-1-60706-836-5
$9.99

VOL. 2: BOOKS OF THE DEAD TP
ISBN: 978-1-63215-046-2
$12.99

VOL. 3: DEATH WISH TP
ISBN: 978-1-63215-051-6
$12.99

VOL. 4: GHOST TOWN TP
ISBN: 978-1-63215-317-3
$12.99

VOL. 1: FLORA & FAUNA TP
ISBN: 978-1-60706-982-9
$9.99

VOL. 2: AMPHIBIA & INSECTA TP
ISBN: 978-1-63215-052-3
$14.99

VOL. 3: CHIROPTERA & CARNIFORMAVES TP
ISBN: 978-1-63215-397-5
$14.99

VOL. 1: "I QUIT."
ISBN: 978-1-60706-592-0
$14.99

VOL. 2: "HELP ME."
ISBN: 978-1-60706-676-7
$14.99

VOL. 3: "VENICE."
ISBN: 978-1-60706-844-0
$14.99

VOL. 4: "THE HIT LIST."
ISBN: 978-1-63215-037-0
$14.99

VOL. 5: "TAKE ME."
ISBN: 978-1-63215-401-9
$14.99